CW01525455

Copyright © 2024 C F Chapman
All rights reserved

This is a work of fiction. Names, characters, places and incidents are either a product of the author's imagination, or are used fictitiously. Any resemblance to actual persons, events or places are entirely coincidental.

Acknowledgements

For Autumn, devourer of words and self-proclaimed 'Honorary Brit'. A dearest friend, confidante, and writing muse.

And for my partner, John, my family, friends, and colleagues, who have all been a constant support in my life. I mean that with the deepest sincerity.

Prelude

Cold. Dark. The unmistakeable smell of damp concrete; musky and mildew rife. The walls – wood? Rusty metal bars, probably iron. A chain, also rusted, heavy, and cold. Painfully chilly against Dan's fragile skin. His wrists were taped, bound behind his back. It was dark out – or was it just dark within his prison? No; he could hear the distant *hoot* of an owl, the faint rustling of a rodent or a hedgehog going about its business. Definitely nighttime.

He shivered, his left leg beyond all pain and throbbing with a terrifying numbness – how long had he been there? Hours. Many, many hours since they'd left him alone. Trying to ease the numbness of his legs, Dan shifted, only to find that his left was shackled at the ankle, chain digging in deep and rattling with a dull clang against the concrete floor. Back aching, head throbbing, he attempted to crack open his eyes but only managed one. The other, crusted shut. Swollen at the socket, dried blood cracking, pulling at his eyelashes. Dried tears too where he'd cried. He wished he could have been harder – more composed with his emotions, because they'd laughed. Horrible, echoing, spurred on by his weakness.

Then, something spotted in the darkness. A pair of eyes like hazy orbs, beautiful in a way yet mournful in their watch. Dan wasn't alone.

For once in his life, the black dog's presence was welcome, like a part of Dan himself that had broken away from his mortal form many years ago.

An old friend who'd betrayed him once, but still, better than nobody at all.

It padded over out of the gloom, surrounded in an ethereal fog, and into Dan's failing vision. He didn't fight it; he couldn't. Sniffing at Dan's ankles, his feet, it laid to rest its chin over his lap. It only offered the smallest measure of warmth however, just a reverent apparition like a ghost, its head heavy yet cold through the thin fabric of his tracksuit bottoms.

Confused still as to what was happening and why he was there, Dan feared that this was it – he was dying, caught in what must have been the space between living and passing on, doomed to an eternity stuck in limbo with that God-forsaken dog.

Could one die from the cold, or was he so cold because he was already dead? Surely it shouldn't hurt this much … he remembered then. Masked men. A Sledgehammer. A scream, guttural and hauntingly shrill, falling from his very own lips. His hand. That's where the pain was worst. Fear, like he'd never felt fear before. Was his hand still there? No way of knowing, so frozen and swollen … although, surely his wrists wouldn't still be bound so securely if there wasn't a hand at the end of them, keeping them securely taped behind his back?

The black dog's ears pricked, its head shooting up, alert now.

Someone was coming.

Voices, footsteps, or was he just imagining it?

Heavy doors clattered open causing the black dog to yelp and scarper, skittering away back into the shadows.

Torches, more than one, blindingly bright flares of light. Scuffling soles against the gritty concrete floor. The doors slammed shut, a grinding bolt sliding back into place. The fear returned, sickening. Dan's stomach churned, retching, doubling over as he fell to his side, metallic bile sour and vile and spilling from his mouth and nostrils. His ribcage screamed in protest as he coughed, and he couldn't breathe, he was drowning ...

The black dog growled, but was nowhere to be seen. Figures approached, with Dan screwing his only working eye shut against the glaring light. A familiar voice, filtering its way through the all-consuming panic Dan was feeling; "*Daniel, son ...*"

Wavering between reality and a nightmare, Dan's head started to spin. It had all started so well, coming back home for a quieter existence just a couple of months ago. He was fading, fast, about to succumb to the pull of unconsciousness, when a pair of rough hands grappled at his shoulders, forcing him up against his will to a sitting position. This was it. Time's up.

They're going to finish with you now, whilst the one person in your life who's ever really believed in you watches as you're sentenced to death – all because you've failed so badly at your job.

And what Dan wouldn't have given then, to be back in that field where it had all begun, wishing that he hadn't been so damned inquisitive as to who had dumped all that rubbish onto some farmer's land ...

Fly-Tippers

There was a distinct waft of shit in the air – one that only someone who had frequented the countryside for quite some time could distinguish. An outsider would just say that it smelled of shit, but there were many possibilities as to what could have produced that specific aromatic waft – it could have been chicken, cow manure, or even human. But not Dan, because he knew what that smell gracing the freshly turned fields was. It was sweet and sour and pungent, and currently all over his shoes. Pig shit.

He should have known better, really, but he supposed that eight years spent treading the comparatively cleaner streets of East London proved to be too much of a habit to break when it came to choices of suitable footwear. But then again, where would one even go about searching for a pair of shoes that were smart, yet functional enough for trudging about the Norfolk countryside on a daily basis? And no, he was *not* going to buy himself a practical pair of walking boots. No way.

But this was his life now, whether he liked it or not. He was home, and it was going to take some getting used to. He was busy frowning down at his shoes, drifting, when he realised that he should have been listening to the man standing before him, currently leaning against his suitably mud-stained four-by-four, rattling off some story about a chest freezer.

"So, as I said, see, that freezer, I took it home on 'back of the trailer, an' I just thought, well tha' look in pretty good nick …"

Dan was drifting again. Saunders, the farmer's name was. He couldn't quite recall his first name, if he'd even told him in the first place. His accent was strong – an accent that Dan himself had spent his time in the Met trying desperately to quash, ever since it had become a source of ridicule that had begun during his training down in Kent. *Shit kicker.* Another thing Dan was struggling to get used to, because it didn't matter anymore, did it? *You're not going back to London. You can speak how you wish, because everyone else here does.*

Perhaps it wouldn't be such a bad thing anyway; country folk were wary of 'outsiders', even if *outside* meant a mere county between, and eighty miles up the road.

Some people from around these parts never even crossed the border unless strictly necessary, and that wasn't just the older generation. But again, ten years of expertly picking up an East London twang would prove to be a hard habit to break – as was remembering that the majority of his work was now spent visiting farmers and their fields when the increasingly bold fly-tippers came to call.

Mr Saunders continued, "... An' then old Holmes, up the road, he hit this deer, see? Big old bastard, it was. But I said, well, I got this chest freezer dumped up on my land, in right good nick, an' it still works, so we got that deer in there, no problems ..."

Dan really didn't see the point in taking notes, but he pretended to be taking in every word that Saunders was slowly drawling out nonetheless.

Was that ... it was. Orange baling twine holding the man's trousers up. He was gesticulating now, a full-on demonstration worthy of an amateur dramatics prize, about how he and his mate had managed to manhandle that poor deer into that freezer. He jotted down in his notepad: *Deer in freezer. Sometime in the early 2000s.* He tried not to laugh, only just managing to contain himself.

"So, um, Mr Saunders. You have no idea who might have dumped all of this on your land?" It was a right old mess; Dan couldn't deny that. There was tons of the stuff littering the entrance to one of Saunders' fields, and no doubt it would cost a fair few quid to have it all disposed of. It was the third shout of a similar nature that week.

"Nope, 'hent got a clue. Your guess is as good as mine, officer. Although I wouldn't put it past those bloody travellers – is that the right term for them now? Thas' gonna cost me some in all, all those oil drums over there, special disposal, they'll need."

The truth was, Dan just knew that this incident would be logged and filed away, never to be seen again – just like the rest. They just didn't have the resources to be chasing up on anonymous cases of fly-tipping. Or the money – it just wasn't worth the funding in the eyes of the powers above. But he would take a courteous look anyway, take a couple of photos for the record, and then spend the rest of the afternoon monotonously logging it onto the system … fantastic.

"Mind if I take a look?" he said, out of courtesy more than anything. It was a stinking pile of rubbish – anyone could see that from a mile off.

"You go right ahead, mate."

Dan's shoes were already ruined, so he supposed it wasn't even worth trying to pick his way around the pig-shit-infused slush at the field entrance. He grimaced as some of it sloshed over his trainer and soaked into his sock.

It felt almost futile, his attempt to find even a shred of evidence that may lead to a perpetrator. Scrap pallets mostly and lots of plastic wrapping, half of it currently making its way up the field and the other half blowing down the road, on a chilly gust of wind that was not uncommon for this time of year. It was late April, but spring and early summer had yet to grace them with their presence.

The oil drums though, they *had* piqued Dan's interest. They looked like something which would perhaps be used by a restaurant? He knew they had to pay to dispose of old cooking oil, so maybe he did have a lead after all. Giving one a little kick, his suspicions were confirmed when it clunked over onto its side, expelling a copious amount of dirty brown oil into the sloppy mix of mud and slurry.

He crouched to take a better look at the drum. Unmarked and unlabelled. Of course it was. Criminals weren't stupid after all. But after a bit of rooting about, pulling at a particularly stubborn strand of plastic wrapping too hard and causing the whole pile to come clattering down, Dan had his lead. He laughed to himself. Was this really what his career had come to; searching through a heap of rusty oil drums in a sodden field, getting excited over revealing a grease-stained, peeling old label?

Yeah. Looked like it was. Better take a photo or two.

"Wassat you got there? Looks like Chinese, that does." Perhaps old Saunders was a bit more well-versed in the wider world than Dan had first assumed – or maybe, more likely, he was partial to a Chinese takeaway on a Friday night. He looked like a chips and chicken balls sort of bloke … but that was just a hunch. Dan rather fancied a Chinese, actually. Anyways. Back to the label.

"Yeah, looks like it," Dan replied, taking his photos before peeling away at the label and just about managing to unstick it from the drum in one piece. He slid it safely into an evidence bag, always making sure to keep a couple spare in his jacket pocket, just as a dog owner seemed to always have a spare poo bag in every item of clothing they owned. Dan liked to be prepared – part of being a good detective sergeant, that was.

Another gust of wind hit, this time with a hint of rain. Dan was done, already dreaming of a change of socks, his desk and a hot cup of tea.

He stood, Saunders joining him.

"Right, well. You've got my number, yeah? If anything else gets dumped on your land?"

"Yes, officer. Right you are."

Dan had expected Saunders to kick up a bit more of a fuss; question as to what the police were going to do now, and was he supposed to clear up the mess off his own back? But he didn't, and perhaps this sort of thing was now so prevalent, so common, that it was now just one of the occupational hazards of being a farmer with roadside land.

Dan wrapped his jacket a little tighter around his torso as the windy rain started to take hold. He trudged back to his car – a black saloon with those special lights hidden above the windshield, and it was a four-wheel drive. He liked it. One of the few perks so far of his new position away from the Met.

He still missed it, the grime and the noise and the thrum of the city, the nights out after work and his even nicer flat to come home to after another long day chasing the bad guys.

He missed his old colleagues too, at least some of them, anyways. But as he'd already said, he wasn't going back. That was one particular chapter of his life well and truly closed.

As he buckled up and switched the heaters onto full, Dan considered whether it was worth him radioing in to the office with his findings, whether any of the team would even care … it was a world away from his past life in that sense too. Things were slower here, and his boss wasn't biting at his arse every five minutes for an update on his whereabouts, which was at least one thing that he definitely didn't miss.

He checked over his shoulder, then glanced towards the rear-view mirror, before pulling away. As he did, he caught sight of an old friend lying across the back seat, staring right back at him with its familiar glassy eyes and empty gaze.

He swore at it grouchily, "'The fuck do you want?"

The black dog just stared ahead, folding its paws over one another and settling in for the ride back to the station.

Alien Invasion

Anticipation. Nerves. Clammy hands around his firearm. This was it – months of planning in the works, near on ten years of fighting to prove himself, that he *could* make it to detective sergeant on merit alone, and Dan was seconds away from heading up one of the biggest drugs raids the Met had seen in recent years. The masked team of AFO's stood poised in flawless unison, awaiting the call from Dan himself to proceed. Seconds ticked by. Dan's hands grew clammier with every thundering heartbeat. And then his earpiece crackled into life. All clear. Risk assessment signed off. Proceed.

Dan gave the signal, and the scene burst into life. Like silent assassins, his team of firearms officers moved forwards as one. Down with the bolted metal door, which fell inwards to the ground with a heavy, reverberating clang. And then they were piling in – *"Armed police, Armed police!"* – the thunder of boots against concrete, officers disappearing beyond the threshold and into the darkness …

An unnerving silence followed. Dan clicked off the safety, his weapon still poised and ready. DCI Walters barked down his earpiece for a Sit-Rep, so loud that he almost flinched. Walters had that effect on him; a force to be reckoned with, his DCI, and more often than not, that force was aimed right in his direction.

"No word yet, sir," Dan cringed, even as the words fell from his lips, in anticipation of the reaction he was about to receive. DCI Walters didn't want him to succeed, he just knew it. Even if it meant months of surveillance, countless late nights away from home and a huge chunk of their department's yearly budget down the pan, Dan could have bet his right arm that his DCI was already setting him up to fail.

The man's opinion of him had always been low, ever since that first meeting when Dan had joined the team as a fresh-faced and newly promoted detective constable. Instead of welcoming him with open arms, Walters had grabbed him by the upper arm and forcibly shunted him into his office. What followed was a wholly unwelcoming introduction to what he expected of his subordinates.

Walters was the sort of bloke whom if he liked you, you would do just fine. If he didn't, well, you were done for from the outset.

"Where's your team, Taylor? Get me that Sit-Rep – now!"

Every ounce of uncertainty over his own abilities, which DCI Walters had relentlessly drummed into Dan's already fragile self-esteem, came crashing down on him like a wave, when his ears were filled with the harrowing echo of screams emanating from the building beyond. He froze. Only for a moment, but still long enough for the nausea to rise and his firearm to slip. Walters was still bellowing down his ear for his *fucking* situation report, but Dan was no longer listening. His feet took over as he entered into the darkness.

It was very dark. He couldn't locate the source of the frenzied screams, nor could he locate his team. It was all echoing around him. He still had nightmares over it and would do for years to come; and not just because the raid had been on the alien themed attraction that was 'Laser Space Adventure', Romford's go-to establishment for a night of alcohol fueled, interplanetary laser shooting fun.

Except it wasn't nighttime. It should have been a dawn raid but according to an anonymous tip off, Johnny Singh (the owner of the business), was apparently running late to the office that day.

So here Dan was at just gone 3pm on a Saturday afternoon, surrounded by the haunting cries of what had to be innocent civilians, along with the resonating shouts from his own men and women. Panic set in. Dan turned a blind corner, only to come face to face with a rather gruesomely fashioned (and twenty years past its best) space being. Large, gaudy eyes stared out at him through the gloom, his vision hindered further by a smoke machine embedded in thing's mouth that decided this would be the perfect moment to expel its stagnant, choking waft of man-made gas.

Everything flashed by in a blur after that. The overhead lights hummed and clunked into life. A herd of children and parents trampled past, followed by Dan's team of AFO's, and again, he stood rooted to the spot, coughing and blinking back the harsh glare of the sudden artificial light.

He fumbled forwards until his hand connected with the nearest armed officer's elbow. The officer stopped and turned, only his eyes visible through his goggles, but nonetheless there was a flash of panic behind them – and it was the lights and the smoke that were making Dan's eyes water. Not tears. Definitely not tears.

"We've gone and fucked this one right up, haven't we sergeant?" the armed officer said, pulling his goggles up over his helmet. It was Matthews. Dan knew him well, and he looked like he was about to bottle it.

Yeah, they had fucked up – big time. And somebody was going to have to take the rap for it, with Dan already certain in his mind who that somebody was going to be. He had to pull himself together though, because Matthews had a wife and a second child on the way. Allen too; she was due to be married soon, her career ahead of her looking promising and bright. And then there was Jonesy, with his PTSD after leaving the forces, and the new family that he had found after signing up with the Metropolitan Police. They were all good people, with real lives and aspirations, and people at home depending on them.

And what did Dan have? A string of failed relationships, that's what. A life in the city that had seemed so exciting and full of possibilities to start with, where he would find his place in the world and prove himself as the man he so desperately wanted to be; to maybe meet that special someone along the way to share it all with …

To be happy – was that too much to ask? Apparently so.

Instead, he was left with a somewhat lonely existence outside of work (with the exception of the odd night out on the town), a boss that had it in for him from the outset, and a team of firearms officers, whom under his instruction, had just performed an armed raid on a children's birthday party. Was there any way that things could have gotten worse at that moment? Most probably. He pulled out his earpiece, letting it dangle down his neck so that DCI Walters' now incessant shouting at him to *'get his sorry arse out of there and face the music'* could give his oncoming headache a break.

"Yeah. We fucked up. On my call though, mate. On my call." Dan had already accepted his fate. There was nothing to be gained by bringing his team down with him. Matthews gave him a very meaningful look, the defiant flare behind the man's eyes saying it all.

"You didn't delay the raid this morning, and you didn't sign off the risk assessment," said Matthews, in a last-ditch attempt to try and convince Dan that they should take the fall together.

Dan appreciated it, he really did. He knew that it hadn't been his fault. Someone had messed up on the intelligence. He also knew that this would be the perfect opportunity for DCI Walters to get him out of his greasy, receding hair once and for all.

As if the genie himself had been summoned from the bottle, there he was, his looming shadow encroaching the threshold of the now destroyed fire exit which Dan and Matthews were slowly making their way towards.

He wished he could have been a stronger presence, and about two feet taller in all, whenever he was in his boss's vicinity. But there was just something about the man, that had his palms sweating and his hackles raised, and his confidence positively crumbling down to dust.

"Dismissed, Matthews. Get out of here." An apologetic clap to the back and a mumbled, '*I'm sorry, mate'*, and Matthews was dejectedly trudging his way out into the afternoon light, back to join the rest of his team – a team that had just performed their first (and last) shout under the command of detective sergeant Taylor.

Walters strode a couple of steps forwards into Dan's personal space, and he was unable to stop himself from shrinking back into himself, withering under the much taller man's overbearing scrutiny. He would have loved to have said that his DCI didn't scare him; that he was strong enough to stand up to him, but he couldn't. Dan would have been lying to himself, and everyone around him, if he were to say there was any truth within that misplaced inclination.

"An armed raid, on a *fucking* kid's party?" Walters' voice was low, which terrified Dan just as much as if it had been shouted in his face, spit and all. And then a threatening hand was reaching out to grasp at his upper arm, hard, too hard …

"And there was me thinking that our young Dan here, cocky young *Danny,* was ready to head up a team of his own. Was I wrong, detective sergeant Taylor? Was my unwavering trust in you misplaced?"

Dan took a shaky breath, his arm throbbing under his DCI's grip. He wanted out. "I … you signed off the risk assessment, sir …" he stumbled in a fruitless attempt to sway his DCI.

"What's that, DS Taylor?" The embarrassing yelp that fell from Dan's lips as his arm was wrenched behind his back, as his body was forcibly shoved against the nearest wall, only seemed to spur his boss on further. The larger man, now pressed into the back of him, whispered low into his ear, "Try getting that wild accusation past the DCS, you jumped up little *shit.*"

Dan was about to blow his top. He twitched his nose in irritation, his upper lip raising in a silent snarl that he hoped and prayed wouldn't give way to a bout of oncoming tears. He was an emotional bloke, something he had never been all that good at hiding, but he was *not* going to cry in front of his senior officer like that. Not when the man had him pinned, pushing for him to break before his very eyes.

Dan's cheek scraped against the bare concrete wall as DCI Walters gave him one final shove, where he remained for a while longer until he was sure that his boss was gone. It wasn't the first time Walters had laid a hand to him, but like the team he had just led into this awful mess, it was sure to be the last.

The soft clack of something approaching from within the alien themed labyrinth had Dan coming back to his senses. Peeling himself away from the wall, he thought for a moment that it was a stray child heading his way, lost in the chaos of it all … but what Dan was met with instead was a pair of hollow, clouded eyes, and a dark shadowy form coming into view.

He cocked his head in question. The black dog mirrored his action. For some reason unknown to him, Dan accepted his visitor, like it had been there all along in some shape or form, lurking just out of sight for quite some time. Only now did it dare to show its mournful face.

They walked out of the back entrance together, the black dog trotting a few paces behind, to face the waiting disarray of sirens and civilians. The noise of it all hit Dan hard – people everywhere; a reporter shoving a microphone in his face, a uniformed officer dragging her back behind the hastily erected cordon, and then there was a hand at his forearm, an unfamiliar touch which he didn't care to whom it belonged, leading him away to face his fate.

Acting Superintendent Broadmeadow

The last of his staff appraisals had just been wrapped up, which left Marcus Broadmeadow feeling rather pleased with himself. Well, pleased if he could ignore the fact that his staffing level was severely dwindling, to the point that it almost counted as skeleton. In fact, he only had two members of staff. And of course, it should have been his chief inspector writing up and delivering the staff appraisals, but it wasn't, because he didn't have one. Broadmeadow was still the chief inspector, technically ...

It had all become so convoluted because their actual superintendent had gone and retired. Oh yes, Alan Richardson was now enjoying his French villa and his vineyard, and his idyllic vision of the perfect end to a hard grafted career. Marcus had dreams of a similar kind, when the time came. That time was a way off though, as he was only 52, having been involuntarily placed into the position of acting superintendent just two years prior.

He was still waiting for that full promotion in order to remove the 'acting' prefix. He wouldn't have said he was entirely ready for the step up to superintendent, but then again, when were you really ready for more responsibility in your life? These things just happened sometimes and you had to go with them; in his case, finding himself heading up Central Norfolk's Rural Crime Unit.

So, superintendent Richardson was gone, and with no replacement on the cards, Marcus had stepped up to the plate out of pure dedication to his team. As an 'acting' superintendent, Norfolk Constabulary weren't obliged to replace his chief inspector position, which left him with a somewhat sparsely numbered team under his control. His highest-ranking officer, Hollie Parsons, was only a detective constable – not that the lass wasn't a fantastic officer in her own right, because that would be doing her a huge disservice, but it would have been nice to have at least one senior detective to work alongside.

Marcus looked across at his empty cup, then up at the clock above the door, before catching sight of a framed photo – one which bestowed him with a pang of sadness every time he looked at that smiling face. They *did* have a detective inspector, who had started out his career as a specialist dog handler before the unit had been disbanded for good, but all that remained of DI Wright was just that, a fixture on the wall that was sure to far outlive them all.

It was late, gone seven, but as he was already committed to getting those appraisals wrapped up, it wouldn't hurt to stay a wee while longer and clear a few emails now, would it?

He wondered if Emily was still working at the front desk; perhaps he could call her to go and put a brew on for him? No, he told himself, gone were the days when he could call on the junior officers to do things like that. Not that she would have minded coming up for a chat with him, but still, he was perfectly capable of getting up and making his own.

In the last three hours, his inbox had piled back up to a healthy two hundred and something. Most of which were addressed for 'all users' informing of system outages, and for the various committee newsletters doing the rounds, but there *was* one that caught his eye. It was from the chief superintendent. Intrigued, he pushed his reading glasses up to the bridge of his nose and clicked it open –

Dear Acting Supt. Broadmeadow,

I have a transfer request that you may be interested in. Detective Sergeant Daniel Taylor, trained firearms operative from the Metropolitan SOC, working apprenticeship obtained from Kent training college. Advanced driving certificate too – sounds like a good catch.

I'll keep it brief. His services are no longer required within the Met, and he is from the local area, which will be to your advantage.

Can I strongly suggest that you consider his appointment to your team. Please find his credentials attached.

Regards,

Romalie Roberts, DCS

Well, that was a bit of good news for a Friday evening. It sounded too good to be true in fact, which meant it probably was. Someone in the force with a CV like that didn't just *ask* for a transfer to leave the heady heights of the city (and what looked to be a very promising career) behind, to come and work for a department in the far back of beyond, where the nearest they came to a criminal investigation was a bit of fly-tipping and the odd back-yard cannabis farm.

Something didn't sound right about it all. The detective in Marcus (that he never took the exams to become) wanted to know more, so he clicked open the attached profile to find out a little bit more about his potential new recruit. Safe to say, the wee face on the lad's ID photo was not what he had been expecting. He looked rather young for a man of twenty-eight years, with his kind face, engaging dark eyes and a slightly furrowed brow. The corners of his lips were ever so slightly turned up, like he was trying his hardest not to smile for a photo that one was definitely *not* supposed to be smiling for.

Marcus read on, returning every so often to that photo for another look. The lad was exactly what Marcus had been looking for on paper, but the question still remained as to why; why was somebody so good being sent his way? What exactly had DS Taylor done to rub his superiors up the wrong way, enough for them to want him out?

His answer came in the form of a bit more delving. There was a file on the lad, but it was locked. A disciplinary, perhaps?

He carried on with his investigation, leaving the database behind to try an internet search engine instead. *Metropolitan police, firearms incident*. He assumed that this must have been a fairly recent decision for transfer, so any major incidents involving a firearms officer from the Metropolitan CID would probably have an article still kicking about somewhere. He added *London Metro* to his search, and about three articles down he had his answer:

Children's birthday party raided by armed police in botched drugs raid.

The Met's already flaky reputation took another hit yesterday, when a popular Romford entertainment establishment was raided by armed police, headed up by the criminal investigations department in what was suspected to be a front for a drugs and weapons cartel. No suspect was apprehended however, as it turned out that an alien themed children's birthday party was in full swing when the Met came knocking on the back door.

There were no reports of fatalities or shots fired ...

Marcus continued to read the article, in which of course no officers were named, but there was a photo taken from behind the cordon of where the incident had occurred, of a rather short, dark haired officer in plain clothes and a stab vest being escorted away from the scene. Towards the end of the piece, there was a brief statement from the DCI in charge of the investigation:

We had solid intelligence that our suspect was present at the time, and no prior knowledge that the establishment was occupied by members of the public. The senior officer at the scene calculated there to be no risk, and therefore made the call to engage. This was a serious miscalculation on their behalf, and an investigation into their conduct at the scene will follow.

Ah, ok. It sounded to Marcus like someone here was about to be pushed into the firing line to save the face of this DCI Walters fella. All it took was another delve back into the police database to find him along with his current team of senior detectives, and there he was, just as suspected – detective sergeant Daniel Taylor.

It stunk to high heaven, the more that Marcus managed to piece together with the limited information that he had on the incident. DCI Walters appeared to be a celebrated officer, with more than one article dedicated to his achievements and commendations. One particular picture of him, receiving an award of some sort from the Met's high commissioner, had Marcus feeling a rather strong dislike towards man.

He had come across many a fella like that in his career; the sort of man who says *yes* to the right people and always finds himself in the right situation at just the right time for promotion. The sort of man who has climbed the ladder fast, with little or no appreciation for the people beneath him.

Not acting superintendent Broadmeadow's sort of fella. He decided then that he would take the risk on this young detective sergeant. He would do right by him like he did for all of his team if this was, as he now strongly believed, a case of painful injustice. Taking one last look at sergeant Taylor's photo, he composed his reply to the DCS that he would be happy to accept the transfer.

By the time he'd finished up his email the time was now gone 8pm, and Marcus decided that should really be thinking about heading home for the night. He begrudged the weekends sometimes, because at least when he was at work there was plenty to keep his mind occupied. But he couldn't stay all night. Perhaps he could pick up a takeaway on the way home – the missus wouldn't be in, he knew that already, and he was highly doubtful that there would be any dinner waiting for him in the fridge.

Takeaway it was then; and to try and stop thinking about a young detective sergeant that he had yet to meet in person.

The Deer

The rain was getting heavier so Dan turned the windscreen wipers onto a higher setting and the car heater up a notch, to the point where anyone else would say that he was driving in an oven. That particular gripe had been the source of many a pointless argument between him and his previous partner – for some unknown reason, the fact that Dan often found himself feeling a bit chilly never failed to fuel some form of seething irritation within her.

That was Leanne and she had been a personal best for him; nearly eight months together before things had broken down to the point of no return. But as Dan already knew, there was just something about his personality that seemed to rub anybody he tried to have any sort of relationship with up the wrong way. Whether that relationship was of a personal or a professional aspect, it didn't seem to matter. He was unlikeable to many, for reasons which he had yet to fathom.

But enough of that self-deprecating misery. He was good at that too – putting himself down, that was – and the black dog was fueling it. Lounging across the back seats of his car and looking extremely smug with itself, the shaggy old creature seemed to have grown in size now that it had been fed.

Dan tried to think about nicer things, like the summer and how beautiful the countryside was once the barren hedgerows and skeletal trees lining the roads burst into life. He had a little garden now too, something he could only have dreamed of from his flat in East London, and he looked forwards to long summer evenings sitting out on the patio with a couple of beers, waiting for the sun to set around him. Someone to share it with would be nice too, but he tried again to quash thoughts of that nature because the thought of going through the dating game again made him feel a bit sick. All that effort for a dissatisfying shag or two, before the reality would set in of having to change himself and hide his flaws in order to make things work out – was it really worth it? So far, the answer was a resounding no.

His new team seemed nice so he thought about them instead. On first impressions, his superintendent wasn't a power-hungry dick-wipe, and the two detective constables he was working with seemed down to earth; perhaps he could invite them all round for a barbeque or something in a few months' time, once the weather eventually improved? He knew he had to make an effort with them because what he wanted, more than anything, was to just feel like he was accepted somewhere. Dan really was riding on this transfer working out alright, because he didn't have another plan if relations with his colleagues were to go flying down south like they had within his last position.

He was nearly back at the station, with the bare fields outside slowly fading back to a more urban environment, when in the blink of an eye something big and brown decided to run out in front of him. Hazard perception took over as he swerved to miss it. Muntjac. What was it with the deer today? Firstly farmer Saunders' stag in the freezer, now this little bugger making a dash across the road at just the wrong moment … luckily there wasn't any oncoming traffic, because as he swerved the wheel a little too hard – not hard enough to miss the deer – and then back in an attempt to stabilise the vehicle, he connected the front nearside wheel into the kerb with a nasty, grinding *thunk*.

Mounting the pavement, Dan slammed the car to a halt. The rain continued to hammer against the windscreen. Coming to attention, the black dog looked at Dan with its head slightly turned in question, awaiting his reaction. A reaction that came in the form of two raised fingers to the rear-view mirror. Fucking deer. Fucking dog. And fuck the weather too whilst he was at it, because now he had to go back out in the rain to check on the state of his front wheel, which he already knew was damaged, and the deer, which had ended up on the pavement and wasn't looking too sharp.

Flicking on his hazards, he pulled his jacket tight around his body and braced himself for the downpour he was about to step out into.

Ok, the tyre was still inflated, but the alloy had suffered a little more damage than just a scratch – it had a full-on chunk missing out of it. Right, on to the deer. Shit. Not a muntjac but a roe deer, and it didn't look like it had much life left in it. The poor thing was just lying there on its side, huge dark eyes jittering as it feebly gasped for every laborious breath.

Could he call farmer Saunders – he had his number – to come out with his shotgun and dispatch it? Or could he call for a police officer to come and take it away? No, that one wouldn't work; he *was* a police officer. "*Fuck it ...*" he muttered under his breath, getting more and more drenched by the second …

The black dog appeared, stopping at the deer's trembling body and giving it a sniff. It too was soaked, its dusky brown hide matted and clumped. A car passed by, spraying up yet more water onto the pavement where the deer lay. Crouching down, slowly, Dan reached out, scared that it may find a fresh wind and try to bolt, but it just continued to lie there as he carefully ran his fingers up its neck before lightly stroking its head.

"I'm sorry ..." he murmured, making his decision. He couldn't leave the deer. Unzipping his jacket, he shucked it off and draped it over the stricken animal, proceeding to scoop it up in his arms and carry it over to his car. The boot seemed like the best place for it. Under the safety of his coat, it just sat there once Dan placed it inside like a piece of luggage and stared at him, as if it had found a level of calm in the knowledge that it wasn't going to be left out in the rain to die. "Get you to a vet, ok? Hold on, little man – woman? – whatever you are."

Shutting the deer safely inside the boot, he got back in the car and checked himself in the mirror. His normally well-kept hair (short back and sides, longer on the top) was drenched, laughing ironically at the soggy fringe he was now sporting. Trying to sweep it aside, it refused to sit atop his head where it belonged and flopped back down over his brow.

He thought again about radioing in, and then decided against it. It wasn't just the embarrassment over kerbing his brand-new patrol car that had him nervous, or that he had acquired an injured deer and put it in his boot, or the ribbing he was sure to receive from his new team, as their new Wildlife Crime expert – it was his boss. The gaffer (definitely not 'the guv' as DC Bartlett had already helpfully informed him).

Dan had really, really wanted to make a good first impression with the man. And he had been excited about showing his new gaffer what he had found out on his recce, all because he wanted to prove that he was worth the chance that superintendent Broadmeadow had given him.

Now, as thoughts of DCI Walters started to leak their way through over how *he* would have reacted to him coming back to the station with a damaged car and a deer in his boot, and with the black dog now sitting next to him in the passenger seat suffocating him with its presence, Dan tried his best to get a hold of himself. Telling himself that at least the first meeting with Broadmeadow had gone a damn sight better than his last introduction to a new senior officer – it hadn't involved any physical displays of dominance for starters – Dan then tried to tell himself that acting superintendent Broadmeadow wouldn't come down too hard on him for messing up so soon into his new position, would he?

It was only a bit of surface damage. These things happened, right? He could do this. Go and find a local vet, drop off the deer, and then go straight to the gaffer to tell him what had happened. Then slide the evidence bag under his nose to appease the situation, and show him that you're not completely hopeless at your new job.

A Breath of Fresh Air

Constable Emily Walker was Dan's first introduction to Vancouver Road Station, and from the moment he first laid eyes on her, he knew that he liked her. She was working at the front desk, which in itself was a bit of a surprise to see a uniformed officer there – they had reception staff back at the Met. She had her hair tied back tight, and eyelashes that were definitely pushing the boundaries of the strict police dress code.

"'Y alright? You're sergeant Daniel Taylor, aren't you?" she chirped as Dan made his way up to the front desk. He nodded, smiling. She had a strong Essex accent, and it instantly made him feel at ease; a small bit of familiarity that he could hold onto. She tapped away at her keyboard, with Dan amusedly watching as her jaw visibly dropped before snapping back shut again, "I'm so sorry, sir. *Detective* sergeant Daniel Taylor."

"'S'ok. It's Dan. Dan is fine." That seemed to placate her as she beamed over the desk at him – and those were some *really* white teeth.

"I've been told that you need to go straight to superintendent Broadmeadow. He wants to introduce you to the team personally. Here …" she thrust a lanyard his way, which he accepted with one hand and slipped over his neck. Holding the pass in his hand, he took a quick look at his new photo ID. God, that was a terrible photo. He'd ask to get that changed at the next opportunity, suspecting that Emily would be more than happy to oblige. She seemed nice, leaving Dan hopeful that the rest of the team were of a similar nature.

"Thanks, um, can I get that photo changed at some point?" Dan didn't want to come across as vain (he was, a bit), but that picture symbolised everything he didn't want to remember about his time under DCI Walters. He wanted to move on, new start and all that, and besides, that picture made him look like a child that was posing as an adult. Eight years had passed since that photo was taken and he could at least pass for somebody in their early twenties now; that was on a good day and if he let his stubble grow out a bit.

"Course you can, I did wonder ..." *Did wonder how somebody so young had managed to reach detective sergeant* – but she stopped herself. Emily was learning that opening her big mouth wasn't always the best idea, especially in front of her senior officers, whether they were new to the team or not.

They checked that Dan's automated pass worked the door ok, and then they were in. And if Dan had thought that having no reception staff was a bit strange, it was nothing compared to the office that spanned out before him past that clunky wooden door (no glass sliding ones here). They were on the third floor, with Emily warning him that you weren't to use the lift unless you really had to because it was extremely temperamental, with a devious habit of trapping people inside for hours at a time until an engineer could be called out.

Community Safety and Criminal Justice were downstairs (otherwise known as South Lynn, which was where they were all stationed), and below them were Traffic and Transport on the ground floor. In the basement was the archive and evidence store, a couple of holding cells and the locker rooms. Emily promised Dan that he would have a locker for himself by the end of the day – Dan was sure that she had been tasked with sorting one out for him prior to his arrival and forgotten, because as soon as he asked about where the showers were her face had fallen, which was as good an indication as any that it had slipped her mind up until then.

Central Norfolk's Rural Crime Unit got the whole top floor to themselves, but on first impressions the place seemed rather cluttered for what should have been such a large space. The desks were scattered about all over the place, topped with mismatched computer monitors – some of which looked like they belonged back in a decade gone by. The windows were covered by dusty old vertical blinds, sunlight just about making its way through the slats in a way that only highlighted yet more dust in the air. The carpet tiles were grimy, and the strip lights across the ceiling were a nasty, sickly shade of yellow (that was, the ones with working bulbs still in them). A single office with a large-paned window sat at the far left of the room, and what looked to be a small kitchen area next door.

Dan wondered where the interview room was. He wasn't to know yet, but the interview room actually doubled up as the archive cupboard. Or the other way around. Rural Crime didn't do much in the way of physical interrogations, with any arrest they did make usually being handed downstairs for Criminal Justice to deal with.

They crossed the floor, Dan with his hands shoved in his pockets in a well-used (albeit subconscious) tactic to show that he wasn't a threat. There weren't many officers present, for such a large department. A petite, plain clothed officer with blonde hair looked up from her screen to greet him with a welcoming smile, introducing herself as DC Parsons. They carried on towards the office at the back of the room.

A bloke, also plain clothed, waved as they passed. He had his feet up on his desk and was scrolling away on his phone. Under his desk, and Dan had to do a double take, was a large German shepherd with soft brown eyes and a greying muzzle, all black except for its forepaws which were an amber tan and looked like a pair of socks.

They gazed at each other for a second, the dog sniffing at the air before cocking its head to the side as if asking Dan a question.

"Alright Chester, he's cool mate. All good." Chester gave out a raspy huff before laying his head back down between his massive paws.

"He can sense you're nervous, mate. Clever boy, our Chester. The gaffer doesn't bite though, don't worry. Unless you really piss him off ... DC Bartlett by the way and it's nice to meet you, mate." DC Bartlett extended his hand and Dan took it.

He would normally have been addressed as 'Sir' by a subordinate officer, but instead of feeling peeved by the detective constable's lack of formality, if anything it felt like a breath of fresh air. And the way that he shook his hand, firm but not in a hand-crushing, '*I'm more of a man than you*' sort of way, made Dan feel so much more at ease with his new surroundings.

"Thanks. Dan. I'm Dan. Nice to meet you, and Chester."

Ok, maybe he was still almost sick with nerves as he stumbled over his words – so nervous that even the black dog had taken a back seat as it trailed quietly behind him.

He had good reason to be, though. He was about to meet his new boss and he hoped and prayed that he was a decent bloke, having only spoken via email prior to that moment with no solid indication over what the superintendent was really like as a person.

Right on cue, the far office door swung open and the man himself appeared. He was tall. Very tall, with lightly greying hair and piercing blue eyes. His uniform was pressed to perfection – white shirt, black tie, black trousers, polished shoes and very big feet, which Dan realised a little too late that he'd been staring at for a prolonged amount of time, wondering what size they must be …

"Thanks, Emily." There it was again, the complete lack of formal address towards one's rank as the superintendent dismissed constable Jones. "DS Taylor. Nice to meet you, son. Come in, come in."

Dan shuffled past his new boss and through the threshold of the office, hands clammy with nerves and now firmly back inside the safety of his pockets. Broadmeadow clicked the door shut behind them before making his way around to his desk. It was nothing fancy, much like the ones out on the floor.

Broadmeadow sat, and gestured for Dan to do the same.

*

The poor wee fella looked like a complete bag of nerves – a surprise to Marcus, because compared to the ID photo that he kept returning to after receiving the transfer request, DS Taylor was a shadow of the man that he had imagined.

There was no cock-sure expression threatening to break into a grin, and those dark eyes were skittish as if he were about to bolt and run at any moment.

Marcus had always prided himself on being an approachable sort of fella; the sort of man you could come to with your problems without any fear of repercussion. He wanted his new recruit to feel at ease in his company, maybe even to share at some point his own side of what had sent him away from the city, but he supposed that would come with time. Trust went both ways after all, didn't it?

"So, I suppose this is where I welcome you to the team, DS Taylor? We're not a big department, as you've probably already guessed, but we are a very close-knit team. So – all I ask of you? Work hard. Try and get on with everyone, and don't be afraid to come to me, yes?" Broadmeadow explained to him and Dan nodded, meeting his new gaffer's eyes for the first time. He had an accent, but he couldn't quite put his finger on what it was. All he could deduce was that the man wasn't born and bred in these parts.

"Ok, sir. Thanks."

Marcus tried to keep hold of the lad's gaze, but as soon as he replied those eyes were back down and focusing instead on the hands that we clasped tight together in his lap.

"I was hoping for you to take over the role of 'wildlife crime expert', does that sound like a role you'd be happy to take? And have you got any questions, fella?" he said softly, trying to coax him out of his shell.

"Uh, no, I don't think so, sir."

Marcus would definitely have his work cut out with this one; the lad had a wall built up around him so high that he could barely see over the top.

"Good lad. Well, shall I show you to your desk? And then perhaps DC Bartlett can give you the run down on our current cases? Sound good to you?" Marcus leant across his desk on his elbows in a conscious attempt to bring himself down to his young sergeant's level, trying again to catch his eyes, which Daniel eventually did when he realised that his superintendent wasn't going to let him leave until he complied.

"Yeah. Thank you, sir."

"I don't bite you know. And I don't know what happened before, Daniel – or do you prefer Dan? Anyways, you can trust me, ok? I'm on your side." He reassured, thinking that he caught a flicker of emotion behind those dark brown eyes as they fixed upon his own, a moment passing between them …

"Right. Come on then, Daniel. Let's get you settled in, eh?"

The lad waited until Marcus stood before following suit (they really must have followed the rules over how to act around a senior officer at the Met), making him feel a tad uncomfortable at the formality of Daniel's actions. A wee bit sad too, because that wasn't how Marcus liked to run his own ship, preferring instead a much more relaxed approach towards his staff.

"Sir?"

Marcus stopped and turned to see his sergeant with his hands back in his pockets, his whole demeanor screaming with anxiety, but was that – was that the hint of a smile playing at the young man's lips?

"Yes, Daniel?"

"You asked if I prefer Daniel or Dan – It's Dan. Sir."

Marcus rather preferred Daniel, with the name already having stuck in his head, and he could foresee himself getting it wrong forever more from that moment. He laughed to himself at his innate inability of getting his team's names right (perhaps he was just getting older), earning himself a questioning look from his new sergeant which he tried to brush off with a friendly smile. Striding on towards the lad's new desk, Daniel obediently following behind without another word.

Chester

The late spring sun was filtering through the slatted blinds as Chester readjusted his position to soak up the best of it, rolling his eyes up to check that Paul was still there. Yep, still there. Chester liked Paul; he was kind and affectionate and fed him meat from a tin with his biscuits when they got home in the evenings. DI Wright didn't give him tinned food when he was still alive because "it was bad for his teeth", and he understood because in his old job he needed to be in top condition. Not so important now though, which he guessed was why Paul gave him all the human food that he shouldn't really be having, as well as his tinned meat.

DI Wright and Chester used to go out in the special police car, and he would get excited because it meant he was going to get to be a good boy and catch some of the *bad guys*. That had been their job, he and DI Wright. They were a team. Not all dogs had jobs, but Chester did.

He would go out, and DI Wright would give him the scent of a criminal, and he would go and find them. Sometimes though, it wasn't a criminal they were looking for. There were a couple of times when Chester would have to go and find a body. He didn't like those times so much, but DI Wright would tell him that he was good boy when he found them, and he'd get his favorite ball as a reward. DI Wright (he wasn't a detective, then) transferred over to Rural Crime when the dog unit closed due to budget cuts, with his faithful companion in tow. They tried to take Chester away to be retired and rehomed, but DI Wright wasn't having any of that and kept him on.

Anyways, where was his ball? Ah. Yes, under Paul's desk. He kept it there for safe keeping so that he didn't lose it. There weren't any other dogs to steal it mind you, so at least there wasn't that to worry about anymore. Thinking about it though, he would put up with all the other dogs in the world if it meant he could have DI Wright back with him.

What happened that day would stick with him forever, when their car had been hit from the side and rolled off the road onto its roof. Chester was meant to ride in the back, but DI Wright always let him sit up front with him because he was so well behaved, which in hindsight had probably saved his own life. The car that hit them didn't stop to help. They had ended up in a ditch that ran alongside one of those straight, narrow roads out to the West which were high up above the fields. 'The Fens' was what they were called. With the car on its roof, Chester had landed on top of DI Wright, who wasn't moving. He could smell blood too, long before he saw it.

He had nosed and licked his face, but when that hadn't worked, he had barked as loud as he could, over and over. But that didn't work either. DI Wright was still alive, but his breathing was faint. He was in trouble, and he was fading, and still nobody had come to help them. He had to do something.

That's when he remembered the radio (the thing that the police officers all spoke to each other through), so he had pawed at DI Wright's chest where the radio was strapped to his vest and much to his disbelief, the green light had flashed on. That meant you had to speak. He barked, again and again, until an officer at the other end had replied, so he kept barking, and kept whining, only quieting down when he was sure they got the message that something was terribly wrong.

Not long after that they had been rescued, but DI Wright was gone. The paramedics in the ambulance kept trying to bring him back but Chester knew that it was too late for that. Paul had been there, and he had taken him away. He was crying as he grappled with him to get him in the back of his car. Chester understood why he was so sad, because he felt sad too.

Paul was his new human now anyways, and whilst he didn't actually do any proper work anymore, Chester knew that he still held a license to do so should the opportunity arise. Despite his age, Chester wasn't yet retired. Paul, *his* Paul, had taken the necessary training and certification in order to handle him after DI Wright had gone. It was an unconventional arrangement, but somehow the gaffer had managed to gain the relevant permissions to allow it, just like he had with DI Wright.

When he said the gaffer, he actually meant the boss – that was just what everyone else called him. The gaffer had been very stressed recently. Paul and Hollie couldn't see it because he was very good at hiding it, but he couldn't hide it from Chester who could sense the tension that he carried upon his shoulders.

The last few weeks though, since the new detective sergeant had arrived, Chester noticed a distinct change in the man's spirit. He seemed happier; less stressed, which was nice. Maybe he could sense that the detective sergeant seemed to have his own weight upon his shoulders in the form of a strange black dog that followed him around, although not like any dog Chester had met before. It had these hollow, white eyes and long shaggy fur, and it didn't smell right. He couldn't tell if it was male or female, and when he tried to engage with it, it just stared right through him as if hadn't even seen him there.

At least it hadn't tried to steal his ball.

Chester didn't have that much of a sense of time, but he did know that it was nearing the end of the day because of which window the sun was shining through. He roused when he saw the detective sergeant appear, followed by his ever-present black dog. It looked bigger today than normal, and its head was hung low as it walked. Chester stood and shuffled underneath Paul's desk to guard his ball, just in case the black dog was thinking of stealing it.

The detective sergeant was nervous, and he smelled like – deer? Although Chester wasn't sure why. He didn't greet them like he normally did, instead heading straight for the gaffer's office and disappearing inside. Chester liked the new detective sergeant. He reminded him of himself in a way – he had this air about him that he really, really wanted to be a good boy, just like Chester did.

He wished he could tell him that he had nothing to worry about; the gaffer liked him and didn't think he was bad – even letting out a strong whiff of protective pheromones when the detective sergeant was around, which were a lot stronger and *different* smelling than when he was around the rest of the team.

Hollie appeared (he liked Hollie a lot too, she gave him treats when nobody else was looking) and started speaking to Paul. They were wondering why the new sergeant had showed up all soaked to the bone, and why he hadn't even looked their way as he went straight in to see the gaffer. They were worried that something was wrong but they couldn't sense things as strongly as Chester could, which he found very confusing sometimes. And they also couldn't seem to see the big black dog that was patiently waiting outside the gaffer's office.

Peeking out from under Paul's desk, Chester aimed a low growl towards the black dog to warn it that he wasn't going to stand for any trouble, but unsurprisingly, it just gazed right through him.

Black and White

"Come in, Daniel. What can I help you with?" the gaffer called out from within the realms of his office.

It felt like Dan's tongue was about to get stuck down his throat, his plan of telling the gaffer straight up what he had done going straight out the window. He shivered, still soaked through and dreaming of clocking off for a hot shower and some warm clothes. Broadmeadow observed him as he sidled his way into the office, with one eyebrow raised as he slipped off his reading glasses and neatly folded them on the desk. The man made him so nervous, although he couldn't pinpoint as to why exactly that was, because Broadmeadow had shown him nothing but appreciation for his services since joining their little department. Maybe it was just authority in general that had him clamming up and losing his nerve?

"I, um, I found some evidence as to who might have dumped all that rubbish at farmer Saunders' field, sir," he exclaimed, which made Broadmeadow smile, clasping his hands together atop his desk and looking at him rather expectantly.

"And?"

"I'd like to investigate further, sir. If you're happy for me to do so."

"Well that's great news, fella. Good work. What did you find then?"

Dan rifled about in his jacket pocket and pulled out the evidence bag containing the label he had pulled off one of the oil drums, stepping forwards to present it to his gaffer. Broadmeadow took it, his long fingers momentarily brushing against Dan's. They were warm. He squinted at the soggy old bit of paper in the bag, nodding; "You think you can get that translated? Looks like Chinese, doesn't it …"

"Yeah. I think so, sir. But yeah, I'll get it translated, although I suspect it's just a list of ingredients, but still. It might point us in the right direction of where it came from," Dan replied, deliberately stopping from himself rambling off on one, yet still unable to eloquently string his words together. Broadmeadow hummed and nodded again. He looked to be deep in thought, staring again at the evidence bag before handing it back to Dan. Their fingers brushed again, this time instigated by Dan himself, curious, the superintendent frowning before pulling his hand away.

Why did he have to go and do that? Stupid.

"Daniel?"

"Yeah?"

"Did you get caught in a shower out there, eh? What happened to you?"

Shit. *Shit*. He'd completely forgotten about that, distracted it would seem by his gaffer's big, warm hands (as he had been with his big feet when he'd first met the man). He should have stuck to his initial plan and told him about the accident and the deer first, before easing the blow with his positive lead on those pesky fly-tippers, but he was just too damned nervous. "I … I hit a deer sir. On my way back."

"Oh?"

"Damaged the car, sir."

"And you? Are *you* ok?"

"Yeah."

"What about the deer?"

"It's fine, I think. I left it at the vets."

Dan waited. And waited. But the shouting never came. The gaffer didn't round on him; didn't storm around to his side of the desk and take a fistful of his collar at the throat, with intentions of marching him out into the wider office for a public dressing down. When he dared himself a look, all that Dan could see upon his gaffer's face was a mild concern for his general wellbeing.

The rain had subsided some, as Dan and the gaffer made their way out to the staff car park. The acting superintendent had slung on a jacket. Dan hadn't. He felt a bit sick like a naughty child in trouble, having to go to the headmaster and own up to a misdemeanor. Hanging back, hands in his pockets, he let Broadmeadow go on ahead to his car, and waited for the outcome.

"From the way you were talking, I was thinking you'd gone and taken the front bumper off or something, lad," the gaffer said after finishing his inspection of the vehicle.

"Nah, just kerbed it." Dan shifted uncomfortably from foot to foot as he watched his boss further inspect the damage to his front wheel, thanking the Gods above that his brush with the deer hadn't caused any further devastation to the bodywork. He'd been lucky, and he knew it – it was extremely rare for one to come away from a collision with a deer without so much as a scratch to one's vehicle.

Broadmeadow was crouched on his haunches, running a finger along the missing chunk of alloy. Dan wasn't looking at that though – he was looking at the way his gaffer had to practically fold himself in half to get down to the floor due to his immense height …

"Well, I'm guessing you don't want to leave it *as is*, so if I give you the number of the garage we normally use you can give them a quick call, get it booked in?" the gaffer concluded, which certainly wasn't what Dan was expecting. At the very least he'd been preparing for a disapproving word or two, or a threat that it was going to come out of next month's pay, but no, nothing of the sort from old Broadmeadow who seemed as calm and collected as ever.

Dan liked that about the man; how relaxed he was. Now that he'd somehow escaped without a telling off he was starting to feel a little more at ease with him too. But Dan, being Dan, still couldn't manage to shake the crushing insecurity that had followed him around his whole life –

"You sure it's ok, sir? I mean, you're not annoyed with me?" – *Or disappointed, regretting your decision to take me on?*

Broadmeadow turned, unfolding his limbs and getting back up to his feet. God, he *was* tall. And rather handsome, in a middle-aged man with greying hair and a bit of a gut sort of way. There was an elegance to the man that reminded Dan of a heron parading up and down the office, commandingly so but not about to swoop down and peck your eyes out either – not unless you got on the wrong side of him Dan suspected, because it was always the calmest of people who were the ones most dangerous once provoked.

He internally cursed, as soon as he realised that he was admiring the older man and his somewhat stately semblance.

What? You just observed that the man was handsome, nothing more. Is that not allowed?

"Of course not, lad. It would take a wee bit more than a scuffed wheel trim to send me off the rails. Look, you'd know if I was angry, ok? Black and white I am, nothing in-between," the gaffer assured him. He was leaning now with his back against the car. Dan wanted to know what it would take to make the gaffer blow a fuse. They stared at each other for a moment. Dan shivered, still soaked to the bone and hoping to slip away soon for a hot shower down in the locker room. He didn't know what to say next, like his gaffer was waiting for a line of conversation to follow, but there was nothing forthcoming.

A glob of rain hit Dan's face – it was getting heavier again. He blinked the water away from his lashes. Broadmeadow leant back off the car and extended his lanky frame back to full height. Dan flinched, when a large hand came out to clap him on the shoulder, but it wasn't there to cause him harm. It was warm. Really warm. The gaffer noticed his adverse reaction; the way Dan's muscles seemed to ripple and tense under his hand, and swiftly pulled away.

"You're soaked through, lad. Have you got a change of clothes? And I tell ye', a good pair of walking boots wouldn't go amiss, you know, keep your wee feet dry in future?"

No, he didn't. And no, he still wasn't going to buy a pair of walking boots. It was getting on in the day with only a couple of hours 'till clocking off, so he'd be ok, making a mental note with himself to starting keeping a change of clothes in the locker. Another mental note made – amusing himself with the image of his gaffer in a pair of sensible hiking boots, and deciding that the man could undeniably pull the look off.

"Nah. I'll be alright, sir. Might go for a shower though, if that's ok?"

Broadmeadow started striding off back towards the station. Dan guessed that he was supposed to follow, stepping into line just to the right and a little back from the gaffer's shoulder. Looking down at Dan, who was at least a head shorter than the taller man, he gave him a smile. His eyes crinkled into deep divots at the corners, giving away the fact that the gaffer definitely wasn't a young man like himself. They spoke of a career hard worked and a past that Dan could only wonder of.

"You could always raid the spare uniform bin; I shan't promise there'll be anything of the extra short variety in there though," he remarked, still smiling, and Dan found himself smiling back at the gentle teasing that held no malice behind it.

Broadmeadow swung open the door to the main entrance, holding it agape for Dan to pass by and back into the warmth. "I'd rather be soaked than have to go back into uniform, sir."

"Ach. Suit yourself, fella."

The gaffer made his way past the broken lift to head up the stairs, leaving Dan staring up at his retreating form. His great, gangly legs were so long that he could take two steps at a time with ease. Then he realised that he was staring, and snapped his eyes away, also realising that he may have just insulted the man with the whole uniform comment. As Dan headed down towards the locker room, he continued to stew over whether he'd unintentionally put his gaffer's position down as inferior to his own.

The familiar *click clack* of heavy paws echoed behind him. The black dog had left him be for a while but it was back now, the solemn creeping of doubt like a daylight shadow falling over his every move.

Dan couldn't be bothered to turn and fling it an insult.

Going Home

There was a satisfying crunch of gravel under Broadmeadow's tires as he pulled up onto the driveway outside his house. They were going to get it block paved to match the rest of the street, the subject having been brought up many a time. And every time it had been brought up, Marcus had reminded his wife that gravel was better for deterring thieves – statistically, houses with a gravel driveway had an 80% less chance of being burgled. Especially where they lived, where crime on the big houses was rife, whether that be the travellers raiding the shed for your power tools or the addicts poking about the front windows to eye up your telly; you couldn't be too cautious, in his opinion.

He was actually home at a respectable time for once, because he'd made a point of leaving work on time that evening. The hallway light shone through the corners of the thick curtain behind the front door. With a bunch of flowers hanging from his left hand, keys jangling in the other, chocolates and a card tucked under his arm, Marcus battled his way through the heavy curtain keeping the heat in and blocking the door.

"Rona? You in, love?" he called out. Silence followed. The hall lamp was on atop the wooden side table, with the little bowl that Marcus chucked his keys into. They clattered noisily against the intricately painted ceramic. They'd brought that bowl on their honeymoon in Venice. Rowena's choice. It had been nice, the city of romance only second to Paris – so romantic that looking back now it had almost felt forced from the outset.

He called out again, his heart sinking with disappointment – a disappointment which he had grown so accustomed to that it didn't hurt him anymore – when his wife emerged from the kitchen with the most stoic of expressions cemented across her face. She didn't step forwards into her husband's arms, and there was no loving peck on the cheek to welcome him home. The kitchen doorframe propped her up, her arms folded about her chest.

"So you remembered then? Blow me down, I'm shocked, Marc." She sounded tired. Bored with it all. Disappointed that he had in fact remembered their twenty-fifth wedding anniversary, because now she'd have to find an alternative excuse to resent the man that stood before her with his supermarket flowers and his hastily written card.

Marcus put on a cordial smile, as if he could still find a chink in her armor and break his way through. "Of course, love. I thought you might want to head out for something to eat, maybe that Italian place down at the quayside?"

"Have you booked?" she quipped, knowing that he hadn't. She didn't want to go out. What was there to celebrate, anyways? The flame that burned for her husband had died out many years ago now, where all that remained were the burned-out ashes in which her and Marcus played at drawing pictures in of what a proper, Christian marriage should look like. Having both been brought up under the Catholic faith, Rowena knew that they only held onto what they still had because of the stain that divorce would leave upon their names.

Marcus cursed under his breath. He always tried with every best intention; and always came up short. "No."

"Well you know there won't be any tables." Under a mask of annoyance, Rowena was secretly pleased that she wasn't going to be subjected to a meal out over forced conversation and overbearing silences in between.

"I could give them a call, just to see?" Marcus trailed off towards her retreating form. She turned on her heel back into the kitchen. Marcus followed. He could see that there was already something slowly bubbling away in the slow-cooker – nothing special, a stew or something, nothing to mark their milestone anniversary. It said it all, really. Rowena didn't bestow him with an answer; she didn't need to. She started retrieving plates and cutlery from the drawer. Marcus automatically went to the cupboard for glasses, placing the unwanted flowers and chocolates on the side as he went.

He may as well have not bothered with them at all.

"We got ourselves a wee bit of a lead today on those fly-tippers – my new sergeant, Daniel, proved he's worth his salt by uncovering a label with an address on it. I reckon it could lead us to a perpetrator if we're lucky …"

Even as he said it, Marcus shot himself in the foot. The missus didn't care for his talk of work. It bored her. But what else did her husband have to say? What else did *she* have to say, for that matter? It no longer seemed worth the effort of trying to make conversation over the small things – that had eluded her interest a long time ago.

"Our wedding anniversary, and you're talking about work?" It came out flat and disinterested. She couldn't even be bothered to make it into an argument, as even that had lost its appeal after she had realised that Marc wasn't willing to take the bait. All he ever did was bounce back with a pathetic apology or a firm foot down that he didn't want to fight.

"Sorry, love," Marcus finished. He had nothing else to say.

They ate in silence after that.

Rowena tried to remember the last time she had taken any form of joy within her husband's company, or when they had last shared a laugh together, or partaken in any sort of physical contact that didn't have her reeling away from his touch. Ten years, perhaps? When they'd last gone back home to bonny Inverness together; when she still believed that there was a chance her husband could let sleeping dogs lie to take a job opportunity back on home soil. She resented him for that, in a way that had slowly crept up and constricted around her heart. There were reasons beyond what Marc had ever shared with her, why he wouldn't go back, and she resented him for that too.

The job had taken over, like she knew it always would. The Rural Crime Department had become the third party in their marriage, Marc's overriding passion in life, and though he tried his hardest to be the devoted husband and do right by his spouse, Rowena just couldn't bring herself to stick with it any longer. Whatever they once had, it was gone. Her husband refused to see it, but to her, it felt like they were drowning.

Marc barely even held onto his proud Scottish accent anymore, so long spent down south now that only fragments of it remained. She wanted to go home. An overwhelming pull like the rugged, crashing tides of the Moray Firth. Her parents were getting old, her sister with her nieces and nephews that only saw her twice a year, the pebble-dashed grey stone buildings, the ferocious coast lines and endlessly changing weather – her heart ached for those things.

"Did you fancy a trip down the coast this weekend? We could go for a walk, perhaps stop at that lovely pub with the garden on the cliff for something to eat?" Marcus suggested after they had finished their meal. At least he'd still held onto his love of the coast; one thing that hadn't been lost to her husband over the years. She felt sorry for him, and was sorry for what she was about to do.

"I'm going home, Marc," she said bluntly.

"What? When, love? Has something happened?" Concern fell over his features – again, she felt sorry for him, for not being able to read between the lines of her statement.

"No, nothing's happened. But I want to go *home*, Marcus." Rowena watched as her husband's face went from mild confusion to quiet acceptance. He looked down into his glass of wine before sadly meeting her gaze across the kitchen table. With her hands around her own glass, it was only then that he realised her wedding band no longer sat around her finger.

"I see. Without me, I'm guessing?" Marc spoke softly, an underlying poignancy to his tone that spoke of a man who had been anticipating those words for quite some time now.

"Yes, just me."

"When?"

"Tomorrow. My flights already booked," she said with a stark finality. She wanted him to put up some sort of fight; to shout at her or throw something or threaten her into staying because that would have made it easier on her guilt. But Marc would never do anything like that. He was soft and he was inexplicably loyal, and he would take it lying down as if he were the one who had gone and done her wrong.

Marc downed his glass and gathered up their plates with a nod in her general direction. She watched as the man she had once loved loaded the dishwasher with a set to his broad shoulders, and only when he left the kitchen and headed upstairs did she allow herself a tear or two to mourn for the finality of the decision she had made.

Runaway

Marcus had chosen to take the spare room that night – he knew when he wasn't welcome in his own bed. It briefly crossed his mind if he'd even go back to their marital bedroom once Rowena was gone, however he packed that thought away for the time being as it hurt to much to think about. The reality hadn't full sunk in yet. How could it, when your missus tells you she's leaving the very next day out of the blue like that? Not only leaving, but not coming back either.

Tomorrow, I'm leaving tomorrow.

It wasn't a shock, per say. Their marriage had been faltering for so long now that he couldn't remember a time where things had been *good*. He couldn't even remember the last time they'd shared something as simple as a cuddle on the sofa, let alone the last time they'd shared matrimonial relations. At some point it had dwindled down to strictly birthdays and anniversaries, and even then, it had been an act of formality rather than one of any real love; in, out, done.

Their marriage had been built on a secret from the very start – a secret that Marcus had never once shared with his dearest wife. Nobody this side of the border knew. Not a soul. For the first time in thirty-two years, in the solitude of the spare bed and with a shallow emptiness filling his heart, he allowed himself to think about Johnny.

*

Fresh faced and proudly donning his new uniform, constable Broadmeadow had joined Police Scotland at the age of nineteen. He'd eventually won his father round after the shock decision not to follow in his fisherman's roots, when he'd grudgingly attended the passing out parade and witnessed his son becoming a man. His father had told him he was proud of him. His mother had cried, smothering him against her breast. Not long after that was the last time they had spoken, because his father had passed before the year was out – a stroke, out alone on his boat. They didn't find him until two days later, when the small fishing vessel had washed ashore.

Even as far back as then Marcus had his secret. Ever since meeting a young man called Johnny, he had been plagued with feelings that no red-blooded fella should ever be having, let alone a good Catholic like himself. He had been naive. He'd let his guard down, just once, and by god had he paid the consequences. He and Johnny went through training together, passed out together, recruited into Police Scotland Inverness together – they were pals. More than that, they were devoted companions. Johnny had made the first move. Their feelings had just been too strong – a couple of young lads full of testosterone and the rebellious freedom of youth, with farfetched notions of a world that hadn't yet caught up.

Johnny was the most gorgeous fella Marcus had ever set eyes on, with his golden-brown hair and freckles dancing up his cheeks and chestnut eyes that could melt any poor soul he came across into submission. They'd been careful, or so they thought. A stolen kiss down a back alley on the Friday night beat, a quick passing touch at the end of their shift when the locker room had cleared, spending their downtime off together down the local, and even going as far as to rent a flat together – they were hiding in plain sight. As he'd already said though, they were young and full of the restless fire of youth, and they hadn't been careful enough in a city steeped with the antiquated conceptions of men like them. It was a time when the 'gay-disease' was still rife and wildly misunderstood; when they could both be dismissed from duty and lose their place in society at the tip of a hat, all without a single repercussion.

But despite it all; despite the very real dangers, Marcus and Johnny had followed their hearts.

"I think I love you, Marc ..."

"You soft shite ..."

"I mean it."

A kiss so tender in the dark, chafed lips and last night's stubble lingering over a promise to each other that they'd be ok ...

"I love you too, Johnny-boy."

Notions of spending a lifetime together were painfully short-lived. Whispers started between fellow colleagues. Rumours spread. Backs to the wall in the showers. And then it all came crashing down, leaving Marcus questioning everything that he ever was and ever would be:

Young officer murdered on beat – police appealing for witnesses.

There were no witnesses; no investigation as to why their shifts had been swapped at the last minute, why Johnny's partner that evening hadn't been present at the time of the attack. Nobody questioned it. The case was filed away almost as fast as it had hit the headlines in the first place, and that was the moment when Marcus had lost his faith and trust in the force that he believed was only there to do good. Johnny didn't matter, because Johnny was a dirty little shit-stabber and the world was better off without him.

Marcus knew that it was only a matter of time before he was next. It was a warning that there was no place in the force for men like him. He didn't have time to grieve; didn't even make it to the funeral for fear of what that would imply. Self-preservation was top of the agenda now.

The village of Culloden Moor was where Marcus grew up. It was a small village just east of Inverness, a passing place for hikers and cyclists touring the North, and more famously, the site of the final confrontation of the Jacobite rising where the battle of Culloden took place. Marcus started to frequent the local pub where he knew the landlord's daughter worked behind the bar. Safe to say, Rowena had been swept off her feet by the tall and handsome young officer who made it his mission to spend every evening off down the Old North Inn. Marcus liked her. She was fierce like the waves against the cliffs of the Western Firth and a pretty wee lass like the spring flowers surrounding the Clava Cairns.

He could learn to love her, and he did. Not in a way that ever felt true to his soul, but he did love her in the best way he could.

Thoughts of Johnny were safely stored away to a corner of Marc's heart like precious artefacts, akin to a painting in a museum that was so revered it had to be locked away in the dark for fear of the paint becoming damaged. As a painful reminder of who Marcus truly was, Johnny's ghost still remained, following him around and visiting him in his fervent dreams, where he would wake with a cold sweat and pounding heart, with only his unbeknownst wife by his side.

As soon as the opening came up to join a department in a foreign land of flat rolling fields and soil made of clay, with the lucrative offer of extra pay and a car to go with, Marcus had packed up his life, his doting young wife in tow, and left his past behind for good.

*

For nearly twenty-six years, he had expertly lived a respectable life. But now, just as he was reaching middle age and was contented with his lot in this world, Marcus found himself facing that life alone. His heart ached for Johnny, a wound that he long thought to be healed peeling open again, stitch by carefully placed stitch. For Rowena he mourned too, for the comfortably married life he had tried to provide.

In the spare bed, with the unused sheets that were still as fresh and crisp as new, and the mattress that felt solid and foreign under his weight, Marcus willed himself not to cry.

Car Chases and Hard Arrests

Holding the title of 'detective' in front of her rank wasn't always what it was cracked up to be, as Hollie was soon finding out. They'd been staring at the same row of commercial bins from across the street for what felt like far too long now – it was a warm evening too, which made the stuffy interior of the idle car even more stifling. Dan had already cracked the windows but it wasn't making much of a difference, even as the evening started to draw on into the night.

Four nights already, they'd been staring at the bins down the side of the Imperial Garden. Four nights of trying not to doze off in her seat, of watching customers come and go, and four nights spent getting really hungry over the wafts of Chinese food that kept drifting in through the windows. Surely they had to empty those bins at some point? Either that, or they would have to change tactics and move on to staring at them come daybreak instead.

Luckily for them the town only had one Chinese restaurant, which substantially allowed them to narrow down the source of their fly-tipped barrels of cooking oil. Thank God. Imagine if they covered a big city? They would have been at it for weeks ...

It was the first time during their extended stint of surveillance that she'd had Dan for company. It was also the first time since his arrival that she'd spent more than a passing pleasantry in the kitchen or a quick chat over case notes in his presence. She shifted in her seat to try and ease the encroaching numbness to her behind. It was going to another long night as they watched the restaurant close up for the day.

"Did you have to do stuff like this in the Met, then? Or have I been sold short by all the police dramas on TV where being a detective is all car chases and hard arrests?" Hollie tried after a long silence. She wasn't too good with new people; even worse when it came to making conversation with a senior officer who didn't seem to be the best of conversationalists either.

Dan continued staring across the street as he replied, "Much the same, really. The cases were a bit higher profile I guess, but most of it was just surveillance and paperwork."

He turned his head to give her a smile then, his eyes crinkling ever so slightly at the corners, which gave Hollie a small glimpse of the young man behind the rather serious facade. She wanted to ask why he'd left it all behind, and what had made him choose to join their small department in the arse end of nowhere, but she didn't want to pry. She liked him. Everyone did, with the gaffer especially having taken a shine to him, even if he wasn't the most forthcoming of blokes from the outset.

The trouble was though, he didn't seem to want to believe it himself; that his new team liked him, and God forbid, actually wanted to get to know him.

"I want to move somewhere and join a bigger force one day, have you got any tips for me?" Hollie asked. She had dreams, and ambition. She wanted to be the best she possibly could at her job.

Dan laughed; a laugh that was tinged with dejection and void of any humour, which had Hollie wondering again what young Dan was holding back from sharing with her.

"Just be prepared to fight for your place because there'll always be someone pushing you from behind. And whatever you do, don't piss off your senior officers ..."

"I think I can handle it," Hollie said as she caught Dan's eye again, and the smile he gave her in return was genuine.

Perhaps she's made of more than what you are, Dan thought. "I have no doubt, Hollie ... oh, hang on ..."

A flatbed van had just roared its way up the street, its trailer base banging loudly as it mounted the pavement before reversing back up the side alley beside the restaurant.

"Looks like it's your lucky day, Hollie." Dan drew his binoculars to his eyes. Hollie shifted the long-range camera into focus, poised and ready, the monotony of their hours of waiting suddenly taking a back seat and giving way to a steady, pulsing rush of adrenaline. They couldn't see a whole lot except for two men, a right rough looking pair, exiting the van and disappearing behind the vehicle that was now blocking the bins from view.

Hollie felt like one of the detectives off the TV, finally. The mug shots she captured of the suspected perpetrators were spot on, with all the angles they could possibly need for identifying the men. Minutes passed, silence except for the shutter clack of the camera, when eventually the men got back into the van. The engine spluttered back into life. Hollie glanced at Dan. He nodded right back at her in a moment of silent communication shared between them.

And then the men were off, the flatbed trailer laden with grimy, oil filled drums as it rattled off up the road, heading straight towards Hollie and Dan.

Hollie held her breath, lowering her camera out of view as the van drew closer. They were going to see them. Dan didn't seem fazed however, slipping the car into gear pushing down the handbrake in one casual move. The engine of their patrol car softy thrummed. She watched on with bated breath as he slowly fixed his gaze at the driver of the van when they passed. The man stared back momentarily – and put his foot down.

They gave chase.

Hollie came back to her senses. She fumbled for the radio; "Request for assistance, in pursuit of vehicle reg. Yankee Oscar 1-4, Golf, Alpha, Bravo ... yes, assessing risk in pursuit ... yes, two male suspects ..."

It would have been rather exciting, her first proper pursuit, if it wasn't for the fact that Dan's driving was erring on the wrong side of questionable. Not *bad* as such, just ... fast. The order to stand down crackled down the radio. Hollie looked across at Dan but he appeared not to have heard – or chose to ignore it. They narrowly avoided another vehicle as it pulled up on the kerb to let them pass. Friday night partygoers started to appear in their droves as they neared the built up quayside that was lined with bars and restaurants. Their suspects knew what they were doing; they were forcing them to back off rather than continue their pursuit.

But Dan's jaw was set in a fixed determination. He didn't want to let them go, and it took all her courage to pipe up, praying that she wouldn't be reprimanded for questioning a senior officer's discretion. "Dan, sir, you need to slow up a bit, we're in a built up area ..."

There was a pause, before Dan gripped the wheel hard and swore under his breath.

"Yeah. Sorry mate." Dan's foot pulled back off the gas. They were moments away from the quayside on a relatively busy Friday night, and about to jump a red light. No. Hollie was right. It wasn't worth the risk. Had they have been pursuing a suspect back in the city, they would have had aerial assistance by now to keep track of the flatbed van. Back-up patrol cars would be closing in to cut the suspects off. But alas, all they had for support here was an officer from Central Control barking at them that the risk to civilian life was too high, and that they needed to concede.

"Fuck it," Dan cursed again as he slowed for the light, watching in vain as the van they were tailing was lost to the flow of traffic ahead. Hollie released the breath she hadn't realised she'd been holding. As she did, she thought she saw a large black dog, bear-like and solemn standing at the side of the road.

A double take in the mirror though, and it was gone.

"We still have the vehicle reg, and some good mugshots," Hollie reasoned as she sighed back into her seat, with Dan slowing up to a more respectable speed and standing down the blue lights.

"We'll find that van burned to the ground tomorrow, guarantee it," Dan said, deflated, turning a left to head back towards the station. He seemed to be in total disregard of the good progress they'd just made towards catching their – until now – unknown fly-tippers.

"Probably. They're probably razing it to the ground as we speak along with those oil drums. But we've got stuff to work on now, yeah? My guess is they're not the only ones involved, anyways. Yeah, we could have done them for dangerous driving and evading an arrest, but we wouldn't of caught them in the act of what we actually wanted to catch them for." She eyed Dan, cautious yet curious as to whether she had gotten through to him. It was one of Hollie's greatest strengths, that. She had the gift of verbal diplomacy, without coming across as patronising or one-sided.

"You know what, Hollie? You're spot on there." Dan was smiling, which made her brim with pride, any preconceptions of the man that DS Taylor really was laying to rest. He valued her opinions and that mattered. Something had just changed between them, she could feel it. They had just crossed the threshold of mere colleagues to allies, and all it had taken was an evening stuck together in a stuffy car and a disappointingly short pursuit.

"Do you fancy stopping for some chips before heading back?" Hollie asked, feeling her stomach grumble.

"Yeah, ok. Shall we whack the blues back on?" Dan's smile had given way to a grin at the mention of his favourite food. She wasn't sure if he was joking about the blue lights part or not, but soon had her answer as Dan stepped on the gas and flicked the switch for the emergency sirens.

Stepping out of Line

"A word please, Daniel." The gaffer's tone was flat, his facial expression stoic. Once satisfied that his sergeant was indeed dropping whatever it was he was doing and making his way over to his office, Broadmeadow stalked back inside and took a seat behind his desk.

Dan didn't like being summoned. It brought back memories of DCI Walters letting loose on him, the relative privacy of the four thin walls and closed door that Dan was always instructed to lock behind him, that gave the man free reign to push him around as he saw fit. He could feel Hollie and Paul's eyes following from behind their screens and over lowered paperwork, as he timidly rapped on the gaffer's open door before stepping inside.

The black dog followed him in. It quietly sat at his feet, emanating a soft whine from somewhere in the back of its throat. Broadmeadow was slowly tapping away at his keyboard, one key at a time with his long fingers purposely punching out each letter, which he would have found amusing had his guts not been squirming in anticipation; worrying over what sort of grilling he was about to receive.

"Tell me something, DS Taylor ... do you understand what an order to stand down means?" the gaffer asked, finally turning his attention towards him. He looked tired, and certainly not in any mood for an argument. Dan bowed his head. His nose twitched. If there was one thing that he hated more than being summoned, it was being spoken to like he was a child.

Somehow, he managed to reign the brewing sarky comment back in before it slipped from his lips. He knew his place. "Yes, sir. I do."

The gaffer pointedly looked up at him over his reading glasses. "Could you explain it to me then?"

Dan knew where this was heading, feeling himself flush with embarrassment at having to spell out to his boss exactly why he'd let his stubborn head get the better of him. He felt like a right tit as he tried work his vocal cords without his voice cracking, staring down at his feet as his hands found their way into the safety of his pockets; "It means a senior ranking officer has given an order that must be followed, sir."

The office was all of a sudden taking on a stifling atmosphere, not unlike that of the car they had been stuck in the Friday just gone. He'd underestimated acting superintendent Broadmeadow – the older man's relaxed attitude towards his team had lulled him into a false sense of security that he wasn't actually capable of administering a reprimand. The black dog grew larger, leaning heavily against the side of Dan's legs. It was whining louder now, like a gust of wind repeatedly whipping around a corner.

The gaffer's blue eyes were boring into him, but he couldn't meet them. He just couldn't. Because his lower lip was starting to wobble and if he cried now, that would be it. Any respect that he had built up over the short time they had known each other would be shattered.

However, the gaffer wasn't done with him yet. "Good, Daniel. Except, there was me thinking that surely, a clever young lad like you would know that when such an order is given, as you *do* in fact know what it means, you are to follow it without question, no?"

"Yes, sir. I just ..."

Broadmeadow picked up his pen, the nearest thing to hand, and started waving it in Dan's general direction, cutting him off mid-sentence, "You just, *what*, exactly? Thought that chasing after some two-bit, bottom of the ladder pair of reprobates was worth you causing an RTA? Killing someone? What were you *thinking*, lad?"

"I wasn't, sir. 'M sorry," Dan cowered, hoping and praying they were done. He felt ashamed, upset, and about two feet shorter than he already was after his gaffer's verbal berating. Of course he knew better. He wasn't stupid.

"No, bloody right you weren't. I want your word, Daniel, that if such an order is ever given again, you will follow it. I've got enough of my plate right now lad, without having to try and explain the actions of one of my team to the head of OPS on a Monday morning, ye' hear me?" He stood then, and God was he an imposing man, towering above Dan, causing something to trigger in his mind that there was going to be more than just a rhetorical chastising.

The black dog flinched before drawing itself up to its feet, hackles raised at the ready. Dan drew back into himself. "You have my word, sir. I ... I promise." The wobble to his voice was uncontrollable now, beyond the point of no return. Dan was crying in front of his boss and there was nothing he could do to stop it. He waited for the next blow, for letting slip his weakness, but it never came. The office descended into silence, bar the steady hum of the gaffer's computer and the ticking of the clock behind him. Every second that passed felt like an age, before he eventually mustered up the courage to glance up at his gaffer.

Broadmeadow was the picture of a man who was in over his head, staring at Dan with a lightly furrowed brow, bemused in his expression which was far softer than it had been moments ago, concerned yet unsure over how to proceed. Dan's hand left the safety of his pocket to wipe his nose. The gaffer made to say something but the words he was trying to compose weren't forthcoming, his mouth opening and closing again before his brow furrowed even further.

He tried again, as a couple of stray tears ebbed their way down Dan's furiously flushing cheeks, "Go and sort yourself out, son. Dismissed."

The look of bemusement clouding his gaffer's face at his sudden outburst remained imprinted across Dan's mind as he scarpered, head down and on a mission to make it to the toilets without causing any further embarrassment to himself. Two paces behind and slowly swaying in its gait, the black dog followed. Chester growled from beneath DC Bartlett's desk, but it didn't have the desired effect – the black dog didn't care about Chester, only Dan.

Later that day, with the black dog now nestled at his feet – *don't worry Dan, I'll always be by your side, you don't need anyone else* – he buried himself in his work. Clicking his way through the criminal records database with a printout of his suspects on the desk in front of him, he resigned himself to the monotony of his task. There were thousands. Literally thousands, even with his search filtered down to males between the ages of 20 to 40, of a certain height bracket and sporting dark hair.

He didn't mind. At least with his face buried in his screen and earphones muffling any outside noise nobody would disturb him. Dwelling on every detail of a troublesome encounter was something he was good at; analysing every word and reaction, every interaction, turning it over and over in his mind until he was satisfied that he had made the wrong move at every turn. This time though, it hurt even more than usual, trying to put it down to the fact that he was so desperate for his new gaffer's approval that any step out of line was bound to cut deeper.

"You're a clever young lad ..."

It was that part, one small and meaningless sentence that he couldn't stop returning to. A shred of a compliment that was most likely not even intended as that, and Dan was clinging to it with both hands. The words curled around his heart like a warm embrace, and the more he let thoughts of Broadmeadow creep inside, the smaller the black dog at his feet grew.

The shaggy old beast, with its grey tinged fur and clouded orbs for eyes tried to bring Dan's attention back to it, laying heavy at his feet with its whistling whine for attention, but Broadmeadow's character was too strong. It was worried then, for the first time since they'd met, that it might lose Dan to the other man altogether.

Tea, Two Sugars

Marcus was no stranger to reprimanding his staff. It wasn't something he particularly enjoyed but he understood that it was a necessary part of the job. He also understood that with every reprimand came an opportunity to mentor and guide; to steer his young team in the direction of what a properly unified unit could achieve. He lived for his job, and the *good* that he could do for the corner of the country that he now called home.

Was there some guilt in there somewhere, a partially subconscious attempt to make right of his former wrongs? Probably. Was he softer with his team than an acting superintendent should be because of that? Definitely. That was most probably why he felt so bloody rotten, too. Daniel deserved the reminder that an order was an order; that much was true. But perhaps he *had* been a wee bit harsh on him, seeing as he was so new to the department and had only acted with the best intentions.

If that had been Paul or Hollie he'd dragged into his office, there wouldn't have been any waterworks to throw him off kilter, and they certainly wouldn't have flinched like a cornered animal the way Daniel had done when he'd rose to his feet and delivered his message of authority. His young sergeant hadn't been crying in a forced attempt to make Marcus go easier on him either – those were genuine tears of remorse that he had laid witness to, and he felt sorry that he hadn't known how to react to it other than sending him away to go and clean his face.

Something didn't sit right about how Daniel had reacted, even though Marcus couldn't recall anything he had done in particular to make the lad so skittish in his presence. He was under the impression that he had been nothing but kind to the lad up until then, and in return, Dan had repaid him with nothing but hard work and an astute keenness to learn. Which led him to believe that the niggling suspicion he had was correct – that someone other than himself, in Daniel's past, had left a resonating impression on him, and not in a good way. And he'd bet good money on that person being his former commanding officer.

Out of his office window, he had a clear view of Daniel's desk, and the young man himself currently residing there. He decided to leave him be for the time being, as he wasn't yet prepared to acknowledge the way that the sight of him made something warm and soft around the edges stir within his chest. God help him, he just wasn't.

Time was getting on in the day, Marcus only realising that he'd been sat there wool gathering for lord knows how long when Hollie tapped on the window to give him a wave. She was giving him a dazzling grin, having picked up on the fact that he'd been daydreaming under the rouse of being deeply embedded in some important emails. That was because, he realised with a start, that his computer screen had gone to sleep. He gave her a tired, apologetic smile through the glass and received a knowing look from his constable in return, pointing at the clock and shaking her head. Marcus waved her away. It was gone five. Paul and Chester had already gone home and Hollie was now leaving, which just left he and Daniel with the office to themselves.

Looking out the window again, he saw something then in the rather short statured young man that he could have seen in himself; that he still did in fact – a man who had been knocked down who was about to work late into the evening to redeem himself. A man who perhaps had nothing else to go home for, which rung particularly true to Marcus.

Marcus could see that Daniel had earphones in. He was lightly tapping his foot to some unheard beat, his face pressed so close to his screen that he wondered if he should be sending the lad off for an eye test ...

Was he sitting there all alone because he was waiting for Marcus to knock off home in order to escape under the radar? Entirely plausible a notion, but Marcus decided that he wasn't having it. Racking his brains, he tried to remember if it was tea or coffee that was Daniel's preferred drink.

"Tea, two sugars, thanks sir ..."

Of course. Marcus had been making mental notes about the lad's likes and dislikes since that very first day, without even realising what he'd been doing. Except now, perhaps it was making a bit more sense, now that his heart was pointing in the right (or wrong) direction. And the gravity of that revelation hit Marcus like a near head-on collision.

Rivalry

Chester was furious with the black dog. He'd had enough of its *blasé* attitude towards him – did it not know that he was supposed to be the top dog around here? At first he thought it would just go away once the new detective sergeant got himself settled, but it was becoming more and more obvious that it was thinking of sticking around.

Chester liked the new sergeant. Dan was his name, although the gaffer, the real top dog, liked to call him Daniel. No one else called him that but Dan didn't seem to mind, moreover, he seemed to like it when Broadmeadow got his name wrong. Chester could sense his change in energy whenever the boss called him Daniel – the jittery waves that he constantly emitted would momentarily soften and the black dog would step back and take pace behind.

The gaffer liked Dan, very much so. But the black dog liked Dan too, perhaps just as much as the gaffer did. It seemed to feed off his ebbs and flows of emotion, growing stronger every time something bad happened. Like today, when Broadmeadow had called Dan into his office and shouted at him for being a bad boy. When he'd emerged with tears in his eyes, the black dog had grown in size and strength; so much so that Chester knew he would be stupid to try and pick a fight, even though he desperately wanted to go up to Dan and make sure he was feeling ok.

"Chester, come on mate. Home time," Paul instructed at two-minutes to five, but he didn't want to leave Dan alone with the black dog. Chester wanted to stay and help lick his tears away because it always helped on the few occasions he could remember when Paul had cried. He'd clambered onto his lap and tried to lick his cheeks, which had made Paul laugh and then he wasn't crying anymore. Paul only cried at home though, when it was just the two of them. He would talk to him about DI Wright when he'd had too much to drink; how much he missed him ... they both missed him. But they had each other so it was ok.

However, Dan's black dog didn't want to comfort him. It liked it when he was sad because it too was sad. Chester didn't know why exactly, but it was.

"Oi, Chester! Whatcha' staring at Dan for?" Paul couldn't see the black dog, but Chester could sense that he knew something wasn't right. He could feel his concern for the sergeant, but also something akin to apprehension or embarrassment that was holding him back from approaching. Chester gave Paul a look, a little wave of his tail, before trotting over to where Dan was sitting at his desk with his earphones in. He was tall enough to rest his head on the desk and nose at his hand. Dan looked down, surprised, and greeted him with a ruffle to his head.

"Hey there, boy." Dan proceeded to tickle his ears, and then he pulled his eyes away from the computer monitor to brush their noses together. The black dog growled a low warning, pulling its lips back in an ugly snarl and whipping out from under the desk. It wanted to start a fight, lunging forwards, but as it lunged towards him, Chester realised that it couldn't actually touch him – it snapped and snarled again, but when it made contact with his neck to try and pull him away, he didn't feel a thing. If dogs could laugh, Chester would have done.

A moment or so later, Paul quietly shuffled his way over. He wanted to say something to Dan, but at the same time

Chester could feel his confliction – male humans were funny like that. They were very good at hiding how they were feeling, and they were equally terrible at offering comfort where required. Chester found it all very strange.

Paul wanted to ask Dan if he was ok, if he wanted to talk, not to feel stupid for crying and that he didn't think any less of him for it, but instead coming out with, "Fancy coming out for a pint, mate?"

If there was one thing male humans were very good at, it was trying to avoid a subject in the way of *'having a drink or two'*. Paul did that a lot, before. He did it a lot less now though, which Chester was thankful for.

"Nah, think I'll stay a bit longer here. Thanks, though," replied Dan, only giving Paul a fleeting glance before focusing his attention back to his computer. Chester thought it would be nice for Paul and Dan to be friends. They were both lonely. He whined, nuzzling again at Dan's hand.

"Come on Chester, leave him be, will ya'?" urged Paul, not understanding what had gotten into his furry companion.

"He really wants me to go for a pint, doesn't he? Another time, hey? Just not ... not today," Dan said. He understood, even if Paul didn't. Chester could sense that Dan meant it. He wanted to be friends with Paul, but the black dog, now sulking under the desk, had too strong a hold over him that day. It was laying over his feet, a heavy weight that was stopping him from rising, even if he wanted to.

"Alright, mate. I'll hold you to that, Dan." Paul smiled, clipping Chester's lead to his collar. Chester got excited then. Hopefully they'd get to go for a walk before heading home? He wagged his tail, waving it like a great fan. He didn't want to leave Dan with the black dog, but then he remembered that the gaffer was still there, and he was waiting for everybody else to leave before coming out to try and make amends with his sergeant. That filled Chester with a great sense of relief as he and Paul headed off home for the night.

An Apology

It was the cup of tea that he saw first, sliding across the desk into his field of vision. He nearly jumped out of his skin when he turned to see the gaffer looming at his side. Not threateningly so, it was just that his height and stature made him look a bit awkward in his own skin. Dan slowly pulled out his earbuds. Broadmeadow was lurking, clearly unsure whether to stand or sit.

"Alright there, Daniel? I'm not used to having company after hours, should you not be heading off home?" Broadmeadow begun when he saw that he'd been noticed, cautious over where he trod with his words whilst he gauged the current mood of his sergeant. Dan was still reeling with self-loathing and still utterly convinced that the gaffer thought he was weak. Incompetent. Not a proper bloke like the rest of them.

But then again; the cup of tea did feel like a peace offering of sorts, which gave him the smallest flutter of hope that forgiveness may still be on the cards. He met Broadmeadow's eye, unable to resist the tenderness he found there. "Just thought I'd stay and make a dent in these records, sir."

"Fair enough, fella. Fair enough. Mind if I take a seat?" The gaffer already had his hands at the back of the nearest chair to pull it round which told him that he didn't really have a choice in the matter, but Dan didn't mind. He couldn't deny, that despite having been given a good dressing down by the man that morning, there was something that he just liked about his company. Broadmeadow was so calm, his defined accent compelling, and it was catching.

"Nah, go ahead." Dan turned back to his screen. The gaffer pulled the chair closer and folded himself down into it. His knees audibly creaked as he fell into the seat – he wasn't expecting it to be set that low.

"Some short arse has been sitting here, eh?" Broadmeadow smiled, before his face dropped. He was meant to be making amends after all, not digging his hole even deeper.

"A short arse like me, sir?" Dan laughed, feeling more like himself all of a sudden. Like that peace offering in the form of a cup of tea, made just how he liked it (Broadmeadow had taken the time to remember he took two sugars and lots of milk), was enough to temporarily set his mind at ease.

"Well, that's not exactly what I ..." the gaffer stuttered, fighting to turn what he'd said into what he'd actually meant, which was that his chair was very low and that his legs were very long – what he hadn't meant was for it to sound like he was poking fun at Daniel's shorter than average height.

"Because I think even if that chair went any higher, which it doesn't because it's broken, you'd still be pushed to comfortably fit in there ..." Work forgotten for now, his gaffer proving a welcome distraction, Dan looked across for his reaction with a bit of a cheeky smile. He was met with a raised eyebrow – had he overstepped the mark? Thankfully, this time, no.

"You've got some cheek, haven't you? And no, we don't have the funding to be running round buying new office furniture, if that's what you're getting at. I suppose you had fancy – what do you call them? 'Ergonomic' chairs, down in the Met?" said with only a mock sternness though, Broadmeadow's lips turned up at the corners as he spoke.

"We had wireless keyboards too, sir. And double monitors that matched, not like these ancient old things." It was a casual banter, a bit of gentle teasing which made Dan feel at ease. The gaffer had moved closer too with his legs spread wide in his seat, and his knee was only inches away from Dan's. Then he leant forwards to rest his elbows atop his thighs. Again, he reminded Dan of a heron, like one in an oriental brush painting with his sharply angled limbs, his piercing gaze and somewhat beaky nose.

His smile slipped then to something more serious, and Dan knew that he was preparing himself to tell him why he had really come over for a bit of a chat. The gaffer paused, took a slow breath, and then came out with it. "Look, I wanted to apologise, Daniel. I know this place is a wee bit of a step down from the Met, but do know that I want you here. I didn't mean for you to feel, uh, intimidated earlier, and if you've had a bad experience with a senior officer before, just know that I'm not like that, ok? I'm on your side, son."

Was it really that obvious? Like he had a sign above his head that read, 'victim'? An uncomfortable knot swelled and constricted inside Dan's stomach. He didn't want to talk about it. "Thanks, sir."

Straight away, Broadmeadow could sense Daniel's discomfort over the subject so he expertly steered back away to something they both found more comfortable; "Are you getting anywhere with that search of yours, then?"

"No, not really. There are thousands of blokes between the ages of twenty to forty, and that's even if they've got previous, which for all we know they don't ..." Dan said dejectedly.

"But you're going to keep looking, eh?"

"Yeah. S'pose so." He would keep looking until his eyes grew heavy with fatigue. He would redeem himself and come up with a result.

"How about we get Paul and Hollie on board too, tomorrow? I know I can't force you son, but I would suggest that it may be better for you to head home soon. I don't like the idea of you rattling about here on your own," Broadmeadow said every so softly, much to the contrary of what DCI Walters would have made him do. He wouldn't have cared. He would have bullied him into staying, without overtime, until he produced a positive lead.

"What time do you normally leave, sir?" Dan tried to sound as flippant as possible, like it wouldn't have bothered him either way. But for some reason it did. He didn't want to be left alone, because when Broadmeadow was around he felt immeasurably more relaxed. He kept the black dog at bay for him, without even knowing it was there.

The gaffer gently reached over and briefly laid his hand at Dan's upper arm. "Ah, well that'll be whenever I feel like I've spent too long here already. An early night tonight though, I'm thinking. Would you agree?"

Did Broadmeadow not have a wife to get home to, he wondered? Dinner on the table? Dan knew he wore a ring around his finger, but aside from that he had never once mentioned a Mrs Broadmeadow. His curiosity got the better of him. "Does your missus not mind? That you're always here and not at home?" he asked, flicking his eyes the gaffer's way just in time to see the minute set of his jaw; the way his shoulders slumped ever so slightly at the question over his significant other.

"No, Daniel. Not really."

"Oh ... Sorry, sir. I shouldn't have pried like that."

Broadmeadow removed his hand from Dan's arm. "How about I come and get you? We can lock up together? I've just got a few things to wrap up – half an hour ok?"

Changing the subject again. Perhaps they both held things inside that they'd rather not be talking about ...

Dan hardly had a chance to nod an affirmative before Broadmeadow was up and sauntering back towards his office. The black dog shuffled back over to lay across his feet once he was gone.

He shut off his computer long before the clock hit half seven, not wanting to keep his gaffer waiting. Broadmeadow appeared soon after with a backpack and his laptop bag dangling from his shoulder. The warm smile he gave Dan when he saw that he was ready and waiting made the uneasy knot in his stomach return – not because he was frightened of him, not anymore; not now he knew that Broadmeadow was a decent bloke, and that he still wanted to be around him despite having shown his senior officer his soft and vulnerable underbelly.

It wasn't fear that had his stomach playing havoc with his insides – it was something more like affection which was quite possibly just as unsettling.

They walked down to the carpark together. The black dog followed, no longer at Dan's side but a good few paces behind. A few causal comments were shared between them as they walked, about nothing in particular like the weather forecast and how annoying the temporary traffic lights at the top of the road were. Dan reached his car first, and stopped. Why did it suddenly feel awkward, saying goodbye for the night? Dan knew why, of course. The same reason why his belly was knotting and flipping as he tried his hardest to bar his mind from leading him in that direction.

He wondered briefly if the gaffer felt it too – could other people feel an atmosphere, like he could?

"Right, well. You take care of yourself Daniel, yes?" the gaffer spoke first, as they both hovered next to Dan's car.

"You too, sir. Thanks, again."

A traitorous thought crossed Dan's mind, that it would take nothing at all to just step forwards into Broadmeadow's arms. Then he reminded himself that he was meant to be redeeming himself; proving that he wasn't some soft shite who needed a physical display of affection to make him feel better. Broadmeadow *was* lingering though. He should have left for his own car by now. And then he did something wholly unexpected, reaching forwards with that same soft smile and ruffling Dan's hair.

Anyone else and Dan would have been rather petulant over somebody messing up his meticulously combed-over hair. Anyone else and his stomach wouldn't have done a full on somersault, sending little shivers of pleasure running in all directions ...

"Right. On your way, Daniel," the gaffer conceded, or else they might have stayed there all night. Dan knew he was flushing at the tops of his cheeks. He knew he was gazing up at Broadmeadow too, and he must have looked a right idiot.

"Yeah. Seeya tomorrow." Dan was treated to one final gesture, as the gaffer clapped his shoulder without a word before heading off to his own car. When Broadmeadow glanced back, just for a second, he caught Dan staring at his retreating form. And if he wasn't mistaken (which was entirely believable), that was the briefest of winks aimed in his direction.

The Black Dog

That night, as Dan begun his nightly ritual of trying to sleep, the black dog lurked by his bedside. Sometimes it slept under the bed. Other times it wandered the house, eventually taking its place by the front door to stand sentry, fixed and dormant like an age-old gargoyle deflecting the rain from a cathedral roof.

It didn't have a sense of time, it didn't know why or where it came from, it just *was*. There were people before Dan, many people, and there would be people long after he was gone. But it didn't need to leave him just yet – there was still a chance it could bring him back round.

The cracks and chasms that tore at Dan's mind, vast spaces of emptiness emanating a dark and whispering fog were what it lived for. It padded forwards to rest its chin on Dan's pillow – he wasn't asleep just yet. It could fix that, if it wanted to. It could just leave him alone, and then he could rest.

It sniffed at his hair before taking a long inhale of the creeping fog radiating out from within Dan's subconscious inner self – where it gathered inside his lungs and misted out through his half-agape mouth. It didn't quite hit the spot though; the fog's consistency was somewhat watered down and tinged with an opalescent grey rather than its usual swirling black. It wasn't as fulfilling as usual.

The black dog considered this. It was confident at first, that moving with him to this new county would be good for them; confident that Dan wouldn't find what he was looking for. But it was worried now that they'd made the wrong decision. Dan's new team were strong, even when the black dog tried its hardest to suck the life out him, make him a shell of the man he once was, Hollie and Paul didn't seem deterred.

And that was just Dan's colleagues – that didn't include the gaffer. He was the real threat. His degree of care for Dan was strong; very strong. So strong that the black dog felt like it had met its match.

Broadmeadow wanted to take Dan for his own, and the black dog knew that there wouldn't be room for the both of them. But Dan was also somewhat weak of mind – that's why it chose him – and as of yet not tuned into how much the gaffer *really* wanted him.

There was still a chance, then. The black dog needed to try harder at playing on Dan's shortfalls, like his crippling self-doubt and downright inability to believe that people actually enjoyed his company. It would take all its strength, and cunning, but the black dog hadn't been skulking about in the shadows of the earth this long for no reason.

It knew exactly how to survive, and no human yet had managed to escape from its jaws unharmed. The black dog would continue to hound him day and night, silently sucking the strength from him like an ungodly parasite – even if meant Dan's life was the ultimate price to pay.

The Hornets' Nest

The darkened corridor stretched on and on ... it was recognisable, yet it wasn't. The strip lights lining the ceiling intermittently flickered and dimmed, eerily coaxing anyone who set foot on the furlong of grey carpet tiles forwards, enticing one along with every buzz and clink of the dancing halogen tubes overhead. The walls were bare – grey, again. The light nearest above sparked and blew. If one was to look back over one's shoulder, one's eyes would be met with an impenetrable expanse of black.

Dan knew where he was, in the stark yet vague sort of familiarity that only a recurring dream could arouse. And with the first light already gone, there was only one way forwards. Dan knew the drill.

He'd been here before; many a time.

He didn't want to be there, but he walked on nonetheless, his feet carrying him forward one trudging step at a time, his shoes making a dull *one-two* against the carpet. He was making his way towards the light – the frosted glass window. It wasn't a welcoming light. It was cold and harsh. For Dan, it was the very picture of *fear*.

Yet still, he walked on. The door appeared, as another strip light blinked out overhead. His feet became heavier, his legs becoming ponderous and threatening to fall. The corridor became hazy like a thick winter fog, the air cold and damp and it was fading away around him.

Tentatively, Dan knocked on the door. His knuckles rapped muted against the chipped varnish, just above the handle.

There was no answer from the other side, but he knew that in order for the sequence to play out, he had to enter.

The office interior was harsh and bright, only heeding to accentuate the towering figure that was stood there waiting for him.

It was him. It was always *him*.

Dan didn't need a ghoul or a fearsome spectre to haunt his dreams. Not when he had DCI Walters – the ghastly man did a far better job of making him weak at the knees and paralysed with fear. In real life, Dan had managed to convince himself that his former commanding officer meant nothing to him anymore; that he wasn't scared of some stupid old bastard who no longer had a hold over him. In his dreams however, every expertly quashed down hurt the man had inflicted upon him all morphed into one hideous incantation; all of his worst memories melded into a bewildering mix reality and illusion.

First of all, it was the swipe from behind. DCI Walters' favourite move. Dan's arm was mercilessly ripped behind his back, the larger man's fingers at his wrist digging hard enough to bruise, the gold sovereign that was too tight for his fat fingers punching an imprint against his spine. Tears of pain and anger followed as he was forcibly shoved face first into the wall. And then DCI Walters' bulk had him pinned – the man was overweight, but you'd be a fool to underestimate his power and prowess when it came to picking on the smaller man. He didn't like women all that much either; not when they got above their station and started thinking they could do as good a job as a bloke, but he couldn't lay his hand to them like he could to Dan.

Because Dan *was* a bloke, and by all rights – in DCI Walters' book – that meant he could take it. He could take it too when the nasty litany of names started falling from his lips, viscous and sneering.

"Get off me. Let me go, please ..."

Dan had never begged in real life, but in his dreams he did. Everything was worse, inordinately over-proportioned and *so* much more terrifying.

"Get on your knees. Go on. I know you want to."

Walters towered above him in his too tight trousers, belly sucked in and bursting at the bottom button, topped off with that camel coloured woollen greatcoat; the one that made him look like something straight out of the nineteen seventies. The lights burned Dan's eyes as he blinked up through a traitorous flood of tears. He could see the walnut desk overhead, as high and imposing from where he knelt as the man that it belonged to. A rough hand at the back of his head pulled him forwards, so close that he could smell the musk and sweat and feel the fabric of day-old trousers against his nose, and he reeled in disgust at what he was about to be forced to do ...

With a start, the room went back. It was just Dan, and a heavy darkness, and the carpet burning at his knees. He hung his head, hands clasped tight behind his back. An insistent buzzing filled his ears and reverberated against his skull. Had he done it? Was it over?

He tried to stand, but his legs were like a lead weight holding him down. The buzzing sound grew louder like a giant, vehement hornet out for revenge over a tampered with nest. But he still couldn't move. He couldn't see through the tangible blanket of willowing darkness. He could hardly breathe as the swirling fog of black filled his lungs, clogging and swelling inside his throat, and he was crying again, finally able to move in a last-ditch flurry of panic but only down, not up, falling forwards onto his elbows ...

The buzzing sound subsided. The light returned, warmer this time like a sunrise burning away the morning fog across the fens. Somebody behind him was easing him up with certainty and calm. He was safe. It was over.

The walnut desk was gone. The worn old sofa now, against the far wall and welcoming him over, and his Gaffer was there. Broadmeadow, hauling him up and into his arms with soft, muted words of encouragement. He wrapped his arms around him, so warm, so *real* ... and Dan might have cried for the comfort that he was being offered, except the sheer terror and humiliation that he had felt only moments (or hours?) ago had evaporated away. All he felt now was a glorious sense of calm.

Broadmeadow murmured something down to him but he couldn't quite make out the words, just that they were spoken with care; that soft accent washing over him, consuming him. He said something that made Broadmeadow smile and tighten his arms around him. However, when the gaffer replied, all that came out of his mouth was that buzzing sound again.

Dan panicked. Broadmeadow's mouth was moving but that insistent noise was persisting against his eardrums. He tried to pull himself free, to get away from that droning hum, but his legs were tangled amongst his gaffer's gangly limbs and he was trapped ...

That was when Dan woke.

Not Broadmeadow's legs that he was tangled in, but the covers where the duvet inside had come loose. He was hot.

So hot he was sweating – he'd had a nightmare. And his phone was buzzing loudly against his bedside table.

Was it a nightmare? Memories of it all were fading by the second. He could still feel the lingering chill with an undercurrent of panic, but the details evaded him. All he could remember clearly was Broadmeadow giving him a cuddle on the sofa in his office. Groaning in his still semi-conscious state, he aimlessly slapped his hand in the general direction of his phone. It was still dark out, barely daybreak. Surely it couldn't be his alarm going off already?

It wasn't.

Dan's stomach did a traitorous flip when he saw the caller ID. He groaned again, more awake now, because combined with the stark memory of his slowly ebbing dream, seeing that name upon the screen of his phone set his pulse racing, with the addition of a disconcerting tightness burning between his legs.

"Sir?" he answered with his forearm flung over his eyes.

"Daniel, there's been an incident down at the co-operative involving some stolen mopeds, and unfortunately it appears to have ended in a stabbing. I'm on my way down to take a look, but, well, I could do with a detective on hand ... I'm sorry, son, for calling at this hour, but ..."

Dan cut in, wide awake now, "But you wanted me for a second opinion?"

He could hear Broadmeadow let out a low sigh down the other end of the phone. "Again, Daniel, I'm very sorry for calling on you off duty like this, but I really could do with your expertise on this one."

The gaffer needn't sound so apologetic – Dan already knew, somewhere deep down in the back of his mind, that he would do anything the older man asked of him. And the fact that he'd called *him,* for *his* expertise on the situation; well that was a gesture that settled nice and warm around his heart. He was wanted. Needed, even.

Or perhaps his gaffer just knew that he was extremely willing to please, but he tried to push that thought away for the time being.

"I'm on my way, sir," he said, already up and out of bed when he hung up the phone, fumbling around in the half-light of his bedroom to find some clothes.

The black dog had been lurking in the threshold of the landing. Watching, listening, its body hung low in defeat. The strength it had taken from Dan's nightmare, the nightmare it had carefully twisted and encouraged into a torrent of all his worst evocations, had been ripped away the second his thoughts had turned to where his heart truly lay.

It didn't even have the strength to follow Dan down the stairs, waiting instead for him to leave before crawling its way under the bed to dolefully lick its wounds.

Cup Holders and a Sensible Car

Kids hanging around the local supermarkets had always been a bit of a problem, even in Dan's days of youth. He'd done it himself as a passenger in one of his mate's cars, meeting up with other lads in their jacked up vehicles thinking they were the coolest young things in the world. They'd smoke drugs and play their music too loud, disturbing the peace and hanging around until the police moved them on. They were good times, which Dan looked back on with a slightly jaded wistfulness, because that was before there was any memory of the black dog being there.

But what Dan had done in his youth had been fun and relatively harmless, before it became clear to him as an adult what the wider consequences of fuelling the local drug dealers' profits were. To him at the time, it had just been a bunch of lads causing a general nuisance of themselves ... but it had never ended in violence. Never. Things had changed a lot since then. Dan passed it off as a person that he used to be, and certainly wasn't now.

There were some kids still there when Dan arrived, apprehended. Some with mopeds and bikes, some gathered around their cars in little groups, one officer to every three or so. A police cordon with a white tent in the middle had been erected in the centre of it all, making Dan's stomach lurch. He'd investigated stabbings before, even a shooting once, which was sadly the norm when working in the less desirable areas city – not here though.

His mind started ticking away. Counting the civilians. The officers on scene would have to question them all; perhaps someone had filmed the incident? What even happened, come to think of it? Who was in charge here? And why was this case something of interest to the Rural Crime Department? That was Dan's biggest question – why had the gaffer called him down here in the first place?

There was a chill to the early summer air, even with his hoodie and stab vest over the top. And then there was a large hand resting at his shoulder, dissipating the cold and momentarily drawing his attention away from the unfolding scene in front of him. "Thank you for coming, Daniel. Thank you," said the gaffer.

Dan side eyed the taller man, instantly noticing Broadmeadow's attire; namely how bloody enticing he looked. Having grown accustomed to seeing his gaffer in his usual shirt and trousers, rolled up at the sleeves and his clip-on tie always a little off-centre, seeing the man donning his peaked hat and padded jacket with a vest over the top had Dan feeling extremely attentive. Broadmeadow looked the very picture of authority, and Dan was getting distracted.

He reeled it in, taking his eyes away from his gaffer and back towards the scene before them. "What happened then, sir? Is the victim still alive?"

Broadmeadow's hand left his shoulder and folded his arms over his chest instead. He sighed. "For now, yes. Seventeen-year-old, and from what I've gathered there was an altercation over some cannabis. No one's really talking though, as you can probably imagine, eh?"

"Ok. And the constables on scene, are they taking statements?"

"Yes, fella."

"And forensics?"

"Already sweeping the scene."

"So ... why are we here? I'm guessing it's South Lynn running the scene – does this even fall under our department?" Dan quizzed the gaffer, still confused as to what this had to do with them. Broadmeadow was still standing close, right in Dan's personal space. If either of them moved over half an inch, they'd be brushing elbows.

"Ah, because a man's name came up, Daniel. *Walshy*. A known name around here, apparently. A group of his wee cronies showed up and started something, and call it a hunch but I suspect him and his gang are quite something to be feared around here; organised crime, perhaps?"

Broadmeadow was being a bit cryptic. Dan's mind started to try and connect the dots. Then it clicked. "You think there may be a link, sir? Our fly-tippers?"

"Perhaps. As I said though, just a hunch." The gaffer smiled down at him. It felt like that smile was filled with pride at him making the link on his first attempt, and it felt ... good. Really good.

"So what now then?" he asked with a renewed eagerness to please.

"I say we pay a visit to the hospital, see if our victim is in a position to talk. That sound like a plan?"

"Yeah, hang on ..." Dan needed more intel. Call it his natural inquisitiveness and the constant urge he felt to know every detail – it was what made him a good detective. Or at least he liked to think he was, anyways.

What he didn't see was the fond smile and the slow, almost exasperated shake of Broadmeadow's head that was aimed at his back when he made his way over to the cordon. The police constable manning the cordon's access was one who he had seen around Vancouver Road before, under Ackehurst's command – and a pretty one at that. And she was looking at his sergeant with a gleam to her eyes; an unmistakable sign of what she thought of the handsome young detective heading her way.

Dan could be a bit naive sometimes, especially when what he saw as a purely friendly smile had something somewhat more behind it. Broadmeadow wasn't so guileless. Just like the achingly fond smile he'd given to Dan's back, the lad also didn't see the slight frown furrowing across his brow, only there for a moment before he wiped his expression clean. Who was he to judge the constable from South Lynn, and her apparent interest in young Daniel? It couldn't be denied that the lad was quite something to look at, easy on the eye, so to speak; so could he really blame her?

And then he scorned himself, hard. Because they were investigating a serious assault with himself at the helm, and he shouldn't have been having those sorts of thoughts about his wee sergeant in the first place.

You're old enough to be his father, for Christ's sakes ...

He watched on for a moment longer, seeing the way that Dan and the pretty young constable conversed with professional ease, scrutinising their body language. It made something ache, deep within his chest; something Marcus hadn't felt in such a long time that it was all but a distant memory. So he forced himself to look away, refused to let his mind wonder if the pair were going to swap numbers, and started to focus instead on their plan of action; in particular how to get what they needed from the hospitalised young fella, in order to start piecing together if there really was a criminal gang operating on their turf.

Broadmeadow went back to his car, and waited. A knock to the driver's side window signalled Dan's return. It whirred a creaky groan as Broadmeadow pushed down the switch to let it down.

"Did you get what you needed, son?"

"Yeah, think so."

"Do you want to hop in with me? It might be helpful to discuss what angle to approach our victim with on the way over?"

And I wouldn't mind spending a wee bit of time alone with you, either ...

Daniel frowned a little, still stooping at the gaffer's window. His expression made Marcus wonder if his offer of a ride had come out as unnatural – beyond what a senior officer should be doing for his sergeant?

"You'll drop me off later?" he asked, still considering what was being offered.

"Of course Daniel, of course I will. You didn't think I'd be sending you off to catch a taxi now, did ye'?"

"Nah. Gotcha. Thanks." Dan grinned, decision made. He just liked to know the details, that was all. He liked control.

Thoughts of last night's dream were still very much at the forefront, as Dan tried not to do something stupid like tripping over his own feet when he made his way around the bonnet. He wondered if he'd be expected to make conservation as he settled himself down into the passenger seat – whether or not it would come easy rather than it becoming a stilted round of somewhat pointless small talk.

The car was comfortable but not flashy, in stark comparison to DCI Walters who had managed to clinch himself a Mercedes as his company issue car, which spoke volumes about the man himself. Dan suspected there would have been an additional monthly payment for that thing, but it wouldn't have mattered to Walters – it was all about appearances for him. Broadmeadow drove a suitably more understated Skoda. Nice, but definitely not flashy.

Dan reigned in the childlike urge to start pulling open all the internal compartments to find out how many cup holders the Skoda possessed. He took note of the green *Magic Tree* dangling from the rear-view mirror, approving of his gaffer's choice in air-freshener. Dan never bought the boring green one, much preferring to hunt out the more exotic fragrances and colours, but still, *good choice, sir,* he thought. And then, because he was distracted over not showing himself up and keeping his hands to himself, Dan's mouth tumbled open instead. "I like your choice in air freshener, sir. Can't beat a Magic Tree, can you?"

It was most probably pity for him about being stuck in a car with his senior officer, the way that Broadmeadow glanced across with a bemused smile. If anything though, it got the conversation going.

"No, you can't. They hold their smell, eh? Anyways Daniel, do share with me what our young constable back there had to say?" Broadmeadow was focused back on the road ahead, both hands at ten-to-two on the wheel like the upstanding, highway code abiding man he was.

Dan started to reel off everything that the constable had told him. "Not much, really. There were reports of a car fleeing the scene but unfortunately there was no further detail than that, so we'll have to get onto the CCTV when we get back to the office. All they could get out of the other kids at the scene was that it was a drug deal gone awry, cannabis, a couple were taken away with possession, but because this is under South Lynn's jurisdiction she was reluctant to share any more than that."

"I'm going to hazard a guess that their detectives are already at the hospital, then?" Broadmeadow was smiling a wry smile, like he'd been in this situation many a time before. Wouldn't life be so much easier, if departments were willing to share their intel with each other?

Dan understood because he had been there too. Some things didn't change, even when you run away to pastures new.

"I suppose the question is, do I have permission to, um, go against protocol with our own line of inquiries?" As much as Dan was getting to know his new gaffer, he still had that moment of: *have I crossed a line, here?* Broadmeadow was relaxed, sure, but was he willing to stand by him whilst he willingly pushed against the rules?

Broadmeadow held onto his smile, still concentrating on the road but briefly flitting his gaze across with a flash of rebelliousness behind those soft blue eyes; "I'll be right behind you Daniel."

Cow on the Tracks

It wasn't really the biggest surprise in the word to see an officer standing guard to the ward, nor was it a surprise to see two young detectives at the victim's bedside, with the female of the pair taking residence in the visitor's chair, and the male officer standing at her side furiously scribbling down notes into his pad. And the biggest non-surprise of them all? They weren't exactly welcoming towards Dan and his superintendent showing up unannounced for their own run down of events.

Dan couldn't blame them for their hostility. If he had been in their shoes, and the head of Norfolk Constabulary's Rural Crime Unit came barging in with his young faced detective sergeant demanding a piece of the action, he probably would have laughed them right back out the door. Rural Crime had a reputation; a reputation of being a bit of a joke to the wider police community – that they had nothing better to do than kick about in the farmers' fields with the mud and shit under their shoes, their crime of the year actually not a crime at all, just a loose cow wandering too close to the tracks.

That was a true story, the cow on the train tracks. There was a framed newspaper print in the office kitchen of a much younger Broadmeadow posing laughably straight faced for the camera, with a farmer at his side and a safely returned Holstein Friesian. The headline read: 'No *spilled milk* here – Norfolk Police Sergeant keeps rural train services *moo-ving*.'

Dan wanted to ask the gaffer sometime whether it really was the dramatic affair that the local news had made it out to be. Somehow, he doubted it. But it still made him chuckle every time he saw it.

With a flash of their badges, the officer guarding the ward had let them through. Only a constable and painfully young, who didn't have the confidence yet to dispute the motives of the two clearly senior colleagues. Had Broadmeadow not have been there, Dan suspected he might have said something, but his gaffer was an imposing man when he wanted to be – enough so that they had been allowed to enter without further question. As for the two detectives actually inside the ward? Not so easy. They were trained to question, and rightly so.

"Can we help you?" the male of the pair spoke. They had both paused mid-interrogation, fixing them with accusatory, beady-eyed stares.

Dan nearly wilted, forgetting his self-assurance for a fleeting moment. Then he remembered the gaffer's presence at his side, drinking in the fortitude it gave him, letting the man's conviction in him swirl and pulse and fill the cavity of his chest. "We'd like a word with Mr Mitchell – if we could possibly get a quick statement off him?"

Broadmeadow added to the plea, "We shan't be long, detectives. I've already cleared this with superintendent Ackehurst, your commanding officer, no?"

All it normally took was a name drop of somebody from a senior rank, and this was no exception. By the time the two young detectives found out that the questioning of their victim was not in fact cleared with their commanding officer, it would be too late. Dan and his gaffer would be gone.

Broadmeadow let Dan lead as the two detectives from South Lynn left the cubicle, opting to hover two paces back from the bedside whilst his young charge occupied the chair. Out came the notebook. Then the voice recorder.

"Hi, Mr Mitchell. I'm detective sergeant Taylor, and this is superintendent Broadmeadow – we were just wondering if we could ask you a couple of questions over what happened this morning? Unrelated of course, to what you've been questioned over already."

Broadmeadow marvelled over Daniel's softly-softly approach. He had a way of making people feel like he was a mate, an ally even, so bloody effortlessly. He was a natural.

"I've already been charged for possession ..." the young lad said, remarkably 'with it' for someone who'd just been stabbed in the side. He was a bit pale, dark bags under his eyes, but other than that Dan deemed him perfectly fit for giving a statement.

"We're not here about that. We just want to know what happened ... how you ended up here, specifically."

"Honestly, we were just scoring some weed. And then he said the price has gone up, and I was like, nah mate, that's not what my other dealer is selling at. He didn't like that, another dealer on his turf I mean, and then he got mad ..."

"And he pulled a knife?"

"Yeah. Stabbed me. Then jumped back in the car, and they drove off."

"Do you know who 'they' are?" Dan questioned further. His tone of voice was soft without a trace of accusation, his brow lightly furrowed with concern written all over his face. Everything about his body language spoke of openness.

That he could be trusted. Like it came instinctively to him to express empathy over a situation, which was something that no amount of police training could truly emulate if it just didn't come naturally like it did with young Daniel.

Ryan Mitchell looked so bloody young, lying there. He was only fifteen. He looked up at Dan, the uncertainty visible as to whether he was doing the right thing. Dan's posture remained open; unequivocal, and Ryan, slowly, granted him that trust. "Walshy. It was definitely Walshy and his lot."

"Ok. That's great, Ryan. Thank you." Dan nodded, and glanced back at his gaffer. This was the lead they'd been looking for. Broadmeadow nodded back, a slow tip of his head, so Dan continued, "Have you told this to South Lynn?"

"Um, who?" Ryan asked, confused.

"The two detectives – the ones here who took your statement."

"Um, no. Should I of?"

"Nah. Don't you worry about that. I'll pass the information on," Dan affirmed. Now that he had a name, he just needed to put face to it. South Lynn would no doubt come chasing, but by then it wouldn't matter. It wasn't like he didn't want to catch whoever actually stabbed this young man, South Lynn were welcome to that line of investigation, but Dan, like his gaffer, just knew that there was something bigger at play here than a simple altercation over a local drug dealer's turf.

"Right, are we done here?" Broadmeadow said, anxious to get out of there because he was sure that the two young detectives outside were making contact with their own commanding officer, and would surely by now be realising that Rural Crime's finest did not have permission to be there. He didn't much fancy seeing superintendent Ackehurst's obnoxious face that early in the morning either, so it was time for them to leave.

"Yeah. I think so. Thanks Ryan, and all the best for your recovery," Dan said warmly. He'd make sure to check up on his progress.

Broadmeadow gave the Ryan a soft smile. "Get well soon, son."

Dan felt a bit of a thrill as they strode away and out of the ward, like they'd just done something that they shouldn't have, all with his gaffer's rather indecorous backing. Back at the car, and trying to hold back a grin, he looked across at Broadmeadow who was giving him a strange look.

"What are you so happy about, eh? First time I've seen that wee smile on you, Daniel …"

"Nothing, sir. Just pleased we're finally making some head way with my fly-tippers – hopefully." Of course, he couldn't be sure until he got a look at this Walshy man's face, but something just told him that he was their man, or at the very least connected with.

Broadmeadow's lips lilted up at that, his eyebrow raising with them. "Well, it suits ye', that smile." He dithered then, like he was about to reach over and clasp Dan's hand to reiterate his point. But he stopped at the last minute, going instead to switch up the heating – presumably because he knew that Dan suffered with the cold.

Regardless of the diverted move, Dan felt his cheeks tinge pink at the endearing way his gaffer had addressed him. He could blame it on the car's heaters blasting into life, except they weren't yet warm because the engine wasn't running. And maybe he should just accept that he liked it when the older man showed him a bit of affection? Which in turn was just because he'd had such a rough time with his previous senior officer, wasn't it?

Pretty

It wasn't just his former DCI that Dan had experienced a rough time with – it was members of the opposite sex too. Anyone really, that he'd tried to have any sort of relationship with. Growing up, he'd never really had girlfriends. Girls liked him, but it was always more in a way of wanting to mother over him rather than do anything else. That in itself didn't particularly bother him – having a girlfriend wasn't ever a burning need for him until he was older, when his curiosity took over and he wanted to know what it felt like to have a pair of lips against his own; a wanting body pressed up against him. And even then, that burning need was more of a teenaged, testosterone fueled desire rather than a real admiration of the female form.

When he did finally have his first experience, at the age of nineteen, it was over all too soon. It was clumsy. An embarrassment. He didn't know where to put his hands, didn't know what he was doing, and was happy for her to tell him where she wanted him. That was when his mind had ultimately betrayed him; when he'd laid back and closed his eyes, and pictured somebody else entirely riding atop him. The intruder didn't have a face, or a name, but they were definitely not female. And that had been enough to instantaneously send him over the edge.

From there on out, terrified – mortified – Dan had banished that thought from ever coming back to the surface. He'd discovered online pornography, courtesy of his mates, and spent many a night at the PC in his bedroom forcing the female body upon himself, extorting his body to react as it should. It worked, sort of. With enough concentration on the task at hand, he could manage it. Like everything else in his life, he just had to try that little bit harder to obtain something everybody else found easy.

Having an actual relationship with someone was the next challenge, but by then he'd already decided he was going off to training college in Kent on a three-year course, which would gain him entry into the police should he see it through to the end. Dan had never been overly academic, so again, he'd had to try harder than his class mates to keep up, which in turn left no time for anything other than studying hard so that he could scrape past his final exams.

Going back a couple of years to when it came to leaving school, most of Dan's friends were going off to agricultural college or to study mechanics, but he didn't see himself going down either of those paths. Becoming a police officer had always been a dream for him as a young boy, where the idea of wearing a uniform and catching the bad guys seemed like the most exciting job in the world – but it wasn't until Dan had his own brush with the law that the decision to join the force was cemented in his mind.

That brush with the law came long before he even set foot inside the police training college. With a fresh paycheck from his part-time job as a pot-washer, and about to spend the evening with his friends – smoking, drinking and playing music from the tinny little speakers on their phones – their evening had been cut short when a member of the public had reported them. The police officers had told them that much, before demanding that they open their backpacks and empty their pockets – rolling tobacco, papers, lighters and the usual paraphernalia but nothing illegal on his mates' behalf. It was Dan, who had the small amount of cannabis on his person.

"It was all his," they said, *"Better only one of us getting nicked, taking one for the team Danny."*

Some mates they turned out to be.

Handcuffed, absolutely shitting himself and very much on the verge of tears, Dan had been led away and stuffed into the backseat of a police car. The two officers had been kind to him, even trying for a bit of conversation on the drive back to the local station. But he'd been too scared of what was going to happen to him to do anything other than bite at his lower lip in a futile attempt to stop the tremble, and stare listlessly out the window, replaying everything that he would have done differently that evening should he have had the chance. What scared him most was his parents. Would he have to tell them? What if they found out anyways, even if he didn't? His dad would be disappointed, and would possibly (most probably) shout at him. His mum; maybe not so much. He'd call her over his father, if it came down to it.

As it happened, he got away with a brief interview, a stern telling off from the officer in charge about the dangers of drug misuse, a few more tears and a warning on his record which would be wiped clean when he hit eighteen. He never did tell his parents – not until years later.

The whole experience had him more determined than ever; firstly, a realisation that he needed to get his proverbial shit together because he didn't *ever* want to go through all that again, and secondly, those two officers who had arrested him looked really cool with their uniforms and radios and handcuffs. Real blokes, they were, and that was exactly what Dan wanted to be – because even then, he knew that he wasn't quite the same as his peers.

Seven years later, two years on the beat in Kent and another two with the Met, when he was preparing for his first detective exams and a world away from the small town where he'd grown up, Dan had met Leanne. Slim, fiery, blonde, and he was punching. She too was going for the detective rank, and they'd hit it off straight away.

Dan finally thought: *You've done it, mate. You're as good as any other bloke out there. That image you had involving the faceless man was just your teenaged mind misfiring. Your wires were getting crossed in the heat of the moment, and more importantly, you don't fancy other blokes ...*

Leanne was dominant in her nature and liked to be the one in charge, but Dan was ok with that. He liked that in a partner. It worked well because he was happy in his more submissive role. Sometimes though, Leanne could be sharp with her tongue and little too honest with her words. Nasty, even. He remembered one conversation very clearly, towards the end of their short-lived relationship, when he realised that she could possibly see through him better than he would like to admit to himself.

"Saanvi and Helena liked you – especially Saanvi. She said you were *pretty*." Dan should have known better, should have realised that Leanne was leading him up to a bitter lash of the tongue, but his complexion failed him. He flushed, his cheeks tinging red at the compliment.

"Really?" He'd tried to sound flippant in his response and not flattered that somebody had said something nice about him.

"She said you were very *sweet*," Leanne replied mockingly. They were sitting in the back of a taxi, before the days of *Uber,* coming home from an evening out with Leanne's girlfriends. She'd had a few, more than Dan himself could ever put away, and that meant she was undoubtedly raring for a fight. Giving him a look of absolute distain from the other side of the cab, she continued, "Normal blokes don't blush at the idea of being called *pretty*, Dan. A normal bloke would tell me to fuck off ..."

"I ... yeah, I guess," Dan had conceded, shrinking back into his seat for the rest of the drive home. On the inside, he wanted to stand his ground. He wanted to tell Leanne that yeah, ok, I am a bit soft on the inside and I don't mind the idea of somebody saying that I'm sweet, or pretty, or a nice bloke; but on the outside, he didn't want to cause a scene in the back of the taxi, so he reverted back to his well-worn habit of backing down. Leanne was drunk, and he didn't fancy being on the receiving end of a slap, especially after she'd had a set of those ridiculous stick-on things attached to the ends of her fingers earlier that day. Dan had told her at the time that her nails looked nice, however he remembered thinking to himself that they looked more like a very sparkly set of dangerous weapons in disguise.

He didn't get a slap in the end, or even a glass hurled his way – but he had been kicked out the following morning. A lucky escape, he told himself afterwards.

After that there had been a number of one-night stands, but that was purely fulfilling a need rather than anything else. Leanne had left him overtly cautious of members of the opposite sex when it came to relationships, and he decided, over time, that he needed to re-think his stance. He loved his job. That would be enough. If somebody came into his life and swept him off his feet then fine, but he wasn't actively looking. Better to be sad and alone than trying too hard to be something he wasn't – and never would be.

Not that Dan was fully prepared to accept what he really was, because he didn't *know* what he was. Or at least he thought that to be the case, up until he moved back home and acting superintendent Broadmeadow came into his life.

The Misidentified Spaniel

"So you really think this Walshy bloke and his cronies are running some sort of crime gang here in Norfolk? What happened to coming back home for the quieter life, eh?" Paul asked, already halfway through his second pint and curious over the line of investigation his senior colleague had been assigned to. They were in the Greyhound which was a favourite haunt of the local force, and Dan had finally given in to Paul's continued badgering over joining him for a drink after work.

Dan found it funny because the pub's sign outside clearly depicted a spaniel of some sort with a pheasant at its feet, not a greyhound. As to why that was though, nobody had an answer for him. It was just one of those things. Chester was there, lounging under the table with his ball between his paws, apparently not a care within his little world. Emily was with them too, having been freed from desk duty for the night, but no Hollie, of which Dan was a little disappointed – he liked the girl. Liked her company.

"Yeah, I'm sure of it, or at least, I think I am," Dan surmised, sipping at his own second pint which was still nearly full. He couldn't drink like Paul could.

"And what evidence do you have, except for a positive ID on Walshy in that van, and then his name coming up again to do with this stabbing?" Paul looked very interested, despite playing the devil's advocate, a spark of excitement behind his eyes. They hadn't been involved in something big like this since DI Wright had met his untimely end, and even then it had been ultimately passed over to South Lynn, with a suspect for dangerous driving never apprehended. As for the cannabis farming operation discovered prior? Also handed over to South Lynn. They were better equipped, and besides, it better fell under the remit of criminal investigations rather than that of rural crime.

"I just … I've seen it before, how organised criminal gangs work. And what better place to go about your work than here in the heart of rural Norfolk, close enough to London where they're based but far enough away from the public eye and well-funded police forces to just slip under the radar. And this Walshy bloke? Why would his face keep coming up if the fly-tipping and the stabbing weren't linked?"

"He looks fucking rough in all. He's definitely guilty of that," said Paul, having seen a picture of the man for himself earlier that day when Dan was starting to make a file on him. He was definitely the same bloke that Dan and Hollie had seen in the van – the photographs Hollie had taken proved that.

Dan stifled down a laugh. "Exactly. Not the prettiest of blokes, is he?"

Not pretty like you, his inner self echoed back to him ironically.

"What on earth must his poor old dear be thinking, producing that ugly meathead from within her womb?" Paul was laughing too, with Dan revelling in the off-the-cuff banter they shared between them. He didn't have this, back in London. Everyone had been so *serious*; so straight-laced and reading directly off the pages of what you were and weren't allowed to say. Paul was the exact opposite of all that. He was exactly what it said on the side of the tin – quite possibly why he'd never made it past detective constable, even though he was a good couple of years older than Dan was.

The pub was getting busier, unsurprising for a Friday night. The din of voices was growing louder as the establishment filled with officers and locals alike. For Dan, somewhere quieter would suit him better – he hated having to shout over background noise just to have a conversation, but he'd been invited out by his colleagues and was determined to re-enforce the bond they were already starting to form.

"Dunno mate. Perhaps she's just as ugly ..." he sniggered, starting to feel loose, more relaxed within his surroundings. The black dog had threatened for a moment to make its presence known, when Dan had felt the flutter of unease at noticing how full the pub was getting, but it seemed to have backed off for the time being – they had a booth in the far corner, near the back door to the smoking area but also right next to an open fire, staving off the chill of an early summers evening. It was cosy, and he felt safe within the company he was keeping, and that appeared to be enough his troublesome hound at bay.

"Paul! You're encouraging Daniel down to your level, and I'm finding it highly inappropriate." Mock serious, Emily flashed those unbelievably perfect teeth over her own pint as she continued, "Look, do we really have to talk about work? Come on, guys!"

"Come on then Emily, what do you wanna talk about?" Paul nudged against her, clearly already half-cut, "Seen anyone tonight you like the look of?"

She gave him a sharp kick. Everyone knew that Paul liked her.

And everyone knew that Emily just wasn't interested.

"No, *Pauline*. I'm not on the pull – not *here*, christ ..." she said, pointedly swooping her gaze around the pub with a look of mild distain. She was right. The Greyhound wasn't exactly the sort of place one would go looking for a potential suitor. Crowded around the bar and propped up on stools were the true locals – the ones who practically lived there – the old boys and slightly tarty looking ladies chatting and laughing over pints and packets of crisps. To the side, at the pool table, the town's youth (the ones not stupid enough to cause trouble in a pub full of coppers) were starting to gather. Apart from that, it was all members of the force, and Emily categorically would *not* date somebody that she worked with.

Except for Daniel, she thought. The sweet, handsome young man that he was, but she already maintained a strong suspicion that he didn't bat for her side of the field. Besides, the feeling of attraction was more of a maternal one than of any real desire for a relationship.

On that note – maybe now would be a good time for her to find out?

"What about you Daniel? Have you a significant other that you haven't yet told us about?" she asked, testing the water for her theory.

Dan frowned across at her. "Nah, I wish ..."

Paul piped up, saying, "I've seen a couple of nice birds over at the pool table looking your way mate, practically wetting their knickers over you. What d'ya say, shall we go and introduce ourselves? Reckon you'd be right in there ..."

And that, right there, was the moment Dan had been dreading. It had been bound to come up in conversation soon enough, but still ...

He looked down at his hands, reluctant say any more than he had to, and reluctant to share that he really wasn't that interested in chasing down a potential date. Combine that with the recent thoughts over his gaffer which had been intruding upon him, and Dan was left feeling like he really didn't know what an appropriate response to that should be. He didn't want to raise suspicion either, having asked Paul already if they should have invited the gaffer along, to which he had responded: *"Nah, mate. Wouldn't bother. The gaffer isn't normally allowed out – his missus would go mental on him."*

Emily, however, was nosy in her nature. Not in a malicious way, just … curious. Dan knew this, not wanting to make a negative assumption, but the girl did watch that 'only way is Essex' – or was it Newcastle? Whatever. She watched it and that 'love island' thing like it was her religion. What he deduced from that was that she liked people, and she liked to connect with them, like it was a hobby.

"Some nice men over there too Dan, if that's more your thing?" Emily enquired further. There was no malevolence or mocking to her tone, her face soft and trusting eyes.

Fuck it. New start and all that. New job, new friends, new Dan.

"I …"

Or not.

Dan felt his cheeks flush, attempting to mask his face by taking a huge gulp of his drink.

"Like we'd have a chance anyways, Danny-boy. Well, you maybe, but not with my ugly mug in tow, eh?" Paul jumped in to save him, reaching across the table to give Dan's forearm a hearty pat, lingering a little as he tried his best at a sympathetic look that said: "*Sorry, mate.*"

For all of Paul's loud, brash, larger than life personality, he really was an open minded bloke. He liked Dan, enjoyed having another bloke more his own age to work with, and honestly couldn't have given a damn what his sexual preferences were (and it meant that Emily wouldn't be running off with him, which was definitely an added bonus).

The evening drew on into night after that, more drinks consumed than Dan had indulged himself in years (a total of three and a half pints in total), and with good conversation to go with. The three officers stayed 'till closing, with Chester flaked out on the floor but soon rousing into action when he realised it was time to go home. Dan knew, just knew, that he'd drunk too much when they stumbled out of the pub and made to call it a night.

He felt ... he felt like the high of the evening was starting to wane, his head spinning, barely managing to stay upright as he hugged Emily goodbye and into a waiting taxi.

"You alright getting home, mate?" Paul wasn't faring much better, but at least he seemed at little more composed to the naked eye.

"Yeah ... I'll just ... it's not far ..." Dan stumbled. Not far for someone who could walk in a straight line – what was he saying? He didn't even know which way he was supposed to be walking ...

Paul observed him for a long moment before making a decision for them both. "I'll call for another taxi, mate. You're not walking home in that state."

The pub doors swung open, clattering on their hinges as a group of those youths from the pool table spilled out onto the street. Dan swayed and then steadied himself against a lamppost, hearing what he thought was a jeer coming from the group of drunken lads. He squinted, trying to focus, grasping for Paul's arm, stumbling, losing his footing …

Paul caught him by the scruff, hauling him back up to his feet and letting Dan lean against him whilst he re-located his legs and the pavement beneath his feet.

"Wheeyyyy! Couple of *bent* coppers over there!"

Oh, no …

Chester growled, his lip raising up into a snarl.

Paul hastily propped Dan against the wall of the pub and slipped Chester's lead into his hand. He looked down at it, disturbed at how there appeared to be two black dogs at the end of it. Before Dan could realign his vision properly to assess the situation, Paul was squaring up his shoulders and striding up to the sole perpetrator, towering into him with a growl far more ominous than the one Chester had already given. "The *fuck* did you just say?"

"Paul, no …" Dan tried to stop him, tried to stumble over to what he could see was about to unfold, but then his stomach lurched, and he doubled over, his insides roaring with nausea. As he did so, one of the lads from the group now surrounding a furious Paul headed his way. Dan didn't think much of it because he was too busy concentrating on holding his stomach – and trying not to panic.

The lad placed his hand between Dan's shoulders and bent down, lowering his voice down to a hiss as he said, "Back off, alright? You need to start minding your own business, copper. Don't say you haven't been warned."

With that, he patted Dan's back and then faded away. Not towards Paul and his coiled fists, back towards his mates, but around the side of the pub, and gone …

Drunk

Marcus had never *really* learned how to cook. The basics, yes, he could do that; for example a jacket potato, pasta with a sauce from a jar or beans on toast – he could manage those sorts of things. But after a long, late finishing day at work, and having been so used to something already cooked for him to heat up when he came home, he was finding it hard to adjust. Hence why he'd fallen into the routine of buying five ready meals when doing his weekly shop on a Monday night. Saturday night, he'd go down to the local chain restaurant for a couple of pints of stout and a meal. Table for one. Sunday night, he was making an effort to hone his very limited culinary skills, by way of some of the cookbooks Rowena had left behind. Then, come Monday, it was back to the ready meals.

Three weeks since she'd left, with half of their lifetime of possessions now gone because the removal lorry had been earlier that day and cleared them out, Marcus must have fallen asleep on the sofa that Friday night. He woke to some late-night film playing on the TV, and his plate of half-eaten shepherd's pie going cold and dry on the coffee table.

Next to the microwaved shepherd's pie was an unopened letter.

Rowena had driven down that day too to supervise the dividing of possessions – apparently, all of the nice things had belonged to her. She hadn't wanted Marcus there, so he'd worked until early evening to make sure their paths didn't cross, coming home instead to a rather empty looking home. Not that it really looked like home anymore, now that most of the furniture was gone and the walls and shelves were bared, and that deeply hurt. It made the whole situation poignantly *real*.

He'd have to sell the house – his *home* that he'd worked so hard for, if what he suspected that letter contained was correct.

But it could wait.

Not tonight.

Not whilst he was feeling such a deep-seated sadness and an aching in his heart for what had become of his life.

The last thing that Marcus was expecting that night was a phone call at just gone midnight – thinking for moment, just a moment, that it may have been Rowena empathically sensing his pain over that bloody brown A4 envelope, but alas, that was not the case. It was in fact a telephone call from superintendent Ackehurst of South Lynn; a man that he knew well but rarely saw eye to eye with. Marcus thought Ackehurst was an outspoken, pompous old bastard. Ackehurst, in return, thought Broadmeadow was a failed, unimportant waste of space, running a waste of space department.

He answered, clipped in his tone – what on earth could he possibly want at this time of night? "Ackehurst, what can I do you for at this ungodly hour?"

"Broadmeadow. Good evening to you too." Ackehurst sounded like he was outside, with the distinctive sound of a vehicle passing by and muffled voices in the background.

"Well?"

"I would suggest, if you're in a fit state to drive, that you get yourself down to the Greyhound in the town centre. That is, if you don't want me to drag two of your officers away in cuffs." There was an underlying sneer to the superintendent's voice that Marcus didn't like; another thing to add to the list of things he found irritating about the other man. He was tired, and certainly not in the mood for this.

"Haud yer horses, I'm on my way." With that, Marcus disconnected the call.

With only three officers under his command, soon to be two when young Hollie inevitably decided to make tracks and forge ahead with her blossoming career, his options for whom exactly he was coming to drag away were extremely limited. Hollie, anyways, was out of the question. She was far too clever a lass to have gotten herself on the wrong side of superintendent Ackehurst. DC Bartlett was top of his list of three – the man was a wee bit of a loose cannon with his temper at the best of times, having grown more volatile since the untimely departure of his dearest friend and colleague, DI Wright.

With that in mind, unless Chester could be counted as one of their officers, that only left him with young Daniel as the other perpetrator. A deduction that he found extremely hard to believe. Daniel was a such a well-mannered, soft tempered wee lad but perhaps he'd read him all wrong; perhaps he too had another side yet to have been revealed to his superior officer?

All of this was purely speculation of course, the indication that there had been some sort of disorder outside the pub that was, because Marcus hadn't given Ackehurst a chance to further explain the incident at hand ... but he had his suspicions.

Suspicions that were soon realised, as he swung around the corner into the main square at the centre of town, to what looked like the scene of a serious incident. Two patrol cars mounted on the curb, blue lights flashing. Twice as many uniformed officers and Ackehurst in the middle of it all, attempting to keep the two parties at the centre of it all apart. A crowd of patrons from the pub were gathered around, taking in the commotion with great interest. He could make out one of the men, definitely Paul, fighting against the uniformed officer trying to back him away from the confrontation, and by all rights not doing a very good job of it.

His heart fell. And where was Daniel?

A sense of unease washed over him for the lad's safety, which was only marginally relieved when he stepped out of his car to be met with the hulking form of Chester, bounding over to meet him with his lead trailing and clattering behind him. "Hey there, fella. Come here." The great beast of a dog greeted him by butting his head against his superintendent's knee, his tail swishing, before giving Broadmeadow a very serious look – as serious as dog could manage, anyways. Marcus stooped to take hold of his lead, and no sooner than it was within his grasp, Chester started to pull him towards the verging on chaotic spectacle unfolding before his eyes.

"What in *God's name* is going on here?!" Marcus didn't shout as such; more of an angry, raised turn to his voice that was just as assertive. Paul froze, wide eyed at the sound and sight of his commanding officer. Broadmeadow quite clearly wasn't in the mood for any further misconduct. His anger dissipated. He'd never dare to cross his gaffer out of pure respect alone.

"Get in the car. *Now*." Paul didn't need to be told twice, as his senior officer gave him a steely glare that was brimming with disappointment, thrusting Chester's lead into his hand as he passed, the uniformed officer still lightly gripping at his arm as if he might change his mind and go in for another round. Marcus' glare followed his subordinate all the way his car, only refocusing his attention when he was satisfied that Paul was safely contained.

Right. One down.

Marcus scanned the scene, looking for Daniel.

He spotted him soon enough, sighing with disbelief as he saw the lad bent double against the wall of the pub with another officer from South Lynn holding his arm, currently preoccupied with ejecting the contents of his stomach onto the pavement at his feet.

Oh, Daniel, really?

He had to deal with Ackehurst first however, who, as usual, was sauntering over like he owned the bloody place. Broadmeadow would give him that one, this time, because he wasn't entirely wrong – his own officers sure had seemed to have been involved in one hell of a ruckus. He'd be the one dealing with them though, not Ackehurst. They were *his* officers, and he would deal with them as he saw fit.

"You'll be pleased to hear that your DC over there 'didn't start it', which is a bleeding good job. Also a bleeding good job one of our patrols was passing at the time, or I'm almost certain we would've been dealing with an ABH," Ackehurst taunted. Unlike Marcus he was fully dressed for the occasion which added to his air of superiority; not wearing a pair of pyjama bottoms under his police jacket like Marcus was.

"Look, just tell me what happened, ok? And then perhaps we can all lay this down to rest." Marcus wasn't in the mood for a stand-off. He was tired from being called out at now well gone midnight, emotionally exhausted at the finality of Rowena's departure, and rather uneasy over how anxious he felt about seeing young Daniel in such a state.

And why was Ackehurst there, anyways? There was absolutely no need for the superintendent of a division to be attending a Friday night, alcohol fuelled bust up. A rhetorical question, Marcus knew, because he knew exactly why Ackehurst was there – he hated anything and everything to do with him and his team. Why, he wasn't sure, but during every head of department meeting, every time they even crossed paths, there was always a snarky comment or a put-down aimed at his team to go with. Luckily for Marcus, he'd grown a very thick skin over his thirty-four years working on the force.

"An altercation. A case of too much to drink and a homophobic slur, apparently. And your DC there, instead of dealing with the situation in line with correct police protocol, decided to deal with it with his fists instead. The young lad over there is threatening to file a complaint, Broadmeadow."

A homophobic slur – really? What were Paul and Daniel doing, exactly? Surely they weren't …?

Marcus stifled down that line of thought for the time being, because he didn't particularly like how it made him feel inside. "Ok. Have you taken statements from my officers?"

"DC Bartlett, yes," Ackehurst swung a look over to Broadmeadow's car, where it was apparent that a PC was in there with him, taking down notes, "The other one, no. I don't think *he's* in any state right now for anything much at all." Ackehurst sounded flippant towards the poor lad still throwing his guts up onto the pavement, and it made Marcus' blood boil.

"Look. I'll deal with my team. You deal with the rest, seeing as you've deemed it such an important situation that a *superintendent* needed to attend the scene," Marcus growled, anxious now to get to Daniel.

Ackehurst didn't have an answer for that, but it didn't stop him from giving one final passing blow; "*Acting* superintendent in your case, Broadmeadow." Right. Enough of him, the self-important *nyaff*. Marcus as good as brushed Ackehurst out of the way, a hairs breadth between their shoulders as he made his way towards his sergeant.

"I'll take it from here, constable," he said as he approached young Daniel, who was gripping at the poor constable's arm for dear life. As she handed him over, Marcus realised that the lad's cheeks were wet with tears and his eyes were glazed, rolling slightly as he tried to focus.

"All yours, sir," she said as she grappled Daniel over, unable to stand on his own two feet as he fell into Marcus' side. Hauling a pliant arm up and over his shoulder, he manoeuvred the lad precariously into an upright position.

"Alright, Daniel. Come on now, let's get you home, eh?" There wasn't much in the way of a response from the lad, except for an incoherent mumble and an ominous gurgling noise emanating from somewhere deep within his stomach – unfortunately, they didn't quite make it to the car before Daniel found himself doubling over once more, copiously ejecting the last remnants of his stomach down Broadmeadow's legs and over his shoes.

Daniel's legs gave way after that, taking Marcus by surprise as he only just managed to catch the now dead weight hanging from his arms – a dead weight that was apparently now his responsibility. Not that he minded the particular notion of having the wee lad within the safety of his arms too much. He was prepared to admit that to himself in his current state of mental weakness. He really was exhausted, and he couldn't get Daniel into the car on his own.

"Bartlett! Get your arse out here and give me a hand, will you?"

Frozen Goods

Earlier that week, at a premises just outside the small village of Buckshorn, a delivery of frozen goods was due to arrive very soon. Janis would have to deal with it. Mikelis had more pressing matters to deal with.

The yard was quiet – employees gone home for the day. Rows of heavy plant lined up, motionless, like static creatures casting great, looming shadows against the backdrop of glaring security lights lining the barbed perimeter fences. Up the far end of the yard was an office building, which was where Mikelis could be found most evenings, working late into the night. He was a man with several successful enterprises to run, which were only successful because of the hours he was willing to put into them.

Gustav lay on the rug by the door, lightly dozing yet part of his brain ever alert, his eyes closed but his ears poised forwards, always listening as Mikelis' loyal sentry. Cracking open one eye, he heard a car approach long before his master did. No cause for concern though – he knew the sound of the engine and the manner in which the vehicle was driven, tyres turning and crunching against the crushed gravel yard with a casual ease.

At which point Mikelis too heard the approaching car, standing to meet his guest. Moments later, the beam of headlights slowly swept the length of the blinds covering the office window. The vehicle came to a standstill, the engine cutting out. The car door, opening then closing with a dull thud. Gustav puffed out a noisy breath, before plopping his head back down onto the rug and closing his eyes once more.

A middle-aged man entered to office. He was portly in stature, but in no way lacking in confidence – he was older than Mikelis, and clearly out of shape (if he ever was in the first place), but still, he had the presence of a man who wasn't to be caught on the wrong side. Making himself at home, the visitor removed his camel-coloured coat and hung it on the back of the door.

"I'm glad you could make it, boss. Please, sit. I get you a drink. Mr Walsh will be here soon, I think," Mikelis said as he went straight for the second drawer of the off-grey filing cabinet which contained the hard stuff. The boss liked brandy. Mikelis liked vodka.

With a hearty glass of each poured, the two men sat at the large wooden desk that dominated one end of the office.

"It's good to see you, Mikelis. How's business?" the other man said, leaning back and spreading his legs. His trousers were too tight for his encroaching gut.

"Business is good. And it is good to see you too. But alas, we must meet here to discuss other matters, I am afraid." Mikelis' gaze turned serious. Sitting at either side of the desk was for official business. There were two worn sofas at the other side of the office, but that was where proceedings of a more unofficial nature took place, like drinking and playing cards. They wouldn't be using the sofas tonight. They had important affairs to deliberate over.

The other man agreed gravely, "As I feared, my old friend."

A courteous knock at the door signaled the arrival of the third member of their little party. Gustav thumped his tail against the floor in greeting, earning himself a scratch behind the ear and a heavy pat to his abnormally wide head. Walshy didn't need to be offered a drink by their host – he and Mikelis were old acquaintances, friends even. He nodded towards his counterparts before heading straight for the kettle. They waited whilst he made himself a coffee before taking a seat next to Mikelis.

Time to get down to business. Mikelis took the lead – it was his office, after all.

"I will not beat about your bush. We are concerned that our enterprises are under scrutiny from the men in blue. We had incident, with some of Mr Walsh's people. A boy is stabbed, and we think he has grassed," Mikelis exclaimed, placing his drink onto the low table between them, matter of fact.

"And you think this will be an issue?" asked Russel Walters, the visitor and old friend of Mikelis Malinovska. He'd travelled quite a long way to be here tonight.

"No. We have dealt with this already. Someone to take the fall, for a payment, of course. No, there is more." Mikelis wouldn't have called for this meeting if it was something as minor as that. These things happened, and they knew exactly how to deal with them in the most professional of manners. He caught the Walters' gaze again; "We have an enterprise on the side, involving waste disposal. Been doing it for years. Except, there now seems to be a new officer within the Rural Crime Department, who has taken a keen interest in our little operation – seems to think he's the new Sherlock Holmes, or something."

Walshy stepped in, pausing as he swilled his coffee between his teeth; "I've been seen."

Gustav yawned, stretching out before raising up to his feet and padding over to the three men. He was the rottweiler who thought he was a lapdog, planting one of his huge paws over Mikelis' knee as he gazed up at his master, deliberating over whether there was room for two on the chair he was sitting on. There wasn't. But he continued to stare, just in case he would be allowed up into Mikelis' lap.

"Right, ok." Walters took a sip of his brandy, considering their options. "Do we have a name, for this '*Sherlock Holmes*'?"

"No. Not yet. But I saw his face, as clear as he saw mine. Young looking lad, short dark hair but a bit longer on the top. Well styled. He looked like a right cocky little bastard," Walshy sneered, as if this jumped-up little shit they were discussing really wasn't worth their bother.

Walters however – he felt an uncharacteristic churn within his stomach. The given description sounded an awful lot like a troublesome young detective he'd assumed to be a problem of his no longer.

"How easy, to dispose of an officer?" Mikelis considered, already having decided that getting rid of the problem may be their best option, if they were to continue going about their work unhindered. The head of Community Safety and Criminal Justice was already on their books, so that was not an issue, but Rural Crime? A pointless department that only dealt with the most minor of crimes. Yet this wasn't the first time they had caused Mikelis some bother – it wouldn't be the first time they had dealt with one of their officers either, so surely to lose another one wouldn't be so hard?

"Not easy. Not easy at all, boys," Walters reasoned. Being the DCI of his own department, he knew the magnitude of such a suggestion.

"So what should we do with him, then?" Walshy clenched his fists within has hands, finding himself fiddling with his wedding band. The kids would be in bed by now.

"Keep an eye, and keep me updated. As far as we're concerned for now, he doesn't even know who you are, Kyle. Put a lid on the fly-tipping. I'll put the feelers out, get an ID on this officer. And then, hopefully, he'll get bored and find something better to focus his attentions on. If he doesn't? We re-think our options. Does that sound like a plan?" Walters already knew that a certain DS Taylor had handed his transfer request in to join a force closer to home, but he was confident that if he was indeed the officer in concern, that he knew how to deal with him. He wasn't worried.

Walshy, however, was planning on taking matters into his own hands. Russel Walters wasn't his boss; Mikelis was. He couldn't tell him what to do. He would get an ID on the officer in question through his own means, and he would deal with the problem before it became an even bigger one.

"Yes. So not, 'disposal', then?" Mikelis continued, unaware of Walshy's plans for another course of action.

"No. Not yet. So, you can keep your hands to yourself for now, Mikelis. And Kyle? Keep a low profile for a while." Walters really didn't fancy the trouble of having any blood on his hands – it had been hard enough the last time to get everything nicely swept under the rug, and he didn't much fancy hedging his bets at getting away with it for a second time. Too risky. "Anyways, boys – we have a delivery arriving tonight, no?"

Mikelis grinned, flashing three of his solid gold teeth between the jutting gaps where many of them had been knocked clean altogether. "Yes. Frozen goods, amongst other things."

The heavy goods driver, four days on the road from Aknīste, Latvia, would be due to arrive anytime now, his trailer laden with customs declared meat and frozen vegetables which were destined for their network of continental food markets. Produce that would then be carefully unpacked at an on-site warehouse, where another driver would be waiting to deliver the goods up to the Greater London area.

That was where Walters stepped in. Mikelis and Walshy took their cut, DCI Walters took the rest, where he could then sell and distribute with a relative free reign over his jurisdiction.

Taxi Service

"Right – what the bloody hell was all that about!?" Marcus growled, hands clenching around the steering wheel with the whites of his knuckles showing, tendons strung and taught. His blood pressure was already high, but right now it felt like it had reached a whole new level. No superintendent should ever be having to do this with two of his officers, and that was on top of the stress caused by Rowena coming and taking half of their possessions away.

"I'm sorry, sir. I really am. But they was winding us up – insinuating things that aren't true," Paul tried to explain himself, but it didn't have the desired effect when the man was slurring over his words and slumped over in the back seat of the car.

"And of course, you decided to start a fight to resolve the altercation, because that's what a police officer should do, is it? Come on, Paul, what were ye' thinking?" Marcus' voice softened some as he briefly caught the eye of one of his most loyal officers in the rear view mirror. He could see the somewhat drunken remorse of a fella who knew that he'd let his superintendent down.

"I wasn't thinking, was I?" Paul ducked his head, idly fiddling with Chester's ears who was attentively sitting beside him. Broadmeadow was making him feel like a naughty schoolboy, summoned by the headmaster ...

"That you weren't. You'll have to fill out a statement, you know that don't you? With any luck there will be no charges, seeing as you, at very least, managed to keep your fists to yourself." Marcus narrowed his eyes as he spoke, his gaze flitting once again to the rear view mirror; but there *was* the smallest hint of a smile to go with, a minute upturn of the gaffer's lips implying that the verbal chastising was over.

"Yeah, of course. It won't happen again, sir," Paul solemnly promised whilst trying to make himself look as small as possible. Which wasn't easily done for a bloke who was somewhat larger in size.

Properly smiling now, Marcus shook his head. "Ok, Paul. I'll believe it when I see it, eh?"

He had valid reasons for his doubts – this wasn't the first time Paul had resorted to physicality over the power of words (or just bloody walking away). He'd always worn his heart very much on his sleeve during their thirteen years of working together, and especially so after the loss of his best pal, DI Wright, which was why Marcus was always prepared to cut the man some slack. Paul had stuck with him too, since graduating from training, and that sort of loyalty paid dividends in his book.

Heading around to the top end of town, both men's attentions turned towards the source of a miserable groan coming from the front passenger seat. "You going to hurl again, fella?" Marcus asked softly, frankly more concerned over the lad's general wellbeing, rather than whether the car would need a valet service in the morning.

Dan churned out a burp. "Nrgggh ... no ..."

He didn't look too good. Not too good at all. Marcus needed to get him home to bed. There was one problem with that though. "D'ya know where he lives, Paul?"

Good question. "Nah, sir. Outskirts of town, maybe? I know he has a garden ..."

So did every other house within South Lynn ... "Helpful, Bartlett. Very helpful. Thank you," Marcus sighed, turning off onto the old high road, "Daniel, can you tell me where you live, son?"

"Uh ..." Dan's head was glued to the back of his seat, his eyes barely more than a squint, desperately trying to keep the remaining contents of his stomach intact. He waved his hand in the general direction of the windscreen.

Chester grumbled, nudging against Paul's arm. Why didn't the boss ask him? He could sniff out Dan's house, no problem. But he had a feeling that the boss was secretly a bit pleased now that he didn't have much of a choice over what to do with him ...

"Right, ok. Good stuff, everyone." Marcus made an executive decision. It was nearly one in the morning, and he wanted to go home. He'd had enough to deal with already that evening, without being forced to play the dutiful parent to his supposedly responsible pair of officers. First stop, the kebab shop at the top of West Row, because yes, tired and disgruntled as he may have been, he knew that there was no other way to end an evening at the pub on a Friday night, other than to fill up on some takeaway food. Then it was around the corner to Paul's house, swinging up against the kerb outside and waiting patiently whilst his late-night taxi's first punter untangled himself from his seatbelt. "I'll see you at the station in the morning, Paul. And no, I'm not paying you overtime."

At that, Chester blundered forwards between the seats, nuzzling first against the boss with a gaping mouth and lolling tongue, and then to Dan, butting his head against him. The black dog wasn't there, so it was ok. The boss would look after him. Paul ducked down, now out of the car but gently swaying like the pavement was moving beneath his feet, grabbing for Chester's collar to pull him back; "You sure you'll be alright, sir? You're welcome to kip on the sofa Dan, you know that don't you?"

"Nah ... m'good ..." Dan hugged at his chest, before burrowing himself deeper into the passenger seat and moving to hug the warm bag of chips in his lap instead.

"I've got a spare room made up, he'll be fine with me," Marcus said as gently as he could, not wanting Paul to push the subject any further. Would be nice to have a wee bit of company for the night. It would take his mind off the brown envelope that was still sitting on the coffee table, unopened.

Paul frowned. "Just didn't want you getting wrong with the missus, sir ..."

There had been an inkling over the past few months that things weren't too good for his gaffer at home – a throwaway comment here and a wash bag under the boss's desk there ... he felt bad enough as it was, without causing any further tension within Broadmeadow's personal life.

Marcus felt his hands grip once more around the steering wheel. Paul would find out soon enough, but not now. Not tonight. "Thanks Paul, but it's fine. G'wan. Get outta here, before ye' kebab gets cold."

"Alright. G'night, sir."

"Night, Paul."

Staying with engine idle just long enough to see Paul and Chester through the front door, they were off again, back into the night. Dan still had the takeaway bag nestled in his lap like a precious newborn child, but hadn't made an attempt to see what was inside, looking like he was verging on a state of comatose. What on earth had happened to him?

Marcus hadn't dealt with someone that drunk in a very long while, and especially not an adult who really ought to know ones limits a wee bit better by now. He did know however, that when Paul got himself on the drink, there wasn't much stopping him. Marcus himself could keep up, but perhaps not Daniel; he was roughly half the size of Paul, which surely meant he had roughly half the tolerance too. But, even so, it was still rather hard to comprehend just *how* drunk the wee fella appeared to be.

With that in mind, he decided to give it one last try, even though he now had his mind firmly set over where he wanted the lad to be staying for the night. "Daniel, son? Are you sure ye' can't tell me where you live? Be much better to wake up in your own bed, no?"

"Um ... Wist ... Wisterly ..." Dan gave up. He knew where he lived, of course he did, but the words just weren't forthcoming. Every time he tried to engage his brain and form the very simple statement of 'Wisteria Avenue, Number 2', his head stared to spin and the nausea returned with a vengeance. Shitting hell, he was drunk.

The parent within Marcus that never got the chance to become took over; "Ok, son. I'll take you back to mine, sleep it off. Is that ok?" There was no doubt within his mind that he'd have spent the remainder of the night worrying anyways, should he have left Daniel alone in such a drunken stupor.

"M'hm," Dan agreed quietly.

They drove in silence after that, with Marcus deep in thought and Dan slipping in and out of consciousness.

Broken Vows

Rowena lay back, naked, catching her breath. "If that doesn't do it, I don't know what will." Her husband lay at her side with an arm flung over his eyes, softly grinning through the high that was now starting to ebb into the post-coital afterglow.

"Aye, that was good for you, no?" Marcus said on the exhale. She admired Marc's face, what she could see of it anyways, when he realised that she was looking his way and turned to meet her eyes.

Always seeking approval, her Marcus.

He did have lovely eyes. As sharp a blue as a summer's sky, flecked with grey and amber when the light hit them right. His hair too, an ashy, mousy brown, with the odd streak of ginger – he was all contrasts, yet perfectly so, a physical embodiment of the North East coastline where both of their roots lay. "Mmm, yes, darling." She lied. She didn't want to hurt his feelings.

Sex wasn't all it was cracked up to be. That was what Rowena really had to say on the matter, and having grown up within a Catholic family, naturally, Marcus had been her first. Two years married and with numerous attempts under their belt, she had yet to have achieved an orgasm, and was starting to believe that such a thing was purely myth and legend. Marcus tried, bless him, to make it good for her too, but unfortunately, Rowena was a little prudish when it came to matters of the bedroom, finding herself cringe at the idea of speaking aloud about things like 'foreplay' and the like, let alone wanting to try out any position other than her husband up on his forearms above her.

Another thing she disliked was when the woman was left to sort out the mess whilst the man just got to relax back (and probably fall asleep; his job now done). At the very least, it seemed enough to sate Marcus' urges. And if she could just manage to get herself pregnant, then it would all be worth it. She rolled over, her husband's discarded underwear coming to hand first to wipe herself clean.

Marcus laughed, "Really? I could have worn those again, you know ..."

"You've got plenty more in the drawer. I need to put a wash load on anyways." Classic Rowena – back to business. She'd already laid on her back long enough for Marc's gift to work its magic, and she didn't really feel like staying in bed any longer than she had to. She sat up, swinging her legs over the side of the bed. "I'm going for a bath. Do you want me to save the water for you?"

"You don't want to stay in bed a wee while longer?" Marcus asked with a tinge of sadness, reaching out for her hand but she denied the gesture. She knew that Marc was one to crave for a physical connection, having never been a man of many words when it came to showing his affections, but making up for it in his need to touch; to hold ...

Rowena used to savour and reciprocate, when the honeymoon period was still running warm between their veins, but now, only a couple of years into their lifetime together, she didn't share that yearning any longer. Marcus was caring – almost too caring for her liking, and she'd started to find it a wee bit overbearing.

So she left the bed, throwing a gown around herself because the need to be bared was gone; she wanted to be covered. And the guilt, a great wave of it, as she left the bedroom with a parting peck to her husband's cheek, that she had only let him take her to bed after her shift at the hospital because she so desperately wanted to bring a child into their lives.

Positive thoughts.

It wouldn't do her chances any good if she was stuck on a negative. Not everyone got lucky enough to conceive a child straight after the honeymoon was over – not that her and Marc had been able to experience a romantic getaway after sealing their vows.

Pushing down the plug and running the hot tap to full, she lifted the seat and sat herself down on the toilet to clean herself up.

There had been no honeymoon because their romantic getaway had been one of a more permanent kind – to England, and away from whatever it was that had caused her Marcus to flee from everything they'd ever known. The position he'd taken hadn't even been for much more money, hence why she was still a working woman, a newly trained nurse, but not for long, with any luck. They would have their wee bairn soon, and with Marc's news of an opportunity to join a newly formed rural crime department (whatever that was), one income would surely be enough for the both of them.

The bath was nearly ready. Marc was there, hovering in the doorway, speaking to her. "Everything alright there, love?"

Rowena must have lost herself in thought for a moment there. She eyed her husband from where she was sat on the toilet. He was bare arsed naked, and in the past, she would have found the invitation to share a bath highly alluring, but not anymore. Hadn't she already told him? Or had she not been clear enough when she'd asked if he would like the water saving once she was done?

"Yes, fine. I'll save the water for you then?" she clipped. Point made.

A look of quiet disappointment clouded Marc's expression as he nodded, stopping just short of turning around and closing the bathroom door whilst sporting a dejected smile. "That'll be grand, love."

*

The wee bairn never did arrive.

They tried for another year or so, but to no avail, before finally taking the decision to see a doctor. Obviously, it was Marcus who was tested first, with his wife undeniably sure that it wasn't her reproductive organs at fault. Fourteen days later her suspicions were confirmed – her husband could not provide her with the offspring that she so terribly desired.

Sitting at the other side of the doctor's desk, with the bad news read out to them by a GP that they weren't familiar with, was the moment that Rowena had fell out of love with her husband. Marcus had tried, god he'd tried to comfort her, holding her hand within his large palm as she'd sobbed, a lead weight like an anchor dropping to the pit of her stomach.

Marcus had never shared her desire to be become a mother; a parent, despite his best efforts to try and tell her otherwise. The guilt was there, for sure, over his belief that he had failed to provide in the most primitive of ways, but he could never fully share the grief that she would now be forced to live with.

"There are other options, Mrs Broadmeadow ..." their doctor had consoled, but none of his options were the answer that she really wanted to hear. IVF was now a possibility, but only if you had the money to pay for it, and even then success rates were shockingly low. Another option would be the use of a sperm donor, but that would mean ... no, she couldn't do that. Brief talk of adoption followed that, but the conversation soon fizzled down to ashes, with Rowena having already lost all hope and slowly coming to terms with the fact that she would never be a mother.

Years went by, and the resentment grew. Marcus constantly overcompensated his perceived failings as a man by mothering over her, giving her everything she wanted – a second car, a bigger, more expensive house, yearly overseas holidays and a large allowance every month, and yes, she was guilty of taking everything that he had to give. She took advantage of his generosity, knowing full well what she was doing.

All Marcus asked for in return was someone to come home to at the end of the day; someone to love and cherish and provide for, to make him feel like he was needed. She tried, with every Catholic bone within her body, to love him in return. But the damage done through no fault of her husband's own was well beyond repair, until finally, after all those years of enmity, she couldn't keep the facade up any longer.

She filed for divorce, and prayed to their lord that Marcus would let her go quietly. She would go home. She would force him to sell the house in order to buy her out, and obtain half of her husband's pension once he retired – he owed her that much at least, did he not?

Guest for the Night

Young Daniel was at least able to walk himself into the house without too much assistance, just a hand hovering an inch or so from his back to catch him if he were to stumble. When they made it inside, the lad stopped and stared, wide eyed around the kitchen, finding an oak-topped worktop to lean himself against. Marcus headed straight for the kettle, because he didn't know what else to do now that he'd gone and taken his sergeant home with him for the night.

"Nice place ... s-sir ..." Daniel slurred, wobbling on the spot.

"Thank you," Marcus said with a degree of wistfulness. It wouldn't be his for much longer, with the estate agents already booked in for a valuation the following week, and of course the fact that half of his possessions were now starkly absent after Rowena had been and taken her fill. The kitchen was large and long, with contemporary cottage style units and an island in the middle. Faux exposed beams across the ceiling led towards patio doors, where Marc's true love really lay – the garden. This wasn't just his and Rowena's house, it was their home, and it hurt to think that he would be leaving it all behind. "I'll get you some painkillers, Daniel. Try and eat some of those chips, and I'll be right back."

It certainly felt *funny* to have a house guest, let alone the circumstances surrounding it. Marcus didn't really have friends, not since Johnny. A psychologist would see straight away that he was afraid of close companionship outside the comparative safety of marriage. They would tell him that he was scared of suffering another life upending loss.

Was Daniel really a friend? He tried to compartmentalise it into the same way that he saw Paul, as a trusted colleague upon whom he could rely – but he knew that wasn't the truth. Daniel struck him as far more vulnerable a soul. A soul in which Marcus held an extremely strong desire to nurture and protect.

The same as Johnny.

With any luck Rowena hadn't cleared the medicine cabinet out too, because the bathroom was just as empty as the rest of the house. One toothbrush remaining at the sink. One towel hanging on the rail. A pale square of paint on the wall where the picture of an Italian lake scene had hung. Marcus took a minute to contemplate as he caught his face within the mirrored doors of the bathroom cabinet above the sink.

Aside from the fact that it was well gone midnight, there were prominent grey bags sitting under his eyes and chasm-like wrinkles at the furrows of his brow, and it made him look old. Not that he had ever considered himself a bad looking fella, even quite handsome in years gone by, but now he could see that age was certainly starting make its presence known.

He punched the glass with his thumb, releasing one of the cabinet doors to find what he'd been looking for. The Paracetamol was a month or so past its expiry, probably why Rowena had left it, but he figured it would still be fine.

Returning to the kitchen, he found his sergeant braced over the sink, unwrapped chips scattered to the side as he retched. "Christ alive ..." Marcus muttered to himself as he edged up beside him, placing a hand between Daniel's shoulders in an attempt to ease the poor boy.

There was nothing left within Dan's stomach for him the expel. He started to tremble, his knees going weak and a cold sweat consuming him as he took in some deep, stuttered breaths, trying to will the nausea to subside. He hated being sick – it made him panic, an irrational fear attached to it that he was going to die from the exertion ...

The black dog, lurking outside, steered clear. It couldn't do anything whilst Dan's mind was so preoccupied.

"I think we need to get you to bed, don't you?" Marcus murmured, running his hand up and down Daniel's back, soothing him.

"M' sorry ..." Dan sobbed around a hitching breath, "Help me ..." with his voice small, cracking to pitifully high pitch, Dan managed to utter past the rising bile within his throat. He retched again, desperately wanting the feeling to pass.

"Ok, ok. Shall I hold your hair back?" Marcus joked, continuing with the motion of his hand because he didn't know what else there was to do, except try to keep the lad calm. He thought about the last time he himself had been sick, a few years back now when a nasty, flu-like virus had struck him down and left him bedridden for the best part of the week. The whole experience wasn't pleasant, that was a given, and there certainly hadn't been anyone there to hold *his* hair back – Rowena had pretty much left him to it, relegating him to the spare room and avoiding him like he'd contracted the black death.

He'd never seen someone panic so much though, over a bout of nausea. The times that Rowena had vomited, especially during that short time when they thought they had conceived (just before the time when Marcus had been called home early from work to find his wife, crying on the bathroom floor, the toilet bowl filled with blood), she had not wanted him anywhere near her, swatting him away if he even attempted to console ...

"You think you can manage the stairs, Daniel? Perhaps the sofa might be a safer option, actually," he said the last part to himself, more than anything. Marcus was no young man, as he'd already self-proclaimed within the bathroom mirror, and Daniel was sturdier built than he looked upon a first glance. Especially now that he'd had his hand upon him too, there was an undeniable muscular strength to his broad back. Anyways, trying to help the lad up the stairs when he wasn't exactly steady on his feet probably wouldn't be the most well calculated of ideas.

"I t-think ... yeah ..." Daniel mumbled sadly as he tried to find his footing once more.

"Right. Come on then." Now that the first level of physical contact had been broken, Marcus found it of a second nature to take Daniel by the arm and lead him to the sitting room. The lad didn't protest. Once the sofa was in sight, Daniel gravitated himself towards it and fell down into the cushions like a sack of potatoes.

He groaned, curling himself onto his side with his feet hanging off the edge. Marcus smiled – even blind drunk, Daniel had still kept hold of his manners. "Shall I help you with those?"

A noncommittal grunt was Daniels response, so Marcus took that as his permission to proceed. The lad helped himself to a cushion, curling it close into his arms and waving a shoe-clad foot in Marcus' general direction.

"I'll take that as a yes then, eh?" He bent down, grabbing Daniel's wavering ankle and feeling how it went limp and compliant once within his grasp. His feet were bigger than

Marcus had expected, like a wee hobbit. One shoe, and then the other safely removed, leaving young Daniel's socks intact as he manoeuvred the lad's feet onto the sofa. "There ya' go, fella."

A part of Marcus' mind told him that Daniel would be more comfortable still if he helped him to undress – he was still wearing his work clothes from that day, with his smart shirt and trousers, all be it a little more crumpled and worse for wear than earlier at the office. He stopped himself though. Taking his subordinate officer home and putting him to bed was one thing; taking his subordinate officer home and removing his clothes whilst within a drunken stupor was quite another.

Try explaining that one, should Daniel wake tomorrow with no memory of the night before ...

"Sir ...?" Daniel cracked opened a bleary eye, taking a moment to focus it onto his gaffer, "You got a bucket?"

"Yes, of course." Marcus went back to the kitchen, swiftly returning moments later for fear of a ruined carpet, placing a mop bucket on the floor close enough for Daniel to be able to hang his head off the side of the sofa into – of which the lad did, taking a shuddering breath through his nose and out of his mouth.

He let out a pained groan, his head disappearing into the bucket as he hugged it with both arms and heaved. Marcus went down to his knees – they crunched as he went – and found his hand at the back of Daniel's head, lacing fingers through his sweat tousled hair to comfort him; to let him know that he was there ...

The boy heaved, his stomach audibly churning as he regurgitated what could only have been a sickly bile, the aroma pungent and sour as Daniel's stomach lining hit the bottom of the bucket. He hung there for a moment longer before emerging, face tear-struck, and Marcus' heart went and broke for him. He didn't like to see anyone suffering, especially so when they seemed to be so bloody vulnerable.

Gently, fingertips light as they brushed against the fabric of Daniel's shirt, Marcus held his upper arm and slowly teased it away from the iron grip around the bucket. Daniel was trembling, white as a sheet yet burning hot. "Some state you've gotten yourself into eh, Danny boy? Paul said you only had a couple, so I don't ..."

Daniel sniffled, his cheeks streaked with drying tears, letting himself be hauled back up onto the sofa. "'M sorry sir ... so sorry."

"Hey, fella. Don't be sorry. It's ok – would you have a wee sip of water for me, now?"

With his heavy eyes now shut, Daniel nodded.

Marcus left once more, taking the bucket with him to give it a good rinse out before returning to his wee sergeant's side with a cold glass of water and the packet of painkillers, only to find that the lad had slipped off into a drunken slumber. He shifted Daniel's legs, a dead yet compliant weight, to make room for himself at the very edge of the sofa. There was a fleece blanket folded over the back – couldn't have the lad getting cold now, could he?

He thought over the state young Daniel was in, relieved that he had finally gone and passed out from his endeavours as he draped the blanket over him. If Paul had rightly said that he'd only consumed a couple, perhaps three pints, then surely, *surely,* he wouldn't have found himself three sheets to the wind and unable to even string a coherent sentence together?

Something was amiss.

An empty stomach, possibly? Medication, that he had failed to mention? God only knew. Marcus felt his eyes growing heavy. He couldn't leave Daniel alone, not now – what if he found himself on his back, unable to turn himself over should he find himself needing to be sick once more? And it became especially harder to move himself when a stray foot came to rest first against his thigh, before an insistent set of toes nudged their way underneath in search of warmth ...

Folding his arms against his chest, Marcus settled back and let his protesting eyes fall shut, sleep coming easy for the first time in a long while now that he had Daniel safely at his side.

Haud Yer Weesht

The black dog crept around the frame of the sitting room door, blending into the darkened shadows as it stuck close to the walls. This house it found itself in was filled with ripples of sadness, desolate and hidden between the cracks in the floorboards and filtering up, filling the very air it breathed.

It pointed up its nose and sniffed, still sticking close to the wall. There had been love, long ago, its presence barely a whiff amongst the consuming sense of hurt and *loss* – everything the black dog could thrive upon. Until now, it had strongly felt its hold upon Dan waning, like it was shrinking, suffocating under the weight of the newcomer within his life, Broadmeadow, but the black dog hadn't survived this long without a bit of cunning prowess up its sleeve.

Dan hadn't taken the medication he was prescribed to keep the black dog from rearing up to full strength – it was at his home, in the bedside drawer. It hadn't always been kept it in there; he used to leave the box lying around the house, but he'd grown wise to the fact that it kept disappearing the following day, doubting himself as to where he'd left it and growing fearful of his forgetfulness. When the self-doubt had grown, so had the black dog, gaining magnitude and strength and the power to manipulate its surroundings, allowing it to make that box of pills fall to the floor or out of sight behind a sideboard. It knew that when Dan didn't have his pills, the dark fog around him flourished, clouding his vision until he couldn't see a way out ...

Only a matter of time.

It waited, watching from the shadows.

Broadmeadow had slumped down, his chin almost to his chest as he snored through both his throat and his nose at the same time – a loud, rattling noise escaping every time he inhaled. The black dog edged closer, unable to resist. Broadmeadow was dreaming, but he wouldn't remember when he woke, so deep within his slumber as he was. It stuck its nose in, sniffing at his hand. Large, powerful hands clustered with old scars and calloused skin. The most prominent of marks – an oven burn, a Christmas day long since passed, the female partner and her family there and she was stressed, pressing questions over why there were still no young within the fold, a tray of roast potatoes as they stood together at the range cooker, intentionally pressed into her husband's flesh although she had blamed him afterwards, for getting in the way ...

The broken little finger, caught in the car door in his haste to attend to the scene of his officer, patrol car upturned and already deceased, ignored at the time but slightly crooked now where treatment hadn't been sought until the bone had already started to fuse ... and then to his palm, the unassuming extra crease of skin, a wine glass hurled his way when the partner had insisted on returning home, to Scotland, and Broadmeadow had refused, saying he couldn't, *wouldn't*, too many ghosts of the past, picking up the shattered glass, not noticing the sliced flesh at first as his blood had pooled among the stain of pinot noir.

But still, Broadmeadow didn't have his own black dog, where Dan had succumbed through far less. He didn't take adversity within his stride like Broadmeadow did.

Broadmeadow stirred in his sleep, causing the black dog to flinch. The man was still dreaming, but it couldn't quite manage to slither its way in. A white, hazy curtain that couldn't be breached was blocking the black dog's path.

It poked its nose forwards, prodding at the veil of light, falling like a sparkling dew upon its muzzle. The black dog blinked as it found itself mesmerised by the gentle beauty of it, how it felt cool and refreshing at the tip of its snout, a summer morning scent tickling at its nostrils. It sneezed, drawing its head back. Back to the familiarity of the heavy, dead of night shadows.

As if Broadmeadow had heard – or felt – the disturbance, his accent stronger than usual as he mumbled something in his native tongue; "*Haud yer weesht ... thalla!*"

And when the black dog that had always been so *untouchable* didn't move, because the world of the mortals was one within it lived but didn't share, the man swung out his leg to kick the dog away. His club-like foot swilled through its semi-translucent form like a skimming stone through a standing pool, and it startled, its spectral carcass starting to ripple and disperse around the foreign intrusion.

Anger, possession, disparity and despair – those were the things that the black dog thrived upon; what its entire being consisted of. Never an embodiment so strong had managed to breach its being, as its nerve endings tingled and dark fibres glowed, some part of the man that was starting to take Daniel away remaining as he drew his foot away.

For a moment longer its abdomen glowed. Standing stock still, the black dog raised its hackles and growled.

Broadmeadow frowned within his sleep, aimlessly waving his hand and swinging out his foot for a second attempt at shooing the nuisance away. He growled right back at the black dog; "*Go on, away with ye'* ..." his tone low, threatening, and unquestionably stern.

With its disturbed, opalescent eyes fixed on the sleeping alpha male, the black dog slowly crept back until it found the wall, watching on with a degree of jealousy as Broadmeadow readjusted his recumbent stance so that a territorial hand rested upon Dan's calf. Whether the gesture was as intended or not, there was no question towards Broadmeadow's desire to be Dan's sentry, even if he was acting upon his subconscious alone.

The night went on, and with the posed threat now neutralised Broadmeadow fell into a deeper sleep. Dan fidgeted and turned under the blanket, fighting against the constraints and fighting for more space by way of kicking at his gaffer's legs in his drunken slumber. The black dog settled itself down onto the floor, pensively watching over the pair.

It had known Dan for most of his adult life, making its presence known here and there but never really a permanent fixture until DCI Walters had appeared on the scene. Slowly at first, and then more frequently as time went on, and when the bullying became more and more sadistic in nature, it had started to feel like the young man needed its company more than ever.

If Dan was sad or hurt, the black dog would lick his wounds. If Dan was frustrated, or angry, the black dog would rear up and fight his corner. If Dan was lonely, the black dog would encourage him to stay home, because only *it* could provide him with what he really needed – but for all the black dog knew about the man it spent its life with, it didn't quite anticipate what would happen if someone else decided that they wanted him for themselves.

Of which, Broadmeadow definitely did, even if he couldn't quite see it for himself just yet. Dan wanted it too, but had spent far too long running from what he really wanted to be able to turn around and *look* at what was right in front of him. That left the black dog with a certainty that its days were numbered, once he was able to see how much Broadmeadow was beginning to mean to him. With that in mind, it curled itself up on the floor, tucking in its nose and feet and wrapping its long, wispy tail around its body, letting the disconcertion it was feeling settle as it quietly observed the two sleeping men.

The Morning After

Dan's first indication that something was amiss was the blinding headache that had woken him in the first place; one that was undeniably caused by a night of alcohol consumption, and one that he hadn't had the pleasure of experiencing in quite some years.

He couldn't even really remember the last time he had woken with a hangover, because he hadn't had more than a couple of drinks in more than one sitting in a very long time – not since he was maybe fifteen or so, when he'd stolen a bottle of gin from his parents' alcohol cabinet to drink with his mates at the park. He'd wondered at the time why it had tasted so unpalatable, not having realised that it was supposed to be mixed (not drunk straight from the bottle), and even now, he couldn't stomach that taste. That was because after downing half the bottle in a very short space of time because he wasn't feeling drunk enough, Dan had started to feel head-spinningly nauseous, suddenly so inebriated that he couldn't string together a properly formed sentence.

Luckily for him, his mates weren't all about the masculine bravado that so many others of his age were striving towards, especially when they realised that their friend was starting to panic over the adverse effect of too much gin and what it was doing to him, and the further panic when he realised that inevitably, and soon, he was going to throw it all back up again. His mates had acted fast, sensible to a certain degree for a bunch of fifteen year old lads, and had done the one thing any teenager finding themselves out of their depth would do in such a situation: they called Dan's father. Which was in itself a story for another day.

Anyways, the second indication that something was amiss was that Dan didn't remember having all that much to drink – maybe a couple more pints than he'd normally have, but when one has such a drastic fear of vomiting, one learns to restrain themselves when it comes to how much can be safely consumed.

The third indication, and this was surely the most worrying, was that he had fallen asleep on a sofa that wasn't his own, and could only presume at this point that the owner of said sofa was the one sharing blanket with him, holding his feet within their lap.

He had woken on his back, a little stiff and a lingering taste of bile stinging at the back of his throat, with the headache pounding at his temple instructing him to keep his eyes shut for a little longer. Not that he particularly wanted to open his eyes just yet anyways, as that would mean having to reveal exactly who he'd decided to head home with the night before.

And why couldn't he remember what had happened?

It all felt worryingly blank.

He couldn't ... there wasn't anyone at the pub last night, aside from Emily and Paul, that he'd spoken to, let alone been swayed by attraction. He didn't think there had been, anyways.

One good sign was that he was still fully clothed. At which point, the person with whom Dan was sharing a sofa with started to move, shifting slightly, breathing growing more present. And at that point, he was faced with a choice – to open his eyes, or not to open his eyes? That was when his heart nearly stopped. Another shift of the thigh he was resting his feet against and he felt something hard. Something hard and undoubtedly *male*.

"*Christ, alive ...*" a soft grumbling voice, with the lilt of a Scottish accent, had Dan knowing exactly who had taken him home last night. His gaffer stretched out, gently removing Dan's feet from his lap and setting them back down onto the sofa. A pause, an afterthought, covering his toes with the blanket. What was happening? How had he ended up here ...? Better find out, he supposed. He unstuck his eyelids, mouth hanging slightly agape. His gaffer was observing him, also a bit bleary eyed.

"Morning, Daniel. How ye' feeling?" said Broadmeadow. He knew more than him then, judging by the way the older man looked entirely unsurprised over their surroundings.

"What happened?" Dan croaked, oesophagus like sandpaper.

Marcus peered down at him, raising his brow to one side with a slightly amused smile playing at his lips. "No recollections?"

He tried again to wrack his brains for absolutely any remembrance at all; anything significant ...

He'd been sick, he knew that much, the bucket on the floor by his head a sure-fire confirmation. But apart from that, it felt as if there were a void – an empty chasm stretching back and out of reach – as to what had happened between being at the pub with Paul and Emily, to ending up here, on his gaffer's sofa.

"No ..." A look of confusion must have been evident upon his face, which Broadmeadow took pity on. He reached over and gently rested a steady hand over his knee. The touch was grounding and resolute, and that palm, so much bigger than his own.

"You were involved with an incident, outside the pub. Well, Paul more so that you, but still – the police were involved too. I was called out," Broadmeadow said slowly, like he deemed Dan only able to comprehend minimal fragments of information. Rightly so, Dan decided. His head was killing him.

When what his gaffer was saying did sink in, Dan's stomach lurched. This couldn't be right. "What sort of incident? I can't ... I only had a couple ... how did I end up here?"

"You couldn't remember where you lived, son. Couldn't even string and sentence together – I didn't know what to do with you, with you being sick and all." The gaffer's thumb started to trace up and down his knee in a softly reassuring, rhythmic pattern of motion. Dan stared at it, absently.

"But what happened? Why where the police involved? I'm so sorry, sir ..." Dan flitted his eyes up, searching for any sort of disappointment within his gaffer's, but all he could see was a resolute, genuine level of care upon the senior officer's features. A realisation hit at how utterly crushed he would be, should he have unwittingly done something to cause an underlying rift between them. For now though, all appeared to be well. Broadmeadow wasn't angry with him.

"It's ok, Daniel. I'll be meeting Paul down at the station to give his statement, so if you just try and remember anything at all about what happened last night, that would be grand.

Anyways, perhaps a cup of tea will help? How's that sound?" The gaffer's eyes – eyes in which Dan was starting to become fascinated by their complexity – were inherently warm, unwavering in their undivided attention upon him.

"Yeah. I think I can stomach it ..."

Broadmeadow gave his knee a final, encouraging little pat before unfolding himself from the sofa. "Good lad. Nothing a nice wee cuppa can't fix, eh?" He turned, just as Dan was about to lay back for a couple more minutes of precious shuteye; "Would you like an extra sugar to help settle the stomach?

"Yeah, ok. Thanks sir."

*

A moment of contemplation transpired for Dan as he braced himself over the toilet and emptied his bladder. Standing up straight wasn't yet a viable option, thanks to some disconcertingly wobbly legs and an awfully tender abdomen like he'd taken a punch to the gut. As absurd as the situation was (waking up after an evening at the pub on his superintendent's sofa), he didn't feel overly uncomfortable about being there. Broadmeadow had gone out of his way to make him feel welcome, despite him being what he saw as an unwanted house guest.

He wondered where Mrs Broadmeadow was. Of course, he'd seen the band around the gaffer's finger, and purely assumed nothing more of it, except that he was a happily married man. She could be on a weekend away or something? However, Dan's intuition told him otherwise.

Everything about his gaffer's house spoke of a man who lived alone, from the single set of shoes by the front door to the distinct *emptiness* of the decor; it just didn't quite add up.

Anyways, although inquisitive as to Broadmeadow's marital state, there was no way in hell that Dan was going to pry further. That would just be downright rude.

His only real concern right then, as he gingerly pulled his trousers back up, was what the *fuck* actually happened last night that had him ending up in such a dire state of incapacitation? Fragments were there, but he still couldn't fathom anything useful past the point of seeing Emily off into the taxi. The desire to remember more; to be able to give his gaffer a proper course of events yet finding himself unable, was hugely frustrating.

Then, as he tucked himself back into his underwear, he felt something. A sharp sting. Pulling the waistband of his briefs aside at the jut of his hip, Dan lightly fingered at a small, raised area upon his flesh. Frowning, he stretched the skin between his fingers, noticing a pin-prick bruise starting to form, and his heart dropped. A training course back at the Met had him knowing, or at least strongly suspecting, what would cause such a minute yet painful mark upon his skin.

Making his way to the kitchen where he knew that Broadmeadow was still tending over the tea, Dan hovered for a moment, disconcerted and entirely unsettled by what he'd just discovered. For just a moment he noticed a well-tended garden, stippled in early morning light, visible through the large paned window which was steamed with condensation from the kettle.

"Alright there, Daniel?" The gaffer turned, giving him a questioning look before stepping away from the kettle, perhaps because he was worried over Dan's bewildered reappearance, concerned over him doing something unexpected like collapsing right there upon the tiles ...

With slightly shaking hands, Dan unbuckled his belt before working on his button, then his zip. Broadmeadow stepped up to him and stared down with a look of utter confusion. "Daniel? What are you doing there?"

Dan didn't care what he must have looked like, stripping off in his senior officer's kitchen, because his level of panic was now overriding anything else. He needed a second opinion, and he needed it now. With his belt hanging loose and his trousers agape, he stretched the waistband of his underwear down over his hip to bare an expanse of pale skin and a nice side-view of his arse.

"My hip ... look ... please?" The gaffer made a face, straining to see, having to crouch down in what could be construed as a rather compromising position, had it have not been for the surrounding circumstances. Warm fingers ran over his skin, thumbing over the area in question. Dan felt himself breath, awash with a sudden sense of calm. Then he flinched as Broadmeadow poked at the area a little too hard.

Before he could even think about what he was doing, he realised that he was gripping at his gaffer's shoulder for support. With that, Broadmeadow hauled himself back up to his feet and confirmed to Dan what he had been fearing from the start – "Right. Hospital. Now."

Heron by the River

"I still can't remember the details, I'm sorry," Dan exclaimed, growing ever more frustrated with his failure to recall any meaningful details over the night before.

Apparently, if one has been spiked, memories will start to return in fits and starts over time. That's what the duty nurse had told him. Still, it hadn't stopped Broadmeadow from calling it in as soon as the confirmation had been received that all evidence pointed towards a needle stick injury. And his face; the underlying anger present, when a constable had arrived and not a ranking detective to take his statement.

Dan just wanted to sleep it off if he was honest, not yet fully comprehending the fact that he'd been drugged without a clear reason as to why. The gaffer though, he seemed to be taking on the brunt of the concern that he should have been feeling, but wasn't.

"Ok, well, if you remember anything, then just call it in with South Lynn." The constable, a larger lady who was also on the shorter side, closed her notebook, clearly about to wrap things up here.

"What about CCTV? Witnesses? Did everybody involved in the altercation with DC Bartlett get interviewed and logged?" Broadmeadow was still there, overseeing proceedings within the ward that Dan had been transported to, and he wasn't happy.

Still, all Dan wanted to do was sleep.

"Until we get DS Taylor's blood results back, and only then if they show any indication of toxicity, can we escalate this into a criminal investigation. At the moment, we just can't prove that anything unlawful has occurred. I'm sorry, sir."

To be fair, she wasn't wrong, even if Dan was sure within his own mind that something other than alcohol was at play here. All he could think about though was how tired he was. There wasn't any mental capacity available for him to try harder at giving a better statement – he'd truthfully told the constable all that he knew, and now he was just willing her to be on her way so that he could get some more rest.

"Well. Just make it a priority, please? To get Daniel's case number logged onto the system?" Broadmeadow stood, along with the constable from South Lynn, and she nodded affirmative before taking her leave.

"Have a good day, sirs. I hope you're feeling better soon, sergeant Taylor."

That was that, then.

Broadmeadow frowned behind the constable's back as she left the ward, before closing in on Dan after drawing the curtains around his bed. "Well that felt like a complete bloody waste of time, if ever I've seen one – How're you feeling, son? Can I get you anything?"

Dan stifled a yawn. In all honesty he felt ok, except for the tiredness and the beginnings of a headache starting to resurface. This all felt rather overblown a situation, but he understood why it was necessary for him to be there in the hospital. "Would I be allowed a cup of tea, d'ya think?"

"I don't see why not. Can't promise it'll taste any good though." The gaffer craned down over him like a mother hen inspecting her clutch, even reaching out to thumb away a stray hair from his forehead. The gesture made Dan feel a nice, gentle warmth inside.

He decided to try his luck. After all, he was a victim of a serious crime, was he not? "There was a coffee shop downstairs near the entrance ..." trailing off, he blinked up at Broadmeadow, who tutted, but was smiling nonetheless; a soft, caring smile that had Dan's heart doing funny things within his chest.

"The vending machine's offerings not good enough for my wee sergeant, eh?" Broadmeadow teased. His eyes were shining, and by all rights, it almost felt like they were flirting with each other ...

"Go on, sir. Am I not worth a proper cup of tea to you?" Dan blinked slowly as he said it, well and truly caught up in the moment between them as he gazed up at his gaffer's face.

"Ok, ok. But I shall have to be off after that to get down to the station and see to Mr Bartlett. He still owes me a statement for last night, and he'll be damned if he thinks he's going to get away with it just because I'm currently here with you."

As promised, Broadmeadow returned soon after with a takeaway cup of tea, a handful of sugars, a sandwich, and chocolate bar (for later, if Dan started to regain his appetite). It was all very sweet of his commanding officer. Above and beyond too, for what Dan felt like he really deserved.

"I'll be off now then. Try and get some rest, and you know my number if you need anything," Broadmeadow said, dithering, as if the last thing he actually wanted to do was to be leaving.

"'K. Thanks again, sir. I'll let you know if the blood results come through." He felt stupid for going all doe-eyed as he said it – or it felt like he was, anyways – but Broadmeadow's expression remained as soft as ever, when he reached out and patted Dan on the shoulder as a parting sentiment.

*

Something was going on, but Marcus just couldn't seem to piece it all together. The fly-tipping, young Ryan who'd been stabbed, Walshy, Daniel getting spiked – perhaps Paul, he hoped, could provide him with some answers for the latter at the very least.

For once, his detective constable was on time. He'd have to give the man a wee commendation for this – on a Saturday morning, too. Bravo, Paul.

"Morning, sir." Bleary-eyed and seemingly a little bit worse for wear, Paul greeted him with only minimal enthusiasm from where he was sat at his desk, having been there for an hour already waiting for the gaffer to arrive.

"Paul." Marcus gestured with a hand for him to follow him into his office. Looked like it was going to be a nice day – the sun was coming in warm, so he stopped to close the blinds to the window that looked out over the carpark, and beyond to the Weston River. A small body of water as far as rivers went; a brown, silty tributary banked either side by reeds and rushes that led on down to the coast if you followed it far enough. Sometimes, a heron could be seen wading in the shallows looking for a meal. Marcus liked to sit and watch it from his desk.

He pulled the blinds closed. No time for lollygagging this morning. Taking a seat behind his desk and pulling out a blank statement from his tray, Marcus got straight down to the point of the matter. "Right, Paul. From the top, please."

Paul frowned, shifting his weight from one foot to the other.

"Ye' can sit down you know, constable. God knows, being in front of me doesn't normally stop you."

"Thank fuck for that," Paul said as he broke into a smile, all crooked teeth on show as he planted himself down on the small sofa that Marcus had in his office. He'd meant for him to sit with him, at the desk, but never mind. Paul always had sung to his own tune.

"As you were, then. What in God's name happened last night to the pair of ye', eh?" Marcus prompted, whilst trying to put the image of young Daniel in need of his care to the back of his mind.

Paul screwed up his face as he tried to get the events of the night before in order. "Ok, ok. We went to the pub straight after work, the Greyhound so … about half five? Me, Dan and Emily. We had a few, Dan not so much actually, but he tried. Must of been nearing midnight when we left? Emily got a taxi; thas' when I noticed Dan was looking a bit rough, and then this group of youngsters, outside – one of 'em said something, calling me an' Dan *'a couple of bent coppers'*…"

"And you lost your temper, eh?"

"Yeah. S'pose I did."

Marcus continued to scribble down his notes. His thoughts wandered back to the night when he'd been called out to attend the scene of the RTA, his own officer, dead, and how Paul had reacted then, not with sadness but with anger. They'd both lost a friend that night, and then, as with now, it was not within Broadmeadow's morality to berate. Paul hadn't been the same man since DI Wright had left this earth, and he wasn't going to change, especially as he held no ambitions for further promotion so he wasn't worried over marring his record in that sense.

Besides, no physical blows were exchanged, so Marcus couldn't really see any point in discipline, except for going through the proper procedures before filing this one away for good. There was something though, that he was more concerned over – he needed to get to the bottom of why one of his officers was currently sitting in a hospital bed, after what should have been an unassuming night out down the pub.

He wondered; had he of been there, would this have happened? Paul had offered, as always, but Marcus had humbly declined. His usual excuse of; *"I'm too old for all that, you young'uns go and have a nice evening"* falling from his lips before he'd even had time to consider the offer. In the past, lunchtimes and evenings down the pub had been a regular occurrence, but not as of late. Not since Rowena had started to question the finances no matter how small a spend, and not since the accusations of marital abandonment had started. So he had, in order for a quieter life at home, slowly started to slip back from any social occasions until they had become a thing of relative past.

He did wish he had been there though. He *should* have been there. "You haven't heard anything from young Daniel then, since last night?"

Paul cocked his head, attempting to recall if he should have done, or if he had forgotten something important; "No, why? Where is he, anyways?"

Marcus paused. He didn't want what he was about to say to sound more dramatic than the situation actually was; "DS Taylor is in hospital. He was quite unwell last night, and he showed me what looks like a needle stick injury this morning."

A look of disbelief clouded Paul's features before his face dropped. "What? You mean, you think he's been spiked? Here? Why the fuck would someone go and do that? I bet it was those lads, who started the fight. Guarantee it, sir. And Ackehurst in all – what was that prick doing there?"

Marcus raised his eyebrow. *They* started the fight now, did they? Come on, Paul …

And he hadn't forgotten about Ackehurst. That line of investigation was next on his agenda.

"Wait – is he alright?" Paul added with an acute look of concern.

"Yes. The wee lad is being kept in overnight for observations, but he seems just fine now. I'm not blaming you, Paul, let me get that straight right here and now," Marcus assured his constable. The last thing he wanted was for Paul to start feeling responsible for what had happened to Daniel.

"No?"

"No. Anyways, do you have any evidence, rather than just a wee hunch, that those young fellas' may have been involved?"

Paul didn't. But he did know of one way to find out. "Have South Lynn taken on the investigation?"

"I believe so, yes." Marcus would never condone a little side investigation under the noses of their friends downstairs, but as with Daniel and the stabbing (also under South Lynn's remit), if DC Bartlett was to instigate his own private inquiries, then who was *he* to stop him?

"CCTV footage from behind the bar would be a good place to start?" Paul pushed, Marcus already able to see his constable's brain working out a roadmap. He could see a level of hurt there too, of guilt and of anger, which was undoubtedly spurring Paul on.

"That would be a good place to start, I agree."

"Dare I ask if I'm going to get paid overtime for this?" Paul asked, however, already up to his feet with his hand dug into his pocket searching for his keys. Like a dog with a bone, his Paul was. Especially when it was one of his colleagues who'd been hurt.

Cheeky shite.

"Ach, away with ya' – you'll be lucky, son. And Paul? Get that statement written up for me first, will you?"

Hen Pecking

The black dog visited Dan that evening. Not in physical form, but in his dreams. After having slept for some of the afternoon, before waking in the early evening when a nurse came round to bring him a hot meal, he had been positive that he'd be ok to go home. He felt fine. Still couldn't remember much, but other than that he was ok, and he didn't feel it entirely necessary to be taking up a hospital bed. As he'd sat there after finishing his meal, contemplating eating the chocolate bar the gaffer had bought him, a message from Paul had come through:

Alright Danny-boy you fucking fanny. Chester says hi. Gaffer told me what happened. Got some CCTV footage you might want to see. See you Monday if you don't go and pull another sickie on me.

And then, a little later as he was eating the chocolate bar, a message from his gaffer:

Hi Daniel. Just checking in. I hope you're feeling a wee bit better. Let me know if you need anything x

A kiss. There had been a kiss at the end of the message. And he'd gone to bed a happy man after that, telling himself that it wasn't a mere slip of the finger, or a typographical error – which was entirely possible, because Dan had seen for himself the way that Broadmeadow handled his phone. It had probably taken the man an age to type out that short message; he hadn't seemed to have grasped the art of texting with the use of one's thumbs, opting instead for the 'phone perched in one hand, hen-pecking with an extended finger on the other' method of using a touch screen. It made Dan laugh as he pictured it.

He found himself thinking over his gaffer more and more, as of late. He liked the way that the older man made him feel, and he found some of his mannerisms terribly endearing now that he was getting to know him more intimately. Anyways, Dan went to sleep a happy man. Happier than he'd been in a long time, which reflected upon the first half of dream he'd had that night:

In the half light of the early hours of the morning, between sleep and waking, Dan found himself wandering the pathways of his childhood home. A long, low beamed cottage, in a hamlet away from the main village. A place of happiness; of endless balmy summers and of freedom to roam the fields and footpaths beyond. A Christmas one year, he must have still been young, where he'd received a policeman's uniform complete with plastic handcuffs and a baton, and a wallet with a warrant card and badge. Hours he would spend in his own little world, playing copper and catching all the bad guys. His sister would sometimes join in, but she was a year or so older, and unlike him, she had friends. Which at that age was of far greater importance than playing cops and robbers with one's little brother.

It must have been late summer, with the wheat and barley gone from the fields, shorn down to spiky golden stubs that spanned out for as far as the eye could see. The little police uniform no longer fitted him. Dan was too old for that now but he still wore the belt it came with, with his baton and cuffs, as he rode his bike around the narrow lanes surrounding the family home. He was chasing down some bank robbers (how original). They tried to lose him by veering off of the road and onto a farmer's track. Hot on the robbers' trail, Dan followed. He came to the end of the track where there was a copse of trees, which he knew to contain a rotting wooden railway carriage nestled away from prying eyes. That must be where they were hiding.

He dumped his bike at the verge before climbing between the double wired fence and into the shade of the trees. This was somewhere Dan had revisited many a time within his dreams. He didn't know why. Perhaps it was just the carefree memories of a simpler time for him that kept him coming back?

This time though, the mood had shifted.

As Dan trod his way around the trunks of oaks and beech, a clamor of rooks cackled out of sight above his head. A chill whipped past, rustling branches and tired leaves falling. Late summer suddenly felt like mid-autumn, as a gloom descended upon the copse. Dan turned, feeling a tremble down his legs. He didn't want to be chasing down the bad guys anymore …

But the ramshackle fence he'd entered through was no longer there, replaced by an impenetrable wall of tangled brambles and branching holly. He was scared. He wanted to go home. His body grew heavy – a recurring occurrence for him in his dreams. Laboriously, one heavy step at a time, he made his way towards the railway carriage, even though his heart was telling him to take flight and just *run*. His footsteps were the only sound; dull and hollow against the time forgotten woodland floor. A rook swooped down, startling him, its menacing *ka-kaah* piercing the air.

Another noise behind him spurred his legs forwards, too afraid to look back. He started to run, but it was like gravity had been lost and he tripped over his own feet, falling …

The railway carriage was even gloomier than the woods outside. The wooden floor was long gone, replaced by dusty soil and decaying leaves. His fears that he'd been followed were realised soon after as the black dog appeared. It stalked towards him as he backed up into the nearest corner. It was huge – larger than life and far more fearsome than its usual incarnation. Fixing Dan's eyes within its gaze, it bared its teeth; gleaming fangs steeped with yellow, foul strings of saliva exuding from its retracted lips. Dan had nowhere to go.

For all his years spent with the black dog following in his shadow, it had never tried to hurt him, yet now, he was genuinely fearful for his life. He couldn't even speak – his voice had failed him as a desperate, silent scream extinguished before it could tear out from his lungs.

The black dog reared up, finding balance upon its hindlimbs, lumbering closer before its huge paws thumped down at either side of Dan's head. Its saliva dripped against his face, and a caliginous, undulating cloud of fog hindered his vision until all he could see was two lifeless, orblike eyes staring right into his soul.

It was cold. So cold. And he was so scared …

"Please …" His plea for mercy materialised into nothing more than a terrified squeak as the black dog considered him. A low buzzing sound filled his ears as he dropped to his knees.

Wake up Dan. For fucks sake, wake up!

The black dog suddenly turned its head towards the entrance of the carriage.

A man appeared, through the haze of billowing fog.

Just a dream. It's not real. It's not real ...

DCI Walters towered into view. The black dog's lips peeled back into a mocking, wolfish grin as it thudded back down to all fours and took a step back, allowing for Dan's biggest fear to take center stage. The buzzing sound grew louder. He cowered as Walters' large, club-like hand took a fistful of his collar and hauled him up to his feet.

"Look at you, Taylor. Playing policeman now, are we? Pathetic. Pathetic. Useless. *Weak.*" The black dog circled at Walters' feet, and it was laughing at him – a horrible, cackling sound that amalgamated with the *kaawing* cries of the rooks, and the buzzing noise, growing louder still, rattling against the inside of his skull ...

"No ..." Dan's head started to spin, his vision clouding and head pounding. He couldn't breathe. He was crying. He knew that he was crying and there was nothing he could do about it ...

"*Weak. Pathetic.* What's that, Taylor? Crying like a *little girl*?"

Dan's eyes shot open. He was sweating and cramped up with fear. Confusion as to where he was caused him to further panic before everything slowly fell back into place. He was in the hospital; that's right. A quick, wild-eyed swoop around the room confirmed his surroundings. The ward was quiet, early enough in the morning for the four other residents to still be asleep. He couldn't see the black dog. It wasn't there with him, but he could still feel it, like its unpleasant residual fog was still swarming around his brain.

Then he remembered. He'd been standing at the bar next to one of the lads who'd gone on to start the fight with Paul.

Perhaps he was the one who had spiked him? It was all still a bit hazy though, as if all the fragments of memories from that night were loose in the air and yet to settle in the right order – he did remember the gaffer though. That part was as clear as day; how he'd held him steady on the pavement outside as he had uncontrollably emptied the contents of his stomach, and how he'd helplessly clung to the man, trusting that he wouldn't leave him.

Broadmeadow didn't call him weak, or pathetic. He'd cared for him and shown him mercy when he'd needed him the most, and he was ten times the man his former DCI would ever be.

Fuck you, Walters.

With the nightmare now fading, Dan checked his phone. It was nearly out of battery, but there was enough remaining for him to read the message there waiting for him:

Glad to hear you're feeling better, son. Let me know as soon as you hear anything more. Try and get yourself good night's sleep in the meantime x

Soft Spot

"Right, everyone. Eyes over here please – Paul, that means you too," Broadmeadow barked, emerging from his office. Half nine on the dot. Monday morning meant it was time for the weekly briefing, which would then be followed up by way of a Friday afternoon debrief, which usually involved somebody taking everyone's orders for the coffee shop up the road before gathering round for a bit of a social catch-up. The Monday morning briefing was less of a casual event though – more of an opportunity to dish the workloads out for the week, and iron out any potential problems with said assignments.

Not that there was usually a pressing number of urgent cases to get their teeth stuck into, because that just wasn't the nature of their work. Often slow paced at times, especially in their neck of the woods, cases within the Rural Crime Department didn't always equate to much. That was because any initial leads were more often than not passed over to other departments within the force, once it turned out that they were better equipped, or more specialised in their expertise.

"Ok, first up – Bartlett, you're on trying to identify those fellas' from the CCTV footage at the Greyhound, seeing as South Lynn don't seem to think it worth their own time to investigate," the gaffer said, directing the first of the week's tasks to Paul as a wee bit of a priority.

"Anything else, sir?" Paul responded, although everybody knew that he didn't really want anything else assigned to him that week. One case was enough, thank you very much.

"I'll let you know if there's anything else that comes up. Hollie?" He produced a brown file from under his arm. "I've got multiple complaints of illegal green laning taking place out at the gravel pits and surrounding area. Bikes mostly, but there's also been a report of a four-wheel drive using the restricted byways for anti-social purposes, if you could so kindly follow up on that one for me?"

Hollie jumped up from her seat to take the file – grateful to have been assigned something to keep her busy for the week.

"Daniel? I've got a good one for you. Mr King has been biting at my ear again over dog walkers traipsing over his fields and worrying his cows. Could you please go down and show your face? And carry on with the fly-tipping once you've done that. I haven't had any more reports come through, but that doesn't mean they're not still at large. I still want to be able to pin this Walshy fella down to it all."

"Sir," Dan nodded. A slow week ahead for him, then.

Broadmeadow then proceeded to pull up a chair, swinging it around to face the wrong way before resting his large hands upon the top of the backrest. Apparently, it didn't have the desired effect on their small team, as Paul audibly sighed, having thought the already painfully short briefing had run its natural course.

Dan could tell that there was something of a more serious nature to be said though. He could sense the change in mood, even though Hollie and Paul seemed none the wiser. The gaffer's face remained stoic, which had Dan worried that some unpleasant news was about to be dealt. They really didn't have a lot of work on – perhaps he was about to tell them that Central Norfolk's Rural Crime Department was about to be disbanded? Or that the gaffer was announcing an early retirement and would soon to be leaving them?

Dan couldn't help but overthink – that was just the way his brain worked. He glanced across at Paul, who looked like he'd stopped paying attention as he started to tickle behind Chester's ears. Hollie looked mildly concerned, but her expression was somewhat glazed.

Just him then, who was forecasting the eternal doom. He focused back onto Broadmeadow. After being released from hospital on Sunday afternoon with a clean bill of health, they had exchanged a couple of messages, each with another 'x' at the end from his gaffer. Whilst they hadn't actually seen each other, it had been enough to keep Dan going; enough to keep his hopes up that he was still highly regarded by the other man, despite the whole debacle he'd been caught up in.

As if he had spoken his thoughts out aloud, he focused back in on the gaffer just at the right moment to see the man staring right back at him. His cheeks betrayed him as he felt them flush. They held eyes for what felt like an age, but in reality, must have been mere seconds before Broadmeadow turned his focus back to the team as a whole. "Is anybody in this office actually paying me the slightest shred of attention here? Eh?"

A mumbled chorus of 'sir' circulated the group.

"Ok. Well. I'll keep it short, seeing as I appear to be keeping you all from your work. I had a surprise Email waiting in my inbox this morning, from HR, informing me that we will soon have a uniformed officer joining our ranks. Now, as you all know, I have been pushing for an extra head for quite some time now. Her name is Rachael, she's a police constable from South Lynn, and she's looking to tick a few boxes on her CV in order to advance her career. She would like to join the ranks of you detectives, so I would very much appreciate it if you could all give her your best. Understood?"

Of course, it was to be Paul who got the first word in, whilst Dan was busy breathing a massive sigh of relief that they weren't all about to be made redundant. "Is she good looking, sir?"

Hollie's head swung round like a shot, daggers and disbelief firing from her retinas. "Really?!" she exclaimed.

"I'm sure she isn't as gorgeous as you, Hollie. Don't worry," Paul grinned back at her as she reached over and slapped him with the case file she had just been handed, before turning to Dan with a mischievous glint in her eyes; "One for you maybe, Dan? You're not as ugly as Paul, so you may just stand a good chance, hey?"

Dan was about to come out with his own retort, when he was stopped dead in his tracks, nearly jumping right out of his skin when Broadmeadow slammed his hand down onto the nearest desk with enough force for a deathly silence to befall the office. Chester let out a soft whine, forcing himself up and under Paul's legs.

"Enough! Any more talk like that and I'll have you all out to HR, so pack it in, the lot of ye'! Now. She's coming round later, so *please*, don't have her running for the door before she's even got a foot in." His eyes took on a steely tone as they swept between the group of officers like a parent reigning discipline over a band of disobedient children; "Is that everything? Paul? Any more to say on the matter? No? Get to work then. Dismissed."

Nobody dared to even breathe as the gaffer gave them all one final, scathing look before clattering the chair he was leaning against under the nearest desk and storming off into his office. A collective sigh of relief could be heard when Broadmeadow shut the door behind him. Chester emerged first from the stunned silence, beating his tail against Paul's legs as if to ask if it was safe to come out.

"What the fuck was all that about then?" Paul, for the first time since Dan had known him, seemed like the wind had been knocked from his sails, as he bent over to wrap his arms around Chester's substantial neck in a rare display of culpability.

"Dunno. Something's got his knickers in a twist …" Hollie mumbled, cautious over not being overheard by the source of the highly uncharacteristic outburst.

Paul nuzzled up against Chester's crown before emerging with a deep frown furrowed into his brow. "It was you, Hollie. When you said that this Rachael bird could be a potential suitor for our Dan. That's when he flipped his lid."

He wasn't wrong, Dan realised. And how did that make him feel? A little conceited perhaps … mixed in with a healthy dose of misplaced arousal at the thought of his gaffer, for all he knew, feeling a little bit under threat?

Hollie elbowed him out of his wandering imagination. "Maybe he doesn't like the idea of somebody leading his favourite detective away from him, is that right, Dan?"

"Leave it out," Dan muttered, tying to keep his facial expression neutral.

"Aww, come on. We all know that the gaffer has a soft spot for you …" Hollie smirked, teasing him.

"She's right, Danny-boy. Have you really not seen the way he looks at you? He thinks he's being all subtle about it, but it's anything but," Paul joined in. Could they really see something that he couldn't? Or were they just trying to wind him up?

"Uh, no, I don't think I have …" he lied.

Paul stood then, smiling, grabbing his cup from his desk and giving Dan a hearty clap across the shoulder; "If old Broadmeadow takes a liking to you then you know he'll have your back for life. Open your eyes, Dan. You'll see."

And wasn't that one of the most discerning things to have ever befallen Bartlett's vocabulary … loud and brash for the most part, but sometimes, just sometimes, Paul shed light upon his greater inner intellect.

"Who wants a brew, anyways? And who wants to ask the gaffer if he wants one? Dan?"

"Yeah, not me. I've got an important date with an ordinance survey map and a magnifying glass …" Hollie pointedly gave him a sly wink as she made her way back to her station. Talk about the pair of them unashamedly sending him to try and calm the angry bear.

"Take one for the team, ey?" Paul said, pushing his cup into Dan's hands.

"Fine," Dan grumbled, defeated. He would have preferred to have left it a little longer before going in to say thanks for saving his arse that weekend – would have given him a bit longer to properly compose himself, but whatever. No time like the present.

The Water's Edge

A quick look through the window confirmed that the gaffer wasn't on a call. He was sitting at his desk with his head turned, gazing out of the window that overlooked the river. Dan wondered what the man was thinking about; whether he was still fraught with anger or not, or whether he was now feeling a bit calmer?

Memories of performing this same routine with DCI Walters churned at Dan's guts – an unwelcome flashback to a time he would rather forget, when he would spend every working day picking his way around his former senior officer's chosen mood. Having to pay a visit to Walters' office was always the worst, whether it was for a routine question or whether it was for a summons, he could guarantee that he would come walking away with his self-esteem in tatters.

And then there were the times when he would come away with more than just a dent in his confidence – when a visit to Walters' office meant a shove against a filing cabinet, a bruise to his wrist or somewhere else out of sight and easily covered by his clothes. But that wasn't even the worst. The worst of all, was that horrifyingly memorable time his commanding officer had tried to lay a hand on him in the most inappropriate of way of all …

Broadmeadow still hadn't seen him, so he shuffled sidewards out of view should the gaffer go and turn his way. He needed a moment to build himself up.

In a well-practiced instinct of his, Dan shot a look over his shoulder, but the black dog was nowhere to be seen. Come to think of it, he hadn't seen it at all since the nightmare the other night, where it had joined forces with DCI Walters and succeeded is scaring the living daylights out of him.

Hollie and Paul were busy looking busy with their assigned tasks, but Chester? Chester was lying under Paul's desk, and he was intently staring right at him. Dan cocked his head – a move which Chester mirrored, before he silently raised his lip in the beginnings of a warning snarl. Something about it, so uncharacteristic of the friendliest dog he'd ever met, caused Dan to shiver from somewhere deep within his bones, and his mind to cloud over like something dark was attempting to consume him from the inside out.

He snapped his head away, rattled by what had just happened, and as soon as it had arisen, the feeling was gone. The two cups he was holding rattled together, as he took a breath, and knocked at the gaffer's door.

A pause, before, "Come in."

A sigh of relief. Broadmeadow's tone was considerably lighter than it had been a mere ten minutes ago. It gave Dan the fortitude he needed to push down the handle and step inside, where the gaffer was now facing his computer screen and not losing himself in the view outside. When he saw that it was Dan a small smile graced his lips, before he frowned. "Alright there, Daniel? How are you feeling? You're a wee bit pale there, is everything ok?"

"Yeah. 'M fine, sir. Just got volunteered to ask if you fancied a drink?" he started, before realising what it must have sounded like.

The gaffer took all in good gest, however; "Not here off of your own accord then?"

Dan looked down at the two cups within his grasp, then back up at the gaffer. There was a hint of playfulness behind his piercingly blue eyes. "I was gonna come see you, but, just … you seemed like you needed a minute …"

Broadmeadow nodded. "Do you fancy a wee walk, son?"

*

He knew that the lad had his reservations over being invited away for a private chat – it was written all over his face, from the slightly confused expression to the way he held himself as he'd dutifully accepted; with his shoulders subtly hunching forwards to how he'd drawn his arms inwards closer towards his body.

But he had followed along behind nonetheless, as Marcus led the way down to the path that led to the river. The grass lining the footpath was still damp with an early summer dew. In the next month or so, the borders would be tall with cow parsley and hawkweed, and then there was the highlight for Marcus – the bee orchids. An herbaceous rarity that formed in small, sparse clusters, in a clearing behind the bench where he often spent his lunch breaks in the summer months. He knew that young Daniel probably wouldn't find an interest in such things, but perhaps he would mention it when they first came into flower, just in case.

"Looks like it's going to be a nice day, eh?" he commented, turning back to Daniel who was trailing a pace or so behind, no doubt struggling to keep up with those short wee legs of his. He toned down the pace in order to allow for the fella to catch up.

"Yeah, think it will be."

They stopped at the bench, set back from the river where the footpath trailed off into a wooded area which was often frequented by dog walkers and runners. He gestured out with his hand for Daniel to take a seat before joining him. Not too close, but not too far apart either.

"So, I won't be the baby of the team anymore then?" Daniel spoke, looking out over the river.

Testing the water, Marcus flicked an eye over to the younger man. He hadn't forgotten the night they'd spent on the sofa together – how could he? It was practically all he had been able to think about since. "I suppose not, no. You'll still be my wee fella though, eh?"

"Yeah? I'm your 'wee fella', am I?" Perhaps it was just the way the morning sun was hitting his face, but the lad's eyes appeared to shine as he caught his gaze. Daniel did have nice eyes. They were dark but peppered with flecks of amber when the light caught them just right, with pupils that seemed to draw him right into the inner workings of his mind.

"I suppose you are. And you're sure you're feeling ok? You looked a wee bit pasty back there in the office," Marcus asked again, convinced that the lad was hiding something and determined to get to the bottom of it.

Daniel sighed, looking down and starting to pick at the side of his thumb. "Yeah, just a bit … I dunno. The consultant said they're not sure about the longer-term effects of mixing benzodiazepines with alcohol and the medication I already take … I guess, I don't know."

The results of Daniel's blood tests came back the day before, where it was confirmed that there were notable traces of diazepam within his system. As soon as he had received the rather short text message from Daniel informing him of the diagnosis, Marcus had gotten straight on the phone to the officer who took the lad's statement at the hospital, where she had promised to follow it up the next day and open an investigation. He didn't tell her that Paul had already obtained the CCTV footage from the Greyhound, and that they were currently conducting their own lines of inquiry …

"Not feeling quite yourself, hm? You could have taken the day off – you know that, don't you?" he reassured the younger man. In all honesty, he had been surprised at first when Daniel has insisted that he was coming straight back to work, and he wouldn't have been offended if he'd chosen to take a couple of days rest. Besides, if he had of done, Marcus would have had a nice excuse to go and pay the lad a visit at home – out of a duty of care towards a member of his team, obviously.

Nothing more than that.

"I'd rather be here, sir. It gets a bit lonely at home sometimes, you know what I mean?" Daniel's eyes searched him, looking for confirmation that he wasn't the only one feeling in need of somebody to tell him that he wasn't alone. Marcus nodded, curious to know what this 'other medication' was that Daniel spoke of, but he knew that it wasn't really his place to pry too deeply. He wondered too if Daniel was feeling what he was feeling … could the lad sense that there appeared to be something unspoken between them? Did he know that Marcus was currently plagued by highly complicated thoughts over what this boy actually meant to him?

Old, dampened flames were starting to come back to life, as if a furnace had been dusted off and reignited for the first time in decades. It was as frightening as it was invigorating – was he to take the warmth that the fire had to offer, or was he to be more cautious over the flames that promised to burn?

At present, he was inclined to head towards the furnace. It may be able to thaw out his ice-numbed heart. "I do know what you mean, son. Trust me, I do." Marcus too found himself now gazing out over the river, watching the gentle flow of the water and the submerged grasses swaying to-and-fro with the current.

"Where was your wife, sir? When you took me back to yours?" Daniel didn't look his way as he said it, like he already knew what the answer was without even having to say it out loud.

Marcus couldn't blame the lad for his curiosity, and he didn't feel the need to keep it a secret from him either. Not when he could sense that the question was asked out of vigilance rather than interference. "She's gone. Back home. The papers for our separation came through the other day."

A silence fell, both men lost in their own lines of thought.

"What's done is done though. I'd be lying if I said that things were a bed of roses between us, not for a long time now," Marcus continued, surprising himself at the sense of relief he felt from sharing with another what had been weighing so heavily upon his shoulders.

"'M sorry to hear that, sir."

"For the best, son. It was for the best."

"We should get back to the office."

"On your say, Daniel. Oh, would you look at that …"

Slowly, Marcus pointed in the direction of the far bank. The heron had landed, looking at them briefly before stepping down to the water's edge in search of its breakfast.

Rachael

Dan didn't like it when their new recruit, Rachael, had stopped by later that week for an introduction to the team and what sort of work she would be laying her hand to. He desperately wanted to be fair and to forego any preconceptions over first impressions, as he himself knew painfully well what it felt like to be judged on face value, but he couldn't help it. Not this time, because Dan was pretty damned good at sussing a person out the very second he laid eyes upon them.

With her hair tied back in a neat bun, subtle yet immaculately done makeup, taller than Dan with an air of astute confidence as she was led across the floor by his gaffer, and he just knew straight away that she wasn't the sort of person who was going to effortlessly gel with his somewhat laid-back, good-humoured colleagues. She looked like she belonged somewhere else entirely – where the pace was fast and the pressure to perform was high. Where appearances mattered and colleagues fought tooth and nail for the next promotion. Not here.

There was one consolation though. Broadmeadow had said that she was purely looking to gain a range of experiences, so with any luck she wasn't planning on sticking around for too long before moving onto bigger and better things.

"I don't like her," Hollie muttered under her breath, once the new recruit was out of earshot and just after she had contrarily given the girl a polite and cheery welcome.

"That wasn't very nice, Hollie …" Dan grinned up over the top of his computer monitor. Despite the cavernous size of their top-floor office, the only three residents of the main floor area had concentrated their desks together into a small area outside of the gaffer's office, and more importantly, within a few steps' distance of the kitchenette, "… But I concur."

What Dan really didn't like though, was when the gaffer had invited her into his office and closed the door behind, not dissimilar to his own first day within the department. Why didn't he like it? The only reason he could give was utterly feeble in stature – he was jealous. Jealous over Broadmeadow paying attention to someone other than himself; and not a bad looking lady at that. After all, the man had been married for longer than he had been alive, so what on earth had made him think that the gaffer would suddenly be interested in him, a member of the opposite sex to their new constable?

Oh, christ.

Dan didn't even know what he wanted. All he did know was that there was a very strong desire within his being to be something special in the eyes of his senior officer.

He wasn't feeling too well.

The heavy fog within his mind swarmed, and was starting to set in thick. A deep sadness overcame him suddenly and out of the blue, finding that he was no longer able to concentrate on his work. Sinking his head down into his hand, he rubbed at his temple in an attempt to recollect his thoughts. There wasn't any peace to be found though as he slipped his eyes shut for a moment, only to be roused by the sound of a low, warning growl coming from under Paul's desk. He cracked an eye open, meeting Chester's gaze. A single tooth slipped from under his upper lip.

"What's gotten into you, mate?" Bemused over Chester's sudden change of heart towards him, Dan reached out to try and coax the boy over but to no avail – it only seemed to agitate the dog further, his hackles raising slightly in a clear display of an animal that was on the defence. Why? Dan could only ponder. Since the involuntary introduction of a harmful substance to his system he was still feeling the after-effects, so there *was* the possibility that Chester could smell the residual high dose of anti-depressants in his system, and that's what was setting him off?

Dan got up from his chair, having to steady himself against his desk which gained him a funny look from Hollie, but he swiftly managed to recover himself; not wanting to draw any further attention to his current state of unrest.

"Paul?"

"Yes, mate."

"What sort of work did Chester used to do, with DI Wright?" It struck Dan, how Paul's face momentarily appeared to flash with resentment over the mention of DI Wright. The gaffer had spoken of him, briefly, when Dan had questioned who the officer in the photo on his wall was, but he hadn't said much, except that he was Chester's former handler, and that he had died in a car accident.

Mentioning him had clearly been as mistake, with Chester sensing his owner's discomfort over the subject and getting up to stand between himself and Paul, and Paul himself, freezing up, refusing to look Dan in the face. "Searching for and apprehending the bad guys, mostly. I believe he was trained to sniff drugs too. Why?"

"Uh, nothing. I think he's been acting a bit odd around me, that's all," said Dan, wishing he hadn't said anything at all.

"I'll have a word with him."

He couldn't tell if Paul was taking the piss or not – his reaction had been so unlike his usual self that Dan didn't know what to think. Second guessing everything now, he started to grow weary, his brain inside his skull feeling like it was swelling, and he needed to leave, before he started to cry. Something flared up inside of him then, a fight or flight instinct, like he too wanted to bare his teeth and defensively snap back at Paul for closing down on him, or Chester, for deciding that they weren't friends anymore, or the gaffer, for allowing an intruder into their ranks …

He managed to push it down for long enough however, just to make his excuse to leave; "I'm going to get a coffee, does anybody want one?"

Getting out of the office made him feel marginally better. The weather was nice, sun shining, and the gentle breeze playing at his face no longer held the chill of winter behind it. Summer was coming. All he really wanted to do was carry on walking, preferably to his car, and hole himself away at home, but he knew that he couldn't justify to the gaffer why he needed to leave without causing any further suspicion over his current state of mind. And then there was Rachael – it would be downright rude, no, to scarper away without giving her a proper introduction? Knowing that he was Broadmeadow's most senior officer, he had a certain level of responsibility riding on his head with that one. He couldn't leave.

Returning a while later with his hands full of takeaway cups, Dan had to admit that he felt a bit more like himself. Getting outside had succeeded in settling his head. After traipsing up the three flights of stairs to their office, he was just about ready to get back to his desk and start mapping out the boundaries of Mr King's cattle fields (and which one contained the fearsome bull), when he saw that Hollie was busy helping their new recruit to set up her workstation, right next to his own.

Come on, Dan. It's ok. Make a good first impression and you'll be fine.

"Alright Hollie? Got you a latte."

"With syrup?" she smiled, accepting the offering.

Dan smiled back at her. He'd gone for hazelnut this time. Hollie liked a surprise flavoured syrup in her coffee. Flat white for Paul and Tea for the gaffer, an iced fruit thing for Emily down on the front desk and a cappuccino for himself. Rachael though? He had been forced to take a gamble on that one. Going for what he hoped was a safe option, he'd bought her a normal coffee like Paul's, with a couple of packets of sugar. Hopefully she wasn't lactose intolerant of anything like that … or allergic to caffeine?

Oh no – what if she didn't even like coffee? And why did life have to be such a bloody minefield?

"Hi, sir. Or do you prefer 'sergeant'? Rachael took note of him for the first time, eyeing him up from head to toe before standing to attention.

"Um, Dan. Dan is fine. I didn't know what you wanted so I got you a coffee …" He plonked it down onto her new desk before fumbling about in his pocket for those packets of sugar that now seemed to be stubbornly evading him. Recognition sparked in his brain as he realised that he'd seen Rachael before. And then it hit him – she was the constable at the scene of the stabbing that he had spoken to; the one who had been giving him the eye from the moment he'd walked over to question her.

Rachael gave him a nervous half-smile. "Coffee is just fine. Thank you, Dan. And it's nice to meet you properly – the gaffer said that you're still quite new to the team, is that right?"

"Yeah. Only been here a couple of months. You're – when do you start officially?" he asked, finding that the small talk wasn't so hard once he got going.

"Monday. I'm looking forwards to working with you and the team. Very much so."

From behind Rachael's back, Hollie gave him a subtle side-eye. Paul still seemed a bit quiet, but had gratefully accepted his coffee with a crooked grin, giving Dan the impression that he hadn't caused a lasting rift by speaking of DI Wright. He'd still apologise however, later. Chester was giving him a wide berth, curled up in the corner under a vacant desk.

"I hope you know what you're getting yourself into here – do you like cows?" he asked stupidly, as Rachael gave him a funny look, again, with that nervous laugh. She seemed ok, and he instantly felt like a very bad person for judging her so soon. Perhaps he'd take her out on Monday to go and visit Mr King and his prized herd of cattle. That would really get her into the swing of things, and he could only hope that she wasn't in for too much of a shock compared to what they got up to in Community Safety and Criminal Justice.

Dan glanced over to Broadmeadow's office, more on instinct than anything, wondering if the man was going to come out and get his tea or if he was going to have to bring it over to him. What he was met with was a pair of blue eyes upon him, clearly watching his interactions with Rachel with a quiet sort of conflict, before they flitted back down to his computer. Too late. Dan had caught him staring, and it made his heart perform a hesitant little flip, because he couldn't quite decide what that illusive look held behind it.

An Endless Sky

Chester could sense that something had changed, ever since the first day of that week when Dan had arrived at the office without his black dog following in his footsteps. He kept expecting it to show up, but it never appeared. And Dan … Dan was different. He seemed heavier in stature, like something was weighing him down.

He'd tried to get close, to give Dan a bit of reassurance because he was a good, friendly boy who wanted to get along with everyone, but something had stopped him in his tracks. He could sense a level of threat coming from the sergeant, something dangerous and wanting to do him harm, although he couldn't quite put his paw on what.

Having already been on relatively high alert due to the gaffer's outburst at them all over their new team member, when he'd seen Dan approach Broadmeadow's office, Chester's basic training had kicked in – he may be getting old now, but he was still capable of doing his job in order to make Paul happy.

The thing was, Dan smelled strongly of illicit substances. The ones Chester had been taught to detect because they were illegal, and led towards an arrest. He had lifted his nostrils and slowly let the waves of scent drift past his nasal passages, just to make sure that he wasn't mistaken.

Letting out a warning growl, Dan seemed confused. Chester had been very surprised by that. Was he trying to hide his illegal activities?

He'd growled again, quietly, lifting up his lips to show his teeth. He wanted to warn Dan that this sort of thing would not be acceptable if his colleagues found out, but he was willing to let it slide this one time because he did like the sergeant.

That was when the really strange thing happened.

Something dark and scary had flashed behind Dan's eyes. Now, Chester wasn't scared by much because he was brave, but he had never seen anything like that before. For a fraction of a second, he could have sworn on his life that he'd seen the black dog's eyes instead of Dan's, and a low humming noise reverberating from inside of him, causing Chester's fur to stand on end …

It happened again, that afternoon, except this time, Chester had been scared enough to back away and seek solace from his Paul. He honestly thought, for a moment, that Dan was going to bare his teeth right back at him and lunge, which he really didn't understand because Dan was the one who had brought up the memory of DI Wright and upset Paul in the process.

Everything about it was all so perplexing, and beyond Chester's comprehension.

The new team member was there. Chester didn't make judgements like the humans around him did. Hollie especially. He wasn't sure why she didn't like her even though they had barely even met. Rachael. That was her name. Rachael was attracted to Dan – female humans were even worse than male ones at concealing all the smells that they let off. And the gaffer? He was the exception to the rule, because he was letting of pheromones left, right and centre, so strongly that they were taking over any other scent around him.

It wasn't that the gaffer didn't like Rachael as such, but more like he didn't appreciate her being so close to his sergeant. Humans were so baffling and so convoluted in the way that they seemed to want to hide their feelings. Why did the gaffer not just go and give his sergeant a good sniff, lick behind his ears and be done with it? Dan would very much like that, but Broadmeadow too was intent on keeping his mating urges to himself because he felt guilty about it.

That was another thing that Chester didn't understand – did the gaffer know that Dan couldn't bear offspring? Rachael could. They had this all wrong, he realised. Dan and Rachael could have some human children, which would make more sense. And the gaffer would have to find somebody his own age. He *did* have someone, before. But she was gone, her scent fading from the man with every day that passed, which was sad, because she wasn't dead – not like DI Wright – she was just *gone*.

Yet, there were other things that seemed to be more important to humans than having children. Things like a desire for companionship even if complicated emotions were involved, and the urge to mate with one another for the fun of it rather than for practical reasons. Broadmeadow and Dan wanted those things from each other, so he knew, realistically, that his sensible idea of getting Rachael involved wasn't going to happen. Dan wasn't interested in her, and never would be.

There was all so much going on that Chester really was glad when it was time to go home. Dan seemed ok when he and Paul had left; he still wasn't his usual self, but whatever had been behind his eyes had disappeared. Probably because the gaffer was hanging around waiting for him, which always seemed to make Dan a very happy boy. He still steered clear though, sticking close to his Paul's side as they left the office. They said goodbye to Emily down at the front desk, as per usual, where Paul laid on the charm (also as per usual), even though it was never going to have the effect that Paul desired. Yet he still tried, bless him.

Now, usually, after saying goodbye to Emily, they would go to the car, drive to the supermarket where Chester would then wait for Paul to go and hunt for some dinner before they headed home. But this evening they turned out of the carpark and headed in the opposite direction. He looked across at Paul, whining softly between his teeth.

"S'ok, mate. Just taking a little detour."

They headed out of town, past the riverside and through the outskirts until the buildings started to fade back to a sparser scattering of houses with larger gardens and blocks of fields in between. Farmhouses and their barns, huge industrial warehouses, dotted between swathes of yet more agricultural land, all passing them by until all that remained was a vast, endless amplitude of fenland spanning out further than the eye could possibly comprehend. At either side of the road, huge banks ran parallel to deep ditches. The sun, like a great mirage, sat ahead of them within its endless sky.

Chester now knew where it was they were heading.

He cowered in the seat as a van coming in the opposite direction passed them by; too close. Too fast. Paul was careful though. He knew these roads well. Yet still, even the best of drivers could fall foul of The Fens. He started to grow restless.

Paul wasn't helping to appease, because he too was filled with a quivering apprehension as they neared their final destination. There was passing place not far from here, which when they came to it, Paul slowed down the car and pulled inside. It was only just wide enough. Any closer to the edge and they would be toppling down into the gulley. Any further out and they would be sticking out into the road.

"Come on then, Chester. Let's go."

He had to exit from the driver's side, where Paul held him on a close lead until they could skirt around the side of the car and onto the grassy verge. A hollow wind ruffed at his fur, haunting and empty as it swept across the desolate expanse of brown and green terrain. Chester stuck hard by Paul's side as they picked their way along the verge until they reached a white pole, starting at the bottom of the ditch and standing high above their heads – the only landmark for miles around.

Chester trembled, sniffing at the air.

Past the pole lay stake of wood, cracked, with its other half embedded into the long grass, rotten and weathered and succumbing to its harsh surroundings. The haggard remnants of a bouquet of flowers, clinging to what remained of the wooden post by a faded red ribbon, were the only reminder left that DI Wright had taken his final breaths right there in the muddy dyke below.

Although the grass was damp, and the sky above had given way to dark rolling clouds, Paul and Chester sat. Side by side, they gazed out over The Fens, two souls lost in the memory of a dear friend. Chester leant heavily against Paul in a fruitless attempt at shielding his companion from a wind that bit so much harder out here – even in the throes of early summer, it was still able cut through flesh like ice.

"What a place to go, ey? Out here …"

Paul was aching. Chester ached too.

"Should of bought some fresh flowers," Paul commented as he clasped his hand around what remained of the way post. The one that had been destroyed when DI Wright's patrol car skidded off the road that freezing autumn night. It offered little solace, but it was something better than nothing.

Another Farmer, Another Field

Another day, another farmer, another field. With every intention of taking Rachael along with him, Dan had soon found his plans scuppered by the gaffer, who had suggested, as soon as he had caught wind of Dan's initial intentions, that she shadow Hollie instead that day. He wasn't too upset over it, he supposed, feeling like he wasn't really in best frame of mind right now to be entertaining a young officer who had clearly taken a bit of shine to him. Besides, even if he was feeling of sound mind, Dan and small talk didn't really go hand in hand.

Conversation had never been one of Dan's strongest assets, not unless he knew somebody well enough, and even then, he still didn't always have all that much to say. Which could in turn would make him say even less, because he would get himself worked up over how awkward he must be coming across. People who were able to effortless converse filled him with envy – they were always the people who got on well in life, who seemingly didn't have to try as hard at the rest when it came to a social situation.

Speaking of having to actually talk to another human being, as Dan sat in his new truck because his usual car was at the garage having its wheel fixed, he spotted a dog walker approaching at the far boundary of Mr King's cow field, up at Crawley Farm. Now, as Mr King had explained, he used to keep his dairy cows within a row of barns on the yard all year round, but with the rising public interest in ethical farming, he had repurposed some of his arable land in order for the heifers and cows to spend their spring and summers with the grass beneath their hooves.

Then there was the wife – turning her hand to home-made ice creams and cheeses in their new farm shop, in essence turning the traditional business of the dairy farm into something more ahead with the times. All of which was in order to save what could have been yet another farm being boarded up and sold on for housing.

Mr and Mrs King were some of the lucky ones. They had adapted, where others hadn't.

With the cows outside though, other challenges had arisen. Dog walkers who had been using the land for years were now being asked to keep their pets under control, especially as the cows now has their little calves in tow.

Dan loved the calves, with their knobbly legs and huge dark eyes. Mr King had treated him to a tour of the yard last week when he had first come to speak to him about the dog walkers, taking him to the shed where the bull calves were kept. Dan had gone all soft on the things – made even worse when he found out that the little boys would be raised in order to be sold for meat rather than ever getting to live a life out in the fields. It broke his heart, seeing them all in their separate little pens, making him consider for a moment that he should sack off the whole detective thing and buy some land of his own. Then he could rescue all the unwanted bulls (and any other surplus farm animals for that matter), and live out the rest of his days without ever having to speak to another human being.

No doubt his deer would be there too, safely living out its life away from any harmful busy roads and dodgy drivers like himself. He had a phone call from the vets that morning in fact, informing him that his deer was on the mend and being transferred to a local wildlife rehabilitation centre for its eventual release, which surprised him at how happy that news had made him …

As the dog walker moved closer, Dan could see that their canine companion was running loose without a lead. Right. Time for some community liaison at its finest.

The step down from the four-by-four was still a bit of a shock – a damn sight further down to the ground for his vertically challenged legs than his usual car. It wasn't unmarked either; full checkered yellow and blue regalia, with 'RURAL CRIME' stamped across the bonnet. Broadmeadow made him laugh when he'd said that he couldn't understand why none of his team wanted the thing as their regular transport, where it just sat in the yard unused unless in the case of an off-road emergency. Hollie called it the *Crime Wagon*. Paul called it the *Mystery Machine*. Whatever it was, he needed to get his own car back soon to stave off a lifetime of piss-taking courtesy of his dear colleagues.

"Excuse me, could I have a quick word please?" Dan called out, waving the dog walker over. She looked at him suspiciously from a distance.

"Yes, how can I help you – Trudy! Come 'ere, will you?" The dog walker stamped her way up the side of the field to meet him. Dan was forced to hold back a snort of laughter. Trudy? Who on earth calls their dog Trudy?! She was an older lady, perhaps in her late fifties, a bit thrumpy in the way she was dressed, with a scruffy brown dog trotting along at her heel.

"Uh, yeah. Detective Sergeant Daniel Taylor. I had some complaints from the landowner here over loose dogs worrying his cows, especially with the little calves about," Dan explained matter-of-factly.

"Oh, you mean Trudy? She's no harm, I assure you. She wouldn't hurt a fly!" Just as the lady said it, Trudy the terrier pricked her ears at Dan as if to give him an innocent yet cheeky grin, before turning towards the grazing cattle and scarpering off towards the herd before either of them could stop her.

"Oh dear. Trudy? TRUDY!" the walker bellowed after her dog. It fell of death ears.

It was too late. Trudy was off. Absolutely perfect timing for a truck to come roaring up next to Dan's, which of course had to be Mr King. Shit. The cows looked up in unison like a single black and white entity as the little brown dog came running towards them. Mr King, in his flat cap and waxed jacket, tumbled out of his truck with a shotgun slung over his shoulder and started storming with intent towards his cows. Trudy's owner started screaming when she realised what was happening, just to add to the unfolding moment of chaos …

"Fucking hell …" Dan muttered under his breath. "Stay here," he instructed over his shoulder before he started to run towards the herd.

"I'll shoot it. I swear. I'll shoot the little bastard!" Mr King warned as Dan approached, waving the shotgun at him before honing the muzzle in the direction of his herd.

Trudy started circling, spurred on by one of the calves which was threatening to bolt. Mr King raised his shotgun up to his shoulder, trying to take aim at the zigzagging terrier, before waving the barrel back in Dan's general direction; "Move it, will ya'?"

"Put the gun down please, sir. You'll scare the cows more if your fire that at them," Dan tried to appease him, even though his heart had jumped up towards his throat over being faced with a crazy farmer and his shotgun. He could see that Mr King was building himself up into a rage, his face a swollen red as he steadied his stance, a single stubby finger teasing at the trigger ...

"I told you to stay back, ma'am!" Standing between the herd, and the dog walker who had graciously ignored his prior order to remain where she was, and Mr King, Dan didn't have enough arms to outstretch and hold them all at bay. Then he went and did something really stupid, as Trudy swerved again and rushed past his legs. Seeing his opportunity, he dived to the ground, catching her by the stub of her docked tail.

It was a short-lived victory, as she turned, wriggled free, and sunk her teeth into Dan's arm before bolting again – all in a split second before a single, deafening discharge filled the air around them.

Silence befell as the dust settled. A flock of birds spilled out into the sky. Dan, head under his arms, slowly raised himself to his knees, his ears filled with the sound of the dog walker's frantic screams. Daring to look up, ears ringing, he searched the field for any sign of the little brown terrier – and then his heart sank, when he spotted the dog walker kneeling down in the long grass.

Never had he heard such a pained noise coming from another human being.

Before he could make his way over to her, swaying as he scrabbled up to his feet, the dog walker got herself up with Trudy draped within her arms. He watched, as she staggered over to Mr King and started to scream at him like a wailing banshee ...

Coming to his senses over what had just happened, with a strange sense of calm washing over him once everything returned to a normal speed, Dan fumbled at his chest for his radio. He needed another pair of hands for this one.

"Control, 1-323, request assistance, firearms incident, shots fired."

Typical Men

"Sooo ... how come you've stuck around doing this then? I mean, it's not very exciting, is it? I'd have moved on by now if I were you," Rachael exclaimed, picking at one of her nails. Manicured, but subtly so.

Hollie sat in the driver's seat of the patrol car, unboxing her sandwich. After a morning of scoping out potential green laning locations but not actually catching any perpetrators, they had pulled over on the outskirts of town for lunch. Afterwards, the plan was to head out again towards the coast, where Hollie had penned down another known hotspot to take a look at.

"It's not very exciting, I agree. I did have hopes of moving up to London one day to join the Met," she took a bite of her plain cheese sandwich, simultaneously reaching for some crisps, the bag balanced between her knees, "But I don't know now. Part of me still wants to make the move, and part of me doesn't."

"Oh really? Me too. I want to get out of here and join a proper city force, firearms or CID or something, not all this rural backwater stuff." Rachael pulled a face as she said it, gesturing out the car window to their surroundings. "What makes you want to stay then? Please tell me it's not because you actually enjoy all this sitting about and traipsing around in the mud for no real reward?"

Rachael extracted her own shop-bought sandwich from a bag on the back seat. Crusty, seeded roll. Halloumi filling? Something like that. Hollie took a minute to really think about her answer, as she shovelled down a big handful of crisps before formulating her response. "I like my team. And the gaffer – he's so relaxed. I'm not sure I really want all that high pressure stuff to deal with. And then Dan – I asked him about why *he* left London, and he really didn't have the best time of it, from what I can gather. It put a certain level of doubt in my mind, I guess. Grass isn't always greener, and all that."

Rachael wasn't all that bad, she decided. They were never going to be best friends or anything like that, but she was alright on face value. She glanced down at her fingernails. Having seen Rachael's and how perfect they looked, she wondered if she should have something like that done to hers. Her own nails were cut as short as possible, with the odd peeling cuticle and some butter from her sandwich streaked up the side of her index finger.

It summed up how she often felt detached from other members of her own sex, due to her complete lack of interest in anything beauty related – she didn't wear makeup or have her hair done, and certainly avoided any form of overly feminine clothing. It used to bother her that she was cut a little different from the rest, but as she grew older, she found herself caring less and less over what others may think of her and her appearance. Rachael's nails did look nice though, she would give her that one, although she knew that if *she* had something like that done they would surely be ruined after a single day on the job.

"I wanted to ask you about Dan, actually …" Rachael questioned, interest peaking at the mention of Dan, as if she didn't actually care about Hollie and her soul-searching after all, and had been steering the conversation towards their short, dark-haired sergeant all along.

"Hm? What do you want to know?" Hollie replied as she screwed her empty crisp packet up and shoved it back into her lunch box.

"Is he single?"

Wow, Hollie thought. This girl isn't hanging about. "Yeah, I think so." Dan was a bit private actually, when it came to his personal life. He'd never mentioned a significant other so Hollie just assumed that he was available. She held back on airing her suspicions though, over what team he actually played for, because she didn't feel it entirely relevant to be spreading such things with somebody that she barely knew.

Although Dan didn't outwardly come across as a bloke who fancied other blokes (he seemed a bit of a typical *man* to her), she knew far better than to make assumptions. And she saw the way he mooned over the gaffer when he thought nobody was looking – being a bloke though, he probably didn't even realise himself that he was doing it. Strange one that, because although Broadmeadow wasn't a bad looking man she wouldn't exactly call him a sex symbol; he was old, for starters, with greying hair and a tiny bit of a gut, and that was without mentioning those funny long legs of his, that made him look like a giant spider …

Must be the accent that Dan was drawn to, or perhaps his height? Or just his general, caring nature? Shame he was a married man really, because Broadmeadow and Dan would make quite a sweet couple. Dan looked like he needed a bit of a father figure in his life – somebody to guide him, and as far as she knew Broadmeadow didn't have any children, so Dan could be his … urgh, no. Stop that line of thought, right there. Besides, they were *both* typical men, so there was only a slim chance that either of them could actually see how they would complement each other – even if it came up and slapped them both in the face.

She digresses however, because Rachael was saying something, and she wasn't listening. "Sorry, I didn't catch that?"

"I said, I think I might ask him out for a drink, if you didn't already have your eye on him?" Rachael slowly repeated what she had already said, as it had clearly fallen on death ears the first time around.

"Oh, no. You go ahead. I wish you luck – he'll be flattered, I'm sure," she said absently. Prior assumptions over Dan's sexual orientation aside, and although she really couldn't see the pair as a good match from the limited time she had spent with Rachael, she'd hate to think that she had gotten in the way of something that really wasn't any of her business. You never know – for all she knew, Dan and Rachael may turn out to be the perfect match after all.

At that moment, a general call from Central Control came across the radio. Assistance was required from any available units, with regard to a firearms incident up at Crawley Farm.

Wasn't that … that name rang a bell …

"Shit. That's Mr King's farm," she muttered, turning the ignition.

"What?"

"Buckle up, Rachael."

By the time they arrived, the scene across Mr King's field was already swamped with a number of patrol cars and uniformed officers. Hollie spotted the *Crime Wagon* straight away and pulled up behind it with her front wheel half up the verge, anxious to find out if Dan was ok. There wasn't an ambulance in attendance which gave her hope, although it had taken them a near half hour to get there, so if a critical incident *had* occurred, then a team of paramedics may have already been and gone by now.

Surely not, though? Surely the gaffer would have called in already if something had happened to Dan?

She swiftly exited the vehicle, not waiting for a rather peaky looking Rachael who was still sitting in the passenger seat. Stomping off towards the police cordon to find the officer in charge of the scene, Hollie still couldn't see Dan. She could see that South Lynn were overseeing the incident, recognising some of her fellow Community Safety colleagues from the first floor. An older woman with a brown bundle in her arms was making a right old racket, shouting to anybody that would listen that she needed to get her dog to a vet.

A stray cow left the safety of the herd and walked over to the cordon. Instead of stopping at the barrier it carried on walking, with the line of tape stretching tighter and tighter against its front end before the whole thing went and collapsed. The rest of the herd followed in the first cow's footsteps and traipsed right across the crime scene. A pair of forensics officers who were picking away in the grass parted for the group of wayward cattle. Out at the edge of the field, Mr King was shouting and swearing his way into the back of a police car.

That was when she spotted Dan, amongst it all but alive and well, talking to another detective.

And where was Rachael – was she still sitting in the car, not wanting to get her shoes dirty?

Whatever.

Moving over to Dan's side, she smiled as one of the heifers butted against her arm. Reaching out, she stroked its nose. Its breath was hot, nostrils wet, and it gave off a sweet scent of fresh hay and manure. You wouldn't get this working out in the city, she thought to herself.

"Alright mate?" Dan greeted her, nodding Hollie's way as he wrapped up his conversation with the detective from South Lynn. Sergeant Collins, she seemed to remember her name was.

"Trust you to be at the centre of all this ... are you ok?" She noticed that Dan was holding his wrist and that the cuff of his shirt was ripped, with a spattering of blood blotting the light fabric, however it didn't look like a gunshot wound. Had he caught it on a barbed fence or something? Whatever it was, it wasn't life threatening. She breathed a great sight of relief.

Dan reassured her with that unabashed smile of his; "Yeah, I'm fine. South Lynn have got the scene so I'm free to go. Fill you in back at the station?"

Wee Shite

"Do you guys ever actually arrest anybody, or do South Lynn always do the work for you?" queried Rachael as they arrived back at the office. Nobody was really listening though, to take her up on her slightly snarky comment.

Marcus had been pacing up and down the office awaiting his team's return, making a beeline straight for Daniel when the trio of officers made their way through the heavy wooden door at the top of the stairs. Hollie had already filled him in with regard to what had happened, which had left him positively swimming with guilt over refusing to send Rachael out with his wee sergeant that morning.

Sending her out with Hollie instead had been for his own terribly selfish reasons, because there was no denying the fact that constable Hutchinson was an attractive young lass. Perhaps fuelled by what Paul had told him, about Rachael having already set her sights upon *his* sergeant, he knew that he had done something incredibly unprofessional by keeping her away from Daniel for the time being.

Yet, despite the knowledge that he was treading a very treacherous path with regards to his feelings, Marcus couldn't stop himself from gravitating towards the lad who had very nearly gotten himself on the wrong end of a shotgun. Eyeing Daniel up and down, he quickly took note of his bloodied wrist, and without a word, steered him towards his office with a heavy hand at his shoulder.

Closing the door behind them, he directed his sergeant towards the sofa. "Sit down."

Daniel did as he was told, still clutching at his wrist. Ever since the call to Central Control had come to his attention, Marcus had been worried sick – and rightly so. Through no fault of his own, this young man under his command appeared to be a magnet for misdemeanour.

"Honest to God, does trouble come looking for you, or do you go out looking for it? Come here, what happened?" he softened his voice, crouching down to Daniel's level and gently taking hold of his hand. It was so much smaller than his own, yet strong and sturdy within its own right. A perfect fit.

"I need to go and get my statement logged, sir," the lad tried half-heartedly, yet made no attempt to take back his hand. Marcus pulled back his sleeve to reveal a bite wound that was still oozing but not bleeding enough to cause any immediate alarm. He wasn't first aid trained so he shouldn't really be doing this – he should be calling somebody qualified up from another floor or sending Daniel off to see a doctor – but again, selfishly, he wanted to be the one to patch the lad up himself.

"Let me have a look at this first, then you can go, ok?" Marcus bargained, keeping Daniel's hand within his own whilst he assessed the damage that the little dog had done. The lad didn't seem like he was in the mood to share exactly what had happened, so he didn't press. He'd read through his statement instead before it was sent off for South Lynn.

"'K." Voice small, Dan let his gaffer clean the wound with a wipe from the first aid box. It stung. Trudy sure had some vicious teeth on her. Honestly, he was more than happy to let Broadmeadow tend to him; he just felt a bit subdued over having caused, as his gaffer so rightly put it, yet more trouble for him for deal with.

Trudy the terrier had survived the blast which helped with settling his conscience some – she had a few surface wounds but on first impressions it was nothing that a vet couldn't sort out for her. And he couldn't blame her for lashing out either; he *had* practically tackled her to the ground before yanking at her tail. What did concern him was how the little dog had looked into his eyes, just before she had sunk her teeth into his wrist, with a clear expression of fear. Even more concerning was how he had, for a fraction of a second, felt utterly compelled to launch forwards and go for her jugular.

What was happening to him? First Chester, now Trudy …

Going mad, son. That's what, because all these funny turns and ill feelings had only been happening since the black dog had disappeared from his wake, leaving him feeling more and more like the thing was residing somewhere inside of him. Physically, felt ok now, but on the inside there was a growing foreboding – feeling of utter vulnerability – over his current mental state.

"I am sorry, sir," he apologised quietly, as the gaffer pulled out a roll of bandage and set about wrapping it around his wrist. Something was telling him that Broadmeadow was enjoying this, by the look of soft concentration on his face and the careful way he was handling him, as if he were about to shatter like glass.

"Don't be, fella. I'm just glad you're back here safe," the gaffer murmured, securing the bandage with some skin-friendly tape, making Dan's heart perform a little flip against his chest. It made him think he should sustain an injury more often, if this was the treatment he was to receive in exchange.

The gaffer made him feel safer than he ever had before. A father-like figure that he wanted just that little bit more from, who had the power over him to quell the unease that so often plagued his mind. A thought crossed his mind then, whilst Broadmeadow lingered with his hand within his own, that if he were to lean forwards a couple of centimetres, then they could brush their lips together …

Before Dan could be tempted further into doing something very stupid, the pair of officers were interrupted by a sharp rap at the office door. It swung open, and Paul entered the gaffer's office without an invite (nothing new there).

"I've found something," Paul exclaimed loudly before his eyes fell to Broadmeadow, still crouched on the floor with Dan's freshly bandaged hand resting in his palm. Suddenly very conscious of their position, Dan reclaimed his hand.

Apparently unperturbed, the gaffer slowly got himself up to his feet with an amused look on his face. "Great news, Paul. Had you lost something?"

"Ha. Very funny, sir," Paul replied dryly, yet he still laughed, "I've identified one of the lads down the pub last Friday, sir. I thought you might want to know that not only does the footage imply some suspicious activity, but it turns out he has a very interesting family connection."

Dan's interest peaked – there he was thinking Paul just sat at his desk all day doing the very bare minimum … "You mean, you've found something that South Lynn have missed?"

Paul laughed again, this time with all the gaps between his teeth showing, "Not just a pretty face, Danny-boy. Fancy a look at what I've been up to?"

Back out in the main office, Dan and his gaffer huddled around Paul's monitor. The CCTV evidence was clear – throughout the evening, one of the young men at the pub was clearly making exchanges of some description with various other punters, and he was pretty brazen about it too.

Imagine – doing business like that in a pub full of coppers? The audacity of it!

Paul fast forwarded the footage to the point where Dan had gone up to the bar for the final drinks they consumed that evening (he hadn't even noticed anything untoward at the time, which he scolded himself for), where it was obvious that the young man in question then made to walk away, a swift movement of the hand as he passed, a jabbing motion, in the direction of Dan's upper thigh. It was so quick a movement, yet Dan was still disbelieving over how he never felt a thing …

As they watched the footage, Dan felt his gaffer's hand ever so lightly – protectively – brush against his hip. "Unbelievable …" Broadmeadow muttered under his breath with a marked undertone of anger.

"That's not the best bit though," Paul flicked over to another window, bringing up the criminal database, where he had left it open on the face of the young man in the CCTV footage, "I've been trawling through the database for what felt like an absolute age, but I've found him. His record was wiped when he hit eighteen, but we still have his basic details. And more importantly, look at who his cousin is."

Dan could see just fine from where he was standing, but the gaffer had to lean closer over Paul's shoulder because he wasn't wearing his reading glasses. Reading glasses that actually held a proper prescription for short sightedness, that he should be wearing full time, but refused himself, because he didn't want to admit just yet that he really was getting older.

The name on the screen read, 'Jamie Stubbs', with a known alias of 'Stubby'. At first, it didn't ring any bells with Dan or his gaffer. It was the name underneath however, of any related acquaintances, that set Dan's heart racing – Jamie Stubbs was the cousin to a certain Kyle Walsh.

Walshy; Dan's fly-tipper and suspected instigator to the stabbing of Ryan Mitchell.

"That's definitely him on the CCTV footage, isn't it. No doubts there," Dan pondered, wondering what they were going to with this information, because he wasn't entirely sure that it fell within the remit of 'rural crime', "Shall we bring him in?"

Broadmeadow frowned, still squinting at the computer monitor. "We should really call this in to South Lynn downstairs."

Paul nodded in agreement. "We should."

The gaffer straightened back up with a coy expression on his face – the same expression he had graced when suggesting that he and Dan followed their own line of questioning when visiting young Ryan at the hospital; "It's been a wee while since we got to use our interview room, however."

Paul nodded again. "It certainly has, sir."

Dan looked between the two men; a bit confused to what was really going on. Hollie was watching over intently from her desk next to Paul's, whatever she was actually doing long forgotten. Rachael joined them, sidling up beside Dan to try and get a look over Paul's shoulder.

Broadmeadow turned to Dan, clapping a heavy hand over his shoulder, "What do ye' say, Danny-boy? Paul? Fancy having a word with the wee shite?"

Stubby

Bringing Stubby in felt like a bit of gamble. The CCTV footage wasn't enough without any hard evidence to go with. Dan knew that. They all did. You can't just go out and arrest someone without having built a case against them first; enough to keep them in and send them in front of a judge. What Dan strongly suspected to be the real reason behind bringing Jamie Stubbs in themselves, rather than sending what Paul had found down to South Lynn, was because Broadmeadow had personally wanted to find out why Dan had been his target that Friday night.

The gaffer was growing to become extremely protective over him. It was becoming more and more obvious, from the first time he had opened up over how he'd had trouble with his former DCI, to when he'd sustained the bite and everything that had happened in-between, it was clear to Dan that Broadmeadow did actually care for him. It was the only plausible explanation, because if he didn't, then surely he would have given up on him by now?

From first impressions, Jamie Stubbs seemed like your typical cock-sure young man, with an accentuated London drawl that they all seemed to have nowadays. He was an apprentice electrician by trade, yet when Paul and Hollie had gone out to pick him up from his house, suspicions were raised when the car parked outside appeared to be well above of his trainee pay grade.

Surprisingly, Jamie had come quietly.

A space had been cleared within the archive cupboard to make it look more like an interview room. The tape recorder had been dusted off with a couple of chairs from the office pulled in for extra seating.

Dan had honestly thought that Jamie wasn't going to provide them with any useful information aside from what they already knew, but under Broadmeadow's scrutiny he had soon crumbled. No kidding, the man could be extremely intimidating when he wanted to be.

Forty-five minutes in and a foray of 'no comment' answers later, the gaffer, along with Hollie at his side, eventually seemed to be getting somewhere.

"You have a good career ahead of you son, and I don't want to see you throw that away. All we need from you right now is to tell us why you felt the need to inject an illicit substance into one of my officers, and where you got it from, and you can be on your way," the gaffer had calmly explained after an intense grilling. Obviously, Jamie was *not* going to be left to go on his way should he confess – he would be taken away for charging.

Dan had been asked to remain outside for the questioning, but he wasn't barred from hovering near the door to listen in, and unsettlingly, he didn't feel a whole lot of anger towards young Jamie. He didn't feel much at all, really – kind of numb towards it all.

Jamie, on the other hand, was close to tears. After the reality hit of him being sent down to serve time was drilled home, leaving his pregnant girlfriend to fend for herself with every chance he would miss the birth of his child, finally – unexpectedly – he admitted to the relationship he held with his cousin; "He asked me to do it. And I need the money, understand?"

"By *he*, do you mean Kyle Walsh?" Broadmeadow pushed, leaning in closer to their interviewee. Jamie nodded.

"For the tape, Mr Stubbs nodded in confirmation to the question. Did he tell you why? Why did he need you to stick a needle into one of my officers, eh?" The constrained anger behind the gaffer's words was evident. He was not happy at all about somebody thinking they had the right to go out and cause harm to one of his own.

Jamie shrugged, "I dunno. All I know is that if my cousin asks you to do something for him, then you do it, you know what I mean by that?"

"So he's threatened you with consequences should you not comply, is that what you're saying?" Hollie interjected, "Is there anything else that you do for him? Dealing drugs, perhaps? Did he supply you with the sedatives needed that night?"

Dan thought he knew why he had been targeted. It made sense now. Walshy had seen his face already, with every possibility that the man had done his own research and knew exactly who he was, and he didn't appreciate this new copper on the scene starting to tread on his toes. Not only that, but the age-old story of his life came into play – he was short, looked younger than his years with his clean-shaven face and his softly spoken accent, which all made him an easy target for attempted coercion. The black dog within him started to stir at that, just as Rachael came up beside him.

"No comment. All I'm willing to say is that you don't want to get on the wrong side of him. And that I need your assurance that my girlfriend – my child – will be safe, because I've said far too much already about my cousin." The meaningful look he gave the gaffer, along with the finality of his words, gave them all the impression that, for now, Jamie had said all he was going to say.

"Ok, ok. Of course we will arrange protection for your girlfriend, if Kyle Walsh is as dangerous as you say he is. Interview concluded. Hollie, could you arrange for custody please?" Broadmeadow concluded, getting up and turning off the tape recorder.

Partly in awe over watching Broadmeadow gain a completely unexpected result through his expert interrogation skills, assisted by the infallible Hollie, Dan managed to push down his own ill feelings over being the victim, forcing the black dog to settle. This all left them with a gaping question though – were they to pursue Walshy as their fly-tipper; an insignificant crime in relation to what was turning out to be a much bigger picture? Or were they to hand it all over to South Lynn downstairs, because the drugging of a police officer and the stabbing of a young man definitely did not fall within their jurisdiction?

For the first time since moving back home, Dan started to doubt if Rural Crime really was the place for him. He missed the satisfaction he would get from helping to convict the worst of the worst. He felt frustrated that they never got to see a case through to the end. He thought; what is the point in what they are doing as a department? Where was the fulfilment, or the knowledge that you'd really helped somebody in need?

The black dog stirred once more, filling him with inner turmoil as his vision clouded, as if he were looking out through a tinted glass. Reaching forward, his forearm connected with the wall, bracing himself. A hand at his shoulder drew him back, but it didn't belong to his gaffer as he had come to expect. It was small and slight and held no real weight or warmth.

"Dan, are you ok?" Rachael's voice came drifting through the haze. The unnerving sensation of having lost a minute of his life overcame him, as the next thing Dan knew, he was sat at his desk. Blinking, he observed his surroundings. Broadmeadow was still in the interview room with Jamie. Hollie was stood in the corner with her back to them, arranging for a custody officer. Paul was in the kitchen making a drink, with Chester observing his every move, hoping to be slipped a biscuit from the tin on top of the worktop …

Everything felt … muted.

Rachael was in his immediate peripheral, stood before him and staring at his face very intently. She wasn't a bad looking girl, he considered, and he also knew that as a younger man, he would have been drawn towards her in the hopes of finding a woman who found him endearing enough to take him under her wing.

Yet now, there was nothing. No urge to flirt or pursue, no physical attraction. Dan's urges had gradually come to be set elsewhere. Instead, he was drawn to the emotional solace that his gaffer was able to give him – even if it was only ever going to be nothing more than platonic.

Closing his eyes for second, he gathered his thoughts and urged the sickness inside of him to dampen. Opening them again, he straightened himself up in his chair and focused back on Rachael. "Yeah, I'm ok. Thank you. We should see if Hollie needs any assistance, come on."

"How about I get you a drink – tea? Coffee? Unlike you, I thought I'd ask first instead of just guessing." It was a bit flirty, the way she said it, but Dan brushed it off as Rachael trying to lay on a bit of banter in an attempt to get to know him better.

"Nah, I'm fine, honestly," he appealed, feeling steady enough to get up to his feet. He needed to see if Hollie was ok. And he needed to be near his gaffer.

Outside, coming up the stairs, were a couple of uniformed officers from downstairs arriving to take Jamie Stubbs away into custody. Accompanying them was superintendent Ackehurst. And he wasn't a happy man. He didn't like it when people trod on his toes, especially when it was something to do with Broadmeadow and his department.

Barging his way through the doors and into the office, face reddened like a swollen beet, Dan only just had time to swerve out of his way as the senior officer made his way straight towards the gaffer.

"You know what? Maybe we should just keep our heads down for a minute …" He made eyes with Rachael, indicating that they return to their desks, as the urge to be closer to his gaffer wasn't as strong as the desire for self-preservation – this wasn't going to end in an orderly conversation, he just knew it, and he certainly didn't want to get himself caught in the crossfire.

With a side glance towards Dan, Jamie was led away in cuffs by the two uniformed officers. As soon as he was safely out of the vicinity, Hollie came scuttling out of the archive cupboard and accepted the cup of coffee that Paul had just passed into her hands. And then all eyes turned towards the cupboard as the door slammed shut behind Ackehurst's back, its reverberation felt right across the floor underneath their feet.

A Few Home Truths

With the door firmly shut, a very angry Ackehurst squared up to his counterpart; "What the bloody hell do you think you're doing, Marcus?! I'm this close to reporting you to the DCS for misconduct of your duties …" he raised his cumbersome fingers and made a gesture like he was trying crush an imaginary pea, "*This* bloody close!"

Broadmeadow squared his shoulders, almost nose to nose with the other superintendent. "I was only performing a duty that your own team failed to pursue, *Neil*."

To be quite honest, Marcus knew that it would only have been a matter of time before Ackehurst came storming up to the third floor to dish out a piece of his mind. What he wasn't expecting was for it to have been so soon. The man must have dropped everything the instant Hollie's call had come through to request supervision of custody, just to come and pay him a visit. That surprised Marcus a wee bit, because he could count on one hand the number of times Ackehurst had actually made a trip up to the Rural Crime Department.

Downstairs, Community Safety and Criminal Justice had a much nicer office than their own, with roughly ten-fold the number of staff. They had expensive computer monitors and ergonomic chairs, with a carpet that wasn't tainted and stained by decades of dirty boots walking over it, and a ceiling that didn't leak next to the kitchen every time it rained.

The budget seemed to start at the bottom where Traffic and Transport took their share, before trickling upwards to Ackehurst on the second floor, who then took the remaining pennies for his own team's pocket. By the time the yearly budget filtered its way up to Rural Crime, there was barely anything left other than that to cover any essential equipment replacements.

Marcus would be lying if he said that there wasn't a small chip on his shoulder over how his department were treated with such little regard – but it wasn't enough for him to understand fully why superintendent Ackehurst held such a disliking towards them. And for that matter, himself in particular. Would make sense if it was the other way around, and he was the one constantly battling for more money, wouldn't it? But it wasn't, and it didn't.

"We did *not* fail. I have two officers assigned to your sergeant's case, and to be quite honest, we do have other more pressing cases on our plate right now that unfortunately, for you, have taken priority," Ackehurst said, also drawing himself up to full height but failing by half an inch or so to contend with Marcus. "And another thing. Are your meagre team of officers so strapped for work that you were forced to send them out to do another department's work? Redundant to your requirements? Why don't you just send them all down now and I would graciously take them onto my own team instead, where they can be getting on with some *real* police work?"

Marcus bristled. His team worked hard for him, and they did partake in real police work, serving the rural community in which they lived in; a community that was so often forgotten about or side lined for the sake of the larger towns and cities. They covered a huge area too, between them. The whole of the county. "One of my officers was drugged.

And we still don't know why. For anybody to assault a police officer like that is a very serious offence in my books – an offence that should be regarded with the utmost importance, ye' hear me? What if it happened to a member of your own team, eh? What then?"

At that, Ackehurst seemed temporarily stumped for an answer. *Gotcha there*, Marcus thought.

Not a man to be beaten however, Ackehurst soon recovered himself; "You always were one to take the matters of your subordinate officers too personally, weren't you? Taken a liking towards sergeant Taylor now, have you? Was the same with DI Wright, wasn't it?"

"You want to watch yourself there …" Marcus snarled, voice dropping lower in a quiet warning. A nerve had been hit. Exactly what the other man had been aiming for.

Ackehurst stepped back a pace, satisfied that he had gained the upper hand. And in his own head, proving that he was still the top dog around these parts. A contriving, superior smile played at his lips; "Why? Because I'm right? Shall I have a word with sergeant Taylor on my way out and ask him if he fancies a transfer to replace constable Hutchinson? I'll be doing him a favour, if you really do care for him that much. Not exactly going to go far under your command now, is he?"

"He's just fine with me, Neil."

A raised eyebrow was all he got in response, of which Marcus wasn't entirely sure what Ackehurst was trying to imply. Did he know? Was it that obvious, that he had been having thoughts of a highly inappropriate nature towards his young sergeant? Or was it just known, as with DI Wright, that they were, and always had been, an extremely close-knit team?

Perhaps he should be exercising some more control over his emotions here – he shouldn't be letting Daniel get so close to him, and he certainly shouldn't have let his anger over the whole situation get the better of him – did he not know better than to try and take the law into his own hands? There was the fear too, of the inevitable letter than would be landing on his desk should he pursue anything greater than a friendship with Daniel, courtesy of the man stood before him, over accusations of favouritism; conflict of interest and abuse of a subordinate to name a few …

Now visibly swollen with his own self-righteousness and on a roll with the snide comments, Ackehurst pointedly glanced down at Marcus' left hand to deliver his final, parting blow; "How's Mrs Broadmeadow doing? Everything alright with her? How rude of me not to have asked."

Marcus' brow knotted into a frown, wondering where such a comment had come from. But then he followed Ackehurst's gaze down, and he understood: Monday night was when he had finally opened the large envelope Rowena had left him, when she had visited to claim the remainer of her possessions. Even though he knew exactly what it contained, holding off from actually opening it meant that he could delay the reality of his situation – to be careening towards older-age with his life falling apart around him. Tuesday night, after pondering over how long he was feasibly able to leave it before physically signing the divorce agreement, Marcus had removed his wedding band.

A reddened indent around his ring finger still remained, from where he had been forced to deploy a large amount of washing up liquid – and a steady stream of cold water – just to get the thing off.

"She's fine. Just fine," he griped, a deep pain starting to rise within his chest. He knew full well that Ackehurst had a loving, doting wife, with three aspiring children and a recently born grandchild to add to his achievements. He drove an upmarket car and had a holiday home on the Costa Blanca, with only five or so more years of work under his belt before he could take his hefty pension, ride off into the sunset, and enjoy a carefree retirement with his family gravitating around him.

Marcus, on the other hand, had no such pleasures to look forwards to. He had a divorce to settle and a house to sell, a conscience to battle with and a life to rebuild with what was left at the end of it …

Small mercies though, as Ackehurst looked like he was about to make his long-awaited exit. Straightening his tie as he laid his hand upon the door handle, he paused, turning his head and fixing Marcus with a steely eyed stare, "Do me a favour and leave my cases to me and my team in future, will you? I wouldn't want you neglecting your runaway cattle, or whatever it is you actually do up here. Oh, just one more thing. I should call you up for not addressing a senior officer correctly – I forget that you're not *actually* a superintendent, are you? Good day to you, Marcus."

Marcus didn't grace the other superintendent with a response; an action which undeniably gave the impression that Ackehurst had succeeded in his intentions. Marcus couldn't bring it within himself to dwell over it. Too many home truths had been uncovered. He was still deeply hurting over the loss of his wife; not in the sense of a love lost, as such, but moreover the sense of being completely abandoned. Not that he didn't deserve it. He was the one who had chased her in the first place, dragging her away from her home and then failing to give her the children she had so desperately desired. It hurt, all of it, and he was seriously considering leaving off early for the day to go and lick his wounds at home, alone.

Then he looked out over the office and saw young Daniel, his wee fella, anxiously giving him the eye from the safety of his desk, and he felt the pain within his heart start to ease. The sensitive young man would have heard the raised voices of him and Ackehurst, and undoubtedly would have heard his own name mentioned, which left Marcus with the strongest of urges to appease.

A drink, perhaps? Purely as friends. Nothing inappropriate.

Yes. He would ask Daniel out for a drink after work, then they could have a good old chat.

But first? He needed to brief his team as a whole, because no matter what Ackehurst had said, he needed them all to know that in his eyes, they had all done the right thing by going out and apprehending Jamie Stubbs.

The Corner by the Window

A different pub to their usual haunt, but to be honest, Dan wasn't sure how he felt about visiting the Greyhound again any time soon, so he was thankful for the gaffer's decision to go somewhere different. The Mulberry was more of a restaurant than a drinking establishment, a little classier than the Greyhound, with its modern yet cosy décor. It was clean, with a hardwood floor and comfortable, mismatched seating, warm lighting and an array of potted plants perched on every available surface. It wasn't full of off-duty police officers either, which was nice considering the company he was keeping. It felt more private – just him and Broadmeadow.

At first, he thought the gaffer was inviting the whole team out to calm things down after Ackehurst's outburst that afternoon, but no, just him. In all honesty, he wasn't feeling all that well. He was even prepared to admit that a depressive episode was oncoming, yet at the same time, there was no way that he was going to turn down a private audience with his gaffer. He liked the man's quiet company. It was easy to be around him, and he was growing to long for the times that they were in close proximity of each other.

Choosing a nice corner by a window that backed onto a pretty landscaped garden area, Dan settled himself down into a small, two-seater sofa. With a low table between them, he was a little disappointed (but not surprised) when Broadmeadow chose the armchair opposite rather than taking a seat beside him.

"I didn't know what to order you. I asked for a coffee like you asked but apparently that isn't an option anymore, so I got you a cappuccino. I hope that's ok?" Broadmeadow eyed him expectantly, looking for approval that he hadn't made a mistake. For himself, he had ordered a measure of whisky.

There was a copious dusting of chocolate powder on the top of his coffee. Dan smiled appreciatively, taking the wide-brimmed cup between both hands, "Did you add the extra chocolate?"

The arches of his gaffer's cheeks tinted red, as he admitted, "I did. I know you have a wee bit of a sweet tooth, am I right?"

"Yeah. You got me," Dan said, ducking his eyes down, suddenly feeling a bit shy. Unless he was spending his life living under a rock, it was very clear to him that there was a low-lying level of flirting going on here – something which Dan hadn't attempted in a very long time indeed, and undoubtedly was even longer for his gaffer, who he knew had been married for longer than he had been alive.

He wasn't opposed to it; he just didn't really know what he was doing. Going back to those troublesome thoughts he'd had as a teenager where a faceless male figure had been the centre of his desires, and the thoughts which he had tried so hard to suppress with a relative degree of success, he now found himself – very surprisingly – quite relaxed over what was happening. He now knew that it wasn't wrong to be attracted to another man.

Admittedly, nobody before now had taken his fancy quite like Broadmeadow had, and he found women attractive too, so that part of things was still a bit confusing for him – the question of; *what was he, exactly*? It didn't matter really, he decided. He liked Broadmeadow, was attracted to him, wanted to be with him – that was all it came down to, which then made any further analysis into his sexuality irrelevant.

He did however find Broadmeadow's stance a little more perplexing. He was a man from a different generation to himself, and until very recently there had been no indications at all that he was anything other than an older, heterosexual man. Saying that, you did hear stories, didn't you? Of people who had been long married suddenly breaking away to find themselves and what they really wanted from life? Perhaps his gaffer was one of those. He didn't know. And again, did it really matter?

"I wondered if you may have heard your name mentioned during my calm and respectful discussion with superintendent Ackehurst, and I suppose I just wanted to reassure you over anything you may have heard. Specifically, that I'm not thinking of sending you down for a transfer or anything like that. Unless you wanted to, of course. I wouldn't try to stop you, if that's what you would like to do, son," Broadmeadow finished with his rambling statement, taking a small sip of his whisky and giving Dan a level look over the top of his glass.

Dan *had* heard his name mentioned, rather loudly in fact, and naturally he had wanted to know why. But other than that, the details of the heated exchange had been unclear behind the closed door of the archive cupboard. He'd have been none the wiser had Broadmeadow not said anything to him now, and he definitely wouldn't have guessed that Ackehurst had suggested a transfer for him. Why though? He hardly knew the man, which was exactly how he responded: "Why would Ackehurst want me to transfer over to his team? Why would I want to?"

That seemed to put his gaffer more at ease. Looked like he wasn't the only one prone to a bit of overthinking …

"Why? Because I worry that Rural Crime isn't the place where you will be able to reach your full potential, and I guess that Ackehurst succeeded in growing those concerns of mine. Please know that this isn't an attempt on my behalf to encourage you to move on, however. I like you, Daniel. And you're proving to be a huge asset to our team," he paused, as Dan took note of the uncertainty upon his gaffer's face, before he continued, "I'd hate to be holding you back, fella. I know that the work we do isn't what most people sign up for when they join the police."

Funny, because only earlier that day Dan had been having thoughts along the same lines. Not serious ones, because he had since decided that he was much happier now than he had been before, even with the troublesome black dog rearing its ugly head as of late. "Not gonna lie, I do miss certain aspects my old job. But I'm happy here, doing what I'm doing now. And I guess more importantly, I'm happy with you, as my boss."

"Just 'happy', eh? Anything I can do to help improve on that rating?" Broadmeadow responded, a smile playing at his lips. Dan liked his smile. It was kind of thin-lipped and crooked with a couple of top teeth on show, cautious, like he was afraid of breaking out in a full-blown grin. Around them, the restaurant started to fill with the first early evening diners. Dan hardly noticed. He was entirely focused on the man sat before him, and what line of conversation he was going to follow up with. Although *almost* certain that a degree of attempted flirtation was going on here, one could never quite be positive, could they? Not without one member of the party having the balls to say it outright.

"I dunno … taking me out for a drink has been a good start, I'd say."

"And there was me thinking the next round was yours, fella," Broadmeadow fired back as he chucked down the remainder of his drink, and there it was again; that wonderfully coy smile that warmed Dan up to the very core. In contrast to his gaffer, Dan had barely touched his coffee – it was still too hot.

"I'll be right back," the gaffer said, leaving for the bar. He returned shortly after with his glass refilled. Dutch courage, perhaps? Dan could have done with a bit of that himself, but after last weekend's events he was trying to stay away from the stronger stuff. The fear of it making him sick again was enough to put him off. Besides, he really wasn't supposed to drink whilst taking antidepressants, even if he had done so without incident many a time before then.

The gaffer lingered for a moment with his drink in hand, hovering between the armchair he'd been previously occupying and the sofa Dan was sitting on, before making his decision and plonking himself down beside his sergeant. His long leg butted up against Dan's knee. Forearms too, brushing together, Broadmeadow's strong and warm against his own. "Is this ok? Not too cramped for you?" the gaffer asked. His voice seemed to have dropped a little lower, his Scottish accent stronger.

"Nah, I'm good," Dan replied, shuffling himself back into the sofa to find a nice comfortable position for himself. It may have been early summer, but he was still more than happy to be getting all cosy with the warmth of another body pressed against him. After a short time of quiet, Dan felt a question that had been playing on his mind exiting his mouth; "What is it between you and Ackehurst, sir? Why don't you two like each other?"

"Good question, Danny-boy. Good question," Broadmeadow mused, settling himself further back into the sofa. Reaching over, in a classic move, his arm wound its way along the backrest behind Dan. As he glanced across at the large hand now hovering very close to his shoulder, he noticed for the first time that the gaffer was no longer wearing his wedding ring.

"It isn't like we have ever had a falling out, as such. I worked with him for a short time, you know. When I first moved down here. We were both sergeants. He's never been anywhere but Criminal Justice, you know that? We got along quite well then. But then an opening came up for a position in Rural Crime, and I thought, hey, nothing like a wee bit of change, so I went for it. Ackehurst stayed where he was – let me think – it was sometime after that, when he was promoted to inspector and then chief inspector. That's when he started really showing an aversion towards me, although to this day I couldn't tell you why."

"I guess if somebody doesn't like you then you're going to start having ill feelings towards them as well? I get that." He was a little biased, he guessed, but still – he couldn't understand why somebody would take a disliking towards his gaffer. He was one of the kindest, fairest and gentlest men Dan had ever met.

"He's like a lot of officers in his position, and I'm sure you will be able to vouch for that one. He says 'yes' to the right people, and he doesn't particularly care for anybody who he sees as a threat towards his end goal. The sort of fella who likes to earn himself a few accolades along the way, you know what I mean?" At that point, Broadmeadow's hand casually dropped down around Dan's shoulders. And Dan's heart curled with the warmth of it.

They smiled at each other for a moment, with an unspoken understanding between them that wasn't there before.

Yes, Dan knew what he meant. Ackehurst was just like DCI Walters. "Yeah. I know."

Quietly, he sipped at his coffee. Even now, with Broadmeadow there to protect him, he still didn't like to speak of Walters. The black dog stirred inside his guts, but he was able to make it sit and stay put for the time being. He was having a nice evening, enjoying getting to know his gaffer a little more personally, and the black dog be damned if it though it was going to ruin this for him.

Quiet Revelation

After sending young Daniel off for the night, Marcus found himself restless. Not just because he had been reluctant to leave the pub where the lad had ended up snuggled against his side by the end of the evening, although that was a large part of it. Especially after that second wee dram, where he had plucked up enough courage to drop his arm down and tuck Daniel underneath it for a bit of an awkward yet fulfilling one-armed embrace. Afterwards, as they had lingered under the lighting of the restaurant carpark, even though the mutual feelings were now clear, neither man had mustered up the courage required for a goodnight kiss.

God, it had him feeling like a teenager all over again. Or a young man, specifically, with Johnny, where they had never really gotten past the stage he and Daniel were at now, before he was so cruelly taken away from him …

His heart was ruling his head, and Marcus knew it. He was very aware of that fact. Aside from being Daniel's commanding officer – an obvious problem in itself – there was the small matter of their age difference. He had over twenty years on the lad, which on paper was just downright criminal. Yet still, despite the obvious challenges, he couldn't stop himself from imagining what the future had in store for them. Daniel made him happy; made him feel like there was some greater purpose to his life other than just surviving. He wanted to protect him from all the contempt in the world; to make him feel special and worthy of everything he didn't think that he deserved.

He wanted to do right by him, like he never had the chance to do with his Johnny.

Sighing to himself, Marcus made himself comfortable on the sofa that he had shared with the wee lad only a week ago. It was late, but a habit had formed since Rowena had left of avoiding their marital bedroom as far as possible, opting instead to sleep downstairs more often than not. The spare room was an option, but that space too held a certain level of trepidation for him – it felt cold around the edges, as if there was a deep-set mould lying beneath the surface of the walls. For him that room felt like the very symbol of the end of his marriage; those last few months where he had slept as if he were a guest in his own home.

Despite his sadness at starting life over again, Marcus couldn't wait for the place to go onto the market. The house no longer felt like it was his own, like Rowena was haunting the air he breathed to the point where it had become unbearably cold, no matter how much he tried to dial up the thermostat.

A job for the weekend would be starting to dig up some of his most prized plants, he decided. The garden was the only place that he did still feel was his own. Having never shown much of an interest herself, the garden was the one place that Rowena's ghost had not yet tarnished for him. Another job would be to get onto the estate agents and actually get the place valued, fully aware of how he wouldn't be left with much – not after the solicitor's fees and the settlement that his estranged wife was demanding.

I'll be working until I bloody die at this rate. So much for all that hard saving to allow for a long retirement; he thought to himself. Not like bloody Ackehurst (the other reason why he was feeling restless that night). He'd be laughing his smug little face off at his current situation.

Turning on his laptop, Marcus decided that he was going to do a bit of digging now that superintendent Ackehurst had sprung to mind. The conversation with Daniel earlier had him thinking; what was it that the man really had against him and his team? It wasn't like Marcus had stepped on his toes for a promotion or anything like that – Ackehurst was the superintendent, not him. Marcus was just a chief inspector in disguise, temporarily promoted because there was nobody else to fill the position at the time when Alan retired, with no indication as to when his period of limbo would be over.

Marcus' most basic instincts as an officer of the law, serving king and country, told him that there must be another reason behind Ackehurst's animosity. There must be.

Starting with the man's basic profile on the police database, he scanned down the page. It only held the briefest amount of information. Current rank, etcetera. That was no good. Marcus knew all that already. Next, he tried the public page for Community Safety and Criminal Justice, which contained a well posed, blown-up image of Ackehurst, resplendent in his full dress uniform. Again, it just contained a paragraph of waffle that undoubtedly wasn't written by the man himself, about how keeping the streets of Central Norfolk safe was his utmost priority; all of which didn't give Marcus much of an insight into the man behind the freshly starched regalia.

Growing frustrated, he brought up an internet search engine and typed in Ackehurst's name. A well-known social media page came up at the top of the list of websites, but it was inaccessible unless you were a member, which Marcus was not. Perhaps Daniel could help him out with that one – he was surely young enough to be au fait with such things.

Going back to the search engine results, he clicked on a link for a local newspaper. Dated three years back, it covered Norfolk Constabulary's own superintendent Ackehurst, going up to a ceremony in Birmingham to give out an award; something to do with making a difference to the community. It was one of those 'suited and booted' occasions that Marcus would try his utmost to avoid at all costs. The sort of gala where one would be forced to socialise for hours on end and boast about all the things that made one superior to one's peers. It didn't come as much of a surprise to see Ackehurst there, soaking up the pompousness of it all, but something at the end of the article did succeed in catching his attention.

He needed his reading glasses for this, the darkened living room and the brightness of the screen straining at his eyes.

Right. Glasses on. The end of the article listed the other awards given out that evening, and more importantly, who received them. And there was a name that sent a jolt of unease through Marcus' veins – DCI Walters, recognised for his services to East London and its surrounding boroughs, by way of a marked decrease in the number of illicit substances finding their way onto the streets. Good for him. Daniel still hadn't shared exactly what happened during his time working under Walters, but he knew that whatever it was, nothing good had come of it, leaving Marcus with the timid, quiet shell of a man who had come out the other side.

To even think that somebody could mistreat his clever, thoughtful and downright captivating young sergeant physically filled him with hurt ...

Going back once more, this time delving into an image search on the awards ceremony, he scanned over the various photos of the evening which were available to the public domain. Scrolling through the reams of images that showed a countless number of unrecognisable faces, he then found what he was looking for. A photograph of Walters and Ackehurst sitting next to each other at one of the large, round tables laid out for the event. Another, with the two men sharing a smile for a picture with the assistant chief constable for the West Midlands. And another, dated a year later, this time at a charity ball somewhere down on Walters' patch, where the two men were photographed together raising a glass.

Suspicions well and truly heightened that Walters and Ackehurst were in some way connected on a more than professional level, Marcus decided that it was time to call it a night. This wasn't a case of a smoking gun – he didn't really know what it was exactly that he was looking for. All he knew for now was that something didn't quite sit right, akin to an undiscovered leak under the floorboards, a feeling of unease over something that had yet to happen.

Before turning in for the night, however doubtful he actually was over getting a decent night's sleep under his belt, he reached for his phone. Half expecting there to be a message from sergeant Taylor to inform him that he was home and safe, like even the mere act of him delving into DCI Walters' affairs may have summoned some unrestful, astrally-projected spirit out to do the lad harm, he found himself sorely disappointed to see his notifications screen blank.

He put his phone back down, going off to get ready for bed. Upon his return, having already decided that the sofa was the place for him that night, he checked again. Still nothing. No way he was ever going to sleep now.

It wouldn't hurt, would it? To just send a quick message over to the lad? Understandable was it not, to want to know that Daniel was ok, considering the number of occasions he had run into trouble already? So, opening up his phone's messaging application, with his first finger poised because typing on such a small screen with one's thumbs was beyond him, Marcus started his composition:

Hi, Daniel. Just checking that you got home ok. I might require some assistance tomorrow with a bit of a private investigation. I think it will be right up your street. Anyways, good night son. I'd hate to be keeping you up x

With that, Marcus pulled the blanket that was folded over the back of the sofa around himself, and settled down against his cushion for a pillow. It still held the faint whiff of whatever aftershave it was that Daniel had been wearing, which served in lulling him away towards another a restless night's sleep.

Ghosts

Filled with a warmth in his belly and a feeling of hope that life wasn't quite so bad after all, Dan made his way home from the pub. With his usual vehicle still at the garage for repairs to its wheel – apparently it wasn't a top priority when he'd phoned up earlier for an update – he found himself slowly getting used to driving the four-by-four. Once you were inside, you forgot about how outlandish the exterior was. Besides, the gaffer said how he preferred him driving it because it gave him better visibility down the narrow country roads that covered the majority of their turf. Whether that was a hint towards his driving abilities or not, or whether it was just a friendly jibe at his height (or lack thereof), he hadn't thought to ask.

All in all, it had been an extremely enjoyable evening spent in his gaffer's company, with the cloud over his mind earlier that day now lifted. He felt good, already thinking over the next time he and Broadmeadow would get the opportunity to spend some more precious time together. If there was a next time – but he felt confident that there would be. The chemistry between them was unmistakeable. Next time, he might even pluck up the nerve for a quick goodnight kiss …

Funny, how it didn't feel *funny*, to be having thoughts like that. Dan had never kissed another bloke, he mused, as he pulled up at the roundabout towards the top of town. But he wanted to. He wasn't sure about doing anything else – not having broached that fanciful detail yet because it was as thrilling as it was scary, all at the same time. Annoyingly, at his exit, there was a diversion sign in place – *Police,*

Accident – so he was forced to follow it round. He knew these roads, and he also knew that the diversion would take him on a twenty-minute jaunt up to the dual carriageway and round, before doubling back down into South Lynn from the coast road.

With that in mind, he took the next exit past the diversion and turned off down towards the small village of Buckshorn, where he knew that he could cut back through at the other end and avoid any build-up of traffic caused by the accident. He turned the stereo down – Lynn Star Radio – in order to better concentrate on the winding, high banked roads he was about to embark along. It had been a good fifteen years or so since he had last come down here. A friend used to live in the Buckshorn, where he would often jump on his bike and cycle down to see him. Bus routes were few and far between around these parts, and even when there was a service it would always be a gamble as to whether it would actually show up or not, so pedal power had always been the most reliable option for Dan and his friends growing up.

Not that he could imagine doing this route now, as an adult. He'd be gasping for breath and giving up come the first hill out of town …

Pulling around a blind bend, he flicked his headlights onto full beam, illuminating the road ahead. A sudden tickle at the back of his throat came out in a dry cough. Perhaps all this feeling under the weather wasn't all in his head after all; it may be that he was actually coming down with something?

A church up ahead came towering into view – Saint Mary's – floodlit from the ground upwards, its great stone spire looming up into the sky as if it were reaching for the heavens. Slowing down for another corner that would take him right up to the front of the church, Dan pulled up onto the gravel entranceway of the surrounding graveyard to allow for an oncoming vehicle to pass.

Slowing to a stop, he was forced to squint at the exceptionally bright headlights coming towards him. Suddenly, he coughed again, drawing his hand up to his mouth to catch it. The lights grew brighter in a slow approach, blinding him.

There wasn't any bad weather forecast that night, yet a low rumble that sounded like thunder in the distance trundled through the air. Probably a fighter jet making its way to the RAF base. Dan flashed his lights, annoyed that the oncoming vehicle still had its full beams on.

Then it appeared to stop, right there in the middle of the road.

"What the fuck are you doing …" Dan muttered to himself, turning his head to the side to try and work out if the other driver was experiencing some sort of difficulty, except all he could see were those two bright lights, unable to make out the body of the vehicle.

The noise up in the sky grew louder – more likely to be a slow-moving surveillance aircraft rather than a jet.

Watching intently, and debating as to whether it would be a good idea or not to get out and see what was going on, Dan blinked in disbelief as the headlights started to grow, morphing into two large orbs that appeared to be floating in a *one-two* bobbing motion, right towards the bonnet of his car.

Transfixed by the peculiar sight, he watched as a blurred shape began to form around the orbs as it neared. A great lumbering body upon four horse-like legs, held aloft upon a set of massive, ursine paws. The orbs of blazing light – Dan could feel the heat of them even through the windscreen – steadily started to shrink until they fell into the face of a beastly looking canine.

For a horrifying moment, as he rasped out another cough, Dan thought he was staring right into the face of a physical, waking embodiment of his own black dog. Only for a moment though, because the black dog was with him, in the car.

Just because he hadn't seen it in a while, it didn't mean it wasn't there, like it had the ability to particulate itself inside of him and wreak its havoc from within. It happened once before, where Dan had foolishly thought he was rid of the thing, sometime in the space between leaving the Met and moving back home. Since the monumental shit show inside of Romford's *Laser Space Adventure* when the black dog had first made its physical presence known, and the weeks afterwards when it had followed him around, it had disappeared again, just like that.

That was right before Dan had been hit with the most helpless feeling of despair, with a fog clouding his every thought and an all-consuming feeling of uselessness rendering him immobile. Even though he couldn't see it, he knew that the black dog was still there with him.

He did get better though, with the help of some medication from the doctor that he still took to this day. Then he'd moved back home which had proved to be his salvation for a time, until the black dog inevitably reappeared. At that point, he understood that this was a lifelong thing he was just going to have to live with.

The monstrous looking thing outside in the road, however? That was definitely not his black dog, and it was craning its neck down, peering through the windscreen like it was considering whether he would make a worthy meal or not. It prodded its nose up against the windscreen, leaving a shroud of mist upon the outside of the glass.

Yet, despite the unexplained appearance of something the devil himself may have conjured up, Dan didn't feel scared. If anything at all, he felt … calm …

Suddenly, its large, pointed ears swivelled before its whole head turned to look back up the road behind. A frightful clap of thunder boomed overhead, causing Dan to flinch back into his seat, followed by a blinding flash of light; so bright that the surrounding countryside became indistinguishable.

Then, as soon as it happened, it was over. The churchyard lay still and quiet. The church itself, its looming tower, now bathed again in the muted glare of the floodlights. The radio inside the car broke into the quiet tune of a well-known song. The engine rumbled idly beneath his feet. Another vehicle approached, a tradesman's van, passing him by and continuing on into the night.

After taking a moment to calculate what had just happened, Dan continued on his way. Through the village of Buckshorn, all was undisturbed. Nothing untoward. No equine-esque hound wandering up the high street. In fact, Dan started to think that he had imagined the whole thing and that he really *was* starting to lose his marbles …

Through the village and out the other side, a large industrial yard came into view on his right. Unlike the church, the floodlights surrounding this place were more like that of a premier league football pitch. Vaguely remembering a crumbling farm building being there before, clearly things had moved on since then. Now the yard was filled with heavy plant vehicles and folded down cranes, with a row of HGVs along the far fence. In the middle of it all was a low bungalow, with two cars parked outside. The lights were on behind the blinded windows.

Dan slowed, curious, as the door of the more expensive looking of the two cars swung open. At this hour, it seemed strange to him that a business would still be operating – even stranger for a meeting to be taking place.

Crawling up the road, he cursed at the fact that he was driving the massive four wheel drive with 'POLICE, RURAL CRIME' stamped across its sides and up the bonnet. Dan watched, as a heavy-set, obviously balding man stepped out of the car, wearing a woollen camel greatcoat.

Dan's heart ran cold.

Even at a distance, the man was unmistakable. As he tried to control another sudden bout of coughing, alarmed to see that a spattering of dark mucus had expelled onto his hand, the man turned, staring right at him from across the expanse of the yard. The floodlights cast a portentous disposition of shadows, jutting out at all angles like a demonic paperchain of adumbral dependents, with DCI Walters at the centre, the puppeteer amongst his spawn. Forget the ghost-hound. That was nothing compared to this on Dan's scale of the most terrifying things known to man.

It wasn't, was it? It couldn't be …

He's not there. You're losing your marbles, remember? Hallucinating. It's the black dog, playing nasty tricks on your mind ...

Dan panicked as the apparition of his worst fear continued to stare him down. Not wanting to hang around, not wanting to find out why the *fuck* his former boss had followed him into his new life, he put his trembling foot down onto the accelerator and sped away without looking back.

Through a Hedge and Back

The phone call that Marcus had received last night had resulted in not only the worst night's sleep of his life, but was enough to have him restlessly pacing around the office like a caged tiger in a zoo, waiting for Daniel to make an appearance. It was still early, only just gone half seven, but he wanted to make sure that he was there when the lad arrived.

"Calm down, son, calm down – start from the beginning. Slowly," Marcus urged down the phone, having only just managed to drop off to sleep, not yet awake enough to comprehend the words of a young man who wasn't making a whole lot of sense.

"DCI Walters? You saw him? Daniel, are you sure you're feeling ok?" He was sure he heard something about thunder and the giant apparition of a dog too, but the latter part of the hastily recited experience was what really concerned him. The wee fella hadn't been quite himself the last week. He seemed distant and troubled, quieter than usual (and that was saying something, because Daniel was a quiet lad on a normal day), only seeming to perk up once Marcus was around. He was worried about him – especially so now that he was having what appeared to be very real, conscious nightmares.

"Can you be sure? Anything on your dash-cam footage?" Trying his best to reassure, Marcus spoke with a level tone. If Daniel didn't calm down soon then he would be left with no choice but to get into his car and drive himself over

there. Thankfully, he could hear the lad's breathing start to even off down the other end of the phone.

"It's ok, ok. You don't have to go back out there now, we can have a look in the morning, yes?" That seemed to appease him further, with the reassurance that he didn't have to go back outside. Daniel coughed. It sounded dry, and raspy. Getting up from the sofa and pulling his dressing gown on with the phone balanced between his shoulder and his ear, Marcus wandered out to the kitchen to put the kettle on, encouraging Daniel to do the same.

"Have ye' locked the doors? Yes? And there's nobody lurking outside; no suspicious looking vehicles parked up? No? Good ... you're alright, son ... no, don't be sorry, you're alright." It went on, sharing a brew down the phone, until the dead of night was well and truly upon them. It pained him when the time came to end the conversation, but they couldn't stay up talking until the sun came back around. Telling himself that it was only a few hours now until they would be up for work anyways, Marcus bade the lad a good night with a final affirmation that if anything else happened, anything at all, he was only a phone call away.

As if they were aware that something wasn't right with one of their own, Paul and Hollie showed up early that morning, shortly after Daniel arrived looking rather dishevelled, with dark rings circling his eyes and a slightly more casual than usual approach to his attire.

Marcus didn't expect his team to show up in suits and ties, but they did generally opt to dress on the smarter side. This morning though, Daniel was wearing jeans and trainers and a hooded sweatshirt, rather than his usual buttoned shirt and boots. He hadn't even done whatever he usually did to his hair – the slightly longer bit on top of his close-cropped sides was all tousled, with a some of it coming down over his forehead like he'd been dragged through a hedge and back.

The temptation was there to go right up to him and sweep those stray strands back into place, but Marcus was forced to hold himself back. Maybe if Hollie and Paul hadn't shown up when they did, he would have acted upon those urges and drawn the lad in closer for a full inspection, but this was not the time or the place for that. They had work to do here, preferably before Rachael showed up because what he was going to ask his team to do was directly against what superintendent Ackehurst had berated him for, and unlike Daniel, she had not earned his ultimate trust from the moment he laid eyes upon her. A nice girl, don't get him wrong, but the trust just wasn't there yet.

"Well, seeing as you're all here so bright and early, gather round please," Marcus instructed. An impromptu circle of office chairs formed, like a coven about to form a devious plot. Hollie was early because she too couldn't sleep; said she'd been up since five just loitering around the house. Paul was early because Chester was being 'a pain in the arse' (in his own words), and kept barking at the front door until he eventually relented and left an hour earlier than he usually would.

With his team of officers present, Marcus got straight to the point. "Right. I'll be completely open with you all – I want us to continue pursuing our investigations into Kyle Walsh, but more specifically, I want us to do a bit of probing into superintendent Ackehurst. But it's strictly need to know only, understand?"

"What's happened, sir?" Hollie questioned, ever curious and striving to understand the full picture.

"Well. Daniel here may want to expand with you both later, and this isn't exactly all related yet, but trust me when I say that I think we're onto something here. There was a sighting last night, of Daniel's former superior officer, DCI Walters. He appeared to be having a rendezvous at a plant hire company just outside the village of Buckshorn. Now, I myself have made a connection between our own superintendent Ackehurst and DCI Walters, and will be digging further into that one. But in the meantime, I want you all to treat this as a wee bit of a covert operation, ok?" Marcus said, sweeping his eyes over the three members of his team. They were all giving him their full attention.

"Wait – I'm confused, sir. That's odd that this DCI Walters has showed up out of the blue, but what's it got to do with Kyle Walsh?" Paul piped up, eager, like Hollie, to absorb every detail of what they were being asked to investigate.

Dan found his voice where he'd been formerly sat quietly at the edge of the circle next to his gaffer; "Don't you think it's a bit strange, that Ackehurst has been so intent on keeping us away from any of his cases, and so reluctant with my own case to pursue a perpetrator even when it was clear that Kyle Walsh was involved? And then last night, when I informed the gaffer that I had seen DCI Walters, and he did a bit of his own research and found that the pair have been seen at a number of social occasions together … I dunno. Instinct tells me at least that something fishy is at play here."

"Right, well said, son," Broadmeadow agreed, smiling down at Dan before falling back into a more serious expression, "Paul, could you be so kind as to do some digging into this plant hire company where DCI Walters was seen? I'll start working on a timeline for you all. We can set up a white board in the back of the archive cupboard, behind the shelving racks, just in case anybody should come snooping up here."

"Gotcha, sir. I'm on it." Paul eagerly accepted his task. His favourite type of job was a nice long sit-down affair; one which involved him not having to leave the office, so this was right up his alley.

"Hollie? I'm really sorry but I need you to look after Rachael for me again. Keep her away from all this, for now. She's still technically under Ackehurst's command so I don't want anything getting back to him at this point in time."

Hollie rolled her eyes. Another case of Broadmeadow acting like a typical *man* – getting her to look after the new member of staff because she was a woman. "Thanks, sir."

"I am sorry, Hollie. Just – just make your job sound as boring as possible so that, with any luck, she will decide to move on sooner than anticipated." He paused, when Hollie started to smile, before adding, "But I didn't say that, ok?"

"Right you are, sir. How about filing of old cases? That should have us both falling asleep by the end of it."

"Good. Good stuff, Hollie. Thank you. Now Daniel, I need you to help me with the Walters/Ackehurst connection. On you go, everyone."

Local Legend

He was a bit surprised that the gaffer didn't berate him over his appearance that morning, but then again, he wasn't. Usually he did make the effort, even if he wasn't feeling at his best, but that morning, he just couldn't. His jeans and hoodie were calling him, so that's what he had thrown on. Dan had even been close to calling in sick, but decided against it at the last minute, knowing that it would do him no good to be cowering away at home on his own.

Besides, Broadmeadow had taken the time to listen to him, hadn't dismissed what he was saying as his imagination playing tricks, so he felt he owed it to the man to at least show up and help open up the wider investigation into what he'd seen at that plant hire yard.

The irritating cough had persisted throughout the night, making it hard for him to drop off to sleep, and that, combined with the black dog trying its hardest to pick away at his sanity, made getting any sort of rest whatsoever almost impossible. His throat felt like sandpaper and his lungs felt tight from strain. His limbs felt sluggish and heavy, body temperature like that of mid-winter. Definitely coming down with something.

Consigning himself to the archive cupboard, Dan was about to make a start on clearing an area at the back of the peculiarly cavernous old cupboard when Paul came inside to join him with a cup of tea in his hand. Ever important, was the constant supply of hot beverages. Hollie would be next on the unwritten rota, then Dan. As for the gaffer? He did make a round on occasion, just to show his appreciation for all the cups of tea that were brought his way throughout the day. The gaffer's tea always tasted the best, Dan decided. Paul's offerings were always a bit weak and watery. Hollie made it strong, but not enough milk. But Broadmeadow – he made it just the way that Dan liked it.

Paul shifted up one of the archive boxes on the nearest shelf to make way for the cup. "You alright mate? You look like shit."

"Thanks. Yeah, I'm ok," Dan responded in the way he always did. Even if it was obvious he was struggling, he never wanted to admit it outright. Blokes didn't do that, did they? Power through it. Don't talk about it.

Paul's expression softened. He wished that Dan would be more open with him – his best mate Callum (DI Wright) wasn't so closed off. They had talked about everything. He missed it. Chester was a good listener, a constant companion to him, but his only flaw was that he couldn't talk back. Apart from his doting canine companion, Paul didn't really have anybody else. Well, that was a bit of a lie because he and Emily talked often, but it wasn't the same.

So, bearing in mind that if neither of them opened up then it was never going to happen, Paul decided to push for a bit more than just 'I'm fine'; "Sounds like you had quite an eventful evening then? Kind of the wrong time of year for that, you know, seeing ghosts and ghouls creeping about the back roads. You getting in early for Halloween or something?"

That seemed to do the trick, as Dan's expression visibly cracked into a bit of a smile. That was before his face fell again as he searched over Paul's. Fucking hell, the man looked troubled. Paul had seen that same look upon his own face many a time, in the mirror, after Callum had died.

"Paul? Do you ... do you believe in ghosts?" Dan said cautiously. Testing the water. Searching for Paul's initial reaction.

"Depends, mate. I do and I don't. Me old ma' always said the house we grew up in was haunted, and I will say that some funny things did happen, but I wouldn't say that I've had any concrete evidence either. Why do you ask?" Paul replied, interest piqued ...

Dan leaned himself against one of the storage racks with his hands digging deep into his pockets. "I saw something, last night. DCI Walters, he was definitely real. I didn't imagine that. But I saw something else. A big black dog, walking in front of my car. But it wasn't a dog, because it had these big, long legs and was the size of a horse. And its eyes – they were like headlights. But it wasn't another car, there was nothing coming the other way ..."

Paul considered the evidence laid before him as Dan looked back down at his feet. When he said that he didn't necessarily believe in ghosts, that wasn't to say that he wasn't interested in such things as the paranormal world. In fact, he was actually a keen enthusiast. And Dan's account sounded peculiarly akin to a certain local legend he had read about in an online forum. "Hey, sounds like you had an encounter with the legendary yet elusive Black Shuck – tell me, where did you see it exactly?"

Dan's eyes rose back up from his feet, looking hopeful that Paul was about to tell him that he wasn't going stark-bollocks mad, as he replied, "Outside saint Mary's church, in Buckshorn."

"Ah, well. You should look it up. There's a legend about that church. If you look closely at the main doors, there's two scorch marks. In the fifteen hundreds there's an account of Black Shuck paying the congregation a visit, bringing a thunderstorm along with him. Two men were killed, the church roof collapsed, and their visitor fled, taking the storm away with it. Afterwards, they find these two burns on the doors, said to have been left behind by yours truly," Paul enthusiastically explained. Dan was surprised, because DC Bartlett was proving time and time again that he was a better educated man than he often made himself out to be. He was pretty sure that Paul wasn't taking the piss either; he was taking him far more seriously than he could ever have expected …

"You really think that was what I saw? I don't think it wanted to harm me though. It seemed merely curious of me, if anything."

"That's interesting, because whilst most descriptions of Black Shuck depict him as an omen of imminent death, there are accounts of him being more of a protector, guiding lost travellers and the like …" Paul seemed to be getting more and more animated by the second which made Dan smile, his own confidence growing that he was in fact being taken seriously.

"Maybe he was warning me that DCI Walters was there?" Dan queried – quietly hopeful now that he hadn't borne witness to his impending doom last night.

"Maybe. Look. It would be awesome if you could share what you saw with the group I'm part of – a real life, modern day Black Shuck sighting!"

Dan agreed. It turned out that Paul attended a monthly meeting of fellow supernatural enthusiasts, and invited him to come along to their next gathering – apparently their numbers were dwindling, so an extra head would always be more than welcome. Perhaps, Dan thought, he should open his mind a little, seeing as he already accepted the other conspicuous omen in his life as pretty much a normality at that point. They agreed to talk more later – Paul had been trying to convince Hollie to take an interest for years now, so with Dan now on board, he was confident that with two of them, they could bring her around to make some sort of holy trinity of supernatural believers.

The *X-Files* sprung to mind. Was that Paul's convoluted plan all along, to covert Rural Crime into Norfolk's own paranormal detective agency? He laughed to himself. Good luck trying to convince the gaffer on that one.

Paul left Dan to it after that. There was a dusty old whiteboard folded at the far wall; looked like it hadn't been wheeled out in years. Upon it, among the faded, half rubbed-out scrawlings, were a couple of newspaper cuttings:

Norfolk Police Detective killed in hit and run accident ... Detective Inspector Callum Wright ... Call for witnesses ... All the usual spiel – no real feeling that the article shed any light on who DI Wright was as a person behind his badge, and no indication that South Lynn were anywhere close to finding an answer. Dan scanned over the other article, dated from just over a week before DI Wright's death:

Cannabis Farm Busted – On Tuesday morning, a dawn raid was performed up at Frog's Farm, near Halestanton. After a lengthy investigation, Norfolk Constabulary's Rural Crime Department raided the property suspected of harbouring upwards of a million pounds worth of cannabis plants, concealed within a shed alongside a legitimate commercial broiler farm, where two suspects were apprehended. Heading the investigation was Detective Inspector Wright, who was not willing to give a statement to the paper at this time. The haul from the raid is set to be incinerated, with the hope that this discovery will lead towards furthering the crack-down on the increasingly prevalent illegal drugs trade within our rural areas ...

It looked to Dan like his colleagues had started to look into the uncanny timing of DI Wright's death; how he had been killed in an 'accident' very shortly after shutting down such a large and lucrative cannabis farming operation. Once again, something didn't add up, especially with the news that South Lynn were the ones to head up the investigation over how a police officer was left for dead in a ditch, somewhere out on The Fens. For some reason though, whoever had started delving deeper – most probably Paul – had clearly given up at some point along the way.

Carefully, he peeled the newspaper cuttings off of the board and placed them aside, with the intention of sorting out their own archive box to store them in later. He was intrigued over the case, and naturally wanted to know more, yet a feeling of slight apprehension surrounded the whole thing, specifically over mentioning DI Wright to Paul again (not after the last time he had brought the subject up).

A knock at the open door roused him from his thoughts, just as he was wiping the white board clean ready for a new investigation to take DI Wright's place. It was the gaffer. He passed his way around the narrow rows of shelving and made his way over to where Dan was scrubbing at the board trying to get the years-old marker off.

"Looking good, Daniel. Could you possibly spare a wee moment – in my office?"

Dan could have taken that whole sentence as a euphemism, but as it was, he knew that for starters, talk of that kind probably wasn't within Broadmeadow's wider vocabulary because he was a sweet, gentlemanly sort of man. And for seconds, he knew that the gaffer actually wanted help with accessing the unfamiliar ground that was umbrellaed under the term: *Social Media.*

Inside Man

Now there was a face that Russel Walters couldn't possibly have mistaken for somebody else. Clearly he'd been wrong when under the assumption that DS Taylor wasn't going to be a problem for him anymore, as he was now filled with an uncharacteristic sense of trepidation over what he'd just seen.

Normally, nothing much worried Walters. Yet for some reason, ever since joining his team as a fresh faced and newly qualified constable, DS Taylor had always been the exception to the rule. Something about him – that *annoying* determination to get to the truth despite a senior officer having told him *no,* was just one of the reasons he disliked the young man so much. Taylor was too good at his job yet not so good at doing as he was told. Walters did like his team to be efficient, but he also liked his team to be compliant. He liked for them to not necessarily *question* his motives when he ordered them to do something.

He was the boss, and they were his subordinates. End of.

So when he saw that jumped up little shit's face peering at him from the safety of his patrol car – a patrol car that was far too big for such a short-arsed man – he felt like a jagged nerve had just been struck. Obviously Walshy's attempt at intimidation (after he'd gone and completely disregarded Walters' firm order not to take matters into his own hands) hadn't paid off, or else Taylor would have been steering well clear.

Of course there was the possibility that Taylor had just been passing because he did live and work around these parts, but that was besides the point. Walters didn't care *how* he had ended up inadvertently snooping about Mikelis' plant hire business, he just cared about neutralising the threat of Taylor finding out *why* his former DCI was visiting there in the first place.

He should have tried harder to get the boy removed from the force entirely when he had the chance. He should have known that he would go running back home instead of handing in his resignation. Not only was Walters concerned over his current business endeavours, but he was also worried – only slightly, mind – that Taylor may go and try to make a case against what he had subjected him to whilst under his command. You heard stories nowadays, didn't you? Especially over senior officers, in the Met in particular, apparently abusing members of their staff.

Not that he was making a confession of any kind there – he never *abused* DS Taylor. Everything he ever did to the boy, whether that was a verbal dressing down or whether that was laying the occasional hand to him when he really crossed him in a foul mood, it was only ever because he deserved it. Taylor was a cocky, too big for his boots young man, who didn't know when to keep his bloody trap shut.

Walters' concerns were all theoretical of course, because he would make sure that Taylor was stopped before any more came of his prying. He just needed to be scared away, which couldn't be too hard a task seeing as he was weak. Weak in strength *and* weak of mind. Easily crushed. Walshy just didn't do a good enough job of it, that was all.

That bloody rottweiler growled at him when he barged his way into Mikelis' office. Should be put down, that thing. Or at least keep it outside.

"Problem, boss?" Mikelis looked up from his paperwork. So much paperwork. It is hard to be a legitimate businessman when there is lots of money to hide within the books. It takes time and much concentration.

"Yes, I have a problem. Not only do I get a call from Ackehurst last night to inform me of Rural Crime sticking their fingers into his pie, but now, *now*, I've just seen one of their officers creeping about outside!" Walters fumed, his face turning a sweaty, beefy red. He made his way straight towards the drinks cabinet and helped himself to a glass.

Mikelis furrowed his brow, outwardly appearing unconcerned, "Why is the finger in the pie?"

"I mean to say that – never mind. Forget the pie. We need to have a serious chat, Mikelis." Walters took a hearty glug of the brandy he had just poured himself, before topping his glass back up and loudly setting the bottle back down on top of the cabinet. He wandered over to the desk where Mikelis sat, and cleared some of his papers out of the way to make room for his glass.

"Ok? What do you want to chat about? I am a busy man, Russel."

"You assured me that you would not go and take matters into your own hands, but now you call me to tell me that your man Walshy has been trying to drug a *bloody* police officer? And now, our little problem just drove past your business here, and he saw *me*, standing in the middle of it. Now, that doesn't sound like he's been effectively dealt with to me. What do *you* think?"

Mikelis set down his pen, pulling out a packet of cigarettes instead and offering one to Walters, before sliding out one for himself and slipping it between his lips. Taking his time with lighting it, inhaling deeply, he considered what the boss had to say. He exhaled, tapping the lit cigarette against the edge of the glass ashtray that had belonged to his grandmother.

"I am not Mr Walsh's babysitter. But have I spoken to him. Besides, you assured *me* that Mr Ackehurst was the reliable inside man. Should he not be dealing with the Rural Crime detective? See? Who has the finger in the pie now, Russel?"

He had a point. Perhaps Walters had overestimated the power that Ackehurst held over his patch. Did he too need a bit of ruffling up? He and Neil were friends, of course, but that didn't mean he wouldn't do what had to be done in order to protect his assets. "I'll deal with him. He's living very comfortably right now and I'm sure that he wouldn't want to give all of that up. But you? I need you to deal with a certain DS Taylor, because if anybody is going to fuck our whole operation up here, it's going to be him. Trust me. He's a persistent little shit."

"You want him finished with?" Mikelis said nonchalantly, like making somebody disappear was as easy as putting the bins out on a Wednesday morning.

"No. Just wreak the fear of God into him. Or the devil. Whatever. I don't care. Just don't kill him." Again, Walters already had one under his belt, courtesy of Mikelis and the company he kept. The risk of another was far too great. Especially with Ackehurst at the helm of South Lynn – he struggled the first time to smooth over the corners and straighten out the rug, so calling upon him again, Walters knew, would be stretching their partnership to the limit.

"Ok. I deal with it. You? You sort out Ackehurst. Deal?" Mikelis thrust out his oxen sized hand with a villainous glint behind his piercing, caucasian eyes.

"Deal."

The two men shook on it. Old friends, sealing yet another pact with one another, of which there had been many over the years; none of which had been broken. Mikelis had been there right from the beginning, when Walters first started to dabble in the world of the offenders he was supposed to be contending. Slowly, things had grown; the odd profit here, the odd suspect 'lost' within the system there, until the money to be made had proved too much of a lure to ignore. Mikelis moved down to Norfolk, a transformation from continental supermarket owner to plant hire business extraordinaire, where it was easier to hide in plain sight and where the police weren't so much of a constant presence. He could separate himself that way, from his supermarkets in the Greater London area. He dealt with getting the goods into the country and then up to the city, where Walters then made sure that his men were immune from the prying eyes of the law.

Walshy had come later. A small-time local dealer who'd applied for a job with Mikelis one day, and the rest was history after that. Now, not only were they players in Greater London, but they were unchallenged in ruling the streets of Norfolk too. That was where superintendent Ackehurst fell into the whole equation – Walters needed somebody on the inside out in the East, and Ackehurst had fitted the bill; power hungry, posted at a central location, and in a position where getting drugs off the streets was one of his main itineraries.

And it had all being going swimmingly until Rural Crime and their team of detectives had started to take the law into their own hands.

Old friends indeed, Walters and Mikelis looked across the desk at each other with a joint concern suddenly coming to light –

"What about the acting superintendent?" Mikelis pried.

"In too powerful a position," Walters replied.

"But if Mr Taylor cannot be persuaded?" Mikelis pushed, knowing that this was a valid consideration.

"Then we rethink." A pause. "Anyways, how are the girls?" Walters added, not concerned enough yet over the acting superintendent to pay him much more thought.

Mikelis relaxed back into his seat. Ah, the girls. Katia is in her last year of school and busy with her GCSE's. Sophia is starting university after the summer. And Charlotte; his darling wife Charlotte. She is working hard with her wedding planning business. One day, when the girls have finished school, Mikelis will give all of this up. Russel will have to take the reins on his own, but for now? The money is too good not stay in the business. "Yes. They are good. Katia is A stars with her exams. Obviously, I am very proud."

He would do anything for his girls, even give himself over to the police if he had to. He's not sure that Russel would do the same because on the inside, he is shallow and conniving. And as for his wife? She is not much better – a stuffy lady who has no sense of humour. Not beautiful and funny like his Charlotte.

Walters asks what Katia is studying for, another cigarette is lit, another drink is poured, and the conversation goes on as if the conversation before had never happened. Just two men, business partners, having a quiet evening chat before heading back home for the night.

Mud on the Seats

Towards the end of the day, Dan was called into the gaffer's office. Nothing surprising there. Since they had lost DI Wright, Broadmeadow had been missing somebody of a more senior position to help with the day to day running of the department. It wouldn't be long before Dan himself would be preparing for a promotion to inspector; that was if the gaffer wasn't already getting him ready for more of a leadership role, which he probably was. Even though he and the gaffer hadn't actually sat down and talked about what he wanted from his career, Dan wasn't entirely sure that he wanted the step up in responsibilities. But that was a conversation for another day.

Broadmeadow looked after his team that way, always making sure that the opportunities were open to them should they wish to progress – the same went for Hollie. She was spending time with Rachael because she needed the experience of mentoring another member of staff. That way an important box would be ticked for her reaching her own goal of detective sergeant, even though she didn't exactly see it that way; honestly, the number of times she had winged about it already … and it had only been a week since Rachael had joined their team on secondment.

Paul knew though. The gaffer told him a lot of things as a trusted confidant.

Paul didn't really fancy the extra responsibilities that a promotion entailed, and it didn't bother him in the slightest that his fellow officers were moving on ahead of him. It was nice to just be coasting along, doing what he was doing. No stress. No targets to hit. Do your job, do it well, and go home at the end of the day.

The last two days had been spent looking into Mikelis Malinovska. He owned the plant hire business where Dan had seen DCI Walters. Unfortunately, as of yet, nothing stood out as untoward. But it was still early days. He was just gathering a bit of a background on the man at the moment.

A family man, Malinovska grew up in a small town in Latvia near the Lithuanian border. He travelled over to the UK as an economic migrant when he was seventeen, where he eventually gained British citizenship. From what Paul could see, after setting up a small supermarket importing and selling Eastern European foodstuffs, the enterprise had grown. At some point, and Paul was still trying to find a way of accessing the finances, Malinovska had moved down to their neck of the woods with his English wife, Charlotte, and turned his hand to the business that he ran now.

By the looks of things, he still owned the three European supermarkets in Greater London – one in Ilford, one in Romford, and one in Walthamstow. That was the same area that DCI Walters covered. Paul took note of the link. Next on his to-do list was to get a hold of his staffing records.

At which point, Hollie and Rachael returned from their day spent out in the field (literally). Still chasing illegal green laners, but to not much success. Paul quickly switched over his screen and closed his notepad upon their arrival – he was heeding the gaffer's warning not to let Rachael in on what he was investigating for the time being, due to her still being under superintendent Ackehurst's ultimate command.

What had he been up to all day then, he tried to think? Technically, he was supposed to be the 'heritage man', and there *was* a report through earlier that day of some illegal metal detecting going on near the Suffolk border that needed looking into, so he pulled up the relevant file and started to have a look into it. Hollie was assigned to the agricultural side of things, whereas Dan was being lined up to take over wildlife, however, their areas of expertise tended to all merge into one at times. Agricultural theft and damage could intertwine with heritage, and wildlife crime could fall into the category of the other two, depending on the case.

Hollie looked grumpy, with Rachel trailing along behind, who was sporting an equally reproachful look on her face as she tried to swat an excitable Chester away. They both had a caking of mud up their boots. Hollie saw him looking and shot him a glare that said, 'Don't even ask.'

Of course, he *was* going to ask.

*

"Sit down, Daniel. Sit down, make yourself comfortable," said Broadmeadow softly, beckoning Dan into his office. He still couldn't shake the feeling of thinking he had done something wrong whenever he was called up by the gaffer, even though, time and time again, there was absolutely no reason for him to suspect that the man had a single ill feeling towards him.

Entering the office as instructed, Dan wondered; did making oneself comfortable mean he should take a seat on the sofa?

Or should he pull up a chair opposite the gaffer's desk? He dithered between the two options, as Broadmeadow raised an ironic eyebrow with a signature, half-lopsided smile, "Or remain standing?"

God, he must make himself look like a right tit sometimes. Pulling up a spare chair, he swivelled it round and parked up opposite the gaffer. So far so good – it didn't look like his senior officer was about to tell him he had fucked up in one form or another. Not really much to mess up though, considering that all he'd really been up to was finishing the start of the timeline hidden in the back of the archive cupboard.

All the whiteboard contained so far were printouts of Ackehurst, Walters (he didn't like looking at that one), 'Walshy', 'Stubby', and later in the day when Paul had brought another mug shot through, Mikelis Malinovska. They were all lined up on the board with notes scrawled down underneath, like they would have done back in CID when working on a complex case.

He and Paul had then started to compile individual case files on the five men, where Dan had then become distracted from his task and started to organise the old case files in the archive cupboard. He'd enjoyed that one, as it had proved to be quite the therapeutic task.

He and the gaffer had earlier agreed that they would conduct their social media search on Ackehurst away from the office, so not to raise any suspicions should IT Central start looking into their online activity. An agreement which he was rather pleased about, because it would mean spending some more time with Broadmeadow out of hours – especially as he was now getting to the point where saying goodbye at the end of the day had started to tug uncomfortably at his heartstrings.

"I shan't keep you for too long, but I've just had an invitation come through from the Rural Crime Committee, for a member of the team to attend a wildlife crime seminar next week. Now, I know it's a wee bit short notice, but I was rather hoping that you would be able to attend on the team's behalf?" Broadmeadow said, gently approaching the subject as he always did with Dan.

"Where is it?" queried Dan, secretly hoping it would be held somewhere exciting and exotic, but also preparing himself for somewhere a little more within the constabulary's budget. It was only the people way above his paygrade that got to go to the fancier locations, like a week away in the south of France, or the Costa Del Sol, for a 'management' seminar. Funny, that, how the budget was able to stretch when the chief constables decided they needed a week away in the sun …

"It's in Scotland. Inverness, to be precise. Now, your travel and accommodation will all be paid for, whether you choose to drive up or get the train. It'll be for four days, Monday to Thursday, back to work on Friday. Does that sound ok with you, fella?"

"Have you already decided I am going then?"

"I would like you to, yes. It'll do you good Daniel, to get away from here for a few days. And it will do you good to use this as a great exercise in expanding your knowledge on the different types of wildlife crime."

"Ok sir," he quietly agreed. The gaffer wanted him to go so he wasn't going to kick up a fuss.

Three nights away didn't sound like such a bad idea, to be fair. It was just the whole 'going away somewhere new on his own' thing that made him feel a little nervous. He would have to talk to new people and make small talk with them … and all that was as long as he was feeling fit and well enough to even go in the first place, although he would actually rather die than let his gaffer down with the excuse of sickness.

Right on cue, he coughed. It was becoming less dry and more throaty, wet with a mucus in his lungs that didn't seem to want to shift. Broadmeadow eyed him, frowning slightly, as he leaned closer over his desk, "Would it help if I told you that I will be attending as well? Or would that make you even more worried than you already look?"

Dan cracked a small smile at that, "No, that makes me feel better about it, sir."

"Good. I'm pleased to hear it. Now, about tonight. Your place or mine, son?"

They could have gone back to the pub and used the Wi-Fi there, which would have been a more professional setting, but Dan understood why it may be a better idea to conduct their investigation into Ackehurst's social life somewhere more private. He wasn't complaining, anyways – having a bit of company for the evening sounded like a fantastic idea.

"You could come to mine? At least that way you will know where I live if I ever get blind drunk again and need a lift home …" Dan grinned, instantly lifted by the news that he and his gaffer would be getting a little trip away together.

"I never want to see you in that state again young man, ye' hear me?" Broadmeadow replied, grinning right back at him.

*

"So, what *did* happen to you then?" Paul sidled up next to Hollie as she washed her cup in the sink. She still had a face on her, which told him that she still wasn't over whatever had occurred out on her travels.

She checked over her shoulder to make sure they were alone, before she sighed and looked over at Paul, "Rachael. That's what."

"I'm gonna need a bit more than that, come on! What'd she do?" Paul gave her an elbow as if to nudge it out of her. Hollie could be extremely stubborn when she wanted to be.

"We stopped a couple of young men riding motocross bikes. Firstly, Rachel didn't want to get out of the car because the footpath to the byway was all churned up. Then, when she did get out of the car, she spent half her time flirting with one of them whilst I issued a warning. AND then – *then* – she put her muddy feet up on the seat when we got back in the car! *My* car!" Hollie griped animatedly in lowered tones, even more enraged now that she had blurted it all out.

"But you caught a couple of green laners?" replied Paul cautiously, trying to lighten her current mood.

She visibly deflated, turning to lean against the worktop in the small kitchenette. "Yeah, s'pose so. Not that I think a written warning will stop them doing it again."

"Next time we'll arrest them then, yeah?"

"I'm sure Rachel won't struggle to get them in the back of the car, with those fluttering eyelashes and that *'come and get it boys'* look …"

Paul laughed at that. Hollie was funny. She wasn't like other women he knew. "Hey, she might fool them but she don't fool me. You're ten times the woman she'll ever be. Anyways, if you've not got somewhere to be, wanna see what I've been up to whilst you've been out doing all the hard work?"

Hollie picked her cup back up and took Paul's from the drainer, chucking two tea bags into them. That'll be a yes, then.

Living Beyond One's Means

"Is that meant to be you, son?" Broadmeadow exclaimed – a genuine question as he screwed his face up trying to make out Dan's profile picture. Granted, it *was* an older photo, but he was sure that it still looked like him, even from a distance. Clearly this was one of the times the gaffer should have been wearing his glasses, but wasn't, because he was at Dan's house and hadn't brought them with him.

"What do you mean, 'is that meant to be me?'" Dan laughed before pausing to look more closely at the picture. It was taken in Ibiza. Dan's first holiday with a couple of mates who he no longer had much contact with – the ones who he used to hang about in the supermarket carparks with, who he was with when he got arrested that one time in his youth. He should get back in contact with them really, even if only to see how things had changed for them all since then.

Anyways, the photo. He was sat on a cliff edge, overlooking the Balearic Sea with the sun setting in the background, sunglasses covering his eyes and a stupid grin on his face as he looked towards the camera. "That was taken on my first holiday in Ibiza. Quite a long time ago now, I guess."

"Looks like you're having a good time there. It's been a wee while since I've been abroad now, I tell ye,'" the gaffer said a little wistfully as he stared at Dan's photo for a moment longer.

"Me too." Dan idly commented, his mind wandering to places warmer. Maybe he should bite the bullet and book something as a solo traveller? The trip to Scotland next week would be a bit of break for sure, but it wasn't exactly going to be a holiday because it was still work. Perhaps he and Broadmeadow could book something up together? Go on their own personal higher management seminar?

Immediately shaking that far-fetched notion out of his head, Dan typed Neil Ackehurst's name into the search bar and scanned down the results. He and the gaffer were sat side by side at his kitchen table (if it could really be called that). It only had two chairs and was barely big enough for two dinner plates.

Dan's house was small. A rented two up, two down. Buying a place of his own had been unattainable with the prices up in London, yet with his rather hasty exit from the city earlier that year he was thankful that he had never tried harder to save up for a mortgage. Now though, feeling more settled than he had done in years, he was hoping to be able to lay down some more permanent roots in the next few years – if he was careful enough with his money.

"That's him." Broadmeadow pointed at the third name down the list of other blokes called Neil Ackehurst. Dan clicked on the profile expecting it to be locked, but to his surprise, everything was available. Somebody wasn't *au fait* with the privacy options available to oneself, clearly. Was it due to arrogance, or ignorance?

It soon became apparent that Ackehurst wasn't short of money. He, unlike Dan and his gaffer, liked a foreign holiday – Italy, Greece, Thailand – and they weren't budget destinations either. They were what Dan would call 'high class', with spa treatments for him and his wife, fine dining and blissful looking pool sides.

It wasn't just the holidays though, that indicated the man's finances – from the watches that he wore to the brand new car bought for his daughter on her 21st birthday; the black tie events up in London including top tier seats at various shows and musical events, and the season ticket that he held for West Ham United with apparent access to a private box. There was somebody with Ackehurst, on the last set of photos. His back was turned, but it was unmistakable as to who it was.

"That's Walters. There." Dan jabbed his finger at the screen to reiterate his finding.

"Interesting," Broadmeadow commented as he took it all in.

Dan wondered whether what he was about to ask may seem a bit like he was overstepping a mark, but then again, it was important to their investigation, so he went ahead and asked regardless, "Would your salary cover all that, sir?"

Broadmeadow responded with an ironic snort. That was Dan's answer right there, but the gaffer was obviously in a mood for sharing; "Perhaps, at a push. But you do know that I am not on a full superintendent's salary, don't you?"

"Yeah. Sorry." Shit, Dan forgot about that.

"And Ackehurst doesn't have a rather spiteful wife to pay off as part of a divorce settlement, so I would say that it wouldn't be correct to compare my own financial situation to his. However, I will say that he does appear to have an abundance of expendable income, wouldn't you agree? And he's not afraid of showing it off, either."

The hurt in his gaffer's tone was painfully evident at the mention of his soon to be ex-wife, and it made Dan feel uncomfortable over his own feelings towards the man. Notably, Broadmeadow clearly still held onto some level of sentiment towards her, and it made him wonder where he stood in all of this.

He sincerely hoped that he wasn't just somebody there to keep the man's loneliness at bay until the divorce was completed, at which point allowing his gaffer to move on with his life. Broadmeadow must have noticed Dan's change in posture, how he sunk back down into his chair a little and tried to conceal a throaty cough, because before he knew it there was a reassuring hand coming out to rest over his knee, big and warm and setting him at ease once more.

"I wonder what his wife does?" he commented. This was almost too easy. One click away and they were onto her profile, some of it locked but enough on show to tell Dan that she worked part-time as a volunteer at a local charity for disabled children. "Only one income then," he concluded, wholly distracted now because Broadmeadow's hand was still resting upon his leg, his thumb unhurriedly running a light circular pattern around the side of his knee.

"It would appear that way, wouldn't it," added Broadmeadow, his voice kind of faraway as if he too were thinking of things other than what they were actually sitting in Dan's kitchen for.

They both stared at the screen of Dan's laptop for some time longer.

"So, what are we thinking then, sir? That Ackehurst is making money on the side somehow?"

"Hm? Oh, yes." Broadmeadow stirred, releasing his hold upon Dan's knee as though suddenly coming to his senses. Every time they got close it seemed; close to something further than an innocent bit of physical contact, the gaffer was always there at the last minute to halt anything more from happening.

Dan's black dog started to stir once more. His lungs constricted, trying to fight it off. Realistically, Dan understood. The man was his boss; a senior figure who should know better than to be chasing after one of his subordinates. That was without mentioning the other dark cloud – whereas seeking a relationship with a colleague wasn't actually against official guidance, a relationship with a senior officer was a kind of murky grey area where terms like 'conflict of interest' and 'ethics' and 'abuse of one's position' came into play. They would have to seek guidance from higher up the chain of command, where even then, it would be likely that either himself or Broadmeadow would end up having to be reassigned to another department.

Dan didn't want that. He believed they were both professional enough to maintain a fair working relationship, but he wasn't so sure what others would have to say about that. He didn't want to cause ill feelings between himself, Hollie and Paul. He didn't want to be the butt of all jokes around the wider station, that he was (theoretically) shagging his much older, same sexed boss …

"We have proved our suspicions that Ackehurst is living above his current means, and that he is on very friendly terms with DCI Walters," Broadmeadow finally concluded after a prolonged period of silence.

"Who we now know is dealing with this Mikelis fella – wait – there's something missing here …" Dan added, brain cells now firing at a rate of knots.

"Kyle Walsh?"

"Yeah." Dan wracked his brains trying to find a link, and then it came to him; "When Ryan Mitchell was stabbed, Ackehurst's team detained somebody with no prior who confessed to it, but didn't go any further as to where the drugs came from in the first place. And when I was spiked by Walshy's cousin – I'm guessing because Walshy saw me when he was collecting commercial waste for illegal dumping, and was trying to deploy some sort of scare tactic, Ackehurst initially wasn't willing to take the case any further – not until we took matters into our own hands. My guess is that Walshy is either working for Ackehurst, or he's working for this Mikelis bloke."

"Or both," Broadmeadow replied soberly; "Before DI Wright was killed, I don't know if you know fella, but we had just completed a successful raid on a large cannabis farming operation. There were two locations. One, which Paul went to – Flax Farm, I think it was called – anyways, by the time he got there, it was abandoned. The other, which DI Wright led a team on, came up trumps. Over half a million pounds worth of cannabis growing there. One week later, Callum was dead. Ackehurst's team were in charge of the investigation, but it never came to anything. No suspects, no witnesses. A tragic accident."

Both men fell into another silence. This was far bigger and a lot more complicated than what they had initially set out to investigate.

Broadmeadow let out a long sigh and leaned back into his seat, "Which leads me to believe that Mikelis Malinovska is at the middle of all this – possibly then too. These fellas are all working together to form some sort of drugs empire, that's my bet."

"My last case under Walters – that was a drugs raid, as you already know. The biggest of its kind in years. Except, at every step of the way, whenever we got close to making the final raid, Walters kept throwing a spanner in the works. Even up to the last minute, when the dawn strike was postponed by five hours due to some mystery 'intelligence' …"

"All makes sense now, eh?"

"Sir?"

"Yes, son?"

"What do we do now? Surely we need to report all of this to an anti-corruption agency?" concluded Dan as he looked to his side and searched Broadmeadow's face for guidance.

"I'll have to – hang on a second …" Broadmeadow reached down to his trouser pocket and pulled out his phone, which was insistently vibrating with an incoming call. The gaffer wasn't quick enough with hiding the caller ID before swiping open the call. Bringing the phone to his ear, at the same time getting up from the kitchen table, he apologetically looked back at Dan. "Excuse me a minute, son."

The black dog growled inside of him as Dan was left sitting there alone with his laptop, his stomach churning as the growl turned into a cackling laugh, which imitated that of a hyena. It was mocking him, and the unfortunate timing of the gaffer's wife deciding now was a good time to pay him a call. Doubling forwards, Dan found himself wrapped in the throes of a nasty coughing fit, unable to control his spasming chest as his lungs expelled a spattering of dark, stringy mucous onto the kitchen table.

Hastily, he jumped to his feet, grabbed a wad of kitchen roll and wiped the tabletop clean before coughing up again into the soiled towel. At that point, Dan really was starting to worry that something inside of him was seriously wrong …

Free

"Excuse me a minute, son," he exclaimed apologetically, as he sharply pushed back his chair and got up in a bid to be out of earshot should Rowena start shouting down the phone at him. Marcus felt terrible for having to answer a call from his soon to be ex-wife in front of wee Danny – principally so because the lad had clearly seen that it was her on the caller ID. Any other time and he would have ignored it, but on this occasion, he knew exactly why she was gracing him with her verbal presence.

"Where are you?" was the first thing she said, and she didn't sound best pleased. Not shouting yet though. Small mercies.

"I'm not home at the moment," Marcus replied sheepishly, knowing exactly what connotations that statement implied. Rowena knew that he didn't have a large social circle. She also knew that he did his food shop on a Monday night – tonight was Thursday – and if he were still at work then he would have said as much.

"Well, I'm at the house. So I suggest that you get back here as soon as you can, whatever it is you're up to right now," Rowena clipped, her tone implying everything that he feared she would, which wasn't fair. Not at all. Even if he was out doing what she seemed to think he was doing, who was she to stop him? They were separated. Soon to be permanently. Was she really trying to retain control over his life like that, even now after all that had been said and done? Unbelievable.

"Alright, love. I'll be home soon," Marcus said before hanging up the phone. Still, the old worn endearment, *love*, fell from his lips, quietly and out of earshot of Daniel – some habits proving too hard to break even though the sentiment behind them was long deceased. Going back to the kitchen, Marcus inwardly cringed as he had hung up on Rowena before she could hang up on him. Daniel was looking at him all wide-eyed, still seated at the table. "I'm sorry son, but I'm going to have to go."

He could see all manner of emotions behind those soft dark eyes. Gods, he didn't want to leave him, wishing he had the strength left inside of him to just say *no* to Rowena's demands. But he didn't. She still had a hold over him as much as it pained him to admit it.

"Ok. You alright, sir?" Daniel replied, his tone quiet with disappointment.

"Yes, I'm ok. That was the wife, in case you hadn't noticed, which I think you did. I have to go and see what she wants. I'd rather not though, would rather stay here with you, you understand that, don't you Danny?"

And when had Daniel started to become 'Danny'? He'd have to watch that one; not call him that when they were at work. And he didn't miss the way that the second slipped endearment of the evening caused a small smile to appear at the corner of the lad's lips (a slipped endearment that, this time, was not without a heartfelt sentiment).

Daniel shut down his laptop and got up, now hovering in the peripheral. It was just like the goodbye at the pub the other evening, except for this time, the circumstances behind Marcus' departure weren't so amenable. He'd been hoping for at least a couple more hours of the lad's company, full of notions of them retiring to the living room after finishing delving into superintendent Ackehurst's personal life, and having a nice, relaxed finish to the evening. He'd also noticed on his way through to the kitchen that Daniel only had one sofa, which meant there would be no option but to sit together on there, had they have made it that far.

But alas, this evening was not destined to be theirs.

"I'll see you out?" Daniel stepped past him, leading the way out to the hallway. He hovered again whilst Marcus sat down on the stairs and did up his shoes, before checking his pockets for phone and keys.

"Right, well. I'll be off then."

"Yeah, ok."

"I am sorry."

"I know. I understand. Really," was the subdued reply from his sergeant. Marcus could see that Daniel meant it. Such a good lad, he was. So full of empathy, always.

Before he consciously knew what he was doing, Marcus was reaching out for the lad's hands and pulling them towards him, noticing briefly that there was a strange dark mark smeared across his sleeve that wasn't there before. Dismissing it at something inconsequential – a leaked biro? – he stepped forwards into the vacant space between them, where his lips found Daniel's forehead, just below the hairline of his brow.

Breathing quietly, taking in his scent, Daniel leaned his head down to gently rest against his chest with their hands still lightly clasped together. "Good night, son," Marcus murmured, his voice catching, knowing that it was now time for him to leave.

*

Rowena was already inside when Marcus arrived home. He wasn't as petty as to have changed the locks, or to have insisted that she turned over her key to the front door. Taking a deep breath, hesitant to enter his own home, he cracked open the front door. This felt rather akin to a time now in the past, when coming back later than expected would send his tail between his legs, carefully treading every word and movement in anticipation of the inevitable verbal lashing.

She was in the kitchen. He saw her before she saw him. She was going through the pile of unopened post on the worktop, turning when he dropped his keys down on the side next to the microwave. "Where were you then?" was the first thing she said, her eyes sending out a cold frost.

"I was out. With a colleague."

"A *colleague?* I see."

"Yes. My wee sergeant, Daniel. Work stuff. I shan't elaborate as I know how it bores you."

An argument was brewing, Marcus could feel it. They had been here before, time and time again. Did she believe him? Probably not. Which led them straight towards the sole reason why she had travelled the five hundred and fifty miles south to grace him with her presence; "Why haven't you signed the papers yet?"

"Because, having read them, I believe some of your statements to be untrue. Come on now, Desertion?

Adultery? Where has all this come from, now?" Marcus felt his voice raise to a slightly higher pitch, finding safety against the worktop when he leaned back against it and folded his arms, intrigued to hear what these claims were actually based upon.

"You tell me, Marcus. Do you really expect me to believe that you were simply 'working late' all those evenings you didn't show up 'till gone nine? And I think that counts as desertion too, don't you? Christmas. Every damned year, for *thirty years* – not once, did you think to let one of your team cover it! You never came home with me. Not once. It's the least you could have done, especially as you couldn't … you couldn't even give me a child!"

Silence rung through the kitchen. Why now? Why had she never spoken to him about how unhappy she was, choosing instead to leave it all bottled up to the point of the glass shattering around her? Marcus wasn't stupid, and he wasn't emotionally stunted – he'd known for a long time that things weren't right between them, but he wasn't blessed with the powers of psychic intervention either. If somebody continuously gave you the silent treatment then how were you supposed to read between the lines?

"We looked at other options, for a wee bairn," he said quietly, his anger fizzling away to a deep-seated ache within his heart.

"We did. And I could see that your heart wasn't truly on board."

"That's not true. I would have done anything for you. *Anything*, to make you happy." True, the pull towards raising child was never as strong as Rowena's – he was able to find contentment in the hand he had been dealt – but he wasn't lying when he said that he would have done anything within his power to give her what she wanted.

"A bit late for that now, don't you think?" Rowena prodded, unable to let the subject go. She was trying to push him so hard that he snapped. Marcus wasn't having it. Not this time.

"Child or not, that was a very long time ago. And it doesn't lead to any truth in the accusation of adultery. I never – *never* – looked the way of another. I stuck to my vows under the eyes of our Lord. I'll tell you what I think," Marcus pushed back from the worktop and took a step towards Rowena, wondering where, exactly, that darling, righteously fierce young woman he had chased all those years ago had gone, "I think, that you are willing to throw any denunciation possible at me, because that way, your settlement will be greater. Now, I am willing to give you half of everything I have worked my whole life for, you would have received that regardless, but I will *not* come out of this as a man who has truly done you wrong."

Rowena stepped forwards too with a nasty, scheming glint behind her eyes; "Are you threatening me, Marcus?"

"No! God, no. Just – don't you think you've taken enough from me already, without taking my pride along as well?"

Rowena backed down as soon as she saw that she had succeeded, subtly resting a hand over the rise of her stomach. She'd hit Marcus where it really hurt. A peculiar feeling settled over her, over how this might actually be the last time she was to ever lay eyes upon him, and funny how she didn't feel a single shred of remorse over that fact. Did that make her a bad person? Certainly. Marcus never really did anything on the scale that she was insinuating. He did try to be a good husband, but there was just something about how *nice* he was, how *hopeless* he was, that had always rubbed her up the wrong way.

Besides, her partner, Robert, was waiting at the hotel in town for her to return with an outcome not only of a signed divorce paper, but a healthy financial backing to her name in order for them to start their new life.

Robert, who she had been seeing for near-on five years now. Robert, who had, despite her age, given her his fertile seed. She was finally going to get everything she ever wanted. "I want you to sell the house. The market is good right now. You'll have to cover the financial support I will be set to lose too, seeing as you are the sole earner. And your pension. Half."

Marcus sighed, defeated. "Fine. Amend the papers to an irretrievable breakdown of the marriage and I will sign. Now, will you please just leave me be?" Marcus gave in, like he knew he always would. Any remaining fight within him was gone. He just wanted it to all be over, regardless of the cost.

She left soon after without another word. She had what she wanted. Marcus took a stiff breath. That was it. Over. Done. In a few days' time, he would be free of her forever. Free too, to pursue the desires his heart was truly leading him towards, like a small, shining light guiding him out of a wall of darkness.

Good Boy

Chester took up his usual spot when the sun was shining – under the window where the slatted blinds cast a square of elongated bands of light across the carpet. Once Paul let him off his lead he had headed straight there and flopped onto his side to have a quick snooze before the day really got going. He slept more than he used to, the pull stronger than ever now to just take life a little slower. He was tired, his limbs unable to support him for very long before they grew heavy and in need of rest. It felt like a natural change of pace for Chester. It didn't worry him all that much, that he couldn't do what he used to be able to do, that his walks in the morning were getting shorter and that he needed help getting in and out of the car some days.

Paul took him to see a vet last week. He didn't like going to see the vet – but then again, what dog did? It didn't scare him, going there, but he didn't like the smell of the place; full of the echoes of so many other fellow companions that had come and never left, prevalent to his extremely sensitive nose. The nurse Paul took him to see was nice though. She gave him these tiny little treats for being a good boy. And these bigger treats, that weren't really treats, that Paul had to hide inside rolls of sliced ham or cheese to get him to eat. Chester would have taken them without, because the big treats made the ache in his back legs go away, but Paul didn't need to know that – if he wanted to give Chester extra helpings of human food then he wasn't going to turn his nose up at that.

Last night, Paul had been happy. Usually, he would send silly messages to Emily (Emily, who still wasn't interested in his advances), yet Chester could sense that his feelings of wanting to mate with her were starting wane. Things felt warmer and more comfortably companionable between them, especially since Emily had met somebody. A solicitor for those who couldn't or wouldn't pay for their own, apparently, who was called up to Vancouver Road on quite a regular basis to represent some of the more unsavoury suspects brought down to the cells. Anyways, Paul wasn't sending messages to Emily last night, because he was sending messages to Hollie.

Paul felt very protective over Hollie, even though Chester knew she was more than capable of looking after herself. More so than Paul was, certainly. There was cup of tea, courtesy of Paul, waiting on Hollie's desk for when she arrived – which would be in about eight minutes.

At that point, and later than usual, Dan arrived. He still wasn't feeling very well. The black dog was making him sick, and Chester wished that he could do something about it. At first, when the black dog had disappeared, Chester didn't understand what was happening. Dan took on a scary new demeanour where everything about him was intimidating, and it made Chester want to defend himself and the people around him. Then he realised where the black dog had gone – it was hiding. It felt threatened.

Dan was now feeling happier though, because the gaffer was treating him like a good boy, and the black dog was struggling to maintain control. That's why it had made its way inside, where it could be closer to Dan. But it was making Dan sick. His body was trying to cough it out, but it didn't seem to be working …

He should go and see the human vet – '*the doctor*' – maybe they could give him a treat like Chester was given, to make him feel better?

He gave Dan a courteous thump of the tail as he passed towards his desk, then slipped off into a doze. The morning sun was warm against his coat, the season now well and truly turned towards the summer. When he woke, the sun through the window had grown too hot for his liking – when one is all black, it's harder to tolerate too much heat.

Dan was busy at his computer, presumably because he wasn't going to be here next week. He was going to Scotland with the gaffer. Hollie was in with the gaffer, also presumably because she was being left in charge next week – something about her working towards a promotion. Paul had wandered off somewhere. It was nearing lunch time, so he had probably gone down to one of the takeaways to bring food back for the team, as was customary on a Friday.

Before, Chester would have insisted on going with him. Now, it wasn't that he couldn't be bothered, but Paul had told him to stay behind. He was worried about his health, insisting to him that he needed to rest. Chester wasn't sick, he wanted to tell him; he was just slowing down a bit.

The whole day was a bit slow, actually. The team were working on a 'secret' investigation that they weren't allowed to talk about around Rachael, but other than that, nothing exciting was going on. Speaking of Rachael – she was currently heading over towards him. He could sense that she was a little nervous around him, like a dog had been bad towards her in the past. He wasn't bad though. He was good. He raised his head to greet her, but she averted her gaze and carried on towards Paul's desk.

What was she doing?

Dan wasn't paying any attention – he had his earphones in and was totally engrossed in whatever he was doing.

Chester got up to his feet, slowly, finishing with a long stretch and a yawn. Hopefully Paul would bring him back something nice to eat. He padded over to where Rachael was scanning over the mess that constituted Paul's desk, nosing up against her hand to let her know that he was there. He wasn't sure about her, but it may just be because the rest of the team weren't sure about her, and he was picking up on that. She didn't seem nasty, or anything like that, but she did give off a scent of somebody who was a little on edge.

"Go away, Chester," she muttered, not looking at him as her attention was still entirely focused on trying to find something atop of Paul's desk. That was rather rude, he had to admit. Not obeying her order, because he didn't have to – she wasn't his human – he nudged his nose harder against her hand, huffing out a displeased breath as he did.

"Really?" she tutted, trying to swat him away without causing too much of a scene. Chester wasn't having that. No. She was up to something. Drawing in a deep breath he barked, loudly, deep and chesty. Rachael flinched, stopping what she was doing and quickly reaching for Paul's cup like that was all she was looking for in the first place. Chester didn't buy it. Dan looked up from his computer, pulling one ear bud out and frowning over at the disturbance.

"Everything alright over there?" questioned Dan. Chester looked his way, letting out a low whine. Dan patted his leg. "Come here, boy."

"Just doing a drinks round – do you want one?" Rachael chimed, holding up Paul's cup to prove that nothing untoward was going on.

Now that Chester and Dan were friends again, he was happy to heed the offer of a bit of fuss for being a good boy. He would have to keep a closer eye on Rachael, especially with Dan and the gaffer away from the office next week. At that point, Paul returned with food and normal service resumed. It smelled like chips, from the chip shop. He excitedly wagged his tail as he trotted over to greet his human, nosing up into the bag in Paul's hand trying to find his battered sausage …

Eighteen Holes

"Wow … is this really the right place?"

After an exceedingly long journey in the car – it had taken them the best part of a day to get up here – Dan couldn't contain his disbelief over the looming country house coming into view.

Although he had looked it up prior to their departure, Chatham Manor Golf Course and Spa looked even fancier in the flesh. A massive, brown stoned house with big pillars lining the façade, immersed in the lush grounds of an eighteen-hole golf course under the backdrop of the sombre grey mountains to the south. Looking north was the Moray Firth, its great waves rippling in the distance below the clifftop that the grounds were set upon.

Marcus laughed over Daniel's amazement. Not only now, but ever since they had passed the border of the North, when he had seen the lad gazing out of the passenger side window for hours at a time, completely fixated on how the land around them was no longer flat. These were the lands in which Marcus grew up upon, yet still, he was not immune to the rugged beauty of his home soil, able to share with Daniel some of that childlike wonder.

"It is. Although I think the seminar may be in a separate conference area. I came here as a wee child you know – it used to be a private house open to visitors before they turned it into a resort."

"You'll have to show me where you grew up. Was it close to here?" said Dan as the gaffer swung around into the already packed car park.

"Aye, it was." Marcus could count on one hand the number of times he'd been back here in the last thirty years. Every excuse under the sun not to return home for longer than he had to.

Something in his heart told him that now was the time though, like this seminar was being held in the North-East of Scotland solely for his own facing of the past. And it felt different to be here with Daniel – like it wasn't so painful to be revisiting a place that held so much regret for a younger version of the man he was now. "Right. Shall we get going?"

The main entrance to the hotel was busy, where Dan found himself clinging close to his gaffer's side as they waited in line to check in. Broadmeadow greeted a few people, presumably other officers that he had brushed shoulders with over his long career. Some were dressed in uniform which made it easy to distinguish their senior ranks, whilst others, like Broadmeadow, were donning a more casual attire. He still couldn't quite get over seeing his gaffer in plain clothes, even if his dress sense was leaning towards the more conservative side of things, with his straight legged jeans and plain buttoned shirt, with an equally plain sweater over the top. He pulled it off well though, Dan thought. Kind of stylish in his own way.

As they reached the front of the queue, Dan hung back and let Broadmeadow do the talking. "Marcus Broadmeadow and Daniel Taylor – Norfolk Constabulary."

The lady behind the desk gave them a look up and down, before cheerfully exclaiming; "Ooh, you two are a long way from *hame!* Let me have a wee look ..." she said as she tapped away at the keyboard under the desk, before her face visibly fell.

"Everything alright there, lassie?" Broadmeadow enquired, leaning over on the desk.

She frowned at the computer screen, tapping away again before shaking her head, "Looks like there's been a double booking on the system, fellas. I'm really sorry but we only have one room under your names."

She peered at them both with her head slightly cocked, clearly hoping that the two police officers weren't going to kick up a fuss over the clerical error. Dan's heart leapt up to his throat. He wasn't – they couldn't – could they? It brought on a bout of coughing that he tried to keep concealed behind his hand.

"Are you sure? Is that really all you have now?" Broadmeadow sounded mildly panicked by the news. Dan couldn't blame him. He was mildly panicked too.

"I'm sorry. We can offer you are free round on the course as a goodwill gesture?"

*

"A free round on the golf course? Really?" Broadmeadow huffed under his breath as he stuck the key card into the door of their room for the next three nights. Trying the handle, the door didn't budge. He tried again, the little light on the electronic lock flashing red and buzzing at him defiantly. "*Bollocks* to ye' then – Danny, give me a wee hand with this, will you?"

Dan quietly laughed to himself at the gaffer's growing frustration. He'd never seen the man so flustered. Taking the key card from his hand, he slipped it into the lock and held it there for a second. Lo and behold, the light flashed green and entry to the room was gained.

The room was large. Tall windows and plush carpet, dark wood furniture and a corniced ceiling. And the bathroom. Just look at that fucking bath in all its roll-topped, golden lion footed glory. Dan, standing there for a minute and taking it all in, then headed straight towards the sofa bed under the window and dumped his bag on top of it. "You have the bed, sir. I'm smaller than you."

Broadmeadow grunted something that sounded like approval before setting his own bag down. This was far from ideal. Slowly making their way towards each other in their own space and time was one thing, but having such close quarters forced upon them was quite another. Dan could sense his gaffer's discomfort over the arrangement, which in turn made him feel all jittery, hyper aware of every move he made, even down to his breathing – was he breathing too loudly?

He coughed, causing the black dog to squirm inside of him. "There's a dinner thing tonight, are we going?" he said, once he'd cleared his throat and caught his breath.

"I suppose we should, yes. Are you ok with that?"

"Yeah. 'S fine." It wasn't fine, really. Dan couldn't think of anything worse than a large room filled with people that he didn't know. The mere notion of it filled him with absolute dread. If it were up to him, an evening spent in the privacy of his room, probably with a takeaway, would be the option he would have gone for. He was here to expand his knowledge on the lesser-known branches of wildlife crime, not to be making new acquaintances with people he was never going to see or speak to again.

At the thought of having to face a difficult social situation that evening, the black dog started to claw at his insides, to the point of a mild nausea.

Broadmeadow was busying himself with unpacking his clothes into one of chests of drawers. Draped over the bed was his dress uniform. Dan eyed it from his perch on the sofa bed, intrigued as to whether he was going to get to see the gaffer wearing it. Now, that was a nice thought that he would like to see followed through …

At that moment, Broadmeadow turned and caught him staring at his hat and jacket, raising a single eyebrow with an amused look on his face; "You did bring some smart clothes, didn't ye' lad? It says in the programme there – there's a wee bit of an event on the last night."

"I did bring a shirt and trousers, yeah." Dan looked down at the programme he was handed along with an ID badge back at the front desk. Broadmeadow was right; *'Dinner and Entertainment, 7pm onwards. Guest speaker, 'Julie Grey'.* Great. More forced socialising. And who was Julie Grey? Although again, if it meant getting to see Broadmeadow in all his finery then he could possibly be swayed …

He leafed through the agenda for the seminar. Although none of it was obligatory, he did see a couple of talks and workshops that looked quite interesting. On the other hand, some of them looked downright dreadful: 'An overview of data and statistics with reference to the impact of the relocation of protected plants' – no thank you. And it was scheduled in for three hours … he knew that Broadmeadow liked plants however, so he could only hope that the gaffer had somehow overlooked it.

"See anything you like the look of?" the gaffer asked, seemingly having relaxed a little as he sat down on the bed, facing him, his long legs hanging over the edge.

"There's a talk on illegal hare coursing. That one looks good."

"May I?" Broadmeadow reached over and took the programme from Dan's hands, "Hm, yes. That one does look interesting. There's one about protected plants tomorrow morning – shall I book us onto that one as well?"

Dan internally rolled his eyes, but managed to keep his face externally neutral with a feign of slight interest. "Yeah, sure."

To be honest, if it interested his gaffer then he was willing to endure the inevitable boredom. He slouched back into his cot, the early start and long car journey catching up with him. Broadmeadow had showed up outside his house at 6am that morning, and it was now just gone 6pm – and that had been a good run, apparently.

"Are you feeling alright there, son?" Broadmeadow enquired, leaning closer until his arms were resting upon his elbows, the programme forgotten, dangling down within a pair of loose hands between his legs.

Dan stifled a cough. It was getting worse. He feared that it wasn't just the tiredness that was taking over his body, even though he had been trying his best pretend that all was well. "Yeah, just … I think I might be coming down with something, sir."

"That cough of yours has been causing you a wee bit of bother, hasn't it? Don't think I hadn't noticed. How about you have a nice bath? And if you're not feeling up for going down tonight then you can stay here and get some rest – I'll get you some room service sent up, hm? Sound good to you?" soothed the gaffer, his words soft and kind. Dan wanted to ask him to stay up here with him, but he knew that wasn't fair. Broadmeadow was here to represent their department, and he couldn't expect the man to cater over his sorry arse, just because he was feeling a bit under the weather.

Dan groaned as he straightened himself back up, about to do as he was told and go and get the bath running, when he was waved back down, "Halt yourself, fella. You stay there, I'll sort it."

As Broadmeadow unfolded himself and got up to his unfeasibly large feet, in passing, he clapped a warm hand over Dan's knee, where the feeling of it lingered long after he had departed in the direction of the bathroom.

When Marcus returned later that evening – not too late, mind – he found young Daniel exactly where he had left him. He hadn't even undressed or pulled the sofa bed out, seemingly having fallen asleep in his clothes after his bath, finished plate of ordered in food on the floor at his feet.

Marcus observed him for a drawn-out moment. It would be so easy for him to just pull the lad up into his arms and carry him over to the bed, where he himself would be sleeping – but he didn't. That wouldn't be right of him. So instead, lovingly, he reached for the blankets and tucked them in around his sleeping sergeant. Daniel stirred, balling himself up tight, sighing quietly as Marcus leaned down to lay the briefest ghost of lips against his temple.

Schedule 8 of the Wildlife and Countryside Act 1981 (As Amended)

"Could you at least try and look like you're paying attention?" Marcus muttered between his teeth, flitting his eyes down disapprovingly to the phone in Daniel's hands between his knees. Undeniably, the talk on protected plants wasn't quite what had been initially anticipated, but that didn't give Daniel license to so blatantly turn his attention elsewhere, even if he was still feeling under the weather.

They were surrounded by Marcus' peers and even by officers more senior than himself. The speaker was slowly droning on about the finer points of 'Schedule 8 of the Wildlife and Countryside Act 1981 (As Amended)'. He'd never seen so many variations of coloured graphs crammed onto one projected slide.

Perhaps he had made a misjudgement on this one, as even he had to admit that somebody or other relocating some bluebells *(Hyacinthoides non-scripta)* from one woodland to another on the other side of the road, back in the mid-nineteen eighties, didn't make for the most riveting of accounts. He looked at his watch. They were only an hour in.

Around the half-filled conference room, there were many glazed expressions, and twice as many others also resorting to other means of entertainment, such as phones in laps, with some officers even with their laptop computers out (who were definitely not using them for taking notes). To his left, a fella was scrawling an intricate, methodical pattern across the lines of his notebook. Marcus watched the tip of his biro moving for a long entrancing moment, observing the black ink mark out the next swirling impression against the page. Sitting at the row in front, a female officer's head lolled down before jerking back up with a start.

Yet, the speaker relentlessly droned on despite his clearly faltering audience.

"You can't tell me that you're actually finding this interesting, sir?" Dan muttered back, nonetheless still putting his phone back into his pocket. Truthfully, he would rather be clawing his eyes out with a teaspoon than sitting here and listening to two more hours of this.

Marcus leaned in close as not to make his words publicly known; "It's not the most enthralling speech I've ever listened to, I will admit that."

Dan shivered, hairs on end at the feel of his gaffer's breath and the curl of his accentuated accent so close against his ear. Was it just him, or did Broadmeadow sound more *Scottish* since they had arrived yesterday?

"You wait 'till he gets to Schedule 9, sir. That's where it will really start to get good," whispered Dan with the start of a cheeky smile gracing his lips.

That was it. Marcus wasn't sure what came over him, but he found himself descending into a stifled fit of laughter. Lowering his head, he muffled it into his hand until it passed. "Quiet, you." He nudged Daniel into silence, aware of a head or two turning their way at the whispered commotion they were causing.

Two hours in, and Daniel started to fidget. Marcus had to admit, this was getting a bit much now – and he had sat through his fair share of skin-crawlingly boring meetings in his time for comparison. This was definitely up there as one of the worst. "One hour to go, fella," he tried his best to reassure Daniel that it was nearly over; that he only had to sit there for a wee while longer.

All he got in response was a discontented huff as Daniel slouched down into his chair and folded his arms about his chest. Marcus' stomach growled. It was drawing on into lunchtime. Schedule 9 never materialised because Schedule 8 was now going into the most intricate of details. His mind started to wander back to that morning ...

In the wee hours before sunrise, he had woken to the sound of Daniel having a fight with the blankets that he'd so carefully tucked around him the night before. At first he'd thought that the lad had just woken prematurely after such an early night. However, when he had raised himself up in bed to squint across at what was going on, he could see that Daniel was caught within the throes of a nightmare. The blankets were balled up and tangled around his feet as he twisted, clutching at his chest; *"No ... leave me alone ... get out ... please ..."*

When the nightmare seemed to persist, Marcus had sighed, getting out of bed in just his t-shirt and pants to see if he could ease the situation. Daniel's eyes had flown open as he'd stood over the lad – not their usual dark hazel, but clouded as if he were blind, whites flaring.

Daniel cowered back at the sight of him, his arms coming up to his face in a defensive move. Taken aback, Marcus firmly told him to wake up, yet to no avail, as Daniel continued to mumble; *"Please ... I don't want to ... don't ..."*

Slowly, Marcus edged himself down onto the sofa bed. The poor boy started coughing so he took a hold of his shoulders and set him onto his side, worried that he was about to be sick.

"Easy now, fella. Easy now …" he soothed, performing a rhythmic, circular motion at his back which seemed to ease the fit of coughing. He noticed, as he looked down at the lad in the dim light of the early morning, that there appeared to be a clouding of dark mucus spattered across Daniel's lips and chin; like the residual vapour of a spray paint, a faint mist clouding out of his mouth and nose every time he exhaled.

Must be a trick of the light, he concluded, rationally.

Still, he wiped away at Daniel's chin with the back of his hand. It tingled as the strange substance fizzled against his skin before evaporating away into thin air. He waited until the lad settled once more before lightly draping the blankets back over him and retiring back to his own bed. Sleep didn't come though. He couldn't relax, unable to take one eye away from Daniel.

When morning did arrive, Daniel didn't mention anything, so Marcus kept what had happened to himself. It left him wondering if the night scares were a common occurrence, or whether it was purely because the lad had woken somewhere strange, caught up in a fever that he was stubbornly trying to fight …

Back to the talk on Schedule 8, and Marcus looked across at Daniel to find that his eyes had dropped shut. He didn't have the heart to force him back awake. Half of the room was already asleep anyways, so it wasn't like he was the only one.

Eventually, when it finally did come to an end (with a muted applause courtesy of the remaining conscious attendees), Marcus and Dan headed straight for the main hall where a buffet lunch was being served. The talk had gone on for an additional half-hour longer than its scheduled slot, which meant there wasn't much in the way of food left by the time they got there. Dan picked at his egg and cress sandwich. The crust had gone dry. "I think I need a week off after that, sir."

"I am sorry, fella. I have to admit, I didn't expect it to be that *in-depth*," Broadmeadow said as he gave Dan an apologetic smile. They had found a table near the edge of the room – what once would have been a grand ballroom for high class social events of a time gone by, with its wood-panelled walls adorned with paintings and shields, to its high vaulted ceiling and its rich oak floor. Dan imagined being in the middle of a rowdy evening event, the ballroom filled with ladies in period style dresses who were gathered together in small clusters, and loud Scottish men in kilts, telling tales of hunting exploits over spilling tumblers of whisky.

At that point, as he was deciding whether he actually did want to eat his egg and cress sandwich or whether he could hold out until dinner, and mid-daydream over his upper-class hunting party, a stout looking man waddled his way over to their table. Within his fat little hands was a plate stacked high with sandwiches and finger-food.

"Well I'll be – Marcus Broadmeadow, is that you, ye' old bastard?" the man excitedly exclaimed.

Dan glanced from the man to his gaffer, seeing something falter behind his eyes before his face fell into a wide smile, "Alastair! Long time no see, how are ye'?"

Apparently that was enough for Alastair to pull out a chair and plant himself down at their table. Dan had never seen somebody so stereotypically Scottish. If you could dress him up with a kilt and a set of bagpipes, he would have fitted right in on the set of a film about the Jacobite rising. "And who are you, wee laddie?" he directed towards Dan whilst stuffing a sausage roll into his mouth.

"Detective sergeant Daniel Taylor. Broadmeadow is my gaffer," he dutifully replied, not knowing whether to address Alastair as a 'sir' or not, as he wasn't in uniform so he couldn't guess his rank. Although, judging by his age, and that he knew the gaffer, he could assume that he was probably far senior to himself.

A stubby hand, covered in pastry flake remnants, came out across the table for Dan to shake. "Well, nice to meet you, son. Marcus may not have told you about me, but we passed out together, didn't we Marcus? Those were the days, eh? Walking the streets of Inverness, clearing up the *nad's* on a Saturday night?"

Something wistful crossed the podgy man's face at the memory. Dan could only guess as to what a 'nad' was supposed to be.

"Aye. All in the past now," Broadmeadow replied, taking on a more sombre stance. Dan knew his gaffer, and could tell that he wasn't really in the mood to reminisce.

"What happened to ye', anyways? One minute you were there, next you were gone, hightailing it for the land of the English," Alaistair jovially pushed, clearly unable to see Broadmeadow's growing discomfort over the line of conversation. Dan looked down again at his sandwich.

"Just needed a change of scenery, old fella. The pay was better down south," the gaffer replied bluntly.

Dan just knew that wasn't the whole truth of the matter; he could sense very strongly that his gaffer was holding back from something. His body language screamed of it. Dan himself had never thought to ask why Broadmeadow had left home so early on in life, although he wasn't so dissimilar himself, he thought, having been desperate to get away from his own home county as soon as the opportunity had arisen. Funny though, how Broadmeadow never mentioned home, as if he had cut his ties with the place many years prior, until it no longer became a place he spared any thought for.

They politely talked a while longer over how both Broadmeadow and Alastair both fell into their own respective Rural Crime Departments, although Dan could feel his gaffer's discomfort every time the conversation steered towards family life or matters of a more personal kind. He stayed quiet for the most part, finishing his sandwich but leaving behind the crusts.

The talk on illegal hare coursing was coming up that afternoon, which was a welcome respite when the time came around for them to make haste and say their goodbyes to Alastair. Dan could only hope that the workshop was going to be a bit more interesting than the last, only realising as they left that he never did find out what the strange little man's rank was.

Something told him that he wasn't going to, judging by Broadmeadow's obvious reluctance to connect with his policing past. And something told him too that they wouldn't be bumping into Alastair again if his gaffer had anything to do with it.

Dan didn't mind that at all, he decided – not if it meant that he got spend the rest of the seminar with his commanding officer all to himself.

Operation Brown Horse

Looking after a team of two wasn't proving to be that hard, really. And on the plus-side – Hollie could leave Rachael under the care of Paul because she had important management duties to attend to. She wasn't required to attend any meetings on the gaffer's behalf as her rank did not allow for it, and knowing that sitting at his screen via a video link did constitute the majority of his working day, she found herself left with the time to start compiling the individual files on their line of covert targets.

Broadmeadow and Dan had briefed her and Paul last Friday afternoon. They needed a strong enough case built up before approaching the Professional Standards Unit for a full investigation, and she was determined to make some headway before the pair of senior officers returned from Scotland.

A call came through that morning over a string of equine equipment thefts overnight, out towards the Waveney Valley, so she had promptly sent Paul and Rachael off to conduct further investigations. It was over an hour's drive away so she anticipated that they would be away from the office until at least after lunch, which gave her plenty of time to start compiling all of the information they had so far with regards to DCI Walters and his wider web of alleged corruption.

Chester lay at her feet. The old boy was getting on a bit now, his muzzle greying and his eyes starting to cloud, spending most of his time sleeping rather than bouncing about the office and causing general chaos with his wide-reaching tail.

Starting with DCI Walters, Hollie typed up into bullet points everything that they knew so far. Perhaps a flow chart would be better? The more that she delved into it, the links to Ackehurst, and that Mikelis bloke, and Kyle Walsh, were becoming more and more web-like.

DCI Walters and Mikelis were definitely at the centre of it all, she knew that much. Then it was just a case of tying everything together with enough proof as opposed to pure speculation. She thought about DI Wright – now, that really had been a bit of a shock, to think that these men had possibly had him disposed of so crudely, after taking down one of their cannabis farming operations. And if it really was Ackehurst who had refused to investigate what had really happened that night – when they all got a call through from the gaffer to say that their colleague had been pulled dead from a ditch out on the fens? It made her blood run cold to think that another officer may have been involved.

And if they were capable of doing it once, then who was to say they wouldn't do it again?

Whatever was going on here, it needed to be stopped. Hollie was sure of that. So, she started to compile her notes:

- DCI Walters?? Ordered Kyle Walsh to seek revenge on DI Wright for uncovering their cannabis farm. Ackehurst involved in failing to conduct a proper investigation.

- DCI Walters and Superintendent Ackehurst have a cross-county border link. Evidence of them having a personal relationship.

- Supt. Ackehurst – questionable financial gains above his current pay grade. Failed again to investigate intimidation tactics against DS Taylor.

- DCI Walters, sabotaged DS Taylor's investigation into one of his main supply routes. Led to an unfair dismissal from Southeast London SOC. No convictions made.

- DCI Walters and Mikelis Malinovska, old friends from before Walters was DCI.

- Malinovska – chain of supermarkets; cover for supply of illicit substances? Has subsequently distanced himself with apparently legitimate plant hire business.

- Kyle Walsh. Fly-tipping. Drug dealing. Works for Malinovska – on his books as a supplies manager. Ordered his cousin to intimidate DS Taylor; get him off their tail? Potentially dangerous individual.

- Conclusion: all parties working together to supply drugs (yet to be confirmed) across Norfolk and East London whilst taking out any competition, including silencing any police investigations leading towards their involvement.

Hollie had a lot of work to do, even though the finer details of a full investigation would be handed over for Professional Standards and beyond to unearth fully.

Getting her head down to the task at hand, the morning soon drew on into afternoon. A call from the gaffer to check in on how she was doing was the only other human contact she had until later, when Paul and Rachael arrived back at the office. Paul didn't seem as riled up as she had been after spending a day with their new recruit, which stirred in her a strange feeling of jealously. She soon brushed it aside. Paul got on with everybody; a trait which she herself did not possess.

"How'd you get on? Anything to lead towards a suspect?" she asked, pleased to have her colleague back to break the silence of the empty office.

Paul thumped down into his chair. "Nah. Sent forensics in to look for fingerprints – hopefully they'll find something, the weather's warm and dry enough. Got some tyre tracks and a van on the CCTV footage from one of the 'questrian centres so I'll try and find it on the database."

They both knew how unlikely it was that they would catch anybody at that point, especially as the value of the equipment stolen came to a relatively low sum. A sad reality of what they were up against when it came to rural crime. There were only three of them to cover the whole county, often having to conduct their investigations individually and then having to place them aside when something more pressing came along.

"Bet it'll be on stolen plates," Hollie concluded. It was always the same.

"Yep. I fear as such. Got to see some nice horses though, didn't we Rachael?" Paul smiled across at their uniformed recruit, trying his best to include her. Honestly, the morning had been slightly lacking in any meaningful conversation which had been rather challenging – Paul blamed it on the age difference between himself and Rachael.

Rachael looked up, smiling unconvincingly. "Yes. We did. Shall I get on with trying to locate that van's number plate?"

"Yeah, crack on," Paul said before lowering his voice down and focusing back on Hollie, "How you getting on with 'Operation Bent Coppers'?"

Hollie couldn't help but laugh at that. "Good. I made a list of main points, and started on the Walters branch. Wait – do you not think we should come up with a better name than that? Isn't the whole point of an operational name for it not to give away what you're actually investigating?"

Paul looked down at Chester, still splayed out across the floor at Hollie's feet. She looked down too, following his gaze. "Operation Black Dog?" he queried, a face of dead-set seriousness.

Chester raised his head. If he could have rolled his eyes, he would have done. Could Paul really not have come up with something more original than that?

"Sounds good to me," replied Hollie, reaching down to ruffle behind Chester's ears. That was that then. Operation Black Dog. "What about today's equestrian theft then? Operation Brown Horse?" she humorously poked at her colleague's lack of originality.

"They were black and white, actually. Gypsy cobs, that's what the lady said. Right. Drink?" It wasn't actually Paul's turn to make the round, but whatever. If he wanted to make her a nice of cup of tea then that was fine by her. She needed to ask Rachael something, actually. The gaffer had forwarded an email across from occupational health requesting a routine check-in, and she needed to make sure that Rachael had booked an appointment with them.

As Paul went off to the kitchenette, Hollie nudged Chester's head off of her feet and walked over to Rachael's desk. Although they were all on the same bank of workstations, Rachael had moved her screens in such a way that they were angled slightly; not facing directly out into the room. She was stationed right by the window, so Hollie just assumed it was to fend off the afternoon sun that came blaring through those blinds that didn't shut properly.

She didn't see Hollie coming, at first. On one of her screens, she was working away at the vehicle registration database. One the other, the one angled away from her, was Dan's personal file. Now, whilst a constable was able to access any other officer's intel file, they wouldn't have full access to details such as date of birth and current address – except, Rachael did appear to have such information to hand.

"What are you doing?" Hollie came up behind her, making Rachael flinch before rapidly clicking her email inbox back up over the personnel file. Too late. Hollie had seen everything.

"Oh, nothing. Sorry, ma'am. I was just ... remember I said before, about maybe asking DS Taylor out for a drink or something?" Rachael quickly covered herself, but Hollie wasn't entirely sold.

Had Rachael really taken that much of a shine towards Dan? Not that Dan had shown even an ounce of interest in return – could she not see that? She'd better tell Paul to watch it – he might be next in the firing line once Rachael realised that she was barking up the wrong tree with that one. "Save it will you, for when you're not on duty?" she clipped, before remembering why she had actually gone to see Rachael in the first place, "You've got an occupational health visit due,

I suggest you get that booked in instead, rather than chasing after Dan like some sort of low-level stalker."

Rachael's face fell like a lead balloon, completely taken aback by Hollie's uncharacteristically sharp mannerism towards her. "Sorry Hollie. I'll get it sorted now."

As Hollie went back to her desk, her suspicions started to rise further. Perhaps it was just a glitch in Rachael's system access that had allowed her to be privy to Dan's personal information, but either way, it needed looking into. She made a note to mention it to the gaffer when she next spoke to him.

One for Sorrow, Two for Joy

Gradually starting to feel worse and worse, Dan was forced to dredge up the energy from somewhere deep within – helped along by the highest recommended doses of paracetamol and ibuprofen – in order to accompany his gaffer on a trip away from the seminar.

Yesterday was a full day of talks, workshops and presentations, with another early night, although Dan had made it down for dinner on that occasion. The morning just gone had been an interactive workshop focusing on protected native species, and the threats from the introduction of non-native species such as the American signal crayfish and the muntjac deer. Dan never knew that the muntjac wasn't a native species, amongst other things, so he'd gone away feeling slightly more knowledgeable than when he'd first walked in – and feeling a bit less like an impostor posing as a wildlife crime expert.

To be quite honest, the challenge of learning about something other than your run of the mill crimes – crimes which he had based his career on so far – felt awfully liberating, and for the first time since moving back home, he felt excited to be taking on something new.

"Where are we going, sir?" asked Dan, wrapped up in a thick hoodie despite the uncannily warm Scottish weather. They had been driving for a short while, out of the rugged coastal countryside and towards the city of Inverness. Broadmeadow had suggested that they take the afternoon off and away from the seminar, but hadn't actually said where it was he was planning on taking him.

"I thought I'd take you to the beach. Some fresh sea air might do that cough of yours some good. But I'd like to make a stop somewhere first, if ye' don't mind?" The gaffer still seemed a bit subdued, ever since the meeting over lunch with that Alaistair bloke. Dan even wondered if it was something *he* had said or done to make the man upset, but he couldn't think of anything in particular, apart from the fact that perhaps he wasn't the best company to be spending four days with alone.

Before he could get too strung up on the idea that he may be shit company, Dan was a bit surprised when they pulled up outside a cemetery.

He stayed put, as without a word, Broadmeadow cut the engine, pulled up the handbrake and exited the car. He watched, reluctantly, as the gaffer walked around to his side and opened the door. "Come on, Danny, come with me, will ye'?"

Going to see somebody's grave who he didn't even know really wasn't at the top of Dan's agenda, even on the best of days, but seeing the quiet hopefulness in his gaffer's eyes when he asked rendered him unable to refuse. The man just wanted somebody for support, he could see that loud and clear.

There was not another soul in sight, as they slowly picked their way along the narrow path through the graveyard, and then across the grass, further up to the back where it started to grow longer and more unkempt. Broadmeadow periodically checked the headstones as they passed, like he wasn't quite sure where they were supposed to be heading. A solitary magpie fluttered down and quietly observed them for a moment, before hopping off behind a beech tree.

Broadmeadow then stopped when they reached the departed soul that he was looking for.

Jonathan P. Cunningham

"Johnny"

1971 – 1991

SON, POLICE OFFICER, MAY THE LORD GIVE REST TO YOUR SOUL

"Alright there, Johnny-boy? Long time, no see ..." Broadmeadow said as he hitched up his trousers and crouched down before Jonathan Cunningham's grave. Dan watched as his gaffer bowed his head, reaching out to touch the smooth grey granite with lightly trembling fingers. Whoever Johnny was, he clearly meant something dear to a younger version of his commanding officer.

"I've missed you, Johnny. Missed you something fierce," murmured the gaffer.

Whilst Dan felt like he needed to remain close, he also needed to allow the man a bit of distance to be with his departed friend. Wandering off to the very corner of the cemetery, kneeling to pull an unruly weed from one of the more unkept graves as he passed, Dan bent down over where a cluster of wildflowers were growing. Large, pinkish poppies he recognised, but the others he couldn't place a name to – should have listened a little harder to the finer intricacies of Schedule 8. Hoping to God that he wasn't about to make the faux pas of disturbing an endangered species, he carefully plucked a couple of stems of the prettiest looking flowers and gathered them into a makeshift bouquet. A strand of long grass pulled last, to loosely tie the bunch together.

Creeping back over to where Broadmeadow was still crouched down at Johnny's headstone, he delicately placed a hand over his gaffer's shoulder to alert him of his presence, offering out his *boutonniere*. Broadmeadow's eyes were looking a little red-rimmed as he tendered Dan a sad yet appreciative smile, taking the gathered flowers and gently, ever so gently, laying them down at the foot of Johhny's resting place.

Silently, bar the crack of his knees, the gaffer raised himself back to his feet and slipped his arm around Dan's shoulders.

"Thank you, Daniel." He paused, quickly wiping at his eyes before quietly reciting something that sounded to Dan like a prayer in a foreign tongue; "*Fois Dhè dha anam.*"

As Dan responded by way of offering his own arm out around his gaffer's waist, Broadmeadow smiled fondly down at him and planted the softest of kisses to his crown. "*M' eudail air do chridhe, a chuilein ...*"

A couple of magpies, a pair this time, landed down on the grass behind the farthest row of headstones.

*

"Was that Scottish you were speaking, before?" Dan asked as they reached their next destination. Parked up across the road, they clambered down a low bank of dunes onto the beach. Nairn, the town was called, just outside of Inverness, on the way back from the cemetery on the outskirts of the city. The sun was shining warm, shimmering bright against the gently lapping waves of the Moray Firth and the coarse golden sand beneath their feet.

It was only then that Dan realised what his gaffer was wearing on his feet – a nice, dark suede, high laced pair of walking boots. He laughed. The man *could* pull it off, after all.

"Gaelic, son. I know the odd phrase or two, that's all," Broadmeadow smiled, all be it a little confused over his sergeant's amusement.

Dan was still in awe, however much his gaffer tried to downplay the fact that he could speak another language. "Well, I'm impressed," he responded genuinely, although didn't ask what exactly Broadmeadow had said to him (he couldn't actually remember the exact pronunciation), but it sure did sound to him like some sort of secretive endearment for his and Johnny's ears only.

They walked across the beach in a comfortable silence, Dan stopping to pick a few weather-beaten shells up along the way as a memento of their trip. Broadmeadow caught on to what he was doing, collecting a piece of round edged, frosted sea glass, slipping it into the front pocket of Dan's hoodie as they made their way towards a small beachfront café. Finding a table that overlooked the water, he waited whilst his gaffer went inside.

"Who was Johnny, sir?" he asked, when Broadmeadow returned with a tea and a hot chocolate in a pair of unassumingly plain white mugs, and took a seat beside him. There was always the concern that the gaffer wouldn't want to talk about it, or that he would grow angry like Paul had done at the mention of DI Wright, but he just got the feeling that this time, it might do the older man some good to open up.

Broadmeadow looked out across the gleaming waves as he started to speak: "Johnny was an old friend of mine. A dear friend. We went through training together, passed out together too."

Dan noticed how his voice started to strain, but he carried on regardless; "One night we were due to go out on patrol together, but my shift was changed at the eleventh hour. Johnny was murdered that night. His partner for the night left him, alone. Five minutes, they said, popped into a local pub for a piss. When he came back outside, Johnny was dead. Blow to the back of his head, hard enough to take his life."

"Is that why you left?" Dan asked quietly, catching the mood and solemnly taking in every word his gaffer had just said. He knew there was more to it than that though. One didn't just up sticks and move five hundred miles south on the back of a traumatic incident – or did they?

Broadmeadow took a deep breath, followed by an even deeper gulp of his tea, "Yes. It was. I feared that I would be next, son."

Dan watched as a small child sat down in the sand near the surf and started to fill a brightly coloured bucket with sand. Her mother, close at hand, poised her phone into position and snapped up the precious memories. Out at sea, a paddle boarder leisurely punted his way across the horizon. "Why? Do you think it was premeditated?"

"There wasn't a place for fellas like us in the police, not back then. I'm not sure that there is now either, but it certainly is a safer time to be living in than it was before," Broadmeadow replied with a grave sobriety.

Dan's heart jumped, and then fell. The black dog, for the first time that afternoon, made him cough wretchedly into his hand. What exactly did he mean, by *'fellas like us'*? Did he mean, like he and Dan? Was he trying to warn him that what they were feeling for each other wasn't ever to be acted upon? He had to know. He couldn't live with an existence of never knowing for sure. "Was Johnny more than just a friend, sir?"

"Aye. He was. Or would have been, if we'd ever gotten that far. I loved him," Broadmeadow said softly, gazing off into the middle-distance as he spoke.

Dan's heart peaked back up, nervously hammering at the inside of his chest. The black dog cowered back down to the pit of his stomach, defeated in its efforts. Broadmeadow's honesty was profound. He wasn't afraid, like Dan was, to admit that he had loved; like it was a pure matter of fact that Johnny was a man, not a woman. Nothing more, nothing less, just somebody, another human being with whom he had shared something special and revered. It gave Dan an immeasurable amount of strength and clarity towards his own outlook – where a man like him fell within the world.

Surveying his gaffer with a searching gaze, barely more than a whisper above the sound of the tide against the shingles, Dan asked, "Could you love somebody like that again, after what happened?"

Broadmeadow thought about it, leaving Dan in a terrible state of limbo, his words hanging thick and heavy in the summer air. But then the gaffer moved closer, seeking something warm and solid and real, as a slight coastal breeze send a soft chill upon the backs of their necks.

He replied, rather elegantly, focusing his vision solely upon Dan's face as he said, "I feel like we mere mortals do not have choice in where the heart leads, Danny-boy."

Twenty-Four Hours

"How long have we got until we're on?" Johnny blearily asked as he sat himself up against the headboard. Marcus appeared with a strong cup of coffee to bring him back to the world of the living. Their first run of night shifts had messed him up some, his body clock all over the place. Tonight was the last stint though, with two days rest to sleep it off now tantalisingly close.

He stretched out his legs, wiggling his toes back to life.

"Two hours," Marcus smiled fondly, slipping the cup into Johnny's waiting hands before heading back towards the door. Johnny had drawn the short straw – his bedroom was the box room, only large enough for a single bed and a chest of drawers, crammed so close to the door that it didn't open properly. Marcus would say that he deserved the bigger room, because he sorted out the tenancy and the bills of their second floor flat within the old tenement block on the outskirts of town. Johnny would say, secretly, that he would be happy with a carboard box on the floor if it meant he and Marcus got to remain residing together.

Their friendship had formed during their time at the Scottish Police College down in Alloa. Two lads, barely eighteen and a long way from home – inevitably, they had bonded over their shared roots up in the Northeast. Now posted at Inverness, Johnny and Marcus had scraped together enough (with the help of Johnny's parents) to rent a place together. It was small, the walls damp and the carpets dank, but it was theirs.

"What's the matter, Marc? You're looking a wee bit somber for a man about to spend a whole shift with yours truly!" Cheerily, and perked up with coffee, Johnny threw himself down onto the sofa – the sofa they had snagged a cracking bargain on at the charity shop downtown – next to a rather thoughtful looking Marcus.

"Just the nights catching up with me. I'm fine," he said as he gave Johnny an unconvincing smile; the lopsided one where only half of his mouth complied with the motion.

"Come on, lad. I know when there's something on ye' mind. Tell me?" Johnny pushed. Marcus could be an extremely quiet lad, the complete opposite of Johnny. He could talk until the *coo's* came home. That's what he loved about him – that they were so different, yet so aligned with each other. But that was getting a wee bit poetic for Johnny's usual vocabulary.

Marcus wasn't quite sure that he wanted to share what he had heard down in the canteen earlier that day, after their shift and whilst gathering a hot breakfast, before heading off home to do it all again that night. Instead, he leant across and nestled down against Johnny's side, where he was accepted into a warm embrace. Johnny was smaller than he was, but he was stockier, more athletically built and able to throw a weighty right hander. Marcus was tall and lanky, still waiting for the body of a man to fill out his jutting bones.

"Or don't tell me," Johnny finished, pulling both his arms around Marcus and nosing down into his crown. Marcus' soft, browny-ginger hair was always a favorite attribute of Johnny's. It tickled at his nostrils and it smelled of *hame.*

It wasn't quite clear when or how it had first started. It just happened, slowly, like the turn of hands upon the face of a clock. At first, Marcus didn't take pause to think what it made him; to find what he needed within the arms of his fellow constable. Johnny certainly didn't seem to care. In one sense, it made Marcus feel carefree and unashamed. In another, it made him feel a churning sense of dread over what their future held.

Marcus' faith in Catholicism was still relatively strong at that point. At least, strong enough for him to still fear the wrath of God should he rebel. And very much strong enough for him to still fear the memory of his childhood priest. Not only that, but in the year of 1991, AIDS was still prevalent and widely misunderstood; Freddie Mercury had just died from complications linked to it. Nobody was safe from its deadly claws – not men like them anyway, and although he and Johnny had never gotten any further than the odd kiss here and there, it still worried him more than he could ever put into words.

He wouldn't have classed himself as '*gay*', as such, like the men that he saw on the news, in their tight-fitting outfits and with their promiscuous natures. He wasn't. He liked women, too. But he liked Johnny more.

It had been Johnny, who first started with the casual touches and lingering embraces when greeting or parting, with his strong arms and stupid grin to go with. Johnny, who was less caring over when or where a physical display of affection was to be gifted. That wasn't to say that Marcus didn't enjoy it, because he did – he was just more grounded with the reality of their situation.

There was still such a thing as the punishable offence of 'indecent or immoral behaviour likely to damage the reputation of the force', with Marcus having heard stories of officers being resigned to back-room duties, or even released from the force entirely. And besides, in the eyes of the law, he and Johnny were still legally underage, which would definitely end in an instant dismissal before their careers had even started.

It scared him, it really did.

But what scared him more, was what he had heard that morning whilst filling up his plate with fried eggs and bacon and a side of beans. At first, he'd paid the group of constables at the condiments station no mind. He knew them. They'd all been on shift together at one point or another. But when he had heard the name 'PC Cunningham' come up, his ears has pricked, senses suddenly set on edge. Swiftly paying for his breakfast, he made his way over to collect some cutlery. Closer now, only a couple of meters away, he could hear them properly:

"He's definitely a wee buftie, that one."

"PC Rattleston – he says he saw Cunningham lurking around outside the Admiral Duncan last weekend. That's where they all hang around, int' it?"

"Fucking faggot. Who let 'im join the force, anyways? Should never av' made it legal, I tell ye' that now."

Marcus barely kept the tremble from his hands as he dropped a knife and fork onto his tray. How did they know? How could they possibly have known? Johnny was friendly with everybody. He could give the banter as good as the rest of them – he was strong, and fit, he loved his football and a wee pint or two down the pub, so what exactly made him so different?

If anybody, Marcus would say that he was the one who was more likely to be targeted. He was quiet and thoughtful, a conservative sort of fella who would shy away from a conflict if he could.

One of the officers, PC Sinclair, turned from the group when he saw that Marcus was looking their way, and he froze. He felt sick. Where was Johnny, anyway? He'd only gone down to the locker room to grab a change of socks before joining Marcus for breakfast ...

"Eh, has he tried anything funny with you yet, Marcus? You wanna watch yourself, sharing a flat with 'im. Back to the wall if he comes at you with a wee bar of soap, eh?" PC Sinclair jibed, jovially nudging Marcus with his elbow. The other constables erupted in a roar of laughter.

Marcus set his shoulders, frowning, "What d'ya mean? I've lost count of the number of lassies he's had back for the night – thinking of asking him for some tips me'self, know what a' mean?" he expertly responded. Out came the lopsided smile that he fought to make reach his eyes with any sort of sincerity.

Sinclair eyed him suspiciously before breaking out into a grin, "Eh, you wanna come out wi' us, how's about it? We'll find ye' a nice wee lassie to take home with ya'!"

At that point, all Marcus could do was accept the loose invitation for fear of getting caught out himself. It shamed him to have lied like that about Johnny, but he knew that it had to be done. He had to protect him – to protect them both.

Back at home, curled within Johnny's arms, Marcus kept what he'd heard to himself. Johnny probably wouldn't care, water off the duck's back to him. But what if he did care? What if he took it all too close to heart and decided that he and Marcus should part ways now whilst they were ahead?

He knew that Johnny would and all, if it meant keeping Marcus safe.

Instead, just soaking up the quiet moment between them, he let himself be held, breathing in the scent of the man he loved. They could move away if they had to. Down South, the English were crying out for new recruits. There were places too where they had a more liberal outlook, like Brighton. Places where they could live their lives without such fear.

Two hours later, suited and booted, Johnny and Marcus arrived at the station for their last night shift of the week, where Marcus was told that *his* shift had been changed at the last minute.

Twelve hours later, Marcus arrived back at the station to start his revised shift, only to find that there was no larger-than-life Johnny waiting for him at the end of his.

Twenty-four hours later, Johnny was dead, and life as he knew it came crashing down around him.

The First Dance

The last night of the conference was in full swing. After a sit-down dinner and an audience with speaker-come-comedienne Julie Grey, (Dan didn't quite get her brand of humour like the rest of the room had), which seemed to go on for hours, Dan and Marcus were finally able to get up and stretch their legs. Some of the tables had been moved aside to make way for a dance floor and a mobile disco, with many of their fellow officers already two sheets to the wind. The majority of the party appeared more than ready to start throwing shapes to the questionable choice of soundtrack – one which was rattling at Dan's eardrums.

Safe to say, he wasn't feeling it. He was exhausted. A Dan in his earlier twenties would have undoubtedly been up there with the rest of them, a little drunk and up for a bit of a dance, but all that had been taken from him at some point along the way – all his energy, his confidence; all gone, and he hadn't even hit his thirties yet.

"Ye' don't fancy a wee dance then, fella?" Marcus quipped playfully, sensing Dan's aversion to where the evening was heading.

Standing at the edge of the hall with the safety of the wall at their backs, they watched as a younger officer took an older colleague by the hand and dragged her onto the dance floor. She soon showed him who was the boss however, breaking into a jive before pulling him into her arms and swinging him around and off his feet. The younger officer stumbled, tumbling down to the floor. A loud cheer erupted as the music turned up another notch, and more people joined in, enjoying letting their hair down after one too many mundane presentations over the last three days.

Dan eyed his gaffer up and down. He was looking rather dashing in his dress uniform, which *was* rather tempting – and far more alluring a sight that what they were currently witnessing. "Like 'An Officer and a Gentleman'?" he responded rather playfully to his gaffer's offer.

Marcus huffed, staving off a blush. "Not sure I quite compare to that now Daniel, but I can give it a good go, if ye' wish …"

Abandoning his glass of sparkling wine atop the nearest table, Marcus stepped in close, swaying slightly as he tentatively took a hold of Daniel's hands. Call it Dutch courage from all the free alcohol, or something pent up inside from sharing a room for the past three nights, or the fresh memories of the man he'd loved who'd been ripped away from him too soon; call it what you will, but Marcus couldn't hold it back any longer.

"Sir, what are you …?" surprised, Dan broke off as he clocked on to what was happening …

Closer still, Marcus placed Daniel's hands at his hips, and looped his arms around the lad's shoulders in a loose embrace, starting to move them both in time with the music. A fleeting look around confirmed for Dan that not a single person was paying them any mind. It didn't help with his jittering nerves though. He couldn't dance, proving his point by stepping over one of his gaffer's pristinely polished shoes, before profusely apologising, as he looked up into Broadmeadow's eyes for any indication that he'd gone and fucked it.

"Hey, relax now. Just move with me, yeah?" Marcus crooned, eyes gleaming in the refection of the disco lights. He pulled Dan closer until they were almost flush, with everything else around them fading away until it was just the two of them, awkwardly swaying off-beat to the music like there was nobody else within the room around them.

Dan melted into his gaffer's arms, deciding that now was the time to take his chances, because if they didn't do it now, would they ever?

Tipping up his chin, grasping a tiny bit tighter at Broadmeadow's hips to steady himself, as he stretched to the balls of his feet, he whispered, "You sure this is what you want, sir?"

Marcus breathed, his eyes full of a soft adoration as he looked down upon the wee lad; the lad who had come along and stolen his fractured, freshly healing heart, "I'll tell you what I want – I want to take you back to our room, if you'll have me?"

Dan didn't need to be asked twice. "Yeah. Let's get out of here."

*

The hotel room was bathed in the dim light of a clear night sky. They didn't stop to close the curtains or turn on the lights. Dan was far too preoccupied to be thinking about that, even forgetting about how unwell he'd been feeling as of late, because his gaffer wearing his dress uniform, closing in for an embrace, was the only comprehendible thought possible in that moment. With Marcus stepping them both backwards, feet tangling as Dan's mouth was forcibly assaulted, they tumbled down onto the bed.

"Can't tell you much I've wanted to get you on here with me …" Marcus gasped between kisses, their legs fighting one another to find an agreeable position as they lay upon their sides, grasping at each other's arms, hips, anything they could get their hands on.

"Was waiting for you to turn me down when I said I'd take the sofa bed …" Dan flushed, a soft noise escaping from his throat as his gaffer's knee inadvertently brushed between his legs. He didn't think much of it, or that it may be a bit strange, to have another man kissing him something silly. In fact, it felt like the most normal thing in the world to be doing, now they'd gone and done it. Different, for sure, but in no way bad.

"Cheeky wee shite. How would that of looked, eh? *'Come 'ere Danny, come get in bed with yer' boss now?'*" Broadmeadow – *Marcus* – drew back, grinning, looking him deeply in the eyes before sinking his lips back against him. He really ought to start calling the man by his forename, Dan thought to himself. Now that did feel a little bit strange. He'd need a bit more practice with that one, he decided.

Marcus' stubble scratched against his face. Their teeth knocked together, Dan fighting with his tongue for more, enjoying the feel of his gaffer's slightly crooked teeth, finding the gap between his gums where a molar had gone astray, and feeling the man smile against his lips …

"I wouldn't have said no …" Dan murmured, eyes smiling, "Just wasn't sure, until now. If I was, I would have just waited 'till dark and crawled up in here with you."

Marcus let out something that sounded like a strained growl as he slung his leg over Dan's thigh, pressing for more contact. His heart burned something fierce; a simmering heat burning down low within his belly. And then something he hadn't really thought much over recently suddenly dropped his heart like a stone – the antidepressants. The unwanted side effects. The inability to ...

"You alright there, son?" Marcus paused his further exploration of Daniel's body, sensing that the wee fella's enthusiasm had momentarily waned. Perhaps they shouldn't be doing this. He shouldn't be encouraging it. Daniel was so much younger than he was, and he was in a vulnerable state of mind – he should be seeking somebody more his own age, shouldn't he? He didn't deserve this. He'd failed himself under the eyes of the Lord, failed Johnny and he'd failed his wife, and now he was about to fail yet another ...

Yet, his body and his heart were saying otherwise. The connection between them was so strong that he couldn't ignore it any longer, no matter how hard he had tried to stop the thoughts he'd been having.

Dan clung to his gaffer's hips, fearing that the man was about to pull away completely. "Yeah, um, I think I have to tell you something ..."

"Ok?" Marcus asked tentatively, but he took courage from the fact that Daniel was still holding him and not pushing him away, or trying to make a hasty exit from the situation.

"You know I take medication, don't you? You know, antidepressants?" Dan took in a steady breath, his cheeks already starting to tinge red, because what he was about to say was something no man ever wanted to have to admit out loud.

Marcus was observing him with an equal measure of curiosity and concern, still lying close though, close enough for Dan to see the lines of age around his eyes even in the dark; close enough for him to really see his defined features, to admire how his light, slightly curled hair was elegantly streaked with grey – he really was a handsome man, Dan thought. Handsome in an almost noble way, with the events in life that had shaped him making him strong and defined in his features.

It made him weak at the knees, even though he was lying down, which made it even more frustrating that his body wasn't able to react in the way it should. "I think it's given me some problems, with my, um, with my …"

He blushed further, unable to say it outright, hoping to God that the gaffer was able to get the general gist of what he was trying to say, despite his complete inability to form coherent words.

"Things not working as they should down there? Is that what you're trying to say?" Marcus asked softly. Dan pulled his eyes down. It was easier to look at his chest than it was his face.

"Yeah. That's it," he mumbled, crushed that they'd come so close, but knowing they couldn't have gone any further without him being truthful about his current situation. If he hadn't, then Broadmeadow may have thought something was wrong, that he wasn't interested – maybe he still did, and thought that Dan was just making excuses …

Marcus moved in closer, sliding one arm in under his neck and the other around his torso, firmly pulling him against his chest. "I'm sorry, Danny. I am. But it makes no odds to how I feel about ye'. None at all. I love you just the same."

Quietly he spoke, winding his fingers into Dan's hair and soothing him against his broad chest. Dan wanted to cry. Never had somebody shown him such compassion; made him feel so loved – and to be told it outright too. Marcus loved him. And it should have felt like a bigger revelation than it did, how easily those words had fallen from the older man's lips, yet it just felt like they were meant to be, so easy and true now that it had been spoken out aloud.

"I think I've loved you since the day I first met you," Dan said as he clung ever closer, wiping his eyes against his gaffer's still buttoned jacket.

They lay there a while, taking it all in, until his gaffer's voice came placidly back into the forefront; "How about we just get ready and then share this big old bed together, how's that sound, hmm?"

"Yeah. Sounds good to me."

Dan did close the curtains, on his way back to the bed after brushing his teeth and getting himself undressed. It felt easier to be doing this in the almost dark. He didn't usually wear anything in the way of pyjamas, but he felt that he'd better slip on a t-shirt seeing as the gaffer was wearing one too.

Broadmeadow was already in bed, waiting for him.

"Move up, then," he said as he crept in under the covers beside his gaffer.

Instinctively, Dan rolled over onto his side. Before he'd even taken a breath to get himself settled, his gaffer's big, warm body had rolled over with him, impossibly long legs sidling up behind his own. Marcus' strong arms closed in to bodily embrace him from behind, with a level of warmth and security that made him feel, for the first time in his adult life, completely at ease within his restless soul. Even the black dog, unseen for the whole evening, seemed to curl itself into the depths of his belly, as if it too was becalmed by the certainty that Broadmeadow unashamedly had to offer.

"Comfortable?" the gaffer murmured against the back of his head, already softly laden with the oncoming approach of sleep. Dan shuffled back, deeper into his embrace, holding Marcus' arms tight around him.

Something told Dan that he too wasn't far off that state either. "Mmm, 'm good. G'night, sir."

Sea Glass

After having been dropped off back home – another twelve-hour journey – Dan decided to just get his bag unpacked, get his stuff ready for work the next day and then call it a night. As he bent over in the kitchen to stuff his dirty washing into the machine, a couple of loose shells fell out of his hoodie onto the tiles at his feet, and bounced across the floor. Pulling his sweater back out the machine, he delved his hand into the front pocket where he found some more shells, and the piece of sea glass his gaffer had found for him. Smiling, he rubbed it between his fingers and thumb. It was smooth and frosted, turquoise in colour; a perfect match for Broadmeadow's eyes.

As they'd walked back along the beach that day, after the heartfelt conversation over his gaffer's past, Broadmeadow had collected a few more treasures for his little horde and passed them too into his pocket. It reminded Dan of the magpies they had seen back at the cemetery, imagining the pair bringing gifts for each other in the form of twigs and bits of rubbish, all special little things to gather together back at their nest.

Dan did not live in a nest though, so he would have to find a nice glass or something to display his invaluable mementoes inside. A tumbler from the kitchen cupboard would do for now, until he found something nicer. Pride of place, upon the windowsill above the sink, where he placed the glass full of shells and beach-finds, wondering when exactly he had become such a sentimental old fool.

Thoughts went back to Broadmeadow, where it had been even harder than ever to part with him this time. With a lingering embrace on the doorstep and a number of 'one last kisses', his heart had wrenched when the time came to say goodnight – even though he knew that both he and Broadmeadow (still hadn't gotten used to calling him Marcus in his head, and still hadn't physically called him that to his face) both needed to just get home and get some rest.

Only one day 'till the weekend anyway, which he was hoping they would be able to spend together. He wasn't overly worried about how they were to act around each other at work tomorrow – they'd had that conversation already on the long drive back down south. They would just act normal. Nothing unprofessional, keep their hands off each other, everything Dan would have expected and wouldn't have dreamed of breaching in the first place. But still, it felt necessary to have laid the foundations out there and then. It made them both feel more comfortable to have a plan.

As for getting his teeth stuck back into building a case against Walters, Mikelis and the others, and seeing Paul and Hollie, he was quite looking forwards to that after his break away from it all.

All in all, Dan went to bed a happy man. Broadmeadow had called him sometime after he himself had arrived back home, and they had chatted for some time. Nothing serious, just gentle conversation over nothing in particular, except for that his gaffer was dreaming of Dan being back in bed with him, at which he had flushed furiously down the phone at him. He was wishing for the same thing, feeling like a lovesick teenager as he'd bedded down for the night with his arms wrapped around his pillow, imagining that his gaffer's solid chest was there in its place.

*

Having felt relatively ok for the last couple of days, Dan woke to his alarm with a start. It felt way too early. His limbs felt heavy and stiff, his chest tight and brimming with phlegm, and his head – not a headache, but a familiar thick fog clouding his mind. He couldn't even lift himself from the pillow, let alone contemplate getting up and out for work.

There was an overwhelming urge to burst out into tears, even though there was nothing to be emotional over. He didn't understand. Why was this happening? Why now? He'd been taking his pills regularly, definitely hadn't forgotten last night, sure of it because he remembered it getting stuck in the back of his throat before brushing his teeth, having to bend down under the tap and wash the bitter taste down.

Curling the duvet around himself, his mind started to betray him.

Broadmeadow doesn't really want you. He didn't ask to stay another night with you, did he? And even if he did, he'll soon realise that having a partner who can't get his prick up isn't much fun for anybody ...

Dan coughed, clutching hard at his chest like something was trying to retch its way up from within –

He's too old for you, anyways. And he's been hurt too badly. What he needs is a nice older woman so that he can regain a normality to his life. He's just reliving his past with you. He'll soon see sense ...

He started to well up with tears, impossible to stop them. Shuddering, Dan coughed again, strained and wretched, this time a black bile spilling out from between his teeth. Heaving himself over the side of the bed, he started to panic. Nausea took hold; head spinning, skin flushing hot and cold, trying the breathe through it but his heart was hammering too fast, like it was about to explode –

And what are you even doing, trying to gain some sort of retribution over DCI Walters? Your colleagues are going to get sick of it in all – sick of you – they never asked to get involved in all of this. They don't really care. You've just come along and dumped all your own baggage onto them, and they haven't had a choice in the matter ...

Dan's stomach churned as he retched again, half choking on bile and cough, with his head hung down near the floor and not caring that his carpet was about to be ruined. His heart reached the point of overdrive. He was going to die. He was dying. He needed an ambulance. And then it came – an echoing belch before everything came pouring out, a level of vomit that Dan had never experienced before, and never wanted to ever happen again. It burned his mouth and throat as a stream of viscous, black liquid poured down his chin and onto the floor below.

Breathing thick and heavy, eyes streaming with tears, Dan watched as it started to fizzle and steam into the carpet. He was sure that he was hallucinating as a mist started to rise from the sticky pool of black vomit, avoiding his face as the cloud of vapour amalgamated into a more solid form: great shaggy legs first, and bitten-off claws, then a ragged chest came into view, with emaciated ribs like it had been starved of the essential nutrients it needed to survive. He didn't dare look up any further. He knew what it was. He didn't want to look at it.

Reduced to a shivering, crying mess, Dan hauled himself back up onto his bed and turned his back on the black dog. He didn't have the strength to bother over the mess on the carpet. Clean it up now, or clean it up later – either way it was going to leave a stain. Curling himself into a ball, uncaring that he was going to be late for work, Dan succumbed himself to the pull of physical and mental exhaustion.

Late

Marcus arrived for work with a spring in his step that morning. His gait felt light. He felt happier than he had done in years, in the knowledge that he and young Daniel had been sharing mutual feelings for each other. Of course there were the underlying worries over his age, and how if life took its natural course then he would be leaving the lad behind at some point in time, but he tried not to think about that just yet. With any luck they would have years together before anything like that was to be faced.

At just gone eight Hollie arrived, eager to hand back control over the department. Dan would normally be in by now, but he put it down to the long journey yesterday and the late arrival back home – not to mention that wee cold the lad seemed to be harbouring. He had a half-hour anyway, before Marcus would be forced to reprimand him for a late arrival.

"Alright there Hollie, how are ye'? Everything running smoothly without me?" he greeted the wee lass as she came into his office and immediately made herself comfortable on the sofa. She looked at bit tired, her skin even paler than usual; but other than that she looked quite well.

"I'm glad you're back, I'll tell you that, sir. It's been harder than I thought to keep on top of everything, all the new cases coming through and that. We had one yesterday from a church up in Wetton – somebody stole half the lead off their roof. I assigned it to Paul of course, as it definitely falls within the remit of heritage crime. How was the trip, anyways? You and Dan have a good time?"

Marcus quelled the skip of his heart at the mention of Daniel's name, putting thoughts of their fledgling relationship away into a safe place for later. "Church roof theft, eh? We haven't had an incidence of that in, what, must be ten years now? And we did have a nice time, thank you. I think young Daniel learned a lot."

Hollie smiled, with something knowing glimmering behind her eyes, which had Marcus wondering if she knew something more than she was letting on. "Good. I've made headway with the file on DCI Walters, working on Mikelis Malinovska now. I'll drop off what I've done so far in a bit, if you wanted to have a read. Is there anything else you wanted me to be getting on with now you're back? Paul and Rachael have taken a report of equine equipment theft already, but I'm happy to take that one back for myself."

Good girl, Marcus thought. Hollie really was a fantastic example of her role. He knew that she had dreams of bigger things for her career, she had never kept that from him, but he secretly hoped that she would change her mind at some point; to decide that fighting rural crime was her true calling in life. "You know what? Take it back if you wish, or leave it with Paul if he wants it. I'm sure the both of you can work it out between you without my intervention, eh? Good work Hollie. Come and drop the file off when yer' ready and I'll have a read through."

Marcus glanced up at the clock. A quarter-past eight. Paul and Chester had just arrived, giving them both a wave before heading straight to the kitchen for a coffee.

Half-past eight and Rachael arrived.

Quarter to nine and there was still no sign of his wee sergeant. The worry that Marcus had been forcing down started to surface. The office phone hadn't rung, and neither had his mobile.

He got up and called out over the office, "Anybody heard from DS Taylor?"

Three heads looked his way, all blankly looking back at him. Ok. He's most likely just having a wee bit of car trouble after leaving it sitting since Monday. The battery may have gone flat, which was a perfectly plausible explanation. Or he'd overslept? Not likely, but a possibility. Retreating back to his office, Marcus decided to give him a call.

It rung, and it rung, until it went to answer phone. He tried again. No answer. On his third attempt, after which he was going to go and drive round there should it ring through again, a rough voice picked up the on the receiving end. Thank the Gods for that.

"Sir … oh fuck. Shit. I'm sorry, sir. I'm late, aren't I?" Daniel hastily explained himself, not so eloquently.

"Hey, hey. It's ok. What happened, fella? Are you ok?" Marcus soothed, hoping that his tone conveyed down the line that the lad wasn't in any trouble.

There was a momentary silence before Daniel admitted; "Not feeling too good, sir. I'm really sorry. I don't think I'm going to make it in today."

Marcus felt a wee bit deflated that he wasn't going to be seeing the lad today as expected, but what was more important was that nothing untoward had happened. He was pleased in a way, that Daniel was actually able to confess that he was feeling too under the weather to come to work – Marcus could have told him that a week ago; that he needed a couple of days off to just *rest* and get himself better. It must have been a remnant left over from his time spent under DCI Walters, he concluded. He couldn't imagine the man taking so kindly as he had to a plea of sickness.

"Look, you stay in bed, yeah? Keep yer'self nice and warm," he turned to make sure nobody was listening in before lowering his voice, "And I'll drop by later after work, does that sound ok with you?"

He could hear the smile behind Daniel's voice as he seemed to brighten up a wee bit; "Yeah, I'd like that. Thank you, sir."

"Alright. Speak to you later then, fella. Get some sleep, yes?"

Daniel reluctantly agreed, even though he sounded like he was half-asleep already and trying to fight it. Every bone within Marcus' body was urging him to just get in his car and go and check that he was ok, see it for his own eyes, but he knew that it wasn't really necessary. The lad would be fine. He'd go and see him later. He'd be able to get into bed with him and treat him to a nice wee cuddle. Besides, he had work to do. He needed to go and catch Paul and ask him how far he'd gotten into Mikelis Malinovska's financial records. And he needed to make a dent in the backlog of emails that had accumulated in his absence –

"Sir?"

A knock at the door. Rachael was stood there.

"Yes, Rachael. Can I help you?"

"I hope you don't mind my asking, but is DS Taylor alright?" She lingered, leaning against the doorframe. Hollie and Paul had both suggested that she may be interested in his wee sergeant, and obviously, on a personal level, he didn't like it. But he had to push any ill-feelings aside, knowing how unprofessional of him it would be to hold such a thing against an officer under his command.

"He's just called in sick, actually. Nothing major, just a cold."

"Oh, ok. Thank you, sir," she smiled, rather apprehensively Marcus noted, before taking leave and scurrying back to her desk, presumably to spread the word to Paul and Hollie. He'd have to call her in later actually – have a bit of a chat over how she thought her first week at Rural Crime had gone. On that note, Marcus logged onto his computer and groaned when he saw how many emails were sitting waiting for him.

A Change of Heart

The black dog bowed down, stretching its legs out in front of its body. Shaking itself off, it clambered up onto the bed and settled itself down over Dan's feet. It felt defeated. Finding its way inside of Dan had been a last-ditch attempt at trying to keep him for itself, but it hadn't worked. Marcus' love for him was too strong, and when he'd said as such, it had confirmed to the black dog that its days were numbered. Of course, it could have remained hiding away. It could have done, but eventually Dan would have grown so sick that he would have perished, in time. It didn't want that, because then it would be left alone again.

And it cared for Dan.

It realised that with a great level of certainty.

Having Marcus around wasn't so bad. He made Dan happy, which, despite its best efforts to fend the feeling off, made the black dog happy too. Whatever the black dog felt, Dan felt. Whatever Dan felt, the black dog felt. That was just the way it worked between them – and Dan was winning the black dog over to his way of thinking.

It liked the feeling of warmth, rather than cold. It found a sense of joy within love and contentment, rather than wallowing within resentment and sorrow. It was starting to contemplate what it would be like to just spend its days as Dan's companion rather than his unwanted shadow, even though it knew what that would mean towards its own expense – if it chose to be *happy*, then it would choose to be mortal.

With Dan it would live, and with Dan, it would ultimately die.

How did humans do that? How did they exist, knowing that every day was a day closer to their last? It was an entirely foreign concept, yet, an alluring one …

It could choose to protect Dan, if it wanted to. It could choose to become his sentry for when Marcus wasn't there to hold his hand, if it wanted to. And it did. It did want to.

As Dan slept through the morning, the black dog remained at his feet. Nothing much happened. The hours passed, but time wasn't an issue for the black dog, so it just waited. At some point, it stretched out, feeling a warmth growing from somewhere within its chest and expanding out, enough so for it to share. Dan's hands were cold, so it rested its chin upon them, giving them a little lick. Dan twitched, but didn't flinch away.

His unconscious mind was preoccupied, dreaming of DCI Walters. A recurring nightmare where he was trapped within the man's office, reliving all sorts of bad memories that were often amplified into far greater horrors. The black dog had joined DCI Walters on more than one occasion, helping to fuel those discomforting dreams into ferocious nightmares.

Thinking about it now, the black dog didn't want to do that anymore.

Careful not to wake him, it crawled in close and curled up against Dan's chest. It felt the warmth within it growing ever stronger, like it was somehow able to channel all the love that Marcus had for Dan, and project it between them like an ever-burning flame. It hoped to give Dan strength, enough so for him to make a recovery from what he'd been through; to banish those fearful memories he had and turn them into something good instead.

Time would tell, but its ultimate decision was already made, for better or for worse.

*

Dan woke to a feeling of utter weakness. The only other time he could remember having felt like that was after catching the flu, many years ago now, when he'd been knocked on his arse for over a week solid. A quick check of his phone confirmed that it was early afternoon.

The black dog was back, curled up with its head resting on his feet. It yawned, rolling over with its belly up and its legs stretched in the air. Dan looked at it curiously. He almost felt compelled to reach over and rub its stomach – the first time he had ever contemplated trying to touch the thing, unsure even if such a thing would be possible, or if his hand would just go straight through it.

With his palm wavering, he decided against it at the last moment, remembering how it had all but burned a hole in his carpet upon forcing itself out from his body. It looked at him from its upside-down eyes. They seemed less cloudy than they usually did, like he could almost make out some sort of emotion or sentience behind them.

The threat of nausea seemed to have passed, and his chest felt clearer, although he did still feel like he'd been hit by a bus. His throat was sore, as if somebody had been going at it with a sheet of sandpaper. Testing his hands and feet, he sat himself up, noticing as he moved that he didn't smell too good. He must have a shower and change the sheets before his gaffer arrived to see him, and then get to work on trying to clean up his own vomit from down the side of the bed. In his haze of what had happened to him that morning, clearly not thinking straight just yet, he narrowly missed stepping right into it as he dragged himself out of bed.

"Come on then," he said to the black dog as he shuffled his way out of the bedroom and made his way down to the kitchen. First off, he needed a drink before attempting to make himself and his house presentable. The black dog happily followed. It was a hot day – the first real hot day of the year – which wasn't helping Dan's situation, so he flung the kitchen door open to let some air in.

He half expected the black dog to go trotting outside to do its business, before he remembered that it wasn't really there; not in the sense of it being a living, breathing animal. It didn't go outside, but it did sniff the air. The smell of summer and the sound of children, an ice cream van tinkling away somewhere in the distance …

Dan's garden was pathetic – his gaffer would be ashamed of him. A roughly laid patio, a small square of lawn, and a shed at the back that could have done with a fresh layer of paint about five years ago. Whilst he wanted to make it nice, have some plants and that, he just didn't know where to start with it all. And of course, the house was rented so the pull to really make it his own just wasn't truly there.

All this standing up was making him feel a bit weak, so he grabbed a glass from the cupboard and turned towards the sink, bracing against it as he let the water run cold. A brief notion of taking a couple of painkillers crossed his mind before he paused, glass of water halfway to his lips. Looking back towards the garden, he noticed that the black dog was standing at the doorframe with its hackles raised. It was trembling, coiled with tension.

"What the ..." he uttered to himself; nerves suddenly set on edge ...

The black dog whined; a low and mournful sound, filling Dan with an unnameable fear and giving him the strongest impulse to take flight -

The glass of water dropped from his hand and shattered at his feet, when two heavy-set men, dark clothing and balaclavas, noiselessly burst into his kitchen.

Some police officer he was, as his legs became frozen in place and rooted him to the ground, raising his hands up in surrender.

One blow to the left shoulder, delivered by a crudely blunt implement, sent him collapsing to the floor.

Falling hard upon his elbow, a sickening crack filled his ears as he felt his wrist bend and snap beneath him.

Another blow to the back of the head sent Dan's world exploding into darkness.

Shattered Glass

Pulling up on the street outside of Daniel's house, Marcus flipped down the sun visor and checked his hair in the mirror. He'd used some of the conditioner Rowena had left behind, because it used to give her hair a lovely soft sheen, and it seemed to have done the trick with his own hair. He ran his hand though it, sweeping a stray, stubbornly curly strand of fringe back, but it wouldn't settle and flopped back down over his brow. He tilted his head to the side, deciding that, actually, he could pull it off as intentional. Take ten years off and he might even go as far as to say that he looked rather handsome …

Ah, well. No point in dwelling on the past as Daniel didn't seem overly bothered by his lack of youth.

The wee fella hadn't replied earlier, when he'd sent him a quick message to let him know he was on his way, but he wasn't concerned over that – the lad was probably still asleep. The poor boy needed it, bless him.

Weaving around Daniel's car on the single-space driveway, he knocked at the front door. No answer. Waiting a moment or two, he tried again. Still no answer. Ok, try around the back. The first thing Marcus noticed was the garden – or lack thereof. Aside from some old pots brimming with weeds by the back door, there was not a plant in sight. He wondered if Daniel would be interested in helping him out with his own garden, once he got a place of his own sorted out? He hoped so; he would love to be able to share his passion with the lad. Plant the seed, so to speak …

Laughing under his breath at his own joke, Marcus noticed that the back door to the kitchen was agape, knocking gently against the wall of the house; a dull *knock, knock* of plastic UPVC against brick. Something then made him pause for thought. Something didn't seem right.

"Daniel, son? You there?" he called out into the empty kitchen.

Eyes adjusting from the bright sun outside to the slightly stuffy feeling interior, Marcus' pulse hammered hard before his blood ran cold, feeling all sensation freeze from the tips of his fingers to the very ends of his toes. The kitchen tiles were covered in shattered glass, and there was blood. Not a copious amount, and it was mixed with the contents of the glass – water – swirling patterns of it like an oil slick, but still, the presence of blood was unmistakeable.

"Daniel?" he called out again, more frantically this time. The glass crunched under his boots as he picked his way across the kitchen and into the hallway. The house was stiflingly quiet. Instinctively, he reached for his chest, but he'd left his radio in his locker at work. He checked the living room. Empty. Light footing it up the stairs, he checked the bathroom. Empty. Spare room? Empty. Daniel's bedroom – empty.

The bedcovers were a mess, thrown back like they'd been vacated in a bit of a rush, and there was a nauseous, pungent smell filling the room. Down the other side of the bed was a sticky black stain on the carpet, which appeared to be where the stench was arising from. Marcus covered his nose and threw the window open. And then he glanced back towards the bed, where Daniel's phone sat on the nightstand; the only thing left of the wee fella, it would appear.

"What in God's name is going on here ...?" he muttered to himself, checking his phone again to see if he had missed a message or a call, but no. Nothing.

Although there was possibly a plausible explanation, Marcus wasn't taking his chances. Clouded perhaps by his feelings for the young man, yet driven by a copper's intuition, he just knew, from the dreadful feeling in the pit of his stomach that something terrible had happened. Urging himself to stay calm however, he extracted his phone and tramped back down to the kitchen, calling through to Central Control.

"Yes, hello? My name is superintendent Marcus Broadmeadow, of Rural Crime. Something has happened to one of my officers – no! I don't need a bloody ambulance! I need ..." he stopped mid-sentence will the call operative still nattering away at him, because from this angle, now facing the back door and looking out, he could see that there were a couple of washed-out footprints, stained with watery blood. He couldn't help it. Thoughts of DI Wright took over, and what they now suspected to have happened to him when he'd stepped on the wrong person's toes. "I have an officer in danger. Suspected kidnap. Request for immediate assistance."

He couldn't believe the words that he was saying. This couldn't be happening. Alternatively, Daniel had dropped a glass, cut himself, and ran down to a local shop for something to patch himself up with, in his haste leaving his phone behind and the back door wide open. That was all.

He could already be dead ... the other traitorous voice inside Marcus' head griped, fuelling his current inability to remain calm.

"Fuck it!" he cried out, marching out of the house as he heard the faint sound of sirens approaching.

*

South Lynn and Forensics were on the case, which didn't fill any of them with much confidence given their prior track record. They did confirm a potential kidnapping incident though, which was something, considering it had been less than twenty-four hours since Dan had last been spoken to.

"Do you really think it was something to do with Walters? Or Mikelis Malinovska, sending Walshy in?" Hollie asked to nobody in particular. Her eyes were red rimmed. She'd been crying. They'd been over it a thousand times already, full of potential scenarios yet coming up with nothing solid to hold onto.

Paul rubbed at his eyes. It was nearing midnight. "I really can't think of any other reason why this would've happened … somebody must have been keeping watch on him, to know that he was at home today."

"He would have noticed though, surely? Dan worked in Serious and Organised Crime for eight years, it's not like he's totally oblivious to his surroundings – quite the opposite, in fact," Hollie added, voice strained.

"I know. Just … I don't know …" Paul trailed off. Broadmeadow had shut himself in his office some hours ago and was yet to re-emerge. They could hear him on the phone almost at a constant, with moments where they both fell silent when his voice would raise to a broken shout, before the sound of the receiver could be heard slamming back down, even from behind his closed door. There was a feeling of utter helplessness surrounding them, as it was not within their rights to go downstairs and lend South Lynn a helping hand, even though they all knew that if anybody knew Dan better than most, it was them.

"Rachael." Hollie said abruptly.

"What about her? You wanna give her a call and let her know what's happening?" Paul looked at her rather stupidly. Honestly, that man sometimes …

Kicking herself, Hollie couldn't believe that she hadn't thought about it sooner; "No! Well, maybe. Remember the other day, when I caught her looking up Dan's personal information? And then today, when she came and told us that he was having the day off sick after asking the gaffer where he was?"

How could they have been so blind? It seemed so obvious now that she really considered the idea. Where did Rachael come from? Ackehurst's team. When had she been assigned to Rural Crime? Right after Dan had been drugged. With all the focus on the men at the top, they had failed to really see the reasoning behind her appointment to their department – a secondment? Really?

"We need to get the gaffer."

Together, they entered Broadmeadow's office. Hollie went first with a brief knock but didn't wait for a call to enter. Chester followed behind them, eager not to miss out on the action. The gaffer was sat behind his desk, bent over and staring at the phone, like if he glared at it hard enough a call would come through to say that Dan had been found.

"Sorry sir, but we need to talk to you. We think that Rachael may have informed somebody that Dan was at home today, alone," Hollie explained concisely, straight to the point.

Broadmeadow raised his head to look at her and Paul. Dark bags hung under his eyes, his hair ruffled and out of place where he'd been constantly running his hands through it. "Dear God ..." he murmured, his tone that of man who was at his wits end, and was about to break down in despair. He was the one who'd ordered Daniel to stay at home that day. He was the one who hadn't gone round to check on him.

"Shall we call her in, sir?" Paul tried.

Broadmeadow shook his head. "No. I would suggest that you two went home and got some rest, but, well, I think it would be safer if you stayed here for the time being. Besides, I've been on the phone to DCS Roberts. She has ordered that my staff remain here until we have an update. If somebody has taken ..." he appeared to choke on his words, clearing his throat before continuing, "If somebody has taken DS Taylor then there's every chance that you two are also in danger. I'm sorry."

The pain behind his eyes was evident.

"Nah, I'm not having that," Paul exclaimed defiantly, "If we're stuck here than I say we go downstairs and kick South Lynn's arses into gear. Dan is one of our own and I can't just sit here and wait for them to fuck about doing whatever is it they're doing – do they even have an ID of a vehicle? Surely they must have something?!"

Paul fixed his gaffer with a determined stare. He understood that Broadmeadow had to do things by the book, and he understood that the man had been hit hard due to his father-like (maybe something more) relationship with Dan, which meant that whilst Broadmeadow was feeling the pressure, he and Hollie had to step up and take some of that weight for him. He'd expect the same from them. His team were more than that; they were his friends, even going so far as to say they were like family …

"Hollie?" he folded his arms about his chest and looked across at his trusted colleague. Her lips twitched, before she nodded.

"Yeah. Let's go. Sorry sir."

Before Broadmeadow could stop them, they were off and out of the office. Chester hung back, torn between following and leaving the gaffer behind. Staring immovably at him, he barked and waved his tail.

"Alright, alright," Broadmeadow sighed in defeat – how could he say no to those eyes? Paul was right. Two detectives and an acting superintendent sitting around for news wasn't going to get them anywhere.

Broken Bones

Pain and fear were the first things that Dan remembered, not really understanding why he was bound at the hands and ankles with a strip of tape covering his mouth, tearing at his lips when he fitfully tried to cry out of help. A cloth bag of some description had been shoved over his head making it achingly hard to breath, as he gave up with trying to scream with every breath that it sucked away from him.

All he could think of in that moment was that he was utterly terrified.

He was in the back of a van, and they had been driving for some time. He was laid on his side with his hands behind his back, but with no recollection of the time between being knocked over the head to where he was now, where he had slowly awoken to a living nightmare.

The van came to a stop and the engine cut. He cringed, as the vibration of the side door rolling open reverberated around the vehicle's metal interior. Then, rough hands were all over him, dragging him by the legs and grappling with his torso. It was no use to struggle. What would they do? Drop him to the ground and then beat him to death right there and then? Kill him off, like they had with DI Wright? Just a suspicion at that point, but a strong one nonetheless – why else would he have been taken? And by whom? It had to be something to do with DCI Walters and his Latvian sidekick; mostly likely courtesy of their mate Walshy, so that they personally didn't have to get their hands dirty.

The warmth of the sun bathed his face and blinded his eyes through the thin fabric covering his face, before that moment of reprieve was taken away, where he was hauled back into the dark. A dank, dusty smell filled his nostrils, like that of an old shed or seldom used outbuilding. His mind flitted towards his gaffer as he was carried like a ragdoll – how he desperately wanted to see him one last time.

Perhaps if he pretended to be dead they would leave him alone, and he would get to live long enough to see Broadmeadow's caring face once more? But then what? They might try to bury him alive …

He whimpered, silently. His wrist was hurting. Back to the gaffer. He'd be arriving at his house soon, wouldn't he? He'd realise that his sergeant had gone missing. That was if he didn't stop by the shops first, or head home for a shower and a change of clothes. Or he was working late after his week away, catching up on his emails …

Or he wasn't coming over at all, having decided that what had happened in Scotland was all a hideous mistake, a message of apology already waiting on his phone, and nobody would even know he was missing until at least tomorrow morning.

In reality, it was only moments before the men that were carrying him – he presumed they were men – and unceremoniously dumped him to the ground. His bound wrists smacked against the floor, causing him to cry out in pain; a strangled sound, muffled against his gagged lips. The sound of his wrist snapping against his kitchen floor sickeningly replayed itself in his mind as he was hauled up to a seated position, his legs cut free, and a chain shackled around his ankle.

The bag over his head was then removed. Turns out, it was a pillowcase. A minor detail. He blinked, squinting, trying to adjust his vision. He was in a barn, or a stable? A stable. He was in a wood-walled stall; an open fronted prison cell, with two balaclava-clad men blocking the only exit. One was taller and heavier set than the other, but aside from that, there weren't really any distinguishing features to make out. The black dog was there. Of course it was. But, newly found kinship or not, it was no good to him now.

"He's very quiet, don't you think?" the shorter one gruffly said to the taller one, with a hint of smugness behind his words.

"For now. We'll see how long you manage to keep that up, is that right, *Danny*?" the taller one mocked, taking a step towards him. Dan cowered back against the wall, drawing the one leg that wasn't shackled up towards his chest. He now strongly suspected that the taller man was in fact Kyle Walsh, and that the other bloke was the one Dan had seen with him in that flatbed truck, transporting cooking oil ready for dumping. They certainly fitted the profile, now that his eyes had adjusted to the limited light.

"What's the matter? Cat got your tongue?" the taller man sneered.

Dan glared back at him with a streak of defiance. He wouldn't give them the satisfaction of trying to speak. Not that he was sure he could, even if he wanted to, unless he wanted to risk ripping the flesh right from his lips. The taller man crouched down in front of him. Dan remained still, forcing himself not to tremble or show any sign of weakness.

Easier said than done, but he was managing ok for now.

"Now, I'll tell you why you're here, if you want? See, you've been prying too close to our personal affairs, haven't you? We tried to warn you off, but you were either too stupid or too stubborn to back off, so we decided that you needed something more to convince you that *our* business, is not *your* business. Understand?" He laid a hand over Dan's extended knee as if he were offering out an olive branch – if Dan complied, agreed to turn a blind eye, then they would let him go and everybody would be happy.

But Dan, being too stubborn or too stupid, just continued to glare at him.

"I don't think he's quite getting the message, do you?" the shorter man said, looming closer and blocking Dan's view of the outside of the stall. The black dog raised its hackles, standing at Dan's side, coiling back as if it were preparing to strike. The accomplice to the taller man reached for something that was propped at the ready against the wall. It soon became apparent that it was a sledgehammer. Its weighty head scraped ominously against the concrete floor like a millstone.

Dan's glare faltered. His stomach dropped, eyes fleeting with panic. So much for not showing any signs of weakness, that notion instantly flying right out of window …

The man presumed to be Walshy agreed with his accomplice; "No, I don't think he is."

Dan tugged at his chained leg in a fitful attempt at escape, but of course, it was of no use. A panicked noise caught in his throat when the taller man stood up and the shorter of the pair passed him the sledgehammer.

He raised it up, as the smaller man gripped at his ankle with an iron hold.

The black dog threw itself over his lap, growling and snapping. Dan fleetingly locked eyes with the man who he suspected to be Kyle Walsh, wild with fright and pleading; *please, don't ...*

The scream that ripped from Dan's throat was deafening in his head yet silent from his lips, as an unimaginable pain blasted from his kneecap, tremoring up through the rest of his body like a shockwave. He fell to his side, protectively hugging at his right knee but unable to tend to the left.

Tears spewed from his eyes. He was going to be sick. It had nowhere to go but out of his nose. He was going to choke on it. He was going to die, choking on his own vomit.

Somehow, he managed to swallow whilst the rest of it trailed from his nostrils.

The last thing he saw was the sole of a trainer, unable to move his head in time before it connected with his face. And then he was kicked again, and again, as he cried, and he wailed, vaguely hearing the words *'fucking piece of shit copper'* before everything faded into nothingness.

*

Coming around to a whole new level of pain, Dan shuddered. There were hands at his shoulders, dragging him back up from the dust. He could only see though a slit between his eyes, because his sockets were swollen and his lids were crusted with dried blood, but he *could* see that the two men were back.

How long they had left him for was anybody's guess – could have been minutes, could have been hours, too dusky inside the stable to tell whether it was evening or night, and he was hurting too much to care about what time it was anyways. Even more scary than the pain, however, was the realisation that he couldn't feel his left leg. He could see it, just about, splayed and limp in front of him, so he knew that it was still attached to his body, but he couldn't feel it. No sensation whatsoever.

"Did you have a nice sleep?" mock-concerned, the taller man asked. He was inches from Dan's face.

Dan groaned with discomfort. His mouth tasted like a dustbin. He was thirsty.

He groaned again when his hands were cut free. It painfully released a pressure around his broken wrist, and he sobbed. He was fucking crying, and the two men were laughing at him.

The black dog was still there, he realised. It was huddling close to his side with all its former vigour gone, like it too had been beaten within an inch of its life. It was something to hold onto though – to know that he wasn't entirely alone in this.

"I don't think you quite got the message, Danny. I need your complete assurance that you're going to run along and stick to what you're best at, which is – what is it that you do? Play about with farm animals all day? Can you promise me that if we let you go, you'll play nice?" the taller man said, signalling towards the shorter man, who crudely took a hold of his wrist and started squeezing.

Dan sobbed harder, his nose and eyes starting to stream as he felt his broken bones crunch and grind together. His head started to spin, unsure whether he was going to make it much longer before he passed out again.

Thumbs dug in deeper. A white-hot pain. His wrist was being crushed; his blood flow being cut off …

"Or shall we just be done with you? Won't be the first time we've made a copper disappear. And you're a pretty pathetic excuse for one, I have to say. Look at you, crying like that. You're an embarrassment."

He didn't have it in him to avoid the glob of spit that was aimed directly at his face. Something that sounded like a pitiful whine could be heard, that he thought was the black dog for a moment, until he realised that it had emitted from his own throat.

Some form of relief came when his wrist was dropped, and his hands were taped again behind his back. One final kick sent him back down to the ground with a face full of dust and old straw cuttings. He wished it could have been a harder blow so that he could have faded back into unconsciousness, but they clearly still wanted him to suffer somewhat further.

Were they really going to kill him? It now seemed more and more likely – a safer bet for them too; that way they could be sure he wouldn't come chasing after them.

Mind going blank as heard the two men leaving him once more, with the black dog curling in against his chest, Dan thought about his gaffer. Not his parents, or his sister – just his gaffer, letting the ounce of warmth it gave him marginally ease his dread over how much longer he had left.

West of the Clayton Bypass

"No, no. You lot shouldn't be down here. Leave, please. Now," was all Ackehurst had to say on the matter. For a man who was usually so full of himself, he seemed flustered. Stressed.

"And get that dirty fucking dog out of here!" he added, glaring across the floor at Chester who had just arrived alongside the gaffer. Chester understood what humans were saying for those most part, and the understood Ackehurst's comment loud and clear, but he chose to blindly ignore it because it was just downright rude. Especially when a sergeant sat at her desk called him over for a bit of a fuss, which earned her a thunderous glare from her superintendent.

Community Safety and Criminal Justice – or better known as South Lynn – was buzzing with hushed activity, despite the hour in which they had all been asked to work. There were at least ten officers working away on Comms, and Intelligence, reviewing CCTV footage and coordinating officers out on the ground. It was a world away from upstairs in Rural Crime.

Marcus felt a small shed of hope at the sight, knowing that every single person in that room was trying to find his wee sergeant. Well, all except one. At that, he strode his way straight over to Ackehurst; "We're not going anywhere. I have two bloody fantastic detectives here who I will not see put to waste. And whilst we're down here," he stood up to Ackehurst, eye to eye and lowered his voice to a threatening growl, "I'll be able to keep an eye on you, eh? Make sure you're doing everything you can to find my sergeant?"

Ackehurst grunted. His eye twitched. Instead of raising his voice to match the rival superintendent, he caved without any further argument. "Fine. Make yourselves busy." With that, he swung around and disappeared off into his office. The detective sergeant who was still fussing over Chester beckoned them over, Marcus recognising her from when they had visited young Ryan Mitchell in hospital – she had been overseeing the case, and had let Marcus and Dan have a word with her witness without making too much of a fuss. Good lass. She and her partner, the other fella from the hospital, were pouring over some CCTV footage of a white van from outside a local newsagents at the end of Dan's road.

"Look at this, sir. We've located a vehicle, first seen driving towards DS Taylor's road at fifteen twenty-two. We think this was around the time he was taken, as there was activity on his phone up until ten minutes prior," she explained as Marcus, Hollie and Paul crowded around her station. She fast-forwarded the footage. Marcus felt like he was going to be sick.

"And then, at fifteen thirty-eight, it leaves in the opposite direction at speed," she said as she paused the footage, "Can you see – there?"

The driver of the van could clearly be seen whipping a balaclava from his face, in a split-second of footage. Blink and you would have missed it. Paul leaned in over the sergeant's shoulder and frowned, focusing his eyes on the blurry image of a face. "That's Walshy."

She turned in her chair to look at Paul. "Who?"

"Hang on, hang on – Kyle Walsh; Jamie Stubbs' cousin? Stubby? He was taken into custody last week for further questioning over the initial attack on DS Taylor?" Paul explained, confused over the blank look the sergeant was giving him.

"Oh, him? That was reassigned to Central Norfolk. Last I heard he was remanded in custody for a random attack on a police officer – I didn't realise it was your sergeant Taylor …"

That proved it, didn't it? That Ackehurst was perverting the course of justice from the inside? How could he *not* have mentioned Walshy's suspected involvement in all of this … Marcus crumbled with despair. South Lynn could have been onto his whereabouts hours ago if that hadn't have been the case.

The other detective sprung to his feet and started calling out orders in the apparent absence of superintendent Ackehurst; "Right, everyone! We're looking for a man called 'Kyle Walsh', and an unnamed accomplice. Any known whereabouts, where he lives, where he works. Get to it!"

Marcus marvelled at the young detective and his proactiveness. He couldn't have been much older than his Daniel, but with more of an assured confidence to him. They'd work on that one, once Daniel was safe and back under his watchful eye.

He felt a lump form within his throat as he took a step back. Daniel. His sweet Danny-boy. Overcome, Marcus blinked back tears. He'd had those same thoughts when he'd first heard about Johnny. *He'll be back soon. He'll wake up soon. I'll tell him how much I love him and not give a shite about who hears it …*

Hollie and Paul got to work with their new acquaintances. A shout came across the office that the van had been identified, driving west on the Clayton Bypass. Detective inspector Adebowale, as Marcus would later find out was his name, called through to officers on the ground, before making arrangements to get a police helicopter scrambled to join the search.

Hollie logged onto a vacant station and started looking up residences of Walshy's family members and known associates, already one step ahead of the game with all that prior research on the man she'd been working on. Paul sat down with the female detective and begun to reel off everything he knew about Mikelis Malinovska, before springing up again to run upstairs and grab the intelligence files they'd been working on.

Marcus would have been so proud of his officers – he *was* proud – but his mind was elsewhere. He wasn't a trained detective, not like they were, fearing that his input on the situation would only serve to hinder.

A thought then crossed his mind. Just a hunch; a wee bit of a stab in the dark, but the sudden inner revelation couldn't be ignored. Leaving his team to their work, with his better judgement clouded with pre-emptive grief, Marcus slipped away unseen and headed down towards his car.

*

"There were two locations. One, which Paul went to – Flax Farm, I think it was called – anyways, by the time he got there, it was abandoned. The other, which DI Wright led a

team on, came up trumps. Over half a millions pounds worth of cannabis growing there. One week later, Callum was dead ..."

Flax Farm. West of the Clayton Bypass, on the back road towards Halestanton. A disused farm up on the coastal marshes that had fallen into disrepair, ravaged by squatters and then later, an implied location of a cannabis farming operation. If Malinovska was involved before, and had gotten away with it, then the chances were that the remote location could be used again. It was about a forty minute drive. Marcus remembered the directions well enough. In the time it would take to coordinate officers to the scene, Marcus could already be close. That was his misplaced reasoning. That was where Daniel was. He could feel it in his bones.

Marcus took Paul's car – swiped his keys from upstairs before he left – it was unmarked and it had blue lights, which he used until he drew close to Flax Farm, after an agonisingly long drive. The thought then crossed his mind over calling in his location, but that would take up yet more precious time. He needed to get to Daniel.

When the abandoned farm came into view, he cut his headlights and drew up the driveway as close as he dared, before performing a ten-point turn in the middle of the narrow track. Parking up, the car was ready for a hasty exit.

Continuing on foot at a hasty jog, Marcus rounded the crumbling farmhouse. It was a clear night, the moon shining high over the abandoned farm which nature had begun to reclaim. The roof of the farmhouse was broken down to exposed timbers. A towering oak tree stood watch over the yard. A rusted old tractor sat dormant, overcome with weeds; in a few more years it would be gone, swallowed by the undergrowth. To the side of the yard was a barn, and next to that, a stable block.

An owl hooted up above. Marcus startled at the sudden noise before laying eyes on the front of a white van, hidden down to the side of the stables. The plates had been removed, but the make and model matched the one they were looking for.

With his heart skipping a beat, Marcus suddenly felt woefully exposed. He patted his pocket to call in his location, with a sense of dread befalling him as he realised that his phone wasn't there – it must have fallen out down the side of the seat in his haste to get up to the farm.

Shit, *shit* …! He'd have to go back. But that would mean leaving Daniel. He turned into a run, but as he did, he heard footsteps coming up behind him.

Stumbling, he swung back to the source of the footsteps, only to find that a man in a balaclava was pointing a firearm directly into his line of flight.

He froze mid-step, raising his hands in surrender – his only viable option as he'd be no good to Daniel if he was sporting a fatal gunshot wound.

"Stay where you are, copper!" The man rounded on him. Marcus remained still as he was grabbed by the scruff and marched towards the stable block, with the cold butt of the firearm pressed firmly against the back of his head.

Lights Out

Torchlight led Marcus towards the dilapidated block of stables. He stepped carefully, slowly, anxious not to make any sudden movements, and to show that he was completely compliant towards the demands of his captor. Once inside, a chill hit him. The place reeked of disuse.

With only the wavering beam of the torch held aloft over his shoulder, he could make out a row of three or so stalls, with high wooded sides and iron wrought bars. The ground was dry and grimy, ancient hay and straw rustling under foot. The muzzle of the gun at the back of his head guided him forwards towards the farthest stall.

That's when he saw the pitiful form of his wee sergeant, crumpled and broken on the floor, one outstretched leg chained at the ankle, hands tied behind his back and a black strip of tape covering his mouth. He saw how the lad tried to open his eyes when the torch beam shone into his face, but they were so swollen at the sockets that Marcus wondered if he could see anything at all, except for the detection of a bright lancet of light flecked with particles of dust.

Daniel scrabbled back like a frightened animal as another masked man stepped out of the gloom and grappled him up by the shoulders, until he was sitting up at an awkward angle, a small sob breaking from behind the tape covering his lips.

"Daniel, son ..." Marcus croaked out, risking antagonising his captor further, but needing to let the lad know that he was there. "What do you want from me – from him?" he cautiously asked the man behind his back.

"We were going to let him go, but then you appeared, so I think we might have to reconsider. On your knees, copper," the man quietly ordered. Unable to stave off a tremble, Marcus sunk down to his knees. Daniel started to frantically struggle and moan in front of him. The man holding him at the shoulders wrestled an arm around his throat in a crude headlock.

"Now, shall I finish with you first?" Marcus' captor, a man who he guessed to be Kyle Walsh, dug the firearm harder into his skull; hard enough to bruise.

Marcus closed his eyes and hung his head. He didn't want Daniel to see his face. He didn't want his fear to be the last thing the lad saw of him. All of his past mistakes flashed before his inner eye, leading right up to this moment, where he'd made the biggest mistake of them all. His desperation to get to Daniel had fatally clouded his better judgement, having gone against every standard policing procedure in the book to the direst of consequences.

The man raised his gun then, and pointed it at Daniel.

The lad loudly started to sob, and Marcus' heart started to break. This wasn't how it happened on the TV, or in the movies, with the calm and collected police officers talking and tricking the inferior captors down until they were able to pull a miraculous turn of events – this was real, and terrifying, and Marcus couldn't think of anything to say or do that would diffuse the situation into an agreeable outcome.

"Or shall I finish with him instead? Either way, neither of you are getting out of here. Let it be a lesson, when they find your bodies, that you people don't have any power over us. We'll always be one step ahead."

"Don't shoot him. Please, *for the love of God,* don't shoot him ..." Marcus pleaded, praying to a faith that had long since betrayed him, that he wouldn't have to witness his dear wee Danny's life being taken away.

Daniel sobbed louder as his own captor held him still to the point of suffocation, as the masked man set his arm out straight and fingered the trigger ...

"Just do it, will you? I've 'ad enough of this one's whining," the man holding Daniel goaded, shuffling back out of the line of fire.

"No!" Marcus roared, throwing himself backwards like a man possessed, sending the balaclava clad man flying.

The firearm went off once – twice – before clattering to the ground along with the torch. Marcus made a dive for it, but the masked man was faster and reclaimed what was his. Marcus felt everything slow down. His movements became sluggish. A phone could be heard vibrating. He felt his arms being manhandled behind his back as he attempted to crawl in the general direction of Daniel, by way of the fallen torch light beaming across the floor.

A Confession

The last person that Hollie expected to see that night was Rachael, but there she was. They'd been hard at work for hours now, and it was actually the next day at that point, although it didn't feel like it. Everything had just merged into one painfully long, emotionally draining and adrenaline fuelled day at the office. Hollie checked her phone. It would be sunrise soon.

Everyone on the team was now tracing as much CCTV and traffic camera footage they could get their hands on, trying to locate the movements of the white van after leaving the Clayton Bypass.

Easier said than done, when there was only one main road throughout the foreseeable search area. The rest of the county was all B roads and backroads, which meant, no surveillance cameras. All units out on patrol that night had been informed to keep watch, including two of South Lynn's own teams that had been deployed, with the sole order of locating the van that had taken Dan. To top off the county-wide search, detective inspector Adebowale had secured a police helicopter at his disposal.

They were going to find him. That's what she kept telling herself. Any missing person – an officer of their own particularly – was of course of grave concern, but this was something more. This was personal. Dan was extremely dear to Hollie, and they had grown close over the time they'd known each other. She saw him as a mentor and somebody to look up to; a man of great inner strength yet unafraid of showing his emotions. Dan was quiet but silly when the time allowed, with many a stupid joke or conversation shared between them over cups of tea in the kitchen, or at their desks when the afternoon was running slow.

Anyways, what was Rachael doing here?

Had somebody from her former team called her and told her what was happening? Because it certainly hadn't been her or Paul. Perhaps the gaffer had decided it was time for her to be questioned – for that matter, where was the gaffer?

Rachael gave her a guarded smile before walking over to where she was sat with sergeant Collins. She was nervously fiddling with one of the rings around her finger; "I heard about sergeant Taylor …"

Hollie raised her eyebrow. She didn't have time for this. "Really? Who informed you?"

"I … the boss. Superintendent Ackehurst."

"Did he now?"

"Hollie, ma'am? Can I have a word with you, like, privately?" Rachael meekly requested, her eyes flitting towards sergeant Collins before back to Hollie with a sense of urgency over the matter.

"Ok. Make it quick though."

They found an empty office off the side of the main floor. Hollie caught Paul's eye as they had passed him by, and he gave her a questioning look. Another wordless look between them was confirmation that everything was ok for now, but for Paul to stay alert should things suddenly go south.

With her back to the closed door, Hollie got straight down to the point. "Well? What's so urgent that it couldn't have waited until your shift?"

Rachael's fidgeting hands grew more erratic. Her eyes were wide, looking completely out of place upon her makeup-free face. Swiftly looking around and out of the paned window, then back to Hollie, she spilled, "It was Ackehurst."

Those were her only words as she awaited Hollie's reaction.

"What was? And is what you're telling me needing to be recorded via a formal statement?" Without waiting for an answer, Hollie pulled her notebook from her pocket and quickly wrote down what Rachael had just said.

"He … he asked me to inform him if I knew when Dan would be at home alone. I had to call a number and give them his address. I don't know who they were. He said I didn't want to find out what would happen to me if I didn't do it …" Rachael trembled out, nigh on close to tears, "He made me feed information back to him. Anything you were investigating to do with a man called Kyle Walsh, and another man, DCI Walters …"

Rachael stopped, unable to carry on because her facial features had twisted and contorted into an expression of pure affliction, her tired eyes spilling with tears. Hollie's heart did something funny at the sight. It betrayed her. Because despite Rachael's admission that she'd aided in Dan's disappearance, Hollie couldn't stand to hear that the young woman stood before her had, by all probability, been forced into such actions by the powers of a senior officer.

A senior officer who they already knew to be a power hungry individual, who was also open to coercion should it provide him with some sort of benefit in return. But first, before she could console, Hollie needed to obtain Rachael's unequivocal word that Ackehurst was a man who couldn't be trusted, and whether anybody else working within South Lynn's walls was working with him.

"You're telling me that Ackehurst orchestrated all of this?"

"Y-yes. I believe so. With my help."

"And is anybody else involved?"

"I don't … I don't think so. They all hate him …"

"And you don't know where they took sergeant Taylor?"

"No …"

Hollie had all she needed, for now. They needed to move fast. Ackehurst needed to be apprehended.

"I'm going to have to take you into custody, you know that, right?"

She watched as Rachael gathered herself, how she took a great, steadying breath and straightened herself up; "Yes. I know."

She fixed Hollie with a genuinely repentant look as she defiantly wiped at her eyes like she was fully ready to face her own fate. "I'm so sorry, Hollie …"

Hollie sighed. All the times she'd told Paul and Dan that she didn't like the girl when really, if she'd just taken the time to learn who she really was, Rachael may have felt comfortable enough around her to come clean sooner. She'd learned an important lesson there, for sure.

"I'll do everything I can to make sure you're looked after." And she meant it. If Rachael was speaking the truth, which she strongly suspected that she was, then she wasn't really the one in the wrong. Hollie knew only too well how devastatingly isolating it could be, when somebody was to intimidate and coerce one into bending to their every will.

Hollie was only eighteen when she'd found herself at the hands of a narcissist within the force, except her own experience had been based on a romantic relationship, and the breakdown of that relationship had caused her to abandon her fledgling career within Central Norfolk's Covert Operations and Surveillance Department. She'd run away, because of him. Rural Crime had given her the freedom she needed to find herself again. Anyways, she sympathised with Rachael and why she'd done what she had done.

"Can I trust you not to do a runner whilst I deal with Ackehurst?" she said, dearly hoping that sympathy wasn't misplaced …

"I'm not going anywhere. Thank you Hollie."

Hollie gave her own thanks before leaving Rachael alone in the office, trusting her word that she was going to stay put. Making her way back over to where Paul was, she wordlessly shoved her notebook under his nose and patiently waited for him to read through the scrawled conversation recorded upon its pages. Paul's lips fell into a silent 'oh'. Then he looked at her. She looked at him.

"Where is he?" Paul glanced over to Ackehurst's office. The lights were on but by the looks of things, nobody was home. He scrambled to his feet to have a proper check, but their fears were only confirmed – Ackehurst was gone.

"Where's the gaffer?" Hollie asked, assuming that Paul had seen him last.

"I dunno – thought he was with you?" Paul replied, assuming that Hollie knew where he was.

"DI Adebowale?" Going for next senior officer down the ranks, Hollie swept the office. He was on the phone, sporadically nodding to whoever he was talking to – then he looked around and beckoned them both over with a waggle of his finger.

"We've got a sighting of the van, heading up towards the coast at about sixteen hundred yesterday afternoon. Units are heading that way now – what's wrong?" the DI questioned, immediately picking up on the anxious demeanour of the two detectives from upstairs.

Hollie let herself fill with a glimmer of hope at the news of a sighting, before packing it away for later consideration, because they now had another matter of urgency to contend with; "Constable Hutchinson has just confessed her involvement with the kidnapping of DS Taylor, sir. And it was superintendent Ackehurst pulling her strings. And to top that off, both he and our own gaffer have gone AWOL. Do we have your permission to locate and apprehend him?"

DI Adebowale rapidly scanned over Hollie's notes before giving the nod. Surprisingly, he didn't look at all confounded by the revelation.

"Ok. I think we need back up from Central Norfolk. I'll call it in now. Has superintendent Broadmeadow taken his phone? Can we get some sort of triangulation set up – on both him and Ackehurst?" He stopped, calling out to the rest of the office, "Gather round, troops. We've got a bit of a lead here."

Time's Up

Outside of his office, the team were busy working away trying to find who had taken DS Taylor, with not a single one of them opting to sack it off for the evening despite his best efforts to encourage it. He'd even warned that it would only be flat rate overtime, but still, they'd all stayed.

All had been going well, when he had delayed calling in Central Norfolk for assistance for as long as possible, and with his team none the wiser over DS Taylor having already been assaulted at the hands of Jamie Stubbs, they literally had to start their whole search from scratch. That added yet more hours on. Twenty-four hours was what he'd been instructed to leave. That's how long they needed before DS Taylor was to be dumped by the roadside in God knows what sort of condition. Only then would he get a phone call informing him of the sergeant's location, and only then would he send a patrol out in that general direction – if a member of the public didn't get to him first.

Russel Walters had assured him that the young man would come out of it alive. He didn't much fancy another murder investigation to deal with. Not after the last. But then again, DI Wright wasn't meant to have been bumped off either, and it had taken all of his prowess to convince everyone around him that the car accident out on the fens was just that – an accident.

Despite his before efforts however, a stick had been thrown in the mud with the arrival of Broadmeadow and his team. So much so, that he was starting to become extremely concerned over the smooth running of the whole operation.

Blaming it on the pressure he was already under, the sight of Broadmeadow storming into their department had unsettled him something proper – he had been under the impression that the other superintendent's (*acting* superintendent, should he say) team had been locked down for their own safety. Add that to the nice little chat they'd had the other week, and Ackehurst had been under the impression that Broadmeadow had been put back into his rightful place; that he wasn't going to create a threat.

The look in the man's eyes though, now that had really thrown Neil off kilter. He'd never seen anything like it. It had been as if a raging fire were burning behind them, at the same time rendering them as cold as ice.

In all honesty, he was more than just a bit concerned. If the plan went to pot then he wouldn't get paid for his troubles. And even worse, Russel had threatened him. He hadn't outright said what the consequences would be, but he *had* said there would be consequences, which was enough for Ackehurst to understand that he wasn't to mess this one up.

Up until now, he and the DCI from Greater London had been good friends. They socialised and even holidayed together; he thought they had a nice mutual, respectful working relationship. He made sure that Russel and his partner Mikelis had free reign over the streets of Norfolk, and in turn, he was reimbursed financially for his troubles.

Tapping his pen against his desk, under the ruse of being agitated over the young police officer in grave danger, Ackehurst allowed entry of his DI, Andrew Adebowale. A good DI, if ever he'd seen one – too good, in fact. Always one step ahead of the game and as of yet, unable to be encouraged to move on in order to 'further his career'. Not like constable Hutchinson, where it had been almost too easy to scare her into bending to his demands. Typical woman. Easily led and easily beaten down.

"What can I do for you, inspector?" Unlike Broadmeadow and his softly-softly approach to leadership, Neil never called his subordinate officers by their given name unless he really had to. It instilled in them who was in charge (he'd learned that one from Russel).

"We've got a positive sighting on a white van sir, and a positive ID of a suspect, courtesy of our colleagues from Rural Crime. Not only that, but they've been working on a file of this 'Walshy' bloke, and another, a Latvian national going by the name of Mikelis Malinovska, who he's working for. I think we need to call the team together for a briefing," Adebowale concisely explained, all the while not even breaking a sweat.

Ackehurst, on the other hand – he felt his heart drop like a stone with a cold, unpleasant feeling of dread dropping all the blood from his face. "Ok. Give me five minutes. Dismissed."

His DI didn't move however, his face set with a steely determination. "Sir. I was hoping you could brief the team now? I fear that time is very much of the essence with this one."

"I said, *five minutes*. Dismissed, inspector!" he snapped, standing up as he did and slamming his hands down onto his desk. He saw Adebowale pointedly check the clock before striding out of the office, the dissentious bastard.

A feeling of one's world crumbling down around oneself befell him. His hands were trembling and his blood pressure was rising, and he needed to call this whole thing off. It was no longer worth the risk. He didn't want to find out what it would mean for him, if Mikelis' men were to be caught in the act of torturing a police officer.

Yanking open his top drawer and agitatedly pushing aside some paperwork, he grasped the burner phone Russel had given him at their last meeting. Holding it within his clammed-up palm, he hastily grabbed his keys, and slipped unnoticed out of the office before his five minutes was up. He needed to warn Russel that officers would soon be on their way, and he needed to see his wife, because it may well be a mere matter of hours before his time really was up.

Just a Scrape

Marcus wasn't aware at first that he'd taken a bullet; just that his shoulder was hurting a wee bit, but nothing to be too concerned over. Like they had done with Daniel, he found that his hands were bound behind his back, and he too was shackled at the ankle by a short chain, bolted to a weighty ring attached to the floor. He realised though, as he tested his hands, that in their haste to neutralise him as a threat, the two balaclava clad men had failed to proficiently secure the tape holding his wrists together.

He tugged at them, feeling the tape start to loosen. Tugging again, he ripped them free. Checking then at the chain around his ankle, he realised that wasn't going to be such an easy fix. It was locked tight, and unless he was to perform an amputation on his foot, there was no way he was getting it off.

Giving up with that for the time being, he noticed that something was leaning heavily against his side; it was Daniel.

Alive – just about.

He eyed the chain around his ankle too, but again, it was wrapped thrice around his leg so tightly, and bolted fast to the floor …

Daniel's breathing was shallow as he wrapped his arms around him; a great sense of relief setting in at having the wee fella back where he belonged – at his side.

Forcing back a grimace at the action of stretching himself, he glanced down in the dim light to see that there was a rip to his jacket, where his epaulette would usually sit upon his shoulder. Apart from the dull pain there where he must have been struck, and the niggling throb to the back of his head, he felt like he'd escaped relatively unscathed. A wee while back, Marcus had heard a bit of a hushed commotion before the throaty engine of the van outside had started up – he'd heard it leaving. He'd definitely heard it leaving, and since then, he knew that by some God given miracle they had been given an unlikely reprieve.

"Danny? You gonna wake up for me, fella?" he spoke softly so as not to startle the boy. It wouldn't do to have him panicking. Daniel grumbled something as he cracked one eye open – the one that wasn't so bruised. "That's it … can you stay still for me now whilst I take this off your mouth?"

The wee fella slowly blinked, before fighting with all his might to get away from him. So much for not startling him …

"Hey, calm down now, it's just me …" Daniel stilled, trembling, but halting with his frantic attempt to escape. Fingers reaching out, Marcus painfully peeled the tape from Daniel's mouth. There was no other way of doing it. Had he have done it slowly, it would have been just as grievous, only more arduous than if he just went and ripped it off.

"Sir …" Daniel croaked out, his voice hoarse with disuse. He shifted uncomfortably with his leg still bent out in front of him, trying to find an agreeable position against his gaffer's side. "My hands …"

"Ok, hang on. One thing at a time," smiled Marcus, giddy with relief that his sergeant was conscious and capable of independent thought, despite the pain he must have been in.

Reluctant to let Daniel out of his arms, he set about working on the tape around his wrists. It was tight, but he managed, after a bit of careful peeling. Once freed, he saw that one of the lad's wrists was near on twice the size of the other, with a healthy spread of bruised skin stretched unpleasantly tight around a misshapen bone.

"Darling, what happened …?" Fingering the injury with the lightest of touches, Marcus' heart cried for him.

Daniel held his limp appendage out and looked at it like it didn't actually belong to him. "I fell on it when they beat me over the head in my kitchen – wait, what happened? Are they gone?"

"Yes. They're gone."

"Is backup on the way?"

"I should think so, fella. They'll be here soon, don't worry," Marcus lied. He actually had no idea if anybody knew where they were, or if anybody even knew that he had gone missing, yet Daniel appeared to blindly accept his answer regardless of its woolliness.

Perhaps he was just too done in to question further, or perhaps he was just happy to accept the vagueness, as it offered a sense of refuge from what he'd been through. To stave Daniel off from asking any more questions over why Marcus was there on his own, without the cavalry bringing up the rear, he decided to change the subject; "Your black dog there seems a bit more amenable towards me today – what have you said to him, eh?"

Marcus hadn't actually seen it in a while now, but it wasn't growling or standing off with him, or skittering away to a dark corner at the sight of him. It was just looking at him from where it lay at Daniel's side, noticing too that its eyes looked more human, with more expression behind them than he'd previously seen them portray.

"You can see it?" questioned Daniel, as he weakly started trying to shuffle his way closer to his gaffer. Marcus helped him, spreading his legs out wide in order for the wee fella to drag himself between them.

Once they were as settled as they were going to get, Marcus unzipped his jacket and pulled the lad against his chest, enclosing him within the open garment and into his arms once more, in an attempt to give Daniel the extra bit of body heat he had to offer. After a moment the black dog followed suit, also slotting itself within the small amount of space left between the gaffer's legs.

"Not at first, out of the corner of my eye mostly, but since we've gotten to know each other better, yes, I can see it. Sometimes I can feel it, too," Marcus spoke softly, holding onto Daniel tight.

Dan was too tired and dazed to fully comprehend what it meant for another to be able to see his black dog, let alone to be able to interact with it like he could – or as to why his gaffer had never let slip before, that he had a permanent canine shaped shadow following him around. It didn't bother him, because Marcus didn't seem bothered. Marcus hadn't been put off by it, or that by committing to him as a person, the black dog came too.

"Something happened to it – I think it likes me now," he murmured, nestling closer into his gaffer's chest. He didn't have any form of higher explanation for it. He didn't know why he had a black dog, and he didn't know if anybody else out there did, as he'd certainly never seen another following somebody around.

Feebly reaching up with his good hand, he wrapped his arm around the gaffer's shoulders. The thought crossed his mind that they might die here, settling over his heart with a strange sense of calm. Everything just hurt so badly, and he was so tired, so thirsty, that he thought about how nice it would be to fall asleep in Broadmeadow's arms right there – how contented he would be for things to end like that …

But as he idly thumbed at the gaffer's shoulder, fiddling with the epaulette on his shoulder and feeling across his rank number, he felt Broadmeadow flinch at the touch. "You ok, sir?"

"I'm just fine. Just a scrape," the gaffer replied indifferently.

Dan investigated further by gently running his fingers along Broadmeadow's shoulder, below the epaulette. What he found was that the man's shirt was sticky, and that there was a deep divot there, that when he poked his finger down into, it made his gaffer wince. He brought his finger up to his uselessly swollen eye, and even in the dark of the stable, he could see that it was covered in blood.

"You've been shot, sir …" Dan said quietly, wrapping himself closer around his gaffer and tightly pressing his hand over the wound. It felt like the bullet had grazed right over him – another half an inch and it would have missed him entirely. Instead, it had taken a chunk out of him as it passed. It was bad, but not fatally bad. Not if he could stem the bleeding.

"As I said, it's just a scrape," Marcus reiterated, however, was unable to hold back a groan as Daniel pressed harder against his shoulder. He leant his head back against the stable wall, breathing through the discomfort. "How's your wee leg holding up, anyways? Are you hurt there too?"

"They hit my knee with a sledgehammer. I can't feel my leg." Dan impotently laughed out loud at the absurdity of it all, pretty sure that he was reaching a stage of shock because it really wasn't that amusing a situation. Reality told him that feeling nothing at all was bound to be worse in the long run, with regard to his shattered kneecap. In fact, even his wrist wasn't hurting all that much … perhaps he should be starting to panic after all? With that in mind, the gaffer started laughing too, grinning as he nosed into Dan's hair and gave him a lingering kiss.

"Ach, we'll get you fixed up, no worries about that. You just keep it nice and still for me, ok?" Marcus squeezed him encouragingly. How could Dan *not* feel like everything was going to be ok, with a man like his gaffer, his knight in shining armour, holding him in his arms?

"I do love ye', Danny," the gaffer murmured into his hair.

For now, Broadmeadow sounded like he was ok, although Dan knew that it would only be a matter of time before the adrenaline would wane, and the pain and exhaustion would set in – then they would both be done for.

He wasn't daft. He knew that if their team knew where the gaffer had gone, then they would be here by now. He knew the man didn't have a phone with him, and he knew that he was just putting on a brave face for his own sakes. He knew that if they had a chance of freeing themselves, then the gaffer would have had them out by now, so he hadn't even asked about that possibility.

At least the sun was starting to rise, yet it had the opposite effect to making him feel like a new day was dawning – instead, he felt dangerously sleepy as he bedded down against Broadmeadow's chest.

"Love you too, sir," Dan whispered with his last remaining ounce of strength.

Caught in the Gorse

"We've got a location. Broadmeadow's phone was last used approximately four hours ago – a GPS map application. It's been left running, which suggests that his position has been stationary since then. I say we go out there. Now," sergeant Collins urgently informed Hollie and Paul, already slinging on her vest and half way out the door.

Paul ran upstairs to grab his car keys, only to find that they had been taken. The next closest to hand were … no, really?

Hollie was already waiting at the bottom of the stairs with Chester excitedly bouncing at her heel. She held out her hand expectantly and Paul didn't argue, thrusting the set of keys into her waiting palm. She'd find out why in a minute, as he grinned to himself despite the urgency of the situation. In return, she pushed a stab vest against his chest, and then they were off, down to the car park where DS Collins and a team of her officers were already tearing off into the night, in a screech of tyres and a screaming wail of blue lights.

"Paul? Where's your car?" Hollie swept the floodlit carpark, but aside from the usual staff cars and a couple of vacant patrol vehicles, Paul's own set of wheels was nowhere to be seen. Pressing the unlock button and holding the keys aloft, she audibly groaned as the Rural Crime Wagon bleeped into life before them. It was set right under a floodlight, like a holy epiphany about to fulfil its God given purpose in life. "For fucks sake … come on then," Hollie groaned.

She glared at Paul, hopping up into the driver's seat as Chester bounded in behind. The Crime Wagon roared into life, and with the sirens whirring, they too set off in search of their fallen colleagues.

With DI Adebowale staying back at Vancouver Road to oversee operations, they both felt safe in the knowledge that everything was finally under control. A dispatch unit had been sent out to locate superintendent Ackehurst, suspected to have headed towards his current address – unfortunately for him he'd taken his allocated patrol car to work that day, which meant a tracker was fitted to the thing, so unless he'd gone and dumped it somewhere, they stood every chance of finding him before too long. And not forgetting Rachael, who was waiting patiently to be taken into custody once an officer became available to deal with her – understandably, not a priority in that given moment as they trusted that she wasn't planning on going anywhere fast.

As they headed up towards the coast with minimal conversation between them, where the land broke out into flat marshland and the sun was starting to peek over the horizon, Paul began to talk. "Hollie – I recognise this place."

He realised, with a crushing sense of familiarity, that he'd driven this road once before. Up ahead, a swarm of blue lights were breaking the dawn where Hollie had soon caught up with the convoy. Up above, a helicopter passed over their heads. Behind them, at breakneck speed, an ambulance brought up the rear.

"Really? What makes you say that? Did you once get lost on your way up to the seaside?" Hollie smiled across at him, but it soon faltered once she saw the look on his face – he looked like he'd gone and seen a ghost. A real one, not just one of those supposed apparitions he discussed at his monthly poltergeist meetings.

"Nah, Hollie. I'm serious. This was where – this was where we went an' busted that cannabis farming operation – well, DI Wright did. This place had already been cleared out by the time we got there." The narrow track that led up to Flax Farm came into view, where the swarm of public service vehicles was already congregated. Hollie swung a right up the un-tarmacked lane, dust and gravel flying in all directions as the Crime Wagon made short work of the loose surface. It sprayed up against a parked white van, half off the road and half into the adjoining field, but neither Hollie or Paul noticed it at that point. They were entirely focused on getting up to the farm building at the end of the long, straight road.

"And you're kicking yourself for not thinking of it sooner?"

"Yeah." Paul clenched his jaw at the admission. For all he knew, Dan could be dead, and the gaffer too, all because he was too slow witted to have remembered such an important piece of information.

Hollie yanked up the handbrake at the end of the track, skidding them to a stop and as she did, waving him into silence as the radio broke into life; *"Two officers have been located. No suspects on scene. All units, hunt for two male suspects, on foot."*

They both breathed a collective sigh of relief, taking a brief moment for it to sink in – Dan and the gaffer had been found.

"At least one of them must be ok if they were able to identify the suspects?" Paul said, unstrapping himself from his seat belt. In the melee of patrol vehicles and flashing lights, he saw his own car parked up, facing away from the farm and back towards the main road. "The old bastard took my car …" he added as an afterthought.

"Do you blame him?" She nodded towards the Crime Wagon as she jumped down and joined Paul – not exactly the best choice for a covert approach. And as for the gaffer's own car? That sensible estate thing he drove? Nope, she didn't blame him one bit for nicking Paul's squad car.

It was the best one in the pool by a mile, and how he'd managed to wangle it for himself she still wasn't sure. She did however, blame the gaffer for heading off without a word in search of Dan. If she were his mother, which she sometimes did feel like towards the lot of them, she'd be giving him a stern telling off as soon as she set eyes upon him. And then she'd give him a big old hug for going out and finding Dan before it was too late.

"Nah, not really. Not when it meant him getting to his Danny-boy," Paul joked as he started striding off towards the farm where a cordon was already being erected.

Hollie gave a knowing laugh. "Yeah … you think they really are, you know?"

"I'd be very surprised if they weren't. And if not, somebody needs to knock their two heads together – wait – what's up, Chester?" Paul stopped dead in his tracks, holding up his hand. Chester had stopped too, having fallen a couple of paces behind and was currently staring intently out across the marshy field to their left.

Chester emitted a low growl. His dark coat ruffled in the slight breeze coming off The Wash. Lifting one paw, he coiled back and tensed his muscles. The silhouette of a small copse of ragged looking gorse was set against the breaking dawn, at the far end of the marsh where the ground raised up into dunes. Here was where Chester's focus was centred. He crouched down on his haunches before briefly turning, giving Paul a *look*.

"Got your torch?" Paul asked Hollie, although he needn't have – she already had her light out and at the ready.

"Yeah, you?"

"Yeah." He turned to Chester, giving him the nod, "Go on then boy. Go get."

Chester took off, stalking down low into the knee-length grass. It was still green, not yet scorched by the summer heat, and the ground was boggy under foot. He weaved around the worst of the sodden terrain like a hairy snake, totally focused on the scent he had picked up by the roadside, trusting in his nose to lead the way. There was no need to check that Paul and Hollie were behind him because he knew they were, at a distance, picking up on the soft sound of their legs brushing against the grassy tufts and breaking reeds.

Soon enough, he reached the edge of the marsh and made his way up the slight incline, setting eyes upon the figure lying down in the gorse, long before he himself was spotted.

Creeping forwards with his vision set dead ahead, he rotated his ears in order to locate his colleagues. They were silently coming up behind him. Good.

The smell of blood tickled against his nasal cavity. The male in the bush was injured. As he heard the snap of dead bracken under foot to his rear, he waited for Paul's signal. "Police! Give yourself up!" Paul boomed, as he and Hollie simultaneously flicked on their torches and shone them in to the shrubbery.

Chester trembled, ready to make a run. The man in the bushes sprung to life, scrabbling to his feet as the sharp branches of the gorse threatened to entangle him.

"Stop what you're doing or I WILL deploy the dog!"

The man paid no mind to Paul's warning, breaking his way free and starting at a stumbling sprint. It was Walshy. No doubt about that, now that he was out in the open. "Chester – get him!"

Before the words had fully broken from Paul's lips, Chester launched into action. He may be getting old but he wasn't past it yet, throwing himself at the suspect like a high calibre bullet, jaw gaping wide and saliva flying …

"*Fucking hell!* Alright, alright! Call him off!" Walshy cried as Chested locked onto his lower arm just like he'd been trained to do. He'd never actually worked with Paul – not out in the field – but it didn't matter. He knew what to do, and Paul knew what to do, and that was the end of it.

As Hollie shouted down the radio that one of the suspects had been apprehended, the helicopter searching the area turned up in the distance. Tripping over his injured foot whilst trying to fight the possessed canine off his arm, Walshy crumpled down to the ground. Chester wasn't supposed to break the skin. But he did. Because the man had Dan's scent all over him – his tears, his fear, his bodily fluid, so Chester felt that a good chomp of his jaws was fully deserved on this occasion.

"Face down, hands behind your back!" Paul bellowed. Walshy complied with the overpowering demand, if only to get Chester off of him.

"You're under arrest, mate," growled DC Bartlett, cuffing him as he started to read him his rights before dragging him up to his feet. Chester could sense that Paul wasn't far off hitting the man.

Dropping his hold now that the man was apprehended, Chester took a step back. The helicopter approached, sending the wind whipping and the ground vibrating, its searchlight illuminating the sky above their heads. The glaring light revealed another man, tangled up in the thick gorse. Chester bared his teeth in warning. The accomplice held up his hands in surrender. There was nowhere to run, and he knew it.

"I need medical assistance, *please*. I've been shot. I can't walk. And there's another bloke down there, in case you hadn't noticed," Walshy griped, trying to shake Paul off. Hollie *had* noticed and was already on the case, dragging him out of the bushes and treating him to the same with Chester's watchful eye over them both.

Paul lowered his voice to an ominously threatening tone, "You'll fucking walk if I tell you to. Come on."

Chester would have to wait to be told how much of a good boy he was, because he could feel every ounce of anger that was coming from his two colleagues towards Walshy and his accomplice. Judging the mood, he knew that the job wasn't done yet. Not until the two men were secured in the back of a police car.

So, scampering up ahead and panting liked he'd run a marathon, with the police helicopter lighting the way ahead,

Chester led the party back through the marsh and towards the dry land, where the rest of his team were waiting.

It'll be ok ...

Dan didn't quite know what was happening at first, when he heard the barrage of noise approaching. It had been so quiet, just him and his gaffer, but now that peace was broken in a cacophony of engines, footsteps, shouting and bright lights. Even though some distant part of his brain was telling him that the cavalry had arrived to rescue them, he found that it was all too much of an assault of the senses, so he curled closer in Broadmeadow's unfaltering embrace.

An officer's voice that he didn't quite recognise was talking to him – or his gaffer? He wasn't entirely sure. His head was hurting. He couldn't focus. How long had it been? An hour, or two? He was pretty sure he'd fallen asleep at some point – or passed out. The voice (a female one) overrode the officers. There was his gaffer's voice too. Dan buried his face further into Broadmeadow's jacket. He could deal with it for him, because what little reserves of energy he had left were just about run down to empty.

It was going to take some convincing on the paramedics' behalf to separate Dan from his gaffer, after a set of bolt cutters had been deployed to cut them both free from their shackles. With shock setting in, Dan's confusion grew, and he just didn't want to let go. Mirroring him, the black dog laid flat against Broadmeadow's legs, pleading with him not to leave them.

"We need to get you to the hospital sir, and to do that we need to get you onto a stretcher – can you do that for me?" the paramedic said kindly, crouched before Dan and his gaffer.

"No ..." he mumbled, gripping onto Broadmeadow's shirt underneath his jacket. What seemed like the whole of South Lynn appeared to be crowded into the stable block by the sounds of things, judging by the turbulence of mixed commands coming through, and the bustle of voices all melding into one overwhelming din.

"You need to do what the wee lassie is asking, fella," the gaffer's own voice filtered through the racket, with a low lilt and reassuringly close to his ear, "You're hurt and they need to help fix you up now."

"Are you coming too?" His voice small, Dan realised how pathetic that sounded. It didn't stop him from whimpering though, as the gaffer took him under the arms and gently started to shift him out of his lap.

"I'll be right with you, son. Got a hole in the old shoulder, in case you'd forgotten?" Broadmeadow light-heartedly quipped, doing something totally unexpected as he took Dan's head in his hands, and pressed their foreheads together, "Come on now. The sooner we get you to a hospital, the sooner I can take you home with me, yes?"

Dan nodded, closing his eyes as some tears started to make their presence known. His gaffer's words were something to cling onto, a much needed promise, as he conceded and let the paramedics ease him down by the shoulders. On his back now, they make a start on assessing his injuries. At which point, as a canula was inserted into the back of his hand and a cool, calming sensation rippled through his veins, everything else around him faded into insignificance.

Forensics descended upon the scene as soon as Dan and his gaffer were moved out of the stall. Under the command of DS Collins, a team of officers started about their work of gathering evidence, with Broadmeadow helping out where he could, filling in the details whilst a paramedic worked on his shoulder.

Outside, Hollie and Paul handed over custody of Walshy and his accomplice to a couple of uniforms, before Paul crouched down and gave Chester the fuss of all fusses. A call from DI Adebowale came through shortly after, to inform DS Collins that Ackehurst too had been successfully apprehended. Over in the distance, the sun broke free of the horizon, for what promised to be another gloriously warm summer's day over the Norfolk countryside.

"Are you ready to go, sir?" one of the paramedics asked, as Marcus chatted away to DS Collins now that the scene was under control.

"Oh – yes, yes. Excuse me, sergeant," Marcus cut the conversation short. She would have to wait for her statement – they could drop by the hospital in a while and take it from him there, because there was no way in hell that he was leaving young Daniel to take the ride alone.

His protective steak flared as Daniel was carried away, all strapped into a gurney. He'd refused one for himself, anxious that he would be barred from riding in the same transport if they deemed him too incapacitated. In reality, his shoulder was killing him, his left arm hanging uselessly at his side where the pain had given way to a lack of feeling, but he hid it well, because he'd made a promise to a certain young man that he would remain right by his side.

In a strange move, Daniel's black dog opted to remain at his side like it was keeping a watch over him. It clung close to his legs as he followed the paramedics outside into daylight, where they saw Hollie and Paul having a wee bit of a conflab near the back of the waiting ambulance. Chester noticed them first, bounding over in a flurry of black fur.

Then Hollie, fixing him with a mock glare. Then lastly, Paul with his usual grandiosity; "Where ya' been, sir? Leaving us to do the hard work, as usual!"

"Only because I know you're both more than capable," he replied, eager to catch up with them, but torn, because right now he needed to be with Daniel. He dearly hoped that they would understand.

Hollie stepped aside from where she'd been leaning against the ambulance, as the paramedics that were carrying a semi-conscious Dan loaded him up into the back. She looked at him, all prior elation over catching Walshy dropping from her face. "Oh my god, Dan ... is he going to be ok, sir? What did they do to him?"

"He's not in any imminent danger, however I will be travelling with him. You two are free to follow on – *ah* – follow on behind," he gasped mid-sentence as a sudden jolt of pain shot through his shoulder, wincing as his automatic reaction was to grasp a hold of it, hence giving the game away that he not as perfectly fine as he was letting on.

"Sir?" Obviously concerned, Hollie frowned at him, stepping closer to take a better look before her jaw dropped and her face went pale. "I think you need to be getting in that ambulance right now, if I were you. They have seen to you too, haven't they?" she added, stepping into her role as mother to the team.

"Hollie. Paul. I'm just fine," he reassured them, trying at a smile, but the pain was starting to magnify. He needed to sit down.

"We'll see you at the hospital, sir. Look after Dan for us," Paul stepped in, giving his gaffer a knowing stare. Marcus nodded curtly, handing him his car keys as he passed, before stepping up into the back of the ambulance. The black dog hopped in behind him.

He was ushered into a jump seat next to Daniel before the doors slammed shut behind them, and not long after, they were off. The nearest hospital was only fifteen or so miles away, as the crow flies, so he didn't anticipate it to be too long of a journey.

As the paramedic sat himself down and begun quietly tending to Daniel's vital signs, Marcus took a long, deep breath. Only in that moment did the events of the last eighteen hours fully sink in – how he'd come so close to losing somebody so important to him. He'd have nightmares over it, he was sure; seeing the wee fella so frantic and scared, and in so much pain – nobody ever wanted to see those emotions upon the face of somebody they loved so deeply …

Reaching out for Daniel's hand (the good one; the one that wasn't strapped up in a brace), where it was sitting motionless across his stomach, Marcus took it within both of his hands and bowed his head. He didn't pray much anymore, but he did say one then, reverting back to old-worn habits of his upbringing. To whom he prayed, it wasn't quite clear, it didn't matter, he just felt compelled to do it. And Daniel's wee hands were so very cold. "It'll be ok, darling. I've got ye' …"

His voice cracked. He swallowed hard, trying to control the wave of emotion that was threatening to overcome him.

"Is his life in danger?" he asked quietly to the paramedic.

"I wouldn't like to rule anything out, but I can say that he's nice and stable right now."

"Ok. Thank you."

Daniel grumbled something incoherent when Marcus squeezed harder at his hand, turning his head towards him where he lay, before sighing back into unconsciousness. At least the lad wasn't hurting anymore, with all that medication pumping through his system. Beside him, the black dog sadly rested its head upon his knee, with its pointy ears flattened down against its head. Feeling the weight upon his leg, Marcus thoughtfully took his eyes away from Daniel, just for a moment, to glance down at the equally sorry a sight.

"He'll be ok, don't you worry," he reassured it, not even stopping to think what it must have looked like to the poor paramedic, to see the police superintendent muttering away to himself like he'd gone and lost the plot entirely.

Clean Break

When Mikelis Malinovska received the phone call from DCI Walters, to inform him of a potential flaw in the plan, he took a very big risk and suggested that they meet up somewhere to discuss things in person. Mikelis travelled up to the city, to one of his supermarkets. Just a routine visit to check on business. Walters would meet him there.

It the back room, between the boxes of stock waiting to go out on the shelves, he waited. Walters didn't keep him waiting long.

"What do we do now then?" Walters questioned him.

Mikelis frowned lightly, as cool as the cucumber; "Nothing. We do not need to. Mr Walsh will not talk. And your Ackehurst man? I trust you have the same faith in him?"

Walters didn't say anything. Didn't even make a comment over Gustav snuffling his nose over an open box of packaged meat.

"Well, whatever. I am not worried. I have something to tell you, Russel. I sell the supermarkets. I have the buyer already." No point in beating about the bush. This would be the last time that he and Walters would meet like this – maybe even the last time they ever saw each other. Old friends they may be, but that didn't count for anything to Mikelis, when it came to his bigger picture.

"You're telling me that you're walking away, if I understand you correctly?" Walters said without an ounce of emotion upon his face.

"Yes, you understand me correctly."

Walters tipped his chin in a gesture of acute clarity over what his Latvian business partner was telling him. Mikelis stepped forwards, extending out his hand.

They shook. And just like that, they were done.

*

The police did come knocking, but by the time they got to him, Mikelis had already been in possession of ample time to sort out all of his affairs. There always had been a plan in place, for if the shit hit the fan, which Mikelis was able to deploy with astute accuracy now that the time had come about.

A man called Janis, a loose acquaintance who sometimes helped with the deliveries, had been bugging him for years over when he was going to sell his supermarkets to him, because why did he need them when his plant hire business out in the countryside was doing so well? Janis had jumped at the chance when Mikelis had informed him that he was ready to sell up.

That was the first part of the plan, already set into motion weeks before the detective from Rural Crime was taken away for an in-depth interrogation at the hands of Mr Walsh. To be honest, Mikelis had seen the walls starting to crumble even before then; even as far back as when the other detective was accidentally disposed of.

Mikelis was hard around the edges, of course, but he was not an evil man. Even though he would openly speak of 'finishing people off' if they didn't bend to his will, it had always been a bit of a front, if he was completely honest with himself. He didn't particularly like seeing innocent people getting hurt, and the young detective by the name of Daniel had really struck a chord with him, because his younger daughter, Katia, had her own dreams of becoming a police officer one day.

Now, how would he feel if she were to be taken and beaten? Aside from going out and smashing some heads in on a trail of bloody retribution, he couldn't even begin to imagine seeing her beautiful face contorted with fear and pain at the hands of some unknown attackers.

Anyways, enough on that subject. Selling the supermarkets was phase one of the plan. The second part of the plan was to tidy up all of his finances. Being the discerning businessman that he was, Mikelis had always made sure that not a single penny of dirty money even caught sight of the plant hire businesses books – it always went through the profits of the supermarkets, which were now no longer anything to do with him.

With the supermarkets gone, there wouldn't be any more heavy goods vehicles passing by the Norfolk countryside, with their bags of cannabis and cocaine and heroin carefully concealed within the frozen foodstuffs. The plant hire business had always been legitimate, except for a select few of his employees, who had only that week been made redundant (with an extremely generous payout), as part of a 'budget tightening exercise'.

The last stage of the plan was to part ways with DCI Walters, where it was up to him whether he chose to carry on with the operation without him, so long as his own name was never to be mentioned. Walters was not a good man.

Mikelis was no saint, and he wasn't saying he ever would be, but he didn't get off on abusing his power like Walters did. The man used to like telling him stories after he'd had a couple of drinks, about how he abused his officers in ways other than using his words and his fists – sick things that made Mikelis want to punch him – and how they were so scared of him that they wouldn't ever dare to report his behaviour.

The detective from Rural Crime was one of them. Walters had taken great pleasure in bragging over that one.

With all aspects of the plan neatly tied up, it still begged the question as to why Mikelis had gone to such efforts to cut ties with an empire he had worked so hard to build up? Twenty years of toil was a long time after all, to now be slowing things down to a halt ...

With Walshy paid off to take the fall, he wasn't going to talk. He'd do, maybe ten years, maximum? Nothing, for a young man like him. And even if the Ackehurst man spilled, there was very little chance that enough evidence could be built up against Mikelis – he'd never even set eyes upon the man, and besides, he worked with Walters, not him.

All in all, he *could* have carried on, with a bit of clever diversifying towards the way he operated, but as the years had gone on, Mikelis found that his heart just wasn't in it anymore.

His girls were growing to become a pair of beautiful, clever young women. He wanted to be around to see them achieve their goals in life; to be the father that he hadn't yet been for them.

And as for Charlotte, his dearest wife? She deserved the world. He loved her so much that it hurt him to think of a life without her.

They had enough money to get by comfortably, no worries on that front. There was enough to send the girls to whatever university they wanted to go to, and they would have a healthy business to inherit one day. As for himself and Charlotte? They could have a nice retirement, if they wanted. All was good. No loose ends.

That was why Mikelis had chosen to walk away, and he did so knowing that only God was there to judge him for what he'd been a part of.

Taking Stock

As Dan slowly came back to consciousness it was evening again. Later evening by the looks of things, as it was getting dark outside. He was parked up next to an expansive window, so had a nice view of the opposite wall of the hospital building, where a central square garden sat in the middle of the square complex. He'd be able to see it, if he wasn't flat out on his back with his left arm and leg encased in plaster.

The black dog was there, sitting upright in the chair by his bedside, and it was staring at him. There was a quiet hum of activity going on around him, coming from behind the closed curtain around his bed; the steady beep of machines, hushed conversation and dull footsteps, wheels clattering past supporting noisy metal trolleys …

All very peaceful.

Some of the machinery beeping away was his own, he noticed noncommittally. There was a catheter stuck in the back of his good hand, and a plastic thing clipped over his finger. Turning his head to the side, but finding that it didn't really want to move, he could see the steady, ebbing lines across a heart rate monitor. He didn't know what all the readings meant, but they were at a constant, and it was quite relaxing watching the little line running across the screen. Soon enough, Dan's eyes grew heavy again, where sleep beckoned him back within its enticing embrace.

When he woke again, he had company other than the back dog, in the real, and very much alive, form of his gaffer. He tried at a smile, as he saw that the black dog had been ejected from the bedside chair and was sitting on the floor, with Broadmeadow now the one who was staring at him instead.

"Alright, sir?" he rasped through his cracked throat. It didn't even sound like his own voice as it fell over his ears.

"Hey there, Danny-boy. How're ye' feeling? Did you have a nice sleep there?" he said softly. The man looked exhausted with his bloodshot eyes and filthy uniform, his whole stature looking rather deflated. Even so, despite him not particularly looking his best, Dan was so very pleased to see him there.

"M'good. Still tired."

The gaffer reached across and found Dan's hand with his own. It was big and it was warm. "You just rest now. You were in surgery for a long time, but they assure me that you're all fixed up and you'll be ready to go home tomorrow, all being well."

"Home?" Dan remembered then. The masked men. The broken glass. The blood. The vomit on the carpet …

The black dog whined, leaning in close against the gaffer's legs. It didn't want to go home either. Broadmeadow squeezed at his hand. "Or if you wanted to come back to mine for a couple of days, just whilst we get your house back in order for you? I must admit, I don't know what state it's been left in after forensics had a good old look around the place."

"Ok," Dan stuttered, mortified over how he still felt so rattled over what had happened to him. It made him feel weak and unsubstantial – more so than usual, even making him reconsider his whole career path as a police officer, because he clearly wasn't quite cut out for it. And then he recognised, as he looked down at his leg, that he might not even have a choice in the matter.

Broadmeadow saw him staring at his cast-bound leg. "You've fractured your patella. They've removed some of it and stuck pins in what was left, but the surgeon will be round soon so she can tell you more. But on the up side, your broken wrist did not require any additional scaffolding, and should heal just fine on its own."

Dan flopped his immobilised hand up and down, glaring at it. That'll be crutches out of the question then. "Will I be able to walk?"

"Yes. I think so. In time. But as I said, you just worry about getting some rest now."

"Ok," Dan said quietly, wishing they weren't in such a public setting so that he could ask for a cuddle. He needed a bit of human contact now more than ever. Then he remembered – things kept coming back to him in fits and starts – the firearm. Broadmeadow's shoulder. More blood. "How are you holding up, sir?"

The gaffer smiled warmly, briefly sweeping his eyes down to his own injury before focusing back on Dan. "This? Ach, it's nothing that a couple of stitches and some antibiotics won't be able to sort."

(And the possibility of a skin graft if it doesn't heal over, and the possibility of brachial nerve damage where the close-range bullet grazed over to take a chunk out of his clavicle.)

But Daniel didn't need to be worrying himself over that right now. As he said, it was nothing really.

"Did it hurt?" Dan asked, concerned for his gaffer, and filled with guilt over how he'd felt so compelled to go out on his own and try to rescue him. If only he'd been bigger or stronger; been able to put up more of a fight when they'd burst into his kitchen and beaten him to the ground. If only he'd been a good enough detective to foresee something like this happening in the first place, then they wouldn't be sitting here now in the state they were both in.

"It did a wee bit, fella. It's ok now though."

"I'm sorry …"

"Don't be."

They sat there for a while after that. Time seemed to have slowed down like there wasn't any rush for anything much at all, with the hospital going on around them, and the outside world beyond that irrelevant. Dan did think to himself, was he feeling hungry? But he decided that he wasn't. There was a slight feeling of pressure in his bladder however, although he wasn't sure exactly how he was supposed to use the bathroom, with only half of his limbs in working order.

Broadmeadow continued to hold his hand. Were they still … actually, what were they? Was the gaffer now his partner because they had kissed and shared a bed? That would be nice, to do that again, the thought of it making something warm and insistent burn within his lower belly.

And then something else came to mind. "Did they catch Walshy? And Ackehurst, and Walters?"

The gaffer laughed at him abruptly breaking the silence like that. "Walshy and his accomplice were apprehended by our very own Chester. The silly bastard went and shot himself in the foot – literally – before their van broke down on them. They're currently on remand with no option for bail. The same goes for Ackehurst. He admitted to perverting the course of justice, but as of yet, there has been no mention of DCI Walters. I'm sorry son, but it's looking like there may not be enough evidence as it stands to link the two men together."

Dan didn't know how he felt about that, as Broadmeadow continued to softly observe him. To be honest, Dan was a realist and he knew exactly how conniving his former boss could be, so he wasn't particularly shocked over the news. But the disappointment was definitely there, that they hadn't had long enough to build a proper case of evidence against him.

"I'd love to be able to say I can't believe it … I'm gonna have to stand in court, aren't I?" he added as an afterthought, going back to Walshy. No pun intended – he wasn't going to be standing anywhere, anytime soon …

"Yes, but you know that. And as for Walters? A battle for another day, eh? We'll get him, one way or another." Broadmeadow softened the blow, and Dan believed him when he said that this wasn't the end of it. Which in turn gave him a rare flash of determination to keep fighting for his arrest, even though he could just let it all lie; leave the man behind as an unpleasant part of his past.

What he really needed to do was admit the details of the physical abuse DCI Walters had dished out upon him, deciding that soon enough, he would tell the gaffer all about it. But for now, as Broadmeadow had rightly said, it was a battle to face another day. At present, he just wasn't feeling strong enough.

"What about that Malinovska bloke?" Dan asked as he shifted, trying to get comfortable. The pain medication must have been wearing off, because everything was starting to ache.

"Here ... shall we sit you up?" Broadmeadow didn't wait for an answer, already up and fussing about with Dan's pillows, before wrapping himself around him for support as he pressed the button at the side of the bed to make the backrest lever up. "He's been questioned, as Kyle Walsh's employer, nothing more."

"Ok."

The gaffer's embrace lingered. Dan was more than happy to let it continue, as he slipped his good around the man's sturdy waist in return. Their position was terribly awkward and not nearly enough, now that his gaffer's arms were around him once more.

"There's probably room for two up here, you know ..." he asked hopefully. "Not you," he added as the black dog flopped a heavy paw up onto the mattress, wagging its tail as if it were about to jump up on the bed with him. It huffed, giving him a hurt look before removing its paw and finding a gap between the bedside cabinet and the wall, curling itself up small and out the way.

Seeing Broadmeadow smile, he already knew what the more sensible man than himself was going to say. "I'm not sure I fancy the wrath of your surgeon if she caught me snuggling up with her patient like that ... save it for when I get you home, eh?"

Nosing his way down, the gaffer tightened his arms around him and confidently captured his lips in a kiss to seal his promise. Dan's heart skipped happily as the kiss turned a little deeper, the way a real lover would lay claim upon what was theirs.

Sadly, they were rudely interrupted by the sound of the curtains around Dan's bed drawing back, with the gaffer grinning against his lips before pulling back, under the ruse of innocently re-fluffing his pillows.

DI Adebowale and DS Collins had arrived to personally take Dan's statement, at the news that he was now awake and well enough to recount his ordeal. No doubt his parents would be around soon to see him too … which meant that his gaffer would undoubtedly feel like it was his time to take a step back, maybe go home to get a shower and some sleep …

"Will you be leaving soon?" he asked quietly, as the reality started to hit that there was still work to be done, and that they still had lives to live outside of the hospital ward he'd found himself on.

"I'll stay for your statement, if you wish. And your parents are on their way – perhaps then I will just nip home for a change of clothes, but I'll be back if you'd like me to stay the night? As an officer of the law, it would appear that there are certain privileges attached when it comes to designated visiting hours." The gaffer winked at him, before stepping back to greet the two detectives from South Lynn.

No Bother

Dan was left in no doubts as to the long road of recovery that lay ahead for him, but for the time being at least, he felt positive. And as for the gaffer? Well, he was making a great show of hiding any doubts over Dan regaining full use of his leg in the long term.

Positivity could only get one so far however, when the realisation dawned that Broadmeadow's older house did not cater for somebody in a wheelchair, starting with the front door. Getting in and out of the car had been challenging enough, but now this?

"It's not gonna fit, sir," grouched Dan, who was tired, aching, and just wanted to get somewhere more comfortable than the public ward of the hospital. He was especially grumpy because he'd been forced to stay there for an extra night, because the surgeon wouldn't sign him off for release until he could get himself in and out of the wheelchair unassisted, which would have been totally fine if he had two working hands at his disposal. The black dog was grumpy too, mirroring his own mood, which really wasn't helping. It did have the sense to back up out the way though, when Broadmeadow tried again at angling the wheelchair over the front doorstep – and failed.

"No, I think you're right, fella. It's ok. No bother …" he said cheerily, as he wheeled Dan's chair back and then stood in front of him, bending down to take the lad under the arms.

"Loop your arms over my shoulders," he instructed. Dan did as he was told, never one to say no to an opportunity of getting up close and personal with the man. He was lifted up laboriously, with Broadmeadow wincing in discomfort over his injured shoulder. Eventually though, he manged to hobble them both inside the house, where, luckily, the living room was situated just past the entranceway. The gaffer eased him down onto the sofa, promptly pulling a footstool over to rest his outstretched leg on top of.

"Now, you make a list for me of what you need from your house, and I'll pop round there in a bit for ye', does that sound ok with you?" Broadmeadow said, as he made his way back outside to get the wheelchair in and fold it up by the front door, then back to the car for Daniel's crutches. When he returned, the lad was just sat there staring at him.

"What's wrong there, fella?"

The truth was, a million and one things were running through Dan's mind. He needed to use the bathroom and he needed help with that. He wanted to have a shower, but again, needed help with that. He was staying in somebody else's house, with no hope of returning to work until his wrist was well enough to use the crutches, which meant Broadmeadow would be leaving him during the day to his own devices. And what if somebody came knocking round to finish off what Walshy and his mate had started? What then? And to top it all off, he didn't even have his phone – it had been taken as evidence, though the gaffer was going to see if he could get it back for him tomorrow at work …

Dan couldn't possibly put all of his misgivings into words, so he settled on; "Just … I feel bad for putting all this upon you, sir."

"It's no bother, Danny-boy. None at all," Broadmeadow soothed as slipped down onto the sofa beside him and pulled him into an embrace, trying to convey every feeling of devotion he had towards the younger man, as he held him nice and tight. Daniel would soon come to realise that Marcus was a natural carer, always had been, and after so many years of having to bottle those feelings up when living with Rowena, he was more than ready to let it all spill out over young Daniel.

His estranged wife had never reciprocated his protective nature, because she was the one who always wanted to be the perceived stronger partner in the relationship. That alone had left him feeling, for many years, that his natural role within the partnership – the place where he felt most comfortable – could not be attained.

Now he had the opportunity to give Daniel everything that he was certain the lad needed from a partner, if only he would just let a bit of his stubbornness drop – let himself be taken care of.

"As long as you're sure? I'm not sure I'm that easy to live with on the best of days, and that's without, well ..." Daniel gestured loosely at his leg.

"Come up here, will you?" Marcus widened his legs and pulled Daniel up into his lap – which was swiftly becoming a favourite position – before setting the lad's leg back out straight along the length of the sofa, carefully batting down any thoughts of anything more. That was despite having something so warm and willing resting right against his ...

"It'll be nice to have the company. I'm happy to have to you here."

He smiled soppily as Daniel gazed up at him, shuffling slightly in his lap to get his arm up and around his shoulders, but careful to avoid his injury. "Could I have a kiss?" he asked sweetly …

"Of course you can, my darling."

*

The time soon came, after having spent a long while on the sofa getting to know each other's mouths, for Dan to face one of his initial fears. Having lugged him up the stairs and then back down for the wheelchair, and then back to find a stool for him to sit on, Broadmeadow apologetically returned to the bathroom, for a third time, to help him with the shower. Well, when he said shower, he actually meant a wash with a warm flannel, because until they could get something large enough to cover the cast around his leg, going anywhere near running water was out of the question.

How he'd have managed all this on his own, had the gaffer not have been there, Dan didn't know. All he did know was that he was eternally grateful for it, despite his initial apprehensions over having to be fully catered for.

If he let the little voice in the back of his mind speak for him, he'd even say that he was quite enjoying all the attention that Broadmeadow was so willing to give him.

"How do you want to do this then?" the gaffer asked, looking a bit uncomfortable now that there was only one thing left to do. Dan's thoughts of enjoying this soon turned to a stark realisation – he was going to have to take his clothes off, wasn't he?

Removing his t-shirt seemed like a good place to start, as he could do that without any assistance (and without too much embarrassment). He pulled it off and handed it over to his gaffer, who folded it nicely for him on the side. The older man visibly snatched in a breath at the sight of his bare chest, before quickly averting his eyes.

Dan just prayed that his prick wouldn't decide that now was a good time to start working properly again. That would be somewhat inappropriate. "I'll need, um, need help with my shorts ..."

"Right. Ok. Let's get them off then." With the gaffer's face burning red, he crouched to lift Dan up into his arms – was getting quite good at that – and instructed him to wrap his arms around his shoulders. Once Dan was steady, Broadmeadow planted his hands around his hips and slipped his thumbs under the waistband of the loose shorts he was wearing. "You ok, son?" he murmured, checking again before continuing.

"Yeah. 'M ok," Dan said a little gruffly, his embarrassment forgotten now that there were two firm hands at his hips about to undress him, at the same time finding it terribly endearing how Broadmeadow was getting himself so flustered over it.

Arousal hadn't really been his prevailing thought when it came to him and the gaffer, having felt entirely contented with the platonic nature of what they had been sharing, yet now, perhaps with their brush with death playing its part, Dan found that he couldn't shift the thought from his mind – never mind the fact that he hadn't *actually* shared relations with another person in a very long time now ...

Not since DCI Walters had ... done what he'd done. But Dan wasn't going to let thoughts of him ruin this.

"Are *you* ok, sir?" he asked cautiously.

"Not if you keep insisting on calling me '*sir*' when I'm about to take your wee shorts off, son," Broadmeadow strained as he pulled Dan closer against him, where he could then feel that they were very much on the same page. The older man was undoubtedly interested in where things were heading, which gave Dan the confidence he needed to push a little harder.

Pressing his weight into him, as Broadmeadow was forced to adjust his footing to keep the both of them upright, Dan whispered up into his ear, "We could just skip the shower, until after …"

"After *what*, exactly? Hm?" playfully, and a little breathlessly, Broadmeadow asked, struggling to hold Dan upright whilst pressed so flush against him.

"You did say we could share the bed once I got out of hospital …"

The gaffer emitted something low from within his chest which sounded like a growl. At that, in a feat of superhuman strength, he hauled Dan up in his arms, backed them both out of the bathroom, along the short hallway, and straight towards the bedroom.

Well Prepared

With all the intentions of grandiosity in the world, Marcus barely made it to the bed without putting his back out. During the short walk from the bathroom to the bedroom, he forced himself to ignore the feeling of his right arm failing him with every step he took. Whilst the wee fella gave the impression of being rather slight next to his own bulk and height, in reality he certainly was a lot heavier than he looked.

Considerate of his injuries, he eased the lad onto the bed, rather than dropping him straight down like his body was telling him to. Romantic a gesture as it may have been, to take Daniel up into his arms like a blushing bride, Marcus wasn't planning on doing that again anytime soon.

One thing Marcus had done, after Rowena left, was to buy a new bed. He wasn't one for splashing the cash usually, especially not when the old one was perfectly functional, but he couldn't have kept it. There were too many not-so happy memories tied up within its frame. So here they were, apparently about to christen the new one, and Marcus was feeling the onset of nerves. Although he'd done all of the necessary research and preparations, this would still be a first for him, as it was for the young man splayed out on the bed before him.

Rather frustratingly, his Catholic upbringing niggled at him, that what he was willingly partaking in was wrong. It was an ungodly sin; unnatural, and he was going straight to the fires of hell for even considering the action.

But then he focused back on young Daniel, who was looking at him like *he* was the one encased within the holy shroud, and the feelings of indoctrinated guilt subsided.

Forcing himself to relax, he unbuttoned his shirt and shucked it off, feeling his face heat up as the lad's eyes fixated on his bare upper body. He was no oil painting. He had a bit of a middle-aged gut, and his grey-haired chest was starting to sag, despite his rather lanky stature.

Daniel, on the other hand? He was downright gorgeous. And Marcus really couldn't see for himself what the young man apparently saw in him. It certainly wasn't for his money, he thought ironically. Daniel's black dog wasn't particularly helping either, with the nerves. It had followed them to the bedroom and was currently snuffling about through Marcus' things. Small mercies though – at least it wasn't staring at him like it usually did.

"Come here will you, sir?" Dan asked innocently, flopping his arm out to the side in an invitation for Broadmeadow to join him. He could see his gaffer's discomfort over stripping off in front of him, so made the executive decision to distract him before he went and bottled it. In hindsight, he should have suggested that they turn the lights off first, but too late now.

Marcus weighed down the mattress as he braced himself over the lad, unable to stop himself from lightly pressing himself against him. Daniel trembled beneath him, a pair of wee hands lacing into his hair, pulling him down to brush their lips together. The cast around his wrist knocked against Marcus' head and he laughed, "You wanna watch that thing now, could do some damage with that, you know …"

Dan spoke between their careful exploration of mouths, "Maybe you need to pin me down instead, save any more accidental injuries …"

Grunting into his mouth, the gaffer rolled his hips against him, and Dan felt things starting to stir down there. Consciously, he reminded himself not to get too carried away with some of the sexual fantasies that went on in his mind – Broadmeadow didn't seem like the type to know too much about such things, let alone having ever acted them out, and he didn't want to scare him off.

There would be time for gently introducing all of that, just not now. Tonight was about something more than just sex, Dan knew.

"Are you telling me you don't know how to keep yourself still, hm?" Marcus grinned against his lips before pulling away and brushing their noses together, "Let us see how well you can do with that one …"

Marcus still wasn't entirely sure what he was doing by way of pleasuring another man, but he used his intuition to guide him, with Daniel's enjoyment at the forefront of his mind. Kissing his neck seemed like a good place to start, which gained an extremely positive reaction, especially when he added some teeth and tongue to the mix.

Spurred on by the amount of squirming the young man was doing, and the noises he was making, he made his way down to his chest, kissing and mouthing at every inch of skin he could get his mouth upon. Stopping at his stomach because he decided that he wasn't to run before he could walk, Marcus drew himself back up. Maybe Daniel could teach him how to perform that act correctly, another time. He did want those shorts off though, especially now there were thoughts of the lad's mouth around him running riot in his head.

"Can I take these off now?" he asked, as he took a hold of Daniel's hips just like he had back in the bathroom, this time with entirely different intentions.

"You don't have to ask …" Dan blushed. Quite honestly, right now, he'd let his gaffer do whatever he wanted with him.

Hooking his thumbs under the waistband of his shorts, Marcus slowly slid them down below the line of his groin. Daniel wasn't wearing any underwear, then …

It took a bit of awkward manoeuvring to free the lad's right leg, where his shorts then became caught over the cast on his left, and he then gave up, deciding that it wasn't worth any further risk of injury.

Daniel went a wee bit quiet then, looking up at Marcus with his hand resting over his jutting hip bone, fingers looking like they about to creep over and cover himself. Looks like Marcus wasn't the only one feeling a little self-conscious, and it made his heart ache for the lad. How could he convince him, that a lack of complete sexual function made no odds to him? There were plenty of other ways to pleasure one another.

Could Daniel really not see how bloody lovely he was? Right from his sweet yet handsome wee face, with his ruffled up hair and ridiculously expressive eyes, to his perfectly proportioned, stocky wee body, all lightly toned muscles and flat lines, with hair growing in places that Marcus had long forgotten enjoying the sight of.

"Would it help if I took mine off too?" he asked softly, working on his belt before kneeling up fully and pulling down his jeans.

Dan gawked at him. Or rather, at the size of him.

Marcus laughed nervously, before sinking back down and finding solace within Daniel's willing mouth. The lad was so responsive to his every move and touch, finding himself taking mental notes every time Daniel made a seductive noise, or trembled up against him at something he had done. Relaxing into it, Marcus pushed his hand between their bodies and took the lad within his palm.

Daniel gasped, pressing up into him. He still wasn't hard, not like he himself was, but it obviously still felt good.

Daring himself to finger down lower, between Daniel's thighs, he inquisitively pressed one finger against the heat he found there – it was positively burning. Drier, and tighter than a woman, but so much more alluring, especially when Daniel started pressing back against him, a strangled noise falling from his lips.

"That good, hmm?" Marcus murmured, pressing a wee bit harder.

"Mhhhm … lube … needs lube …" Dan just about managed to stumble out. It was too tight; too dry.

Marcus chastised himself. He knew that. The internet search he'd performed had told him exactly what he needed to do. Internally, he flushed at the memory – that night where he had pulled out his personal laptop, after realising he and Daniel were heading somewhere with their feelings, where he had tentatively typed into the search bar for what he was looking for. What he'd found had left him feeling more than just a tad hot under the collar ...

Anyway, Marcus' bedside drawer was stocked with everything they needed, and he tried not to feel too embarrassed over it (or too much like a dirty old man who'd come already prepared to perform the sinful act).

Stop it, Marcus. This isn't a sinful act. There's nothing wrong with what you and Daniel are doing.

With a bottle of lubrication and a condom in his hand, Marcus flushed ever further as Daniel piped up; "Glad to see you're well prepared, sir ..."

"Cheeky shite, you. At least one of us was, hm?" he mock-griped as he pushed Daniel's good leg out wider and started working on carefully preparing him, not even sure that either of them was going to last long enough to reach their end goal – not when the lad was starting to make all manner of encouraging noises (and forgetting that he was supposed to be staying still for his gaffer).

Daniel raised his leg up impatiently, with Marcus' finger lodged deep inside of him.

"You sure you want to do this? I don't want to hurt you," Marcus spoke low, his accent lilting, as he pulled down his briefs and poised himself into position.

"I mean, my knee is hurting at bit ... but ..."

Hurting 'just a bit' was an understatement. The ache within his knee that was verging on pain *was* proving a little distracting, and he couldn't quite get into an entirely comfortable position, but the pull towards consummating with his gaffer was stronger. He wasn't going to stop now.

Daniel grinned, his cheeks gloriously flushed as he fumbled on the mattress for the forgotten condom, ripping it open with his teeth because he only had one working hand, and looking rather coy as he took his gaffer in hand. Marcus barely held onto any remaining self-control, as he was handled and nudged back into position. "Christ, lad …" he closed his eyes, holding himself back.

Falling down to his elbows, Marcus slowly sunk himself inside.

Daniel groaned, long and low as he was taken.

Through gritted teeth, Marcus managed to gasp, "I'm afraid I shan't be lasting long, fella."

The lad let out a soft, throaty noise, clawing at his back and pulling him in closer, sinking their mouths back together as they moved against one another in a desperate, needy coming together of two fellas who had finally found what they needed from one another.

The Morning After

Marcus woke to a sensation of utter bliss, with a warm wee body draped over him, and the feeling of reality as far distant as humanly possible. He seemed to remember falling asleep with Daniel curled over into the little spoon, left leg askew, but they must have shifted over in their sleep, as he was now laying on his back, with the lad's arms and legs slung over him like an extremely weighty blanket. Not yet opening his eyes, he pulled his own arms around his sleeping sergeant and placed a soft kiss to his forehead. He smelled of warmth, and it was intoxicating.

Daniel snorted. There was damp patch against Marcus' chest where the lad had been dribbling in his sleep. He shifted under the covers, suggestively nudging himself up against Marcus' thigh whilst incoherently mumbling something or other.

Thinking back to the night before, it was a terribly tempting idea to roll the lad back over and give him a nice wake up to the day, but then he remembered that it was Monday morning, and it wouldn't do to be late for work. Not to mention the realisation over how tender he felt; how he ached in places that he'd entirely forgotten existed.

Then his thoughts went to Daniel – how he'd needed to use the bathroom very shortly after they had consummated, and the wee bit of stomach trouble he'd suffered afterwards (which, with two broken appendages, the lad had needed his gaffer to help him with). Entirely normal for a first time apparently, but Marcus didn't want to go and make things worse for him, or make him feel embarrassed over it – and he didn't much fancy answering to Daniel's doctor either, considering any physical activity at all was supposed to be firmly out of the question.

As Daniel continued to orally perspire against his chest, Marcus took a minute to think about Johnny; how if this would have been life for them, had fate not gone and pulled them apart. He said a quiet prayer to him, hoping Johnny would be happy for him, that he'd finally found somebody to love in the way that he needed. It left a feeling a warmth inside his heart, rather than a gut wrenching sorrow. He knew then that Johnny was giving him his blessing from up above.

It was to be a morning of blessings, it would seem, as he saw that Daniel's black dog was contentedly curled up at the foot of the bed. It wasn't paying them any mind. He was starting to notice, how the more he took the time to really see it, the black dog gave him an extra insight into how Daniel himself was feeling, like the two were one and the same entity. If Marcus looked after one of them, then the other would reciprocate and thrive from it.

It was strange old thing really, but nothing that overly bothered him. It was just a part of Daniel, and that was all he needed to know.

"Good morning, sweetheart," he greeted Daniel as he stirred, stretching out before nestling closer into him.

"Nrgh ... morning ..." the lad grumbled, his voice heavy with sleep.

Marcus had worried that waking up together after finally doing the deed may end in disaster, where Daniel would come to his senses, all filled with regret over what they'd done – and for falling for a much older man which would, in time, bear its own problems – but as of yet, everything felt just fine in Marcus' eyes.

"How's your stomach? All good?"

"Mhm. Fine. Wanna go again?" Dan asked sleepily, fitfully trying to get himself up on top of his gaffer, but finding his movements severely hindered, like he'd gone and forgotten the set of plaster casts restricting half of his limbs.

Again, Marcus was tempted, the body and mind willing. He felt like a teenager all over again – whoever said that one's libido was supposed to fade with age? Because in this case, they were wrong. Ever the pinnacle of sensibility however, and even though his briefs were starting to feel a wee bit tight (and would need readjusting very soon), Marcus settled for a deep kiss instead. He loved the way they just seemed to fit together, and he loved the feeling of Daniel's morning stubble bristling against his cheek; how his hair was all soft and out of place before he'd had a chance to tidy and comb it aside.

He bit back a groan as Daniel's hand started to wander, finding its way between his legs. God, if only he didn't have to get up for work so soon … if that had been the case, Marcus was sure that they'd have soon found themselves spending the rest of the morning in bed.

If only.

"Come on now, fella. Give an old man a wee rest, will ye'?" he said fondly, reaching down and placing the lad's hand across his stomach, rather than between his legs.

The black dog quietly whined first, before he noticed that Daniel was looking at him with a hint of apprehension, like he'd gone and been told off for something he'd done wrong.

"What did your surgeon tell you, eh? You're meant to be resting, young man."

Marcus stole a quick kiss before pulling back to fix the lad's gaze, "If we had more time, then I'd have loved to have given you some more attention, I tell ye' that now."

"Yeah?"

"Mmm, yes." He couldn't get enough of this, as Daniel demanded yet another kiss from him. He was making it harder and harder by the second for Marcus to contemplate leaving the comfort of their newly christened bed.

"What time do you have to get up?" Daniel asked, clinging onto him as if he was indeed going to make it very hard for him to actually achieve that particular goal.

"Ten minutes ago, probably," Marcus said truthfully, yet, still in no particular rush to get moving.

"I'd get up and put the kettle on for you if I could – are you sure I can't come to work too? I feel fine …" Daniel tried, reaching his hand back down to trace a finger down the length of Marcus' spine, finishing at the waistband of his underwear, teasing at the divot of his coccyx …

"No. Absolutely not. You're staying right here I'm afraid."

Dan didn't argue his case further. He knew that it wouldn't really be practicable, seeing as the lift at Vancouver Road Station hadn't worked since he'd been there, sat redundant in a permanent state of 'awaiting repair'. And in no way did he expect the gaffer to be helping him around – literally cringing at the idea of how unprofessional it would come across, should they be all over each other like they were currently.

He'd be ok here. The gaffer had made a trip back to his own house for a bag full of comfy clothes, on top of all the essentials he needed, including his games console that he had permission to set up on Broadmeadow's tiny TV. Marcus said he'd go back and clear the place up for him too, as it was apparently in a bit of state after forensics had done their work. Dan felt extremely bad about that. The man had put himself out so much already.

"Are you getting up then, sir?" he asked, knowing full well that he wasn't making it easy for the older man, and surprised that he still felt so aroused …

He'd genuinely thought, with his 'problems' down there, that his sex life was doomed to be over – still didn't manage a full erection – but it honestly didn't seem to have mattered, especially where the gaffer was concerned. If anything, Marcus took the issue in his stride, seeing it as a challenge to find other ways of making him feel good and loved.

And as for going and actually letting himself be taken? The thought of it had scared him to start with, but under the steady hands of his gaffer, such fears had soon been quelled.

In fact, if only he'd known sooner how good it could feel to be loved like that …

"I do wish you'd call me Marcus once in a while, you know – or Marc? You don't have to keep calling me 'sir' when we're off duty," the gaffer gently berated him. He was smiling however, as he carefully peeled Daniel off of him and sat himself up in bed. The smile briefly broke, as he held in a gasp of pain from his shoulder over the shift in position. Daniel didn't notice thankfully; remaining where he was, suddenly finding his gaffer's navel of great interest, trailing around the downy ingress before poking his finger inside of it.

"Like you insist on calling me Daniel?"

"Ok, ok. Fair point, Danny-boy," Marcus laughed, finding the intrusion a wee bit ticklish and left wondering what exactly Daniel was looking for in there …

Soon enough, the lad pulled out a small ball of fluff from his belly button, examined it between his fingers, then flicked it away. Always so inquisitive over everything around him, his wee fella – presumably why he seemed to always find himself getting into trouble.

Marcus pulled him up for one final cuddle before they really had to get moving, because he had two people to think about now. Daniel needed setting up downstairs with his wheelchair and something leaving in the fridge for his lunch, they both needed their painkillers dishing out, and Marcus needed to iron his shirt at the very least.

Courtesy of Daniel there to distract him, his usual Sunday routine of getting a week's worth of uniforms hung and ready had been neglected. Once the lad was up and running again, conceivably, he could consider bribing him into taking that role over from him … for now though, all he really needed to worry about was getting them both out of bed.

Daniel winced and the black dog went flying, when Marcus abruptly threw the covers back before creaking and groaning his way out of bed like a man of twice his age. Daniel may make him feel younger at heart, but perhaps he should heed to his own advice and take things a wee bit easier going forwards …

Back to Normality

One week later, Dan was able to master his crutches without putting too much weight upon his wrist. Undoubtedly, he wasn't supposed to be doing it, but being wheelchair bound and unable to even get to the bathroom without a fight on his hands, or having to be hauled up the stairs for bed when the gaffer was clearly struggling, made him decide that enough was enough. As long as it was only for short periods of time; that was what Broadmeadow had told him.

One would think that a bit of time off, just to lounge about watching TV and playing computer games would be a dream. In reality, even a week of being stuck in somebody else's home had been a bit of an ordeal, even with the gaffer insisting that it was his home too, as it just didn't have the same comforts of one's own space. It was probably just the knowledge that he couldn't physically leave that left him feeling like he was trapped, having to reason with himself that his only other option would be to go back to his own home.

He didn't want to do that. The thought still made him go all cold inside with fear.

It had been so lonely, and for Dan to say that was something, because he wasn't exactly a social butterfly by nature at the best of times. Sure, the black dog had been there as a constant, but it wasn't the best at conversation, and for the most part it just sat somewhere nearby keeping watch over him. Every day, he'd just found himself waiting until his gaffer returned home, where they then, well, made up for spending the day apart …

His other issue was that he wasn't able to help around the house. There were jobs to do because the estate agents were coming later that week for a valuation, and there were things he could be getting on with, like watering the garden, and cooking the gaffer dinner for when he got home (he hadn't told the man yet that he was a useless cook). Just little things that he longed to be able to do, in order to repay (in some small way) what Broadmeadow had done for him. And there Dan was, he realised with a start, dreaming of a life of simple domesticity at the grand old age of twenty eight.

Today, however, was a very special day, because he had been allowed out. He'd been signed off by Occupational Health for a return to work on a staggered three days a week, and with that, he was to be on strictly limited duties. Dan didn't care. As long as he was back at work in one form or another, he was happy.

First to greet him was Emily at the front desk, and it felt like his first day all over again. He felt like he hadn't seen her in ages, with the conference away and then his extended absence after that. They had a quick catch up over how she'd been, and promising to try and meet up at the canteen one lunchtime – although he kind of knew it wouldn't happen any time soon, because Emily said these things all the time and then never actually committed.

The gaffer ushered him along, not towards the staircase but towards the lift. "Got a wee surprise for you," he said proudly as he pressed the button to call it.

Dan furrowed his brow suspiciously. "Can I trust it? You said it hasn't been working for years."

"Trust me. It's been tested." To prove his point, Broadmeadow stepped in first and then hooked him by the elbow to coax him inside. Looks like he wasn't going to be given a choice in the matter then ...

The gaffer rounded on him once the doors were closed, craning down to steal a quick kiss, which soon distracted Dan over his fears of getting stuck in there for the rest of the day. "Amazing how quick something can get fixed once you mention health and safety, and a less-abled member of staff, eh?" the gaffer grinned as he pulled away, looking extremely chuffed with himself.

"Can we try that one for some new office furniture ... and some new computer monitors, d'ya reckon?" Dan said, as his gaffer reluctantly pulled back to a more respectable distance.

"Don't push it, Daniel. One thing at a time."

Up on the third floor, Paul had to pull Chester back, because he was so excited to see Dan that there was the real risk of him being sent to the ground in a flurry of black fur.

"Alright, sick note?" Paul called out over the office, fighting to keep Chester from breaking free of his grasp. At his desk, Dan could see that there was a helium balloon hovering over it that said: 'Happy Birthday!'

"They didn't have any others, except for 'Enjoy Your Retirement', which I though may be a bit distasteful."

"Thanks, Paul. I appreciate the sentiment," Dan grinned back, at the same time wondering how long he would be expected to keep it there like a giant beacon over his desk. The next thing he knew, Hollie was coming up beside him for an uncharacteristically emotional hug, before helping him into his chair. Two boxes of printer paper had been stacked under the footwell of his desk, so he could plonk his broken leg on top. A very thoughtful gesture from his two colleagues.

They caught up over hot drinks – Hollie and Paul had visited him in hospital but it had been brief, namely because they'd caught him at a time when he was still drugged up on painkillers, and not entirely capable of holding a proper conversation. Now, they had the chance to talk over the details of what had happed the night Dan was kidnapped, and how South Lynn weren't actually that bad now that superintendent Ackehurst was out of the picture. In a positive move for the department, DI Adebowale had been asked to step us as an acting DCI until a new gaffer could be appointed.

They discussed the situation regarding Mikelis Malinovska and how he'd been questioned without further charge. Although none of them had ever met the man in person, it wasn't a surprise to hear that he was set to get away without any involvement at all, after hearing that apart from their suspicions, there wasn't any evidence of wrongdoing when it came to Central Norfolk knocking on his door for questioning. On paper, all involvement of drug running and intimidation came down to Walshy and Ackehurst.

All they could do now was to keep an eye on him from a distance, hoping that one day, he would put a foot wrong under their noses.

"What about Rachael?" Dan asked. He didn't actually feel as angry as he thought he would over how she had betrayed them. Like Hollie, if anything at all, he felt sorry for what had happened to her. That was because he knew exactly what a boss abusing their power could feel like; how desolate and lonely an experience it could be for one to go through.

"Bang her up and throw away the key, that's what I say," said Paul from where he was standing, perched against Dan's desk. Hollie glared at him. "I'm joking. She's been suspended on full pay pending further investigation."

"Ok. What about DCI Walters, has anybody heard from him?"

"Nope, nothing. Central Norfolk have taken over the whole case, and apart from your sighting of him at Malinovska's place, there really isn't anything to go on. It'll be down to the Met, ultimately, and if they choose to open any sort of internal investigation," Hollie replied rather dejectedly.

For every criminal caught, there were always going to be the ones who got away, and as disheartening as that was, it was just the reality of the job they did. Dan thought again over how it would only be right for him to file a formal complaint against the man, and how he'd been treated under his command, but the truth was, he was honestly still so scared of the man. They'd really gotten to him as well, with what they'd done to him – and if it happened again, he surely wasn't going to get away with just a couple of broken bones.

Walters would want him finished off entirely, he just knew it.

Once a court date was set for Ackehurst and Walshy (and the man called Assam who had been the accomplice), Dan would have to give evidence in the dock and under oath, which was enough for him to worry over for now, without the addition of DCI Walters running around his mind, scaring him out of his wits. He tried to put the man to the back of his mind for the time being, and although easier said than done, he'd leave him there for later consideration. He certainly wasn't going to be forgotten – Dan couldn't, because he still wasn't free from the nightmares Walters continued to subject him to.

The gaffer came out of his office then, where the three of them jumped back to their work, in the ruse of looking like they had actually been doing something productive with their morning, rather than just having a nice chit-chat. Broadmeadow looked over his trio of detectives with one eyebrow raised; "Glad to see you're all working hard, eh? I thought I'd just come and tell you all that our very own Chester here has been nominated for an award, for his long service and exceptional bravery. It's a bit short notice, but the DCS has put him through and he's been accepted."

They all turned to Chester who was lying on the floor chewing at his toe nails. Next to him, Dan's black dog was rolling on its back trying to get his attention – nice to see that they'd apparently made peace with each other. Eventually, with his paw still caught between his teeth, Chester noticed them looking at him, causing him to cautiously beat his tail against the carpet.

"Yeah, you're a good boy, mate. Well done," Paul crooned to his loyal companion, which prompted Chester to jump to his feet in search of more fuss, now that the magic words 'good boy' had been spoken.

"There's something else too, so listen up. Central Norfolk will be reopening DI Wright's case in the light of Mr Walsh admitting a few things he shouldn't have, this time with the proposed outcome of a murder investigation. So, I thought you all might want to hear that one first before it gets out elsewhere." Broadmeadow paused, observing Chester who had pricked his ears at the mention of his former handler's name. The sight of it tugged at his heartstrings.

A heavy silence filled the office, and they all took a moment to remember.

"That's great news, sir," said Paul with a sad yet hopeful smile.

"It'll mean a much longer prison sentence for Mr Walsh, and hopefully Ackehurst as well with an additional charge bolted on, so let's hope for the best. Paul – you may be required to help with the investigation, should Central Norfolk require it."

"No probs, sir. I'll gladly be of assistance."

"Good. Right, get back to it, the lot of ye'." Broadmeadow looked proudly over his team before turning on his heel and retiring to his office (he didn't want to start getting too sentimental over them all now, did he?).

Dan settled back into his seat at that, and started making headway on all the emails that had been piling up in his inbox. Everything felt strangely normal, like nothing had ever happened in the first place. Hollie passed him over some information on another church roof theft for him to look over and share his thoughts. In addition to that, there was a waiting report for him over Mr King's cattle being worried again (he'd been released on bail, pending charge for misuse of a firearm), along with some blurry photographs of some dog walkers that didn't really hold any significant context.

He smiled to himself. Everything had definitely fallen back into the slow normality of trying to keep Norfolk's jurisdiction free from rural crime.

Under the Stars

Taking stock, Dan couldn't quite believe how much his life had changed since moving back home only four months prior. When he'd first arrived, they had still been within the lingering grip of a springtime that felt more like winter, and here they were now, sitting out in his gaffer's garden on balmy summer's eve, taking in the serene beauty of the county that they called home.

The far end of Broadmeadow's garden backed onto an uncultivated paddock, where all manner of wildlife could be seen, especially at this time of the evening. Dan particularly liked the barn owl that frequented the grand old oak tree which stood near the boundary, hanging over onto the gaffer's side of the low fence separating them. The sky was a bold watercolour painting of pinks and blues and yellows, where they would get a full view of the sunset over the paddock, before a clear night promised for them to sit under a vast sea of stars.

Watching his gaffer water the hanging baskets with all their lush trailing blooms, he wished ahead to the time when he would be able to learn the ways of the seasoned gardener. His wrist was growing better by the day, which meant he could handle the garden hose, but the same couldn't be said for his knee. Progress was slow and pain was still an issue, leaving him having to trust the surgeon and his physiotherapist when they said it was still early days, and he was young and fit enough to make a full recovery in time.

The estate agent, who visited the other night, had assured Broadmeadow that there would be no problems with selling the house, which made Dan feel extremely sad for his gaffer; knowing that he couldn't take the garden with him when he left. Apparently, contrary to what Dan had thought, you can't just dig everything up and put it into pots, as it was the wrong time of year and the plants may not survive. There you go – already keen to learn.

What was in store next for them, once the house did sell, Dan wasn't sure. There wouldn't be much left after the former Mrs Broadmeadow had taken her cut, with the gaffer stubbornly refusing to let Dan put his own savings into the new house, wherever that may be. Broadmeadow had, however, tentatively asked Dan if he would like to give up his own rented house and move in with him permanently, joint names on the mortgage and all. On one hand, it felt like they were rushing into things too soon, but on the other, it felt like an ultimate commitment, one which Dan was willing to jump at with both hands.

With an assurance from himself that he wouldn't make things hard for the man if things didn't work out, Dan was seriously considering the offer. All he had to do was take into account the fact that, since leaving the hospital, he hadn't actually spent a single night at his own home, and didn't really want to either.

He and the gaffer got on just fine, almost like they were an old married couple.

Laughing to himself at that, how he'd suddenly turned into a proper adult overnight, he looked up as the gaffer made his way over to where he was sitting.

"You alright there, fella?" Broadmeadow checked that Dan's leg was properly positioned upon the patio chair pulled out in front of him, readjusting the cushion beneath it.

"Yeah, I'm good. Just enjoying watching you." Honestly, he'd been following the gaffer around with his eyes for ages. So long so, that the sun had set and he'd missed it entirely. The black dog had been rustling about in the bushes around the perimeter, just going about and doing its own thing. He used to worry when he hadn't seen it in a while, wondering when it would creep up again with its mournful stare.

Now, he didn't really worry over what it was doing, in the knowledge that it was close by somewhere but not out trying to cause him any grief. In fact, Dan had never felt so well within himself, and it felt so unbelievably liberating to have a clear head for once.

"Well I am flattered, *a chuilein*." Broadmeadow gave him that self-conscious, lopsided smile that Dan loved so much. The one that others rarely got to see. The one where the arches of his gaffer's cheeks dappled red making his freckles stand out, where his eyes shone bright like the stars were reflected within them, and the lines of age about his face became more prominent; more handsome …

Broadmeadow went inside for a couple of minutes, but Dan could still see him in the kitchen. There were definitely some issues starting to brew there, over being left on his own. That's where the black dog came in; noticing that the gaffer had left them so it came over to sit at Dan's side until he returned.

"Here." Broadmeadow handed him a cup of tea before placing his own down on the table. Pulling out another chair, he parked it up right next to Dan and slowly slipped his arm around his shoulders. "Getting a wee bit chilly out here isn't it – do you want a blanket?"

Dan snuggled closer against him, revelling in the warmth and security that the older man had to offer. His heart swelled. God, did he love him so. "Nah, you're warm enough, sir."

"What have I said about you calling me 'sir'?" Broadmeadow tutted at him.

Dan didn't think the habit was ever going to slip, no matter how many times he was reminded of it. Besides, the gaffer smiled at him so warmly every time he said it, leading him to believe that he didn't really object to Dan's obscure form of endearment after all. "I think you like it, really," he prodded back.

Broadmeadow hummed, staring up at the sky. As promised, a field of stars expanded out above them, with the moon so large and bright that they could see for miles out ahead. If they were lucky, they may even see a shooting star, because the conditions were certainly right for it. Dan had other things on his mind, however. Things that involved the bedroom, and calling the gaffer 'sir' a few more times, just to see what reaction he could gain from it ...

Leaning in close and brushing his nose against Broadmeadow's ear, before slipping out his tongue and nipping at his lobe, he said, "Actually, I think it *is* getting a bit cold out here, *sir* ..."

"Really, now?"

"Yeah."

Broadmeadow turned his gaze away from the spectacle that was the pure night sky, and focused on Dan instead, reaching up into his hair and holding his head within his hands. "Finish your tea first, and then I'll take you up to bed. Ok?"

Distracted again, Dan focused back on the sky as it was just too beautiful to be ignored. Something flashing, moving slowly across the sky, caught his attention; "Was that a shooting star?"

He pointed in the general direction of what he'd seen, eyes all full of wonder, with Broadmeadow squinting up to try and locate the supposed comet. Hearing the gaffer laugh, he looked at him and frowned; *what was so funny?*

"That's a plane, fella."

"Oh ..."

Now that he looked a little closer, he could see that his shooting star was actually flashing red and green. Oh well. Close enough, he supposed.

Apparently still finding his faux pas highly amusing, the gaffer drew in closer and fervently kissed him, so full of love that Dan found himself practically melting into incomprehensible thought. Something about the gesture told him that the request for him to finish his tea was going to be disregarded entirely, cemented into action when the gaffer, all of a sudden, raised up to his feet and held out his hand for Dan to take a hold of.

Bathed in the light of the moon and swathed in the starlit sky, like a celestial being sent to him from the powers above, Dan grinned up at the poetic romanticism of it all and responsively accepted his gaffer's wordless offer.

Epilogue

DI Georgia Azaria-Beamish, of the Metropolitan Police's Counter Corruption Unit, opened up the latest case that had been assigned to her. It could be anything, from parking ticket fixing, right through to bribery, perverting the course of justice, or overtime fraud – just to name a few.

You name it, Georgia had covered it.

As she opened the file in front of her, it soon became apparent that this particular investigation was going to be a big one. It was with regard to a DCI working the Greater London area, with some serious allegations made against him. They including sexual misconduct, abuse of one's position of power or rank, and suspected (although unproved) waiving of criminal offences.

An officer under the name of PC Kashvi Bhatia had filed the initial complaint. She had witnessed, first hand, the bullying nature of her DCI, and had heard whispers from her colleagues over local drug dealers being deliberately overlooked. As Georgia read on, the accusations got worse – it was one of PC Bhatia's male colleagues that she was really concerned for. He wished not to be named (although Georgia would try her best to get him to come forwards), but he had spoken in confidence with PC Bhatia over an incident where his commanding officer had laid a hand to him – of a physical nature.

Georgia got straight to work on the investigation.

After compiling a list of current staff members, and arranging an informal interview with PC Bhatia, she then started looking back at officers who had left Greater London SOC in the last couple of years. Some had retired, some had moved across to other departments within the Met, and a couple had moved even further afield. One officer in particular caught her attention – a DS who had transferred, rather curiously, to a small Rural Crime department down in Norfolk.

Call it a hunch, or her own intuition as an experienced Counter Corruption officer, but she got the feeling that she definitely needed to talk to him.

Georgia had a lot of work to do on this one. Whoever this DCI Walters was, he sounded like a right nasty piece of work, and more importantly, if these allegations were indeed correct, he needed to be stopped.

A Word About the Author

Caitlin lives in Norfolk – the county where she grew up and loves – with her partner and two cats.

She is a keen enthusiast of British police dramas, a hint of the supernatural and the beauty of the natural world, and above all, reading and writing the m/m romance genre. Focusing on the challenges of real life, human emotions and what masculinity really means, this debut novel was written with the theme of what it's really like to live with functioning depression, and how one can truly find their place within the world with the help of the good people around them.

For writing updates and more, Caitlin can be found and followed on:

Substack: @cfchapman

Facebook: C F Chapman - author

Printed in Great Britain
by Amazon